Praise for Mary Hughes' *Biting Nixie*

Rating: 5 Angels and a Recommended Read! "...Filled with bitingly acerbic humor, endearingly quirky characters, and smolderingly hot vampires *Biting Nixie* kept me enthralled from the opening salvo..."
~ *Hayley, Fallen Angel Reviews*

Joyfully Recommended! "...*Biting Nixie* is a rockin' thrill ride of action, lust, and romance...I adored this book..."
~ *Shayna, Joyfully Reviewed*

"I absolutely loved this book. Please tell me there will be more!"
~ *Angie Gipson, ParaNormalRomance*

Rating: 4.5 Nymphs "...fast and furious, with funny dialogue, great characters and a believable premise..."
~ *Mystical Nymph, Literary Nymphs*

"...a great story..."
~ *Suzi, I Read Romance*

"...entertaining and sexy and fresh. I hope Ms. Hughes writes more, because I can't wait to see what else she brings to the table."
~ *Shannon C., The Good, The Bad, and The Unread*

Rating: 4.5 Roses "This read has a lot of layers you will enjoy peeling off."
~ *Lakisha, A Romance Review*

Biting Nixie

Mary Hughes

A Samhain Publishing, Ltd. publication.

Samhain Publishing, Ltd.
577 Mulberry Street, Suite 1520
Macon, GA 31201
www.samhainpublishing.com

Biting Nixie
Copyright © 2009 by Mary Hughes
Print ISBN: 978-1-60504-437-8
Digital ISBN: 978-1-60504-358-6

Editing by Deborah Nemeth
Cover by Natalie Winters

First Samhain Publishing, Ltd. electronic publication: January 2009
First Samhain Publishing, Ltd. print publication: November 2009

Dedication

To my husband, Gregg. With you, novel research is more fun than a barrel of screaming, sex-crazed monkeys.

To Deborah Nemeth, editor extraordinary, who is far funnier, smarter, and more talented than me. Better looking, too. Thanks for helping me find the sculpture in the stone.

Chapter One

"Waiting's such a pain in the ass."

I was talking to the lady in line ahead of me. Or rather her planet-sized hat, whose fake ostrich feather was doing Pluto's orbit on my face. The hat ignored me.

So I turned to the guy behind. He was skinny with a fat butt and a long nose—like a dachshund in pants. "Life's too short, right?"

Dachshund guy stared at me like I was demented.

And maybe I was. After all, I'd been standing here for—I checked my Juke. Over an hour. Sixty minutes and counting. In sixty minutes a good drama could have solved World Hunger. A comedy would have solved World Hunger, achieved Global Peace, and had a laugh or two besides.

Forget Murphy's Law. Nixie's Law: if you were waiting to make a left turn, there was always *one* oncoming fucktard who sailed through on the red. If you were in a grocery line, which*ever* line you picked would be run by Nimrod the Wonder-Iguana.

Waiting for the burro-cracy (aka the mule-ass government) to move its fat butt was enough to make the Great McHamburger Clown swear.

Standing in line in the mayor's office for an *hour*—to do the government a *favor*—well, please. Just flay my skin off.

I mean, it wasn't like you could do anything while you wait. You gotta be alert—*move up move up move up*—or someone would jack your place in line.

I amused myself by making up sexual fantasies about the people in line. Behind dachshund guy was a shaggy collie of a woman. I imagined them doing it. Doggie style, of course. Teeny wiener-dog frantically humping Lassie. That was good for a few chuckles.

A surgically enhanced 34-DD paired with dachshund guy brought another round of silent laughs. I mean, his face was level with her chest. Imagine his head on a rubber band, playing paddle ball.

That was good for about ten minutes. After that I thought up seven different ways to kill the guy who wrote "Proud Mary". The best was to lock him in a room with every band that ever played a wedding reception, each furnished with a Giant Slugger baseball bat.

But even waiting has to end. It was 4:40 p.m. and dark out when hat lady got called to the counter. I was finally at the front of the line. I was *next.*

Having someone cut in ahead of me was just a fucking insult.

"Excuse me." I reached up to tap the guy's shoulder.

The buzz-cut gray head swiveled. Apparently seeing nobody there, the guy turned back.

I'm used to that. At five-foot-nothing I'm shorter than most fifth graders. I don't make up for it in weight, being a size zero. Don't envy me. The only thing that fits me comes out of the little girls' section at Kmart. Since I'm twenty-five, this is a *major* problem. Never mind trees falling in forests—if the shirt front is flat, do my breasts exist?

"Excuse me," I said again, tugging on my tormentor's suit coat.

He whipped around and seared me with a long glare. Aw, shit. I recognized that sharp nose and ratty face. I knew too well that seersucker suit, new half a century ago and hardened since into a shell of authority.

Mr. Schleck, my high school Vice Principal.

Schleck hated me. Left over from having to deal with my party-animal sister, but he didn't have to enjoy torturing me quite so much.

And he did enjoy it. Schleck was the kind of guy who liked to throw his weight around. Abusive Authority with a capital AA. Break one tiny little rule, and he handed out detentions and suspensions like the Ebola virus. And, from his cutting in line ahead of me, was a two-faced bastard about it.

"Excuse me." I yanked on his seersucker symbol of authority. "You taxed my place. I was here first."

The veep threw me a sneer. "Not now, little girl."

At the counter, Twyla Tafel yelled, "Next!"

Schleck moved.

Enough was enough. Schleck had bullied me as a teenager and got away with it. But I was an *adult* now. He was not going to screw me any more. I grabbed his coat. "Just hold on there!"

Schleck whirled on me, snarling like an angry badger. "Let go of me, you little twerp." His fingers closed around my hand and squeezed.

That *hurt*. But I had stood in that fucking line for a fucking hour. Playing by the rules. I got pissed. "I was here first. *I'm* next. No joust!"

Schleck's face went red as a stoplight. His hand jerked back—to *hit* me. Incredulous, I saw his fat palm rocket toward my face.

I stifled my immediate reaction, which was to Chuck Norris his ass with a roundhouse to the head. Not that I minded shedding a little bully-blood—but not in the *mayor's* office. I would have to take it. I squeezed my eyes shut.

Nothing landed.

"I believe you're out of line, sir."

The voice was deep and cultured. The words resonated with an accent I couldn't immediately place. Proud, almost aristocratic. I cautiously popped one eye open.

Strong, sure fingers held Schleck's wrist in an unbreakable grip. The Vice Principal's face was white as he stared up. And up. I followed that stare, and—

Towering over us both was the most beautiful man I'd ever seen.

Bronzed skin. Black hair and brows. Outrageously long black eyelashes sweeping over laser-sharp blue eyes. Sensuous dark bronze mouth. A jaw made to run your fingers over. Lean muscular body with biteable shoulders and a flat waist. He made a Chippendale look like a cub scout.

Gorgeous Guy stared down at Schleck with cool contempt. He didn't squeeze the Vice Principal's wrist, didn't hurt him in any way. He didn't have to. The man's obvious strength was enough.

Schleck, like bullies everywhere, cut and ran. Gorgeous Guy released the veep-creep as if he were slime.

Wow. Not only man-beautiful, but the guy *oozed* strength. No, more. Power. Power, the kind restrained by a tremendous will. I could have fallen in love. Could have, but not.

The guy was wearing a fucking three-piece suit.

Vest and all. Seriously, had anyone worn those since the ancient eighties? Charcoal gray, looked like worsted wool. Cut like a glove. Reeeeelly expensive. Black Italian wingtip shoes. Shirt so snowy white it glowed. Striped tie, probably from some Ivy League school. Damn. Gorgeous Guy in real life was a straight-laced Suit Guy.

He opened the coat and checked an actual freaking gold pocket watch. "You're welcome." A dry note flavored Suitguy's beautiful voice.

While I was staring at his tailored wool armor he had been looking at me. "Uh, yeah. Thanks."

He smiled slightly. Oh, stars above. What that smile did to my innards was illegal in Georgia. His eyes flicked to the counter. "You're next, I believe."

"Uh, yeah." I couldn't seem to think of anything else to say. "Thanks."

"You're welcome." As he turned away, Suitguy added, "Little girl."

That hit my libido like a bucket of ice water. I gave his broad back an impotent glare. When he didn't instantly burst into flames I settled for stomping all the way to the counter.

Behind the counter, Twyla Tafel watched me approach. My friend Twyla is the mayor's executive admin. She was a hundred forty pounds of competence wrapped in seduction. Men drooled over her and didn't even notice she was doing their jobs better than they did.

I've known Twyla since the day we were sent to Schleck's office for throwing paper wads on the ceiling of the girl's bathroom. Twyla hid us in a supply closet instead. Even as a freshman she had keys to everything.

"What the hell is it with this stupid line?" I grouched at her.

10

"And where's Heidi?" The counter is usually Heidi's domain and she runs it like a POW camp. Or, considering Heidi's affection for spike-heeled boots and black leather, maybe a medieval dungeon.

Twyla shrugged. "Out sick. I'm trying not to mess things up, but everything's hit the fan. Thanks to the mayor's upcoming festival."

The city-wide fundraiser. The mad cow charity event. Just lobotomize me. "Which explains why my short park and fart turned into a Martin Luther-sized constipation."

Twyla cocked her head. "What's got your undies in a bundle, girl?"

"*Girl*," I echoed resentfully. "You're almost as short as me. But no one would mistake *you* for a kid." Twyla's got breasts and hips that stun half the male population into a coma on sight. When she walks, the other half crash. She dresses sharp, wears designer spikes, and carries a lethal bump and grind. I glowered at her. "If I had real breasts instead of these little lumps on my chest—"

"Oh, not that again." Twyla rolled her cocoa brown eyes. She was half black, her mother an African diplomat. She was half German, too, but you'd never know to look at her. It was kind of strange to hear fluent *Deutsche* coming out of the mouth of someone who looked like a voodoo queen.

Of course, everyone here in Meiers Corners was half German, whether they had the genes or not. A small-town thing.

Twyla tapped a long Burgundy Blast-colored nail on the counter. "You're not a skinny-assed kid, Nixie."

"*You're* the one who described me as Shirley Temple crossed with Drew Barrymore." I glowered at Schleck cowering at the end of the line. "Not just you. Everyone seems to think I'm a kid." I looked around for the Gucci god. Suitguy was standing right behind Schleck, which explained the cowering.

"What do you expect, with how you dress?" Twyla waved a manicured hand at my clothes. "You're an adult woman, Nixie. Yet you dress like a punk kid."

I waved my own short pink-and-black nails in answer. "What am I supposed to wear? Two-hundred-dollar Liz Claiborne suits? It would cost another two hundred just to cut them down to my size. That's all daggy."

"Liz charges four hundred these days. Buy a miniskirt. It'd at least cover your knees."

"Ha-ha. Anyway, I'm a *musician,* Twyla. I'm supposed to look rocked up." I glanced down at today's ensemble. Sequined black Skechers. Purple tights. Red bike shorts peeking out from the frill of a skirt ruffle. Garfield hoodie with the sleeves ripped out. A jean jacket, ditto. To show the butterfly tattoo on one arm. And the tiger on the other.

"Thank God you're a lot smarter than you look. Or talk. Speaking of which." Twyla pushed a stuffed manila envelope across the counter at me. "Your instructions. For the festival."

"Thanks." I hefted the envelope. "Why is the city trying to raise money, anyway?"

"We're hiring some hot-shot East Coast lawyer. To protect Meiers Corners from Chicago."

"Yeah, I heard Chicago wants to suck us up. Although I have no idea why."

"Nobody knows. But the big boys are pretty serious about it. They've gone so far as to introduce annexation legislation with the state."

I whistled. "Thus the need for a wonder-shark. But couldn't taxes pay for this legal eagle?"

Twyla arched a perfectly plucked brow. "At five hundred dollars an hour?"

I swore. "That's a lot of Kraft singles!"

"It'll be worth it," Twyla said.

"Worth an HDTV an *hour?*"

"Where do you buy your HDTVs? It'd take him at least two hours to earn one."

Twyla was teasing, but I wasn't. "Why get an outsider—especially at that rate? What's wrong with old Denny Crane?" Yeah, really. We had a lawyer named Denny Crane. Just like *Boston Legal.* Meiers Corners was a magnet for weird. Like Cabot Cove attracted murderers. Okay, that was an ancient reference, but I saw *Beauty and the Beast* as a kid and had a brief hero thing for Angela Lansbury.

Twyla tut-tutted. "You don't want to mess around with Chicago leet, girl. They're top of the food chain. They'd eat

Meiers Corners and spit out the bones if we didn't get someone tough on our side."

"Five hundred per will kill us surer."

"You get what you pay for." Twyla shrugged. "Anyway, it's four-fifty. He's giving us a discount."

"Well roll me on my back and wave my legs in the air. How generous. And who is this playa?"

"Some guy from the firm of Quincy, Emerson and Holmes."

"Great. Sounds like Snobby, Priggy and Prude. Or Dewy, Cheatem and Howe."

"Ha-ha. Anyway, this guy's coming to meet the mayor tonight. I had to order up special cheese balls. You know how the mayor loves his cheese balls."

"Yeah." Five hundred dollars an hour. I was lucky to make five hundred a month. But it explained the big extravaganza. No way little Meiers Corners could pay that much from taxes. "Well, I'd better let you clear out the rest of the line. Thanks for this." I patted the envelope. "Guns and Polkas is looking forward to playing for the fundraiser."

"Playing for it?" Twyla's perfectly arched eyebrows rose. "Girl, you're *running* it."

Chapter Two

After that bombshell, all I could do was stumble away from the counter and collapse. Anywhere. The floor, if I had to. Luckily I found a bench in the hallway. I dropped onto it, gasping like I'd had a heart attack. A manila folder heart attack.

Maybe, I thought, just maybe Twyla was mistaken. I opened the envelope with trembling fingers.

The paper was city letterhead. My full legal name featured prominently. The signature was definitely the mayor's fifth-grade scrawl. Twyla wasn't mistaken.

I rubbed my forehead. Why me? Why not Heidi, or Police Chief Dirkson—or even my mother?

Scanning the text told me. "Your talent for managing...the *only* one...as one of the historic founding families...as a citizen of Meiers Corners..." I had to admire how neatly the letter was done. Inflate me with praise and slap me down with civic duty.

And then came the kicker. The handwritten scribble on the bottom. "You are knowing," the mayor wrote in flawless Deutsche-glish, "how my brother-in-law is having gotten the job for the Milwaukee Summerfest. If you successful raising our money are, I am asking him to find a place for Guns and Polkas in the Miller tent."

Two words stuck out like neon. "Summerfest". And "Miller".

On the shores of Lake Michigan, Milwaukee was the scene for some hot summer festivals. Festa Italiana and Irish fest drew over a hundred thousand people each, and countless smaller fests had tens of thousands.

The crowning jewel was Summerfest.

All the festivals had food, rides, the usual. But the core of

14

Summerfest was *music*. All kinds of music, from punk to bluegrass, from classical to classic rock. Big names, and I mean big, performed every year. Stevie Wonder. Earth Wind and Fire. LeAnn Rimes. Nearly a million people attended each year. It was the musical equivalent of the Kentucky Derby or the Grand Prix.

The Miller "tent" was the Miller Lite Oasis, recently rebuilt, with room for almost ten thousand. Some of it was seating, but most of the audience stood for the heart-pounding, foot-stomping, incredible groups that played there.

And yes. It was sponsored by the beer people of the same name. So you knew it had to be good.

Playing Summerfest was a great gig for anybody. For a local bar band like Guns and Polkas, it was getting a personal invite to heaven from St. Peter.

But...I took to responsibility like a fish to air. Being responsible for the a city-wide event? Cream me and serve me on toast, why don't you?

I sat on the bench, staring at the manila brick of obligation in my lap. Would I do it? If I did, the fate of Meiers Corners would rest squarely on my size-zero shoulders. It felt like a really thick chador, those black cloaks women wear in desert climates. Heavy and suffocating.

"Bad news?" came a deep, sexy voice.

I looked up from my prison papers. It was Suitguy. Stars above, he had broad shoulders. I wondered if they were as yummy as they looked.

His beautiful face was arranged in Genuine Concern. Unfortunately, the concern was framed by a two-hundred-dollar haircut and a perfectly knotted school tie. Damn. Why couldn't he be in Harley leathers and tats? "Yeah. Bad news." I indicated the mayor's letter.

"Grades?" he inquired in that same solicitous tone.

Suddenly he was way less sexy. I stuffed the papers back into the envelope. "You wouldn't understand."

"No? Let me guess. City Hall, mayoral letterhead. Something to do with Chicago annexing Meiers Corners?"

I looked up, surprised. The guy was smart. All those looks, and brains too. If only he weren't packaged in a square box. "It's so *baka*. Chicago rolling Meiers Corners. That's like going all

15

Hulk Hogan on a gerbil."

I waited for a reply. Tall, dark, and suity only stared at me like I was speaking Korean. His stunning eyes tracked a bit as if he was searching his brain for a translation. He 404'd—came up empty. "I beg your pardon?"

"Why's Chicago trying to annex us? We're just a tiny village." Although legally, Meiers Corners was a city. And culturally, we were a city, too, I suppose. We had our own art museum, an independent newspaper, and a truck line. We were the nation's top producer of beer (per square mile). We were the Hemoglobin Society's clearinghouse for the entire Midwest. We even had our own symphony orchestra, consisting of three violins, a flute, a tuba, and a clarinet (I joined last month).

Population-wise, though, we were a Mini Cooper.

Suitguy understood what I said that time. "It's not Chicago doing this, per se. It's a group of back-room businessmen."

"Shady businessmen, uh-huh. Now why am I not surprised? Who?"

"We call them the Coterie."

I had to snort. "The Coterie. Catchy."

Suitguy shrugged. "They're a powerful and exclusive group. So, Coterie."

"And if not for this 'Coterie', we'd be happily tossing like normal."

He gave me that "where's the subtitles" look again. But he answered readily enough, "Chicago suburbs surround Meiers Corners. It would follow that some attempt at annexation would be inevitable."

"Shit. Give me a second to parse that, would you?" Typical suit. Why use one word when fifty would do? I picked out the main—idea, not vein. "Inevitable, right. But who's fault is that? We didn't velveeta-melt into *Chicago's* territory." The Corners began as a tiny independent settlement of 1800's German immigrants, a healthy distance west of Chicago. Acres and acres of farms and fields lay between us and the Big City. By 1900 Meiers Corners had grown to three miles and three thousand people.

During that same time Chicago grew to one *million.*

The giant metropolis oozed around the Corners like a

middle-age spread. Without realizing it, we were soon surrounded. Seven thousand of us. Three *million* of them. The jeans were getting awfully tight.

Unless the East Coast wonder-shark could spring us free.

What a choice. Pay Chicago or pay Mr. Four-K-A-Day. I trust lawyers about as much as I do Vice Principals. I like them even less. I wasn't sure we were picking the right option.

I grunted. "It's inevitable—unless we crank out enough mad skrilla so our shyster can fap on their shyster." Suitglish translation: Takeover is inevitable unless we raise enough money for our lawyer to screw their lawyer.

Suitguy blinked. "Fap?"

Of course he had to pick *that* word. He couldn't have known what it meant. But with his deep, sexy voice, he made it sound pornographic. Which, of course, it was.

Fap was a word used in manga and anime porn for the sound of sex. Think "Bam!" and "Zowie!" with naked pictures.

Before I could explain (if I even wanted to try), a bray like a cheap trumpet snapped both our heads around. "You there! One minute!"

A baseball in a bow tie swept toward us, all broad toothy smile. Lew Kaufman. Lew was the mayor's campaign manager, PR whiz, and cheese ball salesman all rolled into one. Twyla called him Lightning Lew because he zapped anyone in his path. He was Salesman on steroids. Probably had a big "$" tattooed on his chest.

Lew's eyes lit on Suitguy and went *ka-ching!* He grabbed Suitguy's hand and pumped. "Kaufman's the name, welcome's my game. First time visiting Our Fair City? Let me take you on a tour of Our Fair City Hall. Ha-ha!"

Gently, Suitguy tried to extract his hand. But nothing short of a jaws of life was going to make Lightning Lew let go. Lew simply grabbed on with both hands and continued to piston away, like Suitguy was the only water pump in the Mojave Desert.

"Over there's the mayor's office." Lew pointed back toward Twyla's. "You know he's mayor 'cause he uses two secretaries. Of course, the secretaries really run the place, ha-ha!"

"Ha-ha," Suitguy agreed in a dry tone.

Lew stopped shaking long enough to clap Suitguy's broad back. The resulting boom (and the slightly pained look on Lew's face) clued me that Suitguy was even harder-muscled than he appeared. Lew drew back his injured hand and cleared his throat. "Well. You'll want to see the Department of Records, down the hall. You and your lovely wife. This way."

I almost didn't catch it. Lovely—wife? Looking between Suitguy and me, I didn't get it. He was a gorgeous, tall, powerful, tall, obviously rich, tall, conservatively dressed male. And did I mention he was tall?

And here I was, a punk moppet with tattoos.

How did Lew get man-and-wife out of that?

Suitguy and I exchanged a look. For a split second, we shared perfect understanding. Lew had gone psycho.

"Can I carry your papers, little lady?" Lew reached a hand toward me.

Well, at least he didn't think I was a child. "I can carry them. And anything's better than having to read them." I stuck the envelope under my arm and popped up brightly from the bench. "Lead away, Gungho-din."

"Huh?" Lew's eyes crossed.

"That's Gunga Din," Suitguy said.

"Whatever." I turned to Lew, looped my arm through his. "I'd love a tour with my"—I fluttered my eyes at Suitguy—"little hubby."

Suitguy shot me a black look in response. What a surprise, no sense of humor.

"Right this way!" Lew latched his other arm to Suitguy and dragged us both toward the stairs. "This here's the Fire Door. Installed in 1872, after The Fire burned the first Town Hall to the ground. It's Real Steel, solid as a rock." He opened the door and shut it with a clang several times. "Hear it? That's Real Steel."

"Real Steel, honey," I said, beaming at Suitguy.

Suitguy only grimaced. "I've just remembered a pressing engagement. Sorry." He twisted away from Lew and lit out.

Lightning Lew made a grab for him. "But you gotta see this!"

Suitguy was *fast*. Lew barely caught the flappy back vent of

Suitguy's suit coat. But it was enough. When Lew yanked, Suitguy allowed himself to be recaptured. Probably didn't want to risk a rip to his eight-hundred-dollar Armani.

"Now look at these stairs." Lew dragged us through the Fire Door (Real Steel). "These stairs are tiled with gen-yoo-wine imitation marble. Recovered from the original Town Hall after it burned to the ground. Reused in the 1872 rebuilding."

Suitguy looked pained. "Thank you. But really. I must go."

"And the railings! Forged steel. Painted red, see? Now there's an interesting story about the paint."

"How delightful," Suitguy said. A trapped animal could have chewed his arm off. He didn't have that option.

I reached over Lew and patted Suitguy gently on the biceps. "Don't bump the jams, honey." Under the fine wool I felt hard muscle and sinew. And a hum of something. Something that said power, and heat, and...blood.

Blood?

I yanked my hand back. Where the hell did that thought come from?

Suitguy slewed me a look. I pretended not to see the question in his gaze.

Lew grabbed us both and urged us up the stairs. "This is the second floor. Now over here's the Second Floor Closet." Lew released us to fling open the closet door. "Can you believe the space? The organizers were put in in 1988 by Thorvald Heinemann."

Suitguy wasn't listening. He touched my shoulder, lightly, like a butterfly. Incredible how light, considering how strong he seemed. "Are you all right?" he asked under Lew's spiel.

I couldn't help looking up, into his eyes. Framed by those black lashes, the intense blue of his irises stunned me. My whole body clenched, like he'd hit me with lightning.

I shook myself. Blood, and now lightning? What had gotten into me, anyway? "Yeah. Perfectly hawt."

He blinked. "Haute?"

Lew came back, clapped one arm around each of us. "What do you think of Meiers Corners so far, Mr. and Mrs...?" He looked at Suitguy expectantly. Prompted again. "Mr. and Mrs...?"

Lew was trying to coerce Suitguy's name out of him. Names have power, as I well knew. I watched Suitguy's stunning eyes shift from me to Lew, and I could see the electric intelligence behind that gaze. Suitguy was well aware of what Lew was trying to pull.

His intense gaze drilled into Lew's head like an auger. Lew's smile lost some of its toothy arrogance. "I told you *my* name." His tone went pouty, like a little boy.

Taking pity on Lew, I said, "I'm Nixie."

After a slight pause, Suitguy responded. "Emerson. Julian Emerson. But this isn't my wif—"

"Julian *Emerson*! Well, no wonder!" Manhood restored, Lew grabbed Suitguy's hands and pumped like an air riff. Like he'd only been practicing before. "Nice ta meetcha, Mr. Emerson. And little Nixie! I knew you looked familiar. I didn't know you got married."

Neither had I, but it was kind of fun. Though Suitguy...*Julian* was clearly annoyed. His face was stern and his body was all clenched up. Muscles tightened and bunched, straining against the fabric of his shirt, his coat, his pants...yum. Even under all that conservative cover, Julian's body was hot. In what I imagined to be a wifely gesture, I tucked my hip into his thigh. Hard, thick muscle met my touch. Double-yum. "It was a whirlwind romance." I smiled up into his stern, beautiful face.

Something flared in Julian's eyes. Something that said he was suddenly aware I wasn't the child I seemed.

Lew beamed at us both. "Well, congrats, Nixie. You got yourself one of the hottest catches of the century, if *People* magazine is right."

I tore my gaze away from Julian's bright eyes. "Huh?"

"Yes sirree," Lew enthused. "Now I see why you came to help us out, Mr. Emerson. Don't usually get such heavy-hitters in Meiers Corners. But if little Nixie here is your wife, well, 'nuf said!"

Julian's eyes narrowed. "Mr. Kaufman. 'Little' Nixie is not, nor has ever been—"

"—happier!" I wrapped my hands around Julian's arm, batting my eyes at him. Willing him to go along with the ruse just a little longer. "But we haven't been married long, almost newlyweds, in fact. And I want to spend every spare moment with my hubby—"

"Great! I'll show both of you the mayor's beer can collection. Right this way—"

"Alone! So if you'll just excuse us..."

Lew pouted. "I *was* going to show you the Records Department." He added coaxingly, "The file cabinets are Real Steel."

"Next time," I hurried to reassure him. "But now Suitg—*Julian* and I want to be *alone*." Tugging on Julian's arm, I edged away from Lew. "Right, honey?"

Julian, bless him, was quick. He came, even going so far as to put a possessive hand over mine. We escaped into the stairwell.

Once out of sight though, I was in trouble. I felt it before I saw it. Waves of displeasure rolled off Julian like tides of doctor bills.

The man had *no* sense of humor.

"Look, I had to say something," I said desperately. "Lew's like a freight train. Once he gets an idea between his teeth, he's a tornado in a china shop."

"Your metaphors are execrable."

I didn't understand that, but it didn't sound good. I put fists on hips, stuck out my chest. "Yeah? Well, same to you, buster."

For some reason that made him smile. Not a full-out smile, just a kind of lifting of one corner of his mouth. Julian had a spectacular mouth. Bronze lips, not too full. Sleek. Built for kissing.

Seeing my expression, which probably looked like I wanted to eat him, his eyes darkened.

Whoa. So not going there. Not with Suitguy, Defender of the Stodgy. "Well, thanks. For, uh, rescuing me from Vice Principal Schleck. And coming out after and, uh, being nice. But, gotta go."

He let me escape. I ran down the steps and out into the night. My heart was pounding way faster than the exercise merited.

On the sidewalk, I paused a moment to catch my breath.

The cold November air swirled around me, cooling my strangely aroused body. What had almost happened there?

Nothing. Absolutely nothing happened. And it was going to stay that way. I was absolutely, positively, not turned on by Julian Emerson. By *Suitguy*. Suitguy, I rationalized, was probably as seductive as the moan-track of a grade-Z porno flick.

It wasn't working. I started picturing those to-die-for lips shaped around a good moan. Damp thong rapidly became soaked and steamy thong. WTF!

Since a cold shower wasn't handy, I decided to walk my squishy off. I struck out, headed west. Walking was a national pastime in Meiers Corners. You could get anywhere by foot. For example, I lived about a mile from City Hall. Nine blocks west, seven blocks north. Elena O'Rourke's old place, actually, before she married Bo Strongwell. Elena was a cop, but that didn't stop us from being friends.

Of course, Elena and I were friends like an Irish wolfhound and the Taco Bell dog, but looks weren't everything.

A strong hand grabbed me by the arm, yanked me to a stop. "Just *what* do you think you're doing?"

I reacted without thinking. Pivot. Cock back an arm. Strike with the heel of the hand. Smash the nose. Done at the right angle, it drives bone shards into the brain.

Except my hand never got past my shoulder. Vise-like fingers spun me. Arms stronger than bands of steel wrapped around me. I was yanked back against a chest as solid as a concrete wall. Hot breath stirred the hair on top of my head.

I struggled uselessly, until recognition broke through. That deep, cultured voice. Those haughty vowels.

Julian Emerson.

I jerked against him, trying to pull loose. "Emerson! What the hell do you think you're doing?"

"I asked you first, little girl." Julian released me suddenly and I stumbled. His strong hand on my arm steadied me briefly.

I glared up at him. My glare hit his old-school tie. Thirty seconds since I'd seen him and I'd forgotten how *tall* he was. My breasts would rub against that flat belly. My nipples would harden... I readjusted my eyes one foot up and glared fiercely. "I am *not* a little girl."

"I know." He sounded resentful. "But you're not very big, either. You shouldn't be out alone."

"Oh, please! This is Meiers Corners. The worst crime we have is shoplifting."

He glowered at me. "You have gangs."

"*A* gang. *One* gang. East of here, in the bad part of town." As if Meiers Corners *had* a bad part of town, compared to any other city.

"Nowhere in town is safe any more. Especially not for a hu...female." Julian blew a frustrated-sounding breath. "This issue with the Chicago Coterie has upset the balance."

"Upset the *balance*? Well don't you sound all crunchy."

His glower morphed into puzzled annoyance. "I beg your pardon?"

"All feng shui guru-ey. Thanks for the warning, Emerson." I lifted my chin. "But I can protect myself." On that line I swept away, a perfect haughty-yet-dignified exit.

Only to be grabbed and spun back. "You can defend yourself against *normal* adversaries. But not against evil." Julian's blue eyes glowed, burning almost red violet in the yellow street lamp.

"Evil?" I glared back, but it bounced off a stare hard as rubies. So I redirected my glare to Julian's hand, wrapped securely around my arm. And was exceedingly surprised.

Given his long, lithe build I expected long, slim fingers. An ele-gaunt, artsy-fartsy hand.

But Julian's fingers were square, his hand strong. The same bronze as his face, dusted by small black hairs.

His hand would be powerful and sure between my thighs.

Appalled with myself, I shook Julian's square hand off. "Evil?" I repeated. "That's pretty extreme, Emerson. Hitler was evil. Pol Pot was evil. Gangs are bad, yes. But evil? As far as I know no gang has wiped out millions of human beings as if it were their right."

"'Wiped out millions of humans as their right.'" Julian's lean jaw worked, as if he were fighting for restraint. "Yes, *evil* is exactly the word I want."

He *really* needed to lighten up. "And this Coterie is evil. Uh-huh. Are you always wired so tight, Emerson?"

He blew a frustrated breath. "I fail to see what's wrong with being careful. The Coterie is extremely dangerous—"

"An evil and dangerous bunch of *suits*. You're feening, Emerson. I don't like lawyers and bureaucrats either, but I'd hardly call them evil. Well—maybe the lawyers."

Whatever Julian had been about to say in retort died. He gave me a strange look. "Nixie. I should tell you—" A loud pop cut him off. The street light in front of us died.

Chapter Three

As the light died, Julian's jaw kicked up. His eyes narrowed to slits. His nostrils flared like a beast scenting prey.

Suddenly Julian Emerson looked nothing like a suit. He looked like—a hunter. A dangerous, deadly hunter.

"Get behind me." Not waiting for me to obey, he pushed me behind him with sure hands. My fingers wrapped automatically around his waist.

Beyond him I caught the impression of movement. Blurs, three of them, coming in *fast*. I couldn't see much, sequestered behind Julian. He was lean, yes. But big. His chest was solid and his shoulders broad. His waist was easily as big as my hips. That lean, flat waist.

"Get him!" someone shouted.

In front of me, Julian's arms jerked. Cut through the air, hard. His hands almost whistled with the force he used. If he'd held knives, whatever he hit was now sliced, diced, and julienned. I smiled at the image.

Until twin arcs of dark liquid sprayed out on either side of him.

It all happened so fast. I couldn't be sure what I really saw. But the *sounds* sent ice through my veins. The liquid spattered onto the sidewalk like unnaturally thick rain. Plop-plop-plop. Like the sick crunch of car metal, it's a sound I will never forget.

In front of me, Julian's arm went forward, then pulled abruptly back. *Digging something out.* The image was so strong I even heard a sucking, as if whatever it was had resisted coming out. My fingers fumbled under his suit coat, found his belt. I clutched that belt as if it were a lifesaver.

With a sharp motion, Julian threw—something. I cringed, listening for a crunch, or a splat. A sound to tell me what he'd thrown. A sound to confirm he'd...killed...something. Or...someone.

Nothing.

I found my voice. "What...what just happened?" The words were shaky. Under my hands, his belt felt fuzzy.

Not only my voice was shaking, I realized. My vision was going wonky. Julian's broad back blurred, almost as if I could see through him. I blinked.

An instant later he was reassuringly solid. The belt felt fine in my hands, smooth and normal.

He reached behind him, found my fingers. Gently he worked them open. I seized his hand. I must have squeezed his fingers white but he did not protest. Holding my hand securely, Julian turned.

I expected to see dark spray on his shirt. But it was pristine. I looked beyond him, to the sidewalk on either side. Dark dots of thick liquid glistened like oily rain. Nope, I hadn't imagined it. "Emerson. Why is there blood—"

Julian seized me by the shoulders. Skewered me with a stare so intense, I could feel the hairs on my nape rise. "Nixie. I want you to promise not to go outside after dark. Not alone. It's not safe any more."

I slewed another glance at the dark drops on the pavement. "Were those homies from a gang? Is that the gang you were talking about?"

"You see the danger now? Nixie, you have to promise me."

Blood. But no bodies. "What happened to them? Where did they go? Will they be okay?"

"Oh, for...they ran off. Dragging one, but he'll be fine. And back before we know it." Julian looked like he wanted to shake me. "So it's important that you stay home at night. That you stay inside. Understand?"

Maybe Julian was right. Maybe Meiers Corners had become dangerous. "I understand you think it's important. But I can't. I can't stay home nights."

Julian's eyes flared a bright violet. "Do you care so little about your life?"

"No! I'm *not* my sister." His eyebrows raised at that, but I only repeated, "I can't stay home nights."

"Nixie, what does your sister—"

Not going there. "I *can't!*"

His brows raised a notch at my tone. "You must. Whatever parties—"

"Not parties. I earn my pay after dark."

His eyebrows shot up to his hairline.

I winced. "I didn't mean that like it sounded."

The eyebrows stayed up. "What *did* you mean, then?"

"I'm a musician."

He closed his eyes, maybe searching for strength. "A musician."

"Guns and Polkas." Digging in my pocket, I pulled out a card. "Bars, parties, weddings, you name it." The small pasteboard in my fingers made me feel almost normal. "Reasonable prices," I added hopefully as I gave it to him.

Julian opened his eyes slowly, as if he were afraid of what he'd see. "Nixie...Schmeling? N. Schmeling?" He frowned, and his eyes scanned like he was reading an internal PDA. "Not *Dietlinde* N. Schmeling?"

Dietlinde. My daggy first name. Symbol of *everything* I hated. My intro to the power of names, when my parents millstoned me with it. Trying to drag me down into the hell of Normal Life.

I snapped, hearing him say it. Hearing Julian Emerson, Suitguy extra-stodginary, say *Deet*-fucking-*linda*. Any residual shakiness fled in the rush of mad. "Yeah. Wanna make something of it?"

He was obviously surprised by my reaction. But he only held up his square hands. "Peace. We're on the same side."

I wasn't placated. "Oh, yeah?"

"Yes. Nixie...I'm the lawyer who's going to keep Meiers Corners free."

After I picked up my jaw from the sidewalk, I realized I should have known. A fucking HDTV-an-hour lawyer. It was all there. The suit, the money, the classic good looks. I should have recognized the name, Emerson, from Fogey, Stuffy, and Emerson.

And I had responded to him! I thought he was *sexy.* Which, of course, only pissed me off more. Without another word I stalked off. He followed me.

I stomped all the way to my flat. Like a lithe shadow, Julian glided along silently behind. He must have been freezing in only his suit coat but he didn't complain once. Just followed, without a word. He waited silently on my stoop while I fumbled out my key and unlocked my door. He stood without comment when I slammed the door in his face.

He waited, hands folded patiently behind his back, until I locked the damned door again.

And then Julian Emerson, lawyer, suit, melted away into the night.

♫ ♫ ♫

"It was right here," I said, dragging on my captive's hand. I pointed. "Right here. I swear it!"

Detective Elena O'Rourke Strongwell hunkered down and scanned the sidewalk where I had pointed. "Nixie, there's no blood." Her fashion-model face was smooth, untroubled, but her eyes were sharp.

I dug my hands into my jacket pockets, staring at the hygienically clean concrete. A bloody mugging had happened here. Conservative attorney Julian Emerson had gone all violent here. Bloody violent. Ploppy-wet violent.

Nothing showed. "But it happened!" I blurted.

"You're sure it was here?" Elena rummaged in a duffel she'd brought. Her long dark curls whipped in the wind.

Elena was five feet nine inches tall, and every inch was cop. Her Irish father was a public defender. She got her unswerving sense of justice from him. Her Hispanic mother was a model. Elena got her incredible beauty and slender grace from her. But the fierce intelligence and off-beat sense of humor was all Elena. It's why we were friends.

And why, if Elena didn't believe me, no one would.

"Someone must have cleaned it up." I felt bewildered. It was *here.* "Wouldn't there still be traces? Isn't there something you can use to make the blood pop? Please, Elena?"

She rolled her chocolate eyes. "Saints preserve us from TV detectives. Yeah, this." She brought out a pump bottle. "Luminol." She sprayed the sidewalk with quick, sure sprays. I waited for the flash of fluorescence spatter to show.

Nothing.

"It was *there*. We were *attacked*. Maybe it's too bright to see the reaction—"

"Nixie. I'm not saying you're imagining things. But..." Elena shrugged and left the rest hanging.

"Blood was splashing. I heard it!"

"Uh-huh." She rose to her feet. "And how well did you *see* it?"

"Well..." I couldn't meet her eyes, and not just because they were nine inches above mine. "Emerson pushed me behind him and...he's kind of big."

"Julian Emerson?"

At the clear surprise in Elena's voice, I looked up. A frown flashed across her forehead, gone instantly.

Then she shrugged. "Maybe Emerson was faking a fight. Guys do that sometimes to impress a woman."

"Hardly. Emerson's *way* too arrogant to fake anything." Besides, he was Suitguy. Defender of the Hidebound, Righteous Protector of the Old School Tie. He would never try to wow punk little ol' me. "*Someone* attacked us. Three someones."

Elena busied herself with her bag, putting away the bottle. "And Julian Emerson fought them. Three of them. Yet there wasn't a scratch on him?"

"Well..."

"Or any blood?"

I thought of that strange fuzzing out thing. Had that zapped the blood somehow? Fixed any wounds? "I don't think he was injured."

"Nixie." Elena gave me the full benefit of her intelligent dark stare. "You're saying an attorney, a man whose most demanding activity is filing briefs, fought *three* men—and won? Not only won, but didn't have a single injury?"

It sounded impossible, put like that. "He's pretty tall..." I mumbled.

"Nixie, honey." Elena clasped my shoulders warmly. "To

you, *everyone* is 'pretty tall'."

"Fine." I kicked at the stupidly clean sidewalk. Stubbed my toe for my trouble. "So what should I do?"

Elena shouldered her bag. "Well, you could report it. But there's no evidence. And you didn't really see anything. So it wouldn't do much good."

"I suppose not."

"However. I *would* be careful. Going out after dark."

"What? Oh, come on now." First Julian, and now Elena. I put my hands on my beruffled hips. "This is Meiers Corners, not Chicago."

"Yeah, but—hey, do you want to grab breakfast? You'll feel better with some food." Elena started off on her long, strong legs. "How about we go to the Caffeine Café?"

"Don't try to change the subject." I trotted to keep up. "Yeah but what?"

"I'm not changing subjects. You get crabby if you go too long without eating. That tiny body of yours."

"Yeah—but—what?"

"Damn, you're persistent. I can't believe you're not an older sister."

"I babysat. Last chance. Why shouldn't I go out after dark?"

Elena shrugged, looked a little uncomfortable. "With the Coterie moving to annex us, Meiers Corners has drawn attention. And not just from the businessmen and politicians, I'm afraid."

"Who else has noticed—" I stopped dead. "You mean *real* gangs? Like Vice Lords? Or one of the Popes? The 12th Street Players?"

Elena shrugged again. "Probably none of those. But Bo's fielded some threats."

I ran to catch up. "Bo has gotten threats?" Her husband, Bo Strongwell, managed an apartment building on the upper east side. "Why Bo? Why not the police, or the mayor?"

Strangely, that made Elena look even more uncomfortable. "Bo does this neighborhood watch thing. I think that's why he got involved."

I was confused. "What does a neighborhood watch have to do with gangs from Chicago?"

30

Elena's eyes wouldn't meet mine. "Well...I think it's part of a larger network. Bo's, uh, neighborhood watch."

Yeah, I thought. *Suuure.* I could practically hear Jon Lovitz saying, "That's the ticket." Elena might be telling some part of the truth but by no means all of it.

We reached the Café. Before going in, Elena faced me. Her eyes were dark and serious. And lurking beneath, she might have even been worried. "Do me a favor, Nixie. Just be careful."

Elena Strongwell, super cop. Worried. "Are you okay, Elena?"

"Dine and fandy." She turned and pushed open the door.

I shut my mouth and followed. Elena had invoked the Dine and Fandy.

Dine and fandy was a mix-up of fine and dandy. It was what we said when shit was flying but we were coping. When we didn't want to talk about it.

So even though I was deathly curious, I dropped the subject. Besides, we were friends. I could always attack her later about Bo's mysterious neighborhood watch.

Elena made her way to a table in the corner. "So tell me about the fundraiser. Is Guns and Polkas playing?"

I groaned, remembering the manila Pack of Doom. "The band's playing. I guess."

"You guess?" Elena grabbed a chair and put her back to the wall. A cop thing, probably. "Is something wrong?"

I sat opposite. "Yeah. I got mammomashed by the mayor."

Sympathy immediately touched her face. "Tit in a wringer?"

"Yeah."

I broke off as a beautiful, regal blonde sashayed in from the back room. To my surprise the woman immediately hurried over to us. To my further astonishment she rapidly laid gleaming silverware in front of Elena and me. To my absolute shock she smiled and said, "Your usual, Elena?"

This was no barista. *This* was the proprietor of the Caffeine Café herself, Diana Prince. Diana was normally as majestic as her name. Her barstool was her throne. She rarely waited on customers and *never* personally came to a table.

Except, apparently, for Elena O'Rourke Strongwell.

Elena nodded. "My usual's fine. And whatever Nixie wants."

31

I had expected to have to slog in line for my caffeine, to have plenty of time to figure my order out. "Uh," I said, for a moment at a loss. "I guess I'll have a red eye. And a...a scone."

"The orange frosted are very good today." Diana's tone was actually *coaxing.*

"Uh, okay."

"Shall I heat it?"

I blinked. "Yeah. That'd be great."

As Diana the Princessy Proprietor glided away, I transferred my confused face to Elena. "What got into her?"

A blush stole over Elena's fair cheeks. "She, ah, owes Bo."

"She must owe him her *life* to be *that* grateful...no. Not really?"

The flush deepened. "We don't talk about it. So tell me about the fundraiser. I heard it was to pay for that attorney you were talking about. Julian Emerson."

Another thing about friends is that they don't play fair. Wanting to switch subjects, Elena had sucker-punched me. And she knew just where to hit. I launched into my own rant. "We have to raise five hundred thousand dollars. Can you believe it? Half a million to pay for a snarky lawyer."

"Some of that might be for legal research." Elena toyed with her silverware, not looking at me. "And, uh, processing fees."

"Maybe. But you can be sure most of it's going in Emerson's perfectly tailored pockets. There's a reason they're called sharks, you know.

"Oh, I don't know. Emerson seems nice."

I think my jaw dropped. "Have you met him? He's not *nice*, Elena. He's a *lawyer*. The two terms are mutually exclusive. Like military intelligence. An oxymoron, emphasis on *moron*."

"My father was a lawyer," Elena said, turning stiff.

"That's way different. Your father didn't charge five-fucking-hundred dollars an hour."

Elena picked up her fork. Thoughtfully balanced her knife between its tines. "If Emerson can fend off the Coterie, he'll have earned it." Slowly, almost reluctantly she added, "And...I think he might donate some of his fee. To charity."

"And he's kind to small dogs and pigeons. For goodness sake, Elena. Emerson's a bloodsucking monster in an old school tie. A fucking vampire, not a hero!"

The knife clattered to the table. Elena's face drained completely of blood. "A...a what?"

"A leech! A man who enriches himself on the pain and suffering of others. A *lawyer*."

Her color returned. "I don't think Julian Emerson is like that. But," she said, holding up a hand to stop any further argument from me, "it really doesn't matter. All that matters is that he keeps us safe from a takeover. And that we raise enough money to pay him."

Our orders came then. Diana laid cup and plate in front of each of us. Good smells wafted from mine. I was hungry. But I was more upset. As Diana sashayed away I dug a fork savagely into my scone. "I suppose that's all that matters to *you*."

Elena smiled at me over her mocha latte. "Eat. You'll feel better. Not another word on snarky lawyers, okay? Now, tell me about the fundraiser."

I gave her such a glare. "Damn, you're persistent. I can't believe you're not an annoying older sister. Oh, wait. You are."

"Damn tootin'. So get a-shootin'."

"Very funny." I mashed scone crumbs onto the back of my fork. "But since you'll just hassle me to death if I don't...the fundraiser is more like a bunch of fundraisers. This thing's going to be Summerfest, Germanfest, and the Grand Ole Opry all rolled into one. Everything and anything that will raise money. Even cheese balls." I squashed the scone a couple more times with my fork.

"You going to eat that thing or torture it to death?" Elena said, her tone amused.

I glared at her again. Honestly, she should have burst into flames by now. Since she didn't, I shoved mashed scone into my mouth.

Heaven burst on my tongue. Sweet, tart, tangy. Warm oozing frosting, moist scone. Five tons of mad simply...dripped away.

"Better?" Elena's smile turned smug.

I should have resented that self-satisfied smirk, but I did feel better. "Yeah." I washed down heaven with my red-eye. Caffeine and sugar. Perfection.

"You're always a little crabby until someone feeds you."

"Am not," I objected through another mouthful of scone.

"Am too. So we'll have rides, like a county fair? And music tents?"

"No rides. Plenty of music, though. In fact, I'm auditioning bands tonight at the *Kosmopolitisch.*"

"But no rides. Huh. I think I'm disappointed."

"For heaven's sake, Elena." I swallowed. "It's almost winter. You want a bunch of kids slipping out of an icy Ferris Wheel and going splat on the pavement? We've got plenty of other attractions. A beauty pageant. Midway-style games with fussy little prizes. Fudge. Oh—and a sheepshead tournament. You should enter."

"Oh, no." Elena set down her fork. "I'm not playing *schafkopf* against you. You get a handful of fail and still slaughter your opponents."

"*You* don't pick unless you have five queens."

She sniffed, picked up her fork. "I'm just a conservative player."

"Uh-huh. Well, the point is, we need to raise money every way we can. Music, dancing, food—"

"—and beer?"

"Duh, yeah. It's Meiers Corners. A whole tent is just for beer tasting. Five big-names and thirty microbreweries. Bock, pilsner, stout, even raspberry and chocolate. Twenty-five bucks to the public, all you can drink."

"I hope you'll have plenty of porta-potties."

"Um...yeah, sure." I pulled a small spiral notebook out of my jacket pocket, made a note. Winced. *I was making lists.* Like my *mother.* Ye gods. I really was going to do this thing.

But if I was going down, I was taking Elena with me. "I want you to run the beauty pageant."

Elena sprayed muffin. "You what?!"

"I want you to run the beauty contest," I repeated, trying not to get a kick out of her shock. Elena's normally the ultimate of cop cool.

"*You* want me to run...?" She stared at me. "Oh, no. You're joking, right? Like someone died and made *you* Elvis."

"Mayor Meier made me an offer I couldn't refuse. Well, I

could refuse it, but I'd piss off every member of my band. 'Course, the mayor will probably wish *he'd* died when he sees how I run things."

"Wait. You're really in charge?"

"I'm really in charge." I flipped a page in the notebook, wrote "PAGEANT" at the top. "And I really want *you* to run the beauty pageant."

"You're kidding. You've got to be." Elena's brown eyes had gone a little wild. "You're either kidding, or you've gone insane. It's the only explanation."

"Aw, c'mon, Elena. Your mom was a model, right?"

"My mother died when I was an infant, Nixie! I don't know anything about modeling."

"It's in your genes. You'll be fine."

"Nixie, I'm a *cop*. I don't know the first thing about a beauty pageant." She took a slug of latte. Behind the steam rising from the cup her eyes bulged, and I didn't think it was just from the heat of the drink.

"Fine." I shrugged, shutting the notebook. "I'll ask your partner, instead."

Elena started choking. I reached over and pounded her on the back. She gasped, "Dirk!? You want Dirk Ruffles to run...anything?"

"Why not? He's friendly."

"Friendly like a sheepdog! He even drools like one. Nixie, that's nuts. Dirk's clueless. He doesn't know the first thing about being *human,* much less running a pageant!"

"What's to know? Draft a bunch of women, have them wear tiny swimsuits and parade them across a stage. Instant money."

"Oh, for heaven's sake. You're insane, you know that?"

"Does that mean you'll reconsider?"

"Not a chance. But I will help you with the planning. It's obvious somebody has to."

Chapter Four

It was the best offer I'd get, so at four o'clock I hiked over to Elena's on Seventh and Lincoln. The Strongwell apartment building was the weirdest I'd ever seen. It was right in the middle of working-class Meiers Corners, but it screamed money. A palatial entryway opened onto an elegant foyer of polished wood and cut crystal. It was an apartment building with several small units. It also had an institutional-sized kitchen, a gym, and a parlor straight out of the eighteen hundreds.

Like apartments grafted onto a Victorian manor house.

But Elena was happy there with husband Bo. So I figured the weirdness was none of my business. Especially since I wasn't exactly June Cleaver myself.

Elena met me at the door and led me to the parlor. I spread out my Papers of Doom on a table near the window. "Most of the pre-planning has already been done by Twyla." I pointed to the neat list of events with corresponding venues and budgets.

"So our first order of business is picking someone to run each event?" Elena skimmed the list. "How about Granny Butt for the Beauty Pageant?"

Our AARP stripper. "That's worse than Dirk."

"But better than me."

"Anybody's better than you, according to you. How about Buddy to run the Sheepshead Tournament?" Buddy slings drinks at Nieman's Bar.

"Since the tournament's at Nieman's, he'll already be there. Good idea." She marked Buddy's name next to the tournament. "I can't believe the mayor picked you to run this thing. You're not exactly Ms. Bureaucrat."

"I know. I think the cheese ball grease must have hardened all the arteries in his brain."

"A complete brainectomy is the only explanation I can think of."

"Hey, I think I've been insulted. It's entertainment, and I organize bands for a living. I can do this."

"Yeah, but didn't you even ask? Why *you*?"

Because the mayor knew I could, but I didn't want to tell Elena that. "I was too busy having a heart attack at the time." And then having an attack somewhere lower, bumping body-parts with pseudo-hubby Julian Emerson. "See anything Twyla missed, besides the porta-potties?"

"She's done a good job planning. Except...did she get insurance?"

Insurance. Almost as bad as lawyers. "It's just a big party. Why would we need insurance?"

Elena ticked off fingers. "Beer. Visitors. Visitors drinking beer. Expensive equipment. Expensive equipment with visitors and beer. Sidewalk ice. Beer and sidewalk ice. Kids. Expensive equipment and kids. Need I go on?"

Not unless I wanted her to take off her shoes and socks. "Doesn't the city have insurance?"

"It won't cover the festival."

"Fuck. I hate being an adult. How do I get some?"

"Talk to your insurance agent." At my blank look, Elena raised her eyebrows. "You don't have an agent?"

"I don't have insurance. Can I use your agent?"

She stared at me like I was insane. "Thousands of dollars' worth of musical instruments and sound equipment and you don't have insurance?" Elena didn't quite squawk it.

"Insurance is expensive. I'm poor." I shrugged. "Which reminds me. How much do you think I'll need to budget for it?"

"I have no idea." She was still staring.

Only Mom could stare harder. Immediate distraction was in order. Before I got Elena-sized skull piercings. "I'll call for it tomorrow. If you tell me your agent...?"

It sort of worked. Elena went to find the name, which got her stiletto-stare off me. But it backfired, in that she felt the need to review *every* string and clasp of the Packet of Doom. To make sure I didn't forget anything *else.*

Like I hadn't organized bands and music for half my life.

So it was four hours before Elena let me take a break. Then she *finally* went to find her husband while I kicked back on the couch with a soda. I put my feet up on the coffee table and rubbed the cold can against my temples. Shut my eyes.

A *whump* snapped them open again. What the hell? Another *whump* sounded. Overhead. From the ceiling. Crystal tears on the chandelier shuddered. Another *whump* right on top of me.

I sprang to my feet. Dashed up the stairs. *Whump, whump.* The noise was coming from the room directly over the parlor. Cautiously I tiptoed down the hall and pushed open the door.

The room was all narrow lacquered floorboards and wall-to-wall mirrors. Weights and equipment were clustered in one corner.

In the center of the room, naked to the waist, was Julian Emerson.

He stood like some latter-day Goliath, his fists raised over his head. Muscles bunched and strained in his arms and chest. Loose black trousers hung low on lean hips. He slid one bare foot out, legs bent. Crossed powerful wrists in front of him. Pivoted and punched both arms up in a fluid harmony of motion.

My breath punched out as well, like I'd been hit by a truck. Julian's body was beyond gorgeous. His abs were cut like diamonds, his chest was chiseled marble. He turned and his back...stars above. His back made me want to wrap my thighs around him and ride him like a horse.

Twin wings of pure, hard muscle flared from his narrow waist to his immense shoulders. I could see individual muscles work as his fists spun out in a ballet of power. A thin sheen of sweat slicked his skin. I wanted to lick it off.

He turned again and I was overwhelmed by *color.* Bronze skin, deep bronze nipples. Short black hairs feathered up the center of his abs and over his broad chest. Black glossy hair curled around his ears as his two-hundred-dollar haircut absorbed the sweat of his exertion. Laser-blue eyes, made even more startling by his black sweeping lashes, stared—

Julian Emerson was staring straight at *me.*

I jerked back. The door swung gently shut. I checked the corners of my mouth for drool. Okay, I hadn't completely disgraced myself.

The door reopened. Julian stood there, a white towel draped over his broad bronzed shoulders. I took a deep, involuntary breath. The smell of a strong, well-oiled male body came like thick incense. I could practically taste it on my tongue, it was so wonderfully tangy. I nearly swooned.

"Nixie? What are you doing here?" Julian's deep, cultured drawl caressed me like cream. I wanted to melt in its liquid tide.

Which would have been mortifying beyond words. I was drowning in a tide of mindless hormones. What the hell was I doing, lusting after Suitguy? Although he was not exactly Suitguy at the moment. He was Pumped Pecs guy. Taut Ass guy...I struggled to get myself back on some sane footing. "What kind of accent is that?"

"Bostonian." He eyed me strangely. "Is there some problem?"

"No, no." I backed away. "I was working with Elena and heard the thumping." Thumping, pounding, rhythmic and hard. Like bodies pounding into the sand with the surf pounding all around—

Fuck. The guy was a lawyer! Just because he smelled like sex on a Harley didn't make him one iota less proper and dull. "Do you ever wear leather?" I asked, and could have bit my tongue.

"My shoes," he said, clearly confused. "My watchband." He showed me his wrist. Black leather, but connected to a highly conservative, highly expensive timepiece.

"I thought you used a pocket watch." I could have bit my tongue again.

That almost made him smile. "No pockets." He indicated his naked torso.

"Yeah," I breathed, and choked. "Well, I have to get back...to work. Yeah, work. Before Elena has to leave."

Julian frowned. "How did you get here?"

"Get here? Well, I...I walked."

"Walked." The frown became a scowl, and I remembered his telling me not to be out alone after dark. "Well, when you're done working, let me know. I will *walk* you home."

He still thought I was a little kid! Annoyance sliced through the sensual haze. "Who died and made you my keeper?"

The scowl turned into a slight smile. "I did."

He died and made *himself* my keeper. Oh, great. A bloodsucking lawyer, playing babysitter to a twenty-five-year-old. And an autocratic bloodsucking lawyer at that. "For your information, I'm not going home. I'm going to audition bands at the *Kosmopolitisch.*"

"Then I'll walk you there."

Stupid autocratic bloodsucking *tenacious* lawyer. "Well, be warned. I'm in charge of this extravaganza that's paying your exorbitant fees. And I'm putting everyone I see to work. You might find yourself in charge of the cheese judging."

"I'll take my chances." Julian checked his watch. Whipping the towel off his shoulders he started to rub the sweat off his chest. His pecs were really huge for such a lean man and they danced like heavyweight wrestlers. I wanted him to stop with the towel. I wanted to lick his chest dry instead.

No, no, no! I wanted to leave him *strictly* alone. Pristine white shirts and old school ties normally covered that chest. Delectable though said chest was.

I wondered what Julian would look like in only an old school tie...and nothing else.

I was so fucked.

♪ ♪ ♪

Elena and I worked for another hour before she had to leave for the police station. She usually started work at nine. As a detective she had some leeway, but she couldn't avoid going in all night. As she said, "Somebody has to keep Dirkenstein from boring the department to death."

I got out of having Daddy Julian accompany me by dipping out with Elena. Band auditions didn't start until ten thirty, and I needed to go to the cop shop anyway. I had to ask her partner Dirk to chair the beauty pageant.

Elena's husband Bo walked with us, which surprised me. Apparently the threat of Big City Gangs meant not even kick-ass detectives were allowed out alone after dark.

It was so stupid. Like either Elena or I were prissy little girly girls.

If it had to be anyone, I guess I'm glad it was Bo. Elena's husband was built like a Viking, complete with wavy blond hair. But he was easygoing and had a sense of humor. That was refreshing in a town as conservative as Meiers Corners.

Elena chafed under Bo's watchful eye. "Why, Bo? Much as I love your company, why do you have to come? I have my gun. And my backup piece."

Bo only shook his head. In his deep voice, which Elena says sounds like black satin, he said, "Detective. You know a gun and a knife are not enough against a *gang.*"

A word about being a musician.

We lived in a world filled with sound. For us, sound was information. It was as informative as sight for normal people. And in some ways sound was better than sight. You heard things the light wouldn't reveal.

Speech was a marvel of music. Take the phrase, "You're such an idiot". It could be said affectionately ("You're *such* an idiot"), or spitefully (*"You're* such an *idiot"*). Or just plain hatefully ("You're such an *idiot!"*). The same words could take on a wealth of different meanings, depending on the music behind the words.

Bo's words were a symphony of meaning. *Detective* had a lilt that told of deep affection. Bo said *detective* the way another man might have said *sweetheart* or *love.*

But the word *gang* had deep, ominous overtones.

Strangely enough, they weren't the usual ominous overtones. Not that any ominous overtone *was* usual. But Bo's overtones didn't say *dangerous* or *punk* or even *scary.* I wasn't really sure what Bo's overtones meant.

I only knew they were *unnatural.*

And Elena shivered.

Put together with Bo insisting on escorting us, I wondered if maybe snarky old Julian Emerson didn't have a point. Maybe I should be a little more careful after dark.

Just as I had that thought, about halfway to the cop shop, the night thickened around us.

41

Shadows that hadn't been there swirled and coalesced. I jerked to a stop, wondering what was going on. Wondering if I was imagining the dark pressing in on us.

A streetlamp bulb burst ahead of us. The loud pop was followed by glass tinkling to the sidewalk. Elena whipped out her gun. Bo slid fluidly in front of us both. He seemed to flare bigger.

Five men stepped from the shadows. Long leather coats swept around the ankles of three of them. The other two wore expensive-looking suits.

No overcoats, though. The suits must be freezing their heinies off.

But hell, I thought. Emerson was right. Meiers Corners did have gangs.

And here we were, five against three. Five large, very menacing males. Against a Viking, a cop, and a squirt.

We were in trouble.

One of the suits swaggered forward. The guy looked like Der Arnold—from the bodybuilding days, before he became The Governator. He was big, blond, and confident. More than confident. *Contemptuous.* "Fighting us won't do any good, you know. We'll get what we want." His eyes, a curious red brown, drifted over Elena, then me. "*Everything* we want."

A rumble came from Bo's throat. Low and menacing, almost inhuman. "This is *my* territory."

"This *was* your territory." The suit shrugged. "Not anymore."

"You have no right to be here."

"We have every right. Why should we pay for what we need—when we can just take it?" The man's eyes floated disconcertingly over me. I felt my heart beating hard in my throat. "In fact, maybe we should take it *now*."

"That," said a cultured voice, "would be particularly ill-considered."

I whipped around. Julian Emerson strode from the darkness, his face a bland mask of urbanity. He wore his usual suit but at least he'd had the sense to throw a coat on over it. A very nice black cashmere coat. I followed him with my eyes as he took a stand next to Bo.

Oddly, the spokesman flinched. "You can't stop us." He didn't sound nearly as confident. "There are five of us. Only two of you."

My spine snapped straight. "Four of us."

That dropped into the tension like a splatting bird-bomb. Bo frowned. Julian scowled. Even Elena looked a little shocked.

The gang leader *laughed.* I clenched my fists. How dare he? I was small, but trained. In the right place, my fists were as lethal as the next guy's. I stalked forward.

Only to run into Julian's arm barring my way. "Let us handle this."

Wasn't that just typical? "Oh, yeah. Us *men?*" I spat.

Startled blue eyes met mine for an instant. "Not at all." His gaze whipped back to the gang confronting us. "This has nothing to do with gender."

Elena sidled up to me. "Do as he says," she murmured. "There's more going on here than you know."

"Numbers don't matter, Cutter," Julian said to the gang's spokesman. "And you can tell that to your bosses."

"Numbers *do* matter, when it's a hundred to one." The man called Cutter bared his teeth at Julian and Bo. His canines were strangely pronounced. "Or a *thousand* to one."

"Not when the *one* is very old. And very powerful." Julian seemed to swell in front of me, growing taller and broader before my very eyes.

An optical illusion. It had to be. Because of the dim light. Six-foot-something of male could *not* grow half a foot.

But the men facing us fell back. Cutter steeled himself. "Even an Ancient would fall beneath a *thousand.*"

"An ancient what?" I asked, but no one answered me.

"Would you like to test that theory?" Julian asked. And he pumped up again, so big I knew it was no illusion.

Then, in front of my shocked eyes, his hands...his strong, square hands...grew. Lengthened. Sharpened.

Became something like claws.

Julian surged forward. He moved impossibly fast, was on the gang before I could blink. As Cutter quailed before him, Julian slashed violently downward with those claw-like hands. Blood sprayed.

I screamed. My voice stuck in my throat.

Cutter howled, flailed with both fists. Julian slid just out of reach. Almost casually, he reached into his cashmere coat, swept something out. Something that doubled in length with a *ka-chick*. Something that looked like a really big knife...or a sword. It glinted in the moonlight like it was very sharp.

Silver flashed. Cutter fell to the sidewalk with a sick *whump*. The rest of the gang cowered in the shadows of the broken streetlamp.

"Take this back to your keepers." Flicking the blade shut, Julian bent elegantly. He scooped something up and held it out to them.

It looked like a head.

"Tell the Coterie that Meiers Corners is off limits. That it will *not* be annexed to Chicago, not in *any* way. *Ever*." Julian lobbed the thing toward the gang. The other suit caught it, bobbled it like a hot potato.

Julian's cultured voice roughened. Almost growling, he said, "Now *go*."

The gang ran.

"Showy." Bo sauntered over to where Julian stood, fist clenching.

Julian's hands appeared normal now, and I wondered at the trick of the light that had made me see claws.

"I did not intend to be quite so...theatrical." Julian's cultured voice was still rough.

"You can take the man out of the performer, Emerson, but—" Bo laughed. "Take the man out, get it?"

"You have a juvenile sense of humor, Strongwell. Get Elena and Nixie out of here. I'll clean up." Julian jerked a hand toward where Elena and I stood.

I didn't want to go. I wanted to figure out what the hell had just happened. And find out if Julian had been hurt.

And comfort him if he had.

All right, probably a bad idea. But the body—the possibly headless body—of the gang leader looked big and fierce on the ground. Julian was a *lawyer*. A desk jockey. For whatever insane reason, I had to know if he was okay. "Emerson?" I reached out to touch him. "Julian?"

Julian turned so I couldn't see his face. "Go with Strongwell, Nixie. You'll be safe with him."

"But what about you?"

"*Go.*" His voice was strange, hollow. And though I don't follow *anyone's* orders, I found my feet moving.

I had gone half a block before I realized what I was doing. "The fuck!" I dug in my heels and spun.

Julian and the body were gone.

Chapter Five

"So all I have to do is pick some pretty women and have them to dress up in bikinis?" Detective Dirk Ruffles's muddy eyes brightened. "And pick some judges? That sounds easy. Not nearly as hard as being a detective. I know who I'll ask to judge. I bet my uncle'd do it. He likes pretty women, almost as much as I do. I bet he'd say yes. My uncle, and maybe Captain Titus. Or maybe not Captain Titus since Elena found out he's a pimp, which means he's manager to a group of prostitutes—"

"Dirk! Heel!" Elena snapped her fingers in front of her partner's face, stopping the inexhaustible flow.

For about two seconds. Or maybe Dirk was just taking a breath before launching back in. "I was just saying, Detective Ma'am. My uncle the Chief of Police would be good as a judge."

I stepped in. "Your uncle would be great, Dirk. And the women are already expecting the swimsuit competition. All you need to do is, er, well—" All he needed to do was *nothing*. But I didn't want to come out and say it.

"But I get to pick some pretty women, right?"

"Um, no. Actually, all the pre-competition stuff is taken care of." By my good, efficient friend Twyla Tafel. "You don't have to pick the women. They're already signed up."

"But Nixie, I've got an idea!"

Uh-oh. Dirk with an idea was as dangerous as a monkey with a gun.

Now that I thought about it, Dirk sort of looked like a monkey, too. Skinny, with a potbelly. Like an orangutan—well, maybe not an orangutan, because they were apes, not monkeys. Like a chimpanzee...no, wait, those were apes, too.

Like a macaque! Yes, those were monkeys. Except, no...no, he really didn't look like a macaque.

No, Dirk Ruffles looked like Tarzan's chimp, Cheetah, in a bright yellow fedora. On anyone else the hat would have looked all Humphrey Bogart. It made Dirk look like a duck.

Actually, when he spoke, Dirklet reminded me of Huey, Dewey, and Louie, too.

Elena flashed me a sympathetic look. "What's your idea, Dirk?"

"That you'd be a perfect contestant, Detective Ma'am!" Dirk grinned like an idiot. "You'd look great in a bikini, Detective Ma'am! Like a Bond girl. In a bikini with a gun belt strapped across your hips!"

Bo, leaning against the wall, straightened suddenly. *Growled.*

Dirk was either deaf or just plain *baka.* Despite the obvious imminent danger, he continued blithely on. "What a great draw! My uncle would love it!"

Elena put a hand on Dirk's shoulder, keeping a wary eye on her husband. "Maybe that's not such a good idea, Dirk. Um, think of how it would reflect on the department. Captain Titus probably wouldn't like it." She kept her tone mild and reasonable, like speaking to a child. Elena once told me crowd control of a thousand drug-freaked groupies at a rock concert was easier than keeping Dirk in line.

I sympathized. I'd gone to school with the Dirkenator. He'd been clueless then, and maturity hadn't been any kinder to his brain cells.

Under it all, Bo continued to growl.

"You know who else would be good?" Dirk continued happily on. "The Widow Schrimpf. The one you said looked like Lady Godiva? I don't know what chocolate has to do with it, but the Widow Schrimpf sure looks good in a bikini. I think a lot of guys would like looking at her. Even though she's gay. But the guys wouldn't know. And it's just looking. Not like fondling or anything."

"Just looking," Elena repeated soothingly to Bo.

"Not like fondling," I added helpfully.

The growling deepened.

Dirk ignored it. "But you, Detective Ma'am. In a bikini with guns...yum, yum."

Elena shot an alarmed look at her husband. Bo was normally the most placid of men. But at the *yum yum* he bared his teeth. And his eyes had gone that peculiar shade of bright violet that meant he was extremely pissed.

"Dirk!" I rushed between Bo and the clueless wonder. "I've been thinking. Elena is right. Your Captain Tight-ass...um, Titus, wouldn't want the department to call attention to itself in such a, well, commercial way."

Dirk, mouth still moving, blinked. "Oh. Maybe."

"No maybe about it." I saw Bo start to relax out of the corner of my eye. "So instead of you, I think Bo should run the beauty contest."

Bo snapped upright. "What?!"

"No way." Elena gave me *such* a look.

Dirk clapped his hands. "Mr. Strongwell, you'd be perfect. You know all the pretty ladies in town. Elena, Diana Prince, Drusilla—"

Now Elena started growling.

The fact that the Dirkenator endorsed the idea should have warned me. But considering the alternative, I really had no choice. "It's easy, Bo. Contestant applications are already at local stores. Twyla Tafel is keeping track. All you have to do is pick judges. Almost a figurehead, really." I heard my voice drop into pleading.

"You've got to be kidding." Bo gave me a long, dark look. I thought his eyes were going to drill out the back of my head.

I whimpered. "But Elena can help you."

"And it's for a good cause," Dirk chimed in.

Bo's frown slewed to his wife and turned thoughtful. "Maybe...maybe it wouldn't be so bad."

"Not so bad?" Elena shrieked. "Not so *bad*?" She stared at Bo like his brains had dribbled out his ears. "*Not so bad*?" She couldn't seem to think of anything else to say.

"Well, that's settled then." I used my brightest third-grade-teacher voice. "Bo will run the beauty pageant. And Elena will help."

Elena turned her stare on me. She didn't *say* a thing, but

was obviously *thinking* words too blistering to speak. Either way, now was the time to get out. While I still could.

Dirk's muddy rasp stopped me. "But what can I chair, Nixie?"

Bo blinked at Ruffles, then sliced me a grouchy look. "Yes, oh great Fearless Leader. What do you have for Detective Ruffles to do?" Just a touch maliciously he added, "Maybe he should help *you* with planning."

"No!" I shouted. Dirk looked hurt. "I mean...Detective Ruffles can be far more helpful running...the Sheepshead Tournament." Which practically ran itself. Hopefully.

"I don't know," Dirk said. "Gambling. Captain Titus wouldn't like that either. Even though he's a pimp."

"And Buddy at Nieman's Bar is already in charge of the sheepshead competition," Elena said, perversely helpful.

"Yeah, *thanks*. I forgot about that." I thought furiously hard. What could the Dirkenator do? The opening VIP reception? No, he'd bore any potential donors to death. What, then? Not the beer tent. Not the corn 'n wienie roast. Definitely not the kiddie games—that was just a lawsuit waiting to happen. I couldn't think of a damned thing.

I felt frustrated. Not only because I couldn't think of anything that would keep Ruffles happy, yet out of the way.

I was also frustrated because of Elena's and Bo's crabby faces. Because I didn't like how I was behaving. I didn't like cornering friends into running stupid contests. It would serve the mayor right if I just quit. Just because he'd known me since diapers...just because he'd offered my band the break of a lifetime...I didn't *ask* to run this foozley extravaganza. I especially did not ask to corner friends to run an extravaganza to pay for an overpriced, overrated, snooty *lawyer*.

As if the thought brought him, the office door clicked open. Julian Emerson strode in, all graceful power and authority. His cool eyes flicked over the room. Disdain curled in that arrogant gaze. The mighty big-city attorney looking down on our tiny cop shop. Stupid Boston blue-blood. The fact that Julian exuded waves of barely contained sex appeal only made it worse.

All my frustration and self-disgust channeled itself instantly at Julian. It burst through my system as a big, bad mad. "WTF are you doing here, Emerson?"

"I'm here to walk you home." So cool. So confident. So fucking sensual.

My jaw kicked up. "You going to carry my books, too? And I'm *not* going *home*."

He kept coming. Didn't stop until he was standing practically on top of me. He was so close I could have put my nose between his impressively huge pecs. Wickedly, I thought about the smudge of makeup I'd leave on his old school tie.

But my quarrel wasn't with his tie. Well, it was, but right now I was picking a fight with him. I tilted my head so I could glare directly into his eyes. My neck started to kink. I ignored it. "You don't have to stunt, Emerson. I can walk by myself. I am not a child!"

Brightly, Dirk said, "You look like one, Nixie. A child, that is. Next to Mr. Emerson. Him being so tall and you only reaching up to his armpits. Well, not even his armpits—"

"I am not a child!" I said, stomping my foot.

My cheeks burned like a fire when I realized what I'd done.

It was all Julian Emerson's fault. Damn the man! His cool arrogance brought out the very worst in me. He was everything I hated. Puritanical and rigid (which my parents called stability). Pigheaded stubborn (which my parents called tenacity). Stifling anything creative (consistency) or fun (soberness). Julian Emerson was the epitome of rigid, stubborn, boring old male. Sober. Conscientious. Reliable.

No—pigheaded! Pigheaded Julian, fixated on my not being alone at night. Feening on walking me to the auditions, like I was some little kid who'd lose her way.

"Nixie...think about what happened earlier," Elena said reasonably. "You really should let Julian walk with you."

"Safety in numbers," Bo agreed.

Julian, damn him, simply grabbed my elbow. "Are you finished here?" It didn't help that, with our extreme differences in height, he had to look down his nose to see me.

But here was a drama-llama question. Did I defy Julian's smug arrogance and stay? Or did I escape with him—before Dirk cornered me into putting him in charge of something?

In the meantime, Julian's square, competent fingers were branding a hole in my skin.

"I'm finished." I yanked my elbow loose. Julian, unfazed, simply put his strong hand on my waist.

Even though I wore layers upon layers of clothes, his heat burned.

It propelled me into motion. "I'll get back to you later about the pageant," I called to Bo and Elena as I escaped. Dirk I ignored. Hope springs eternal.

Only to be dashed. Dirklet followed us out, chattering. "So what do you want me to do for the fundraiser, Nixie? I could run a kazoo contest. Or should I book the polka bands? You are having polka bands, aren't you? Well of course you are. This is Meiers Corners. Is Guns and Polkas playing? Well, of course they are, it's your band. But will the Elvis impersonator be singing? I like him, though I wish he could play accordion like that nice Lawrence Welk. Do you think Oprah plays accordion, Nixie?"

Julian took his burning hand from my waist to hold it out like a traffic cop in front of Dirk. Still yammering, Dirk ran forehead first into Julian's palm and bounced like he'd hit a brick wall. "Detective Ruffles. You have work to do."

Dirk's muddy gaze met Julian's blue one. "I...I have..."

"Work to do," Julian repeated patiently.

To my amazement, Dirk said, "I have work to do."

"You need to return now."

"I need to return now." Dirk turned slowly around and disappeared back into the detectives' office.

"OMG!" I stared after Dirk. "That was so Jedi." I waved my hand in the universal Obi-Wan. "You don't need to see his identification."

Julian frowned at me. "I beg your pardon?"

I circled my palm at him. "You know. *Star Wars.* Obi-Wan and the Storm Troopers. Before they go into the cantina and meet Han Solo."

His frown deepened. Total incomprehension.

"For goodness sake. Where have you been the last thirty years, Emerson? A coffin?"

Julian blinked. "Do you ever speak English?"

"You're so daggy. Come on. Let's get this over with." I put his hand back on my elbow (better than the waist, and who

51

knew where he'd burn if he couldn't reach that?). And then, because he wasn't going to leave me alone, I started off to band auditions.

Besides, I could grill him on the way about Cutter and his gang.

Slowly, I wormed my fingers through Julian's, anchoring him to my elbow. When I was sure he couldn't get away I launched my offensive. "So what was that back there, with all the fighting and falling bodies and stuff?"

Julian gave an experimental tug. Found himself well and truly hooked. Grimaced. "Dirk looked fine when we left."

"Not Dirk, you moron. Cutter. Remember? Scary gang guys, male chest-beating, ancient blah-blah-blah?"

"Oh. That."

"Yes, that. What was that all about? Who were those guys? How do you know them? And how'd you make yourself look taller? Oh, and your hands. Did you put something on to make them look like claws? And did you really chop off that Cutter guy's head, and was that a machete you pulled out of your pocket and—"

"Nixie, please. One question at a time." Julian's eyes closed like he was developing a headache.

"Well...how'd you do the snarling cat thing? You puffed up about half a foot and I could have sworn you had claws. And you moved like lightning."

"Snarling cat thing." His eyes opened, tracked like he was thinking hard. "Yes, cat thing. How apt. You see, I study kung fu. A form based on animal natures. I appear larger by pumping up muscles, much as a body builder does. Cat-style kung fu also uses something called claw hand." He demonstrated, his fingers becoming rigid curves.

I squinted at his hand. I remembered his fingers looking sharper, but that could have been the light. "Okay, say I believe that. And the foot-long knife in your coat pocket? Or was it a sword?"

"Chef's knife. I do a bit of cordon bleu cooking in my spare time."

"Uh-huh. And you just happen to carry a foot-long thing in your clothes."

Both black eyebrows raised.

"I didn't mean that the way it sounded."

"I'm sure you didn't."

"Yeah. Well. Um, what about Cutter? It looked like you chopped off his coconut."

Julian shook his head. "Nixie. Think how unlikely that is. A human neck has bone an inch thick. Tough muscle. Tendons and cartilage. And I sliced through that with a chef's knife?"

"Well...I saw blood."

"Yes. I hit Cutter in the head with the hilt of my knife. To knock him out. Head wounds bleed a lot."

"Oh. And the thing you tossed to the rest of the gang?"

"A bundle of cash. A bribe. Good heavens, Nixie, I'm a lawyer, not a superhero. You didn't think I physically threatened a dangerous gang, did you?"

I flushed. "No, of course not. Oh, look. There's the club." Conveniently, for my embarrassment. "Time for auditions."

The *Kosmopolitisch* was the Meiers Corners equivalent of the Bronze in the Buffy universe. It had live music all the time. Most of it was pretty lame, but when you were a high schooler, who knew? And really, who cared? For most non-musicians, clubbing was all about drinking and getting laid. The music was just what got you in the mood.

Tonight was normally open mic night at the club. With less than two weeks until the festival, I'd strong-armed the manager into slotting my bands in instead, not that any of the dozen couples making out would notice.

Julian and I got there just as the first band was setting up. It was a group called Death Turkeys—two guys and a drum machine. You can see why I needed to do auditions.

Before they could strike their first chord there was a *click* and the lights went out.

The blackness was so absolute I could *feel* it. Like black cotton balls in my eyes. I remembered the last two times the lights went out and grabbed for Julian's arm. I clutched fine worsted wool. "What is it?" More attackers? More...blood?

"I don't know. Stay here." He rose.

I clutched tighter. No way. No way he was leaving me when there might be muggers, or attackers, or...or something worse.

Julian's warm hand slipped over mine. Gently, he worked my fingers loose. Before he could get away I grabbed on with the other hand. "My dry cleaner is going to hate me," he complained mildly, sitting back down. "I don't suppose I can convince you to wrinkle onto something other than my suit?"

"I can't see." Except I was beginning to be able to see a little. A thin beam of moonlight was just dusting the surroundings into shadowy shapes. The band guys milled in confusion on the stage. Or maybe they were trying to play. They strummed their guitars, getting little toy guitar twinkles for their efforts.

The *Kosmopolitisch's* manager, Cary Grant, was hopping around like a crazed monkey, pointlessly flipping light switches. Yeah, I know. And if anyone was *less* like the debonair actor it was this guy. He was short, he was hairy, and he could have played Gimli in Lord of the Rings. But Cary Grant wasn't the manager's real name. He was born Archibald Leach.

Anyway, Grant was flipping hard, *click-click-click,* but nothing was happening. So he dashed to the bar so fast he did a half-gainer over the edge. "I'm okay!" He jumped up and frantically tried various appliances. Empty clicks told me he had no greater success than he had trying to turn on the lights.

Surprisingly, the couples making out didn't seem to notice anything was wrong. Or maybe that wasn't surprising, considering their preoccupation. "I can see a little," I amended. "But not enough." Not enough to see if bad guys were coming.

"All right. Hang on." Julian rose again, this time taking me with him.

We wound our way through tables to the bar. Cary Grant had given up pushing buttons and flipping switches in favor of more brute force. Right now he was shaking the blender.

"Excuse me," Julian said in Grant's ear.

"Shit!" Grant squealed. Half-blended frozen daiquiri shot up onto the ceiling. Little snottules dripped onto my cheek from above. I wiped them off, absently licked. Hmm. Needed more lime.

"Who's there, and why are you trying to scare me to death?"

Grant wouldn't know Julian, so I spoke up. "It's Nixie, Cary. What's wrong?"

Deprived of the blender, Grant started on the dishwasher, poking and prying. "No phones, no lights, no motor cars. What do you *think* is wrong?"

I *thought* we were under attack. But I said, "Electricity out?"

"Well duh, Sherlock."

"Have you checked the circuit breakers?" Julian asked.

"Um...no." Grant stopped his frantic poking. "I, um, don't know where they are."

"Could they be behind this plate on the wall?" Julian indicated a hinged metal door.

"No, no. That's just the...safe. The safe where I keep receipts...and bills..."

But Julian had already opened the metal door. "You keep your receipts in the circuit breaker box?" Sure enough, rows of black switches were revealed, along with a pile of paper and envelopes. Julian removed the stack and started sifting through it.

"Hey! Those are private!" Cary Grant snatched at the papers but Julian was too quick for him, pulling away at the last instant.

"This could be part of the problem." Julian held up one of the envelopes. I could just make out the Meiers Corners Electric Company logo. He extracted two sheets of paper.

Grant snatched at them. Julian simply raised them higher until Grant couldn't reach. Julian tsked. "How long has it been since you paid bills?"

"None of your business!" Grant jumped. When he realized Julian's height made even pole-vaulting for the papers impossible, he added petulantly, "Besides, it's winter. They're not supposed to cut off your electricity even if you don't pay."

"I believe that's heat." Julian handed Grant his stack of unpaid bills.

"Oh. Yeah."

I put fists on hips, disgusted. "No electricity. Now how will the bands play?" Even if they had their stuff memorized, they'd need power for their amps and keyboards. And, looking over at the Death Turkeys, their drum machines.

"You could pay the bill, Nixie. Since you're the one who

needs the lights." Grant pushed the electric bill under my nose. That close, all I saw was OWE in big red letters.

"*Pay*? Me?" My wild take number thirty-two was lost on him in the sketchy moonlight. "I barely have enough money for my chewing gum habit. Why don't you ask the golden idol Godskrilla here?"

"Can't." Julian gave a curt shake of his head. "My cash is tied up. Long term investments."

I blinked. "You understood that?"

"'Golden idol' is universal. We might as well go, Nixie. Since the bands can't audition tonight."

I meant Godskrilla, but let it ride. "Yeah, but when? I need to audition the bands like *yesterday*. The festival's less than two weeks away!"

"You'll find a time, I'm sure." Julian dragged me out the door of the *Kosmopolitisch*. The moonlight etched his flared nostrils and sharp eyes.

"What," I said as he dragged me down the street.

His eyes were so intense they must have pierced every shadow. When he answered, he sounded distracted. "What, what?"

"You're doing your Elmer Fudd imitation. Do you think the lights-out *wasn't* because Cary didn't pay his electric bills?"

His eyes closed briefly, as if in pain. "Do you ever speak a known language? Sanskrit, perhaps?"

"Look, it's a simple enough question—"

I was interrupted by another streetlamp blowing a bulb. The sharp pop made me jump. "What is it with these cheap-ass lights? Or did Meiers Corners forget to pay its electric bill, too?"

Julian's fingers tightened on my elbow. "Don't blame the city." The hunter face was back in spades. His eyes were bright violet, like Bo's when he got really angry. And he was working his jaw like he tasted something nasty. "Apparently some people don't know a warning when they hear it."

Four figures swirled out of the dark. Three long coats and a suit.

Julian inclined his head toward them. "Gentlemen," he said, his voice dark and thorny.

If I thought by his calm nod he was being all friendly, that dangerous tone would have clued me otherwise. That, and the fact that he was grinding my elbow into powder with his tight grip.

"Emerson." The lead suit greeted him cautiously.

"Did you deliver my message to your bosses already?" Julian was the epitome of cool. He could have been at a Victorian tea party, asking "one lump or two".

The suit shrugged. "We phoned it in."

"It doesn't have the same impact if they didn't see my...little gift."

"We took a picture." One of the leathercoats held up a cell phone.

At least Julian wasn't so digitally challenged that he didn't recognize a camera phone. "Ah. And their response?"

The suit shrugged again. "You die."

"So you waited until I was alone."

"Hey," I objected.

"Yes." The suit smiled. And his canines were *really* long.

I leaned closer to Julian. "Four of them, two of us," I said under my breath. "We'll have a better chance with a plan. You take the toothy Lupin, I'll take the left coat." But as I started to move, something tugged my head forward, and the lights went out.

I was suddenly blind. Couldn't see a damn thing.

Fighting down panic, I realized something covered my head. Something clingy and soft. At least I hadn't had a stroke. Struggling with the thing, I realized it was some sort of cloth. A sack? A hood?

Growling and snarling slashed the air around me. It sounded like a pack of ravenous dogs. I had to do something. But how could I fight without my sight?

A couple quick little snicks were followed by a deeper *ka-click*.

And I realized I could fight—with my ears! I swung both fists. Hit *nothing*.

In front of me came a sound uncomfortably like meat tearing. I flailed at it, again swiping air.

And then came that terrible, awful sound I hoped never to hear again. Wet plopping. Blood, spattering onto the pavement.

Inside my restraint, I gasped for breath. I had to see! I reached for my face but a roar startled me into falling on my ass. The voice was Julian—if Julian had eaten a lion. What the hell was going on? Frantically, I tore at the cloth over my face. It wouldn't come off.

My fingers hit some lumps in the stuff. Gathers, like a tie in a channel of cloth.

It was my hoodie! My own freaking hoodie. I traced down until I found the laces. They were knotted tight.

Blindly I picked at the knot. Around me were sounds of a fierce fight. Four against one. I could only imagine the beating poor paper-pushing Julian was taking. If only I could help! The knot loosened but refused to come free. In impotent fury I jerked at the hood, as if I could rip it open. The cloth remained stubbornly whole.

The sound of fighting died away. What was going on now? Was Julian down? Was he...no, he couldn't be dead. Julian Emerson, Super Suitguy, was too damn arrogant to be dead.

But it was so silent. What else was I to think? And what would happen to me if Julian was...down?

Chapter Six

Hands came around my waist. I went ballistic, hitting and scratching with no finesse at all. Strong fingers grabbed my wrists, restraining me. Arms wrapped around me like steel bands. Lifted me. Caught me tight to an immense chest. My legs curled automatically around a lean waist.

My fight died. Strong fingers, steely arms, concrete wall chest. I recognized these body parts. And the oh-so-lean waist. Panic flamed into instant desire. I tightened my legs, snuggling my crotch up good and close.

Well, hello. Someone was *very* glad to see me.

"Nixie." Julian's voice. But not his usual cultured drawl. No, this voice was tight and strained. The kind of voice you got when all your blood drained from your vocal cords to your baseball-bat-sized cock. Ooh, he really did carry foot-long things in his clothes. I rubbed my hips against Mr. Big Gavel. That drew more blood down. "Nixie," he said again, even more strained. I found I *liked* Julian's voice all stiff and growly.

"Stop that. I'm trying to untie your hood."

Damn. Aroused, but in control of himself. How disappointing.

In my dark cave, I blinked. *Disappointing?* No way. I was not *disappointed* that Julian Emerson, stodgy old hoag, was not interested in me. Well, feeling his big nightstick flex, maybe he was interested. But not enough to be out of control about it. And that was a good thing, right?

Except I was burning up. That thick rod pulsing against my crotch, the smell of fighting male, the feel of his hard body under me...I was wet enough to grease a Cadillac.

So when my hoodie came loose, I took one look at his beautiful, dark-bronze mouth and kissed him good.

He tasted like war. Like fast rides with a powerful motorcycle between my thighs. Like getting drunk on expensive champagne. I ran my tongue over his lips and drank.

Julian's hands, in the process of putting me down, stopped. Came back around me. *Crushed* me to him.

His mouth opened against mine. With a raw groan, he kissed me back.

OMG. Julian hadn't spent *all* his time studying law in law school. His tongue slid between my lips, stroking my skin like wet silk. He tasted me as a man savors the last pressing of summer grapes. Suckled my lower lip like it was sweet, heavy, and ripe.

And as Julian kissed, his hands, those square competent hands, were oh so busy. One slid up and under my shirt. The other stole down the back of my pants.

That wasn't as easy as it sounded. Tonight I was wearing ruffled spandex over jeans cut to my ass over a French thong. But Julian wove his fingers over and under, smooth as a wet dream. Stroked my buttocks. Found that really sweet spot right at the base of my spine. Brushed the downy hairs until my bottom was wide awake and clamoring for more.

My brain filled with images. Me lying on my back, six-feet plus of male over me, all lean muscle and hot satin skin. Blue eyes clouded with desire as he did the passion pushups. Julian would be tender and attentive. Conscientious. Sober. Staid. Deadly dull.

We would have vaginal sex in the missionary position.

Would he even take off his tie?

Lust turned off like a light. I pulled away.

Julian didn't put me down immediately. He lifted his head, looked at me. Intently, as if he could read why I'd cooled in my eyes. It was weird. His hand was still down the back of my pants. I was still breathing heavily. I could feel my lips, still wet and buzzing. But Ms. Malebox no longer wanted any deliveries.

I expected Julian to be angry. I expected him to accuse me of being a cock tease or worse. After all, I had started it. And pulsing against my crotch was an erection as big and swollen as a Usinger sausage. It had to be painful.

But Julian only continued to stare into my eyes. Deeply, as if he could read my thoughts.

And maybe he could, because slowly he bent his head. He pressed warm lips to my neck. As if he had all the time in the world, his tongue came out and tasted me.

Not a little lick or tickle. No, a full, curling hot swipe. Intimate. Wet. Sinfully erotic. And just a little bit kinky.

That hot lick was not staid at all. My motor revved back up, going directly into third gear. I clutched Julian's shoulders. Hard muscle met my fingers. I closed my eyes and enjoyed.

The tongue grew bolder, tracing the line of my throbbing pulse. It slicked over my skin, steamy and questing. Hot male battle-scent spiced the air. Julian's fingers threaded into my hair, pulled my head aside to give him greater access to my neck. His mouth opened over my skin. Fiery breath lanced me.

Oh, please, I thought. Give me the sharp edge of sex. Bite me.

The scrape of teeth hit me like a step-up transformer. My whole body shuddered. My heart started hammering double-time. I grabbed Julian's head and mashed his lips into my neck. Do it again, my fingers screamed. Bite me. Harder.

Needle-like teeth touched my flesh. And then—

He bit me. For real.

His teeth penetrated my neck like lightning rods. My whole body convulsed in shocked reaction.

I shrieked. Electricity tore through my system. Caromed off my brain and knocked me sideways.

My world narrowed to black-edged waves of powerful climax.

When I could think again my heart was pounding and my mouth was dry.

Thin hot threads trickled down my neck. Julian was licking them like a man possessed. His eyes were closed, his lashes long and beautiful against his bronzed cheeks. A deep rumble came from his chest.

"What...what are you doing?" I croaked.

"Mmm?" His voice was half-murmur, half-purr.

"Kinky's good, and all..." I tried to swallow, couldn't get past the hot feeling of being *consumed.* "But if this is sex, it's not anything I've seen on the Internet."

Julian stiffened. The tongue stopped abruptly. With a final, gentle swipe, he set me down. "I need to get you home."

I felt lost. "Home?" What was he talking about? I had just had the best orgasm of my life—with a *lawyer*. And he hadn't even touched my pussy.

And now he was sending me home?

Rejection, horrible and cold, struck me. What made it worse was that I was still incredibly aroused. I jammed my hands into my pockets. "Whatever."

"It's late." Julian's voice was still rough. And he shifted his stance like *something* was uncomfortable.

At least I wasn't the only one to feel the furnace kick in. Not that it helped all that much. I had responded to Mr. Establishment not once but twice. Suit coats normally made me allergic. Had I no pride? I stomped off.

Only to slip in a pool of blood.

I would have landed on my keister were Julian not faster than a speeding bullet. He scooped me off my feet. And he kept going.

After I got over the shock of being carted along like a little kid, I wiggled my legs. "Hey, put me down!"

"Not until we're a little farther away."

I looked back at the rapidly receding scene. Blood was everywhere, splashes and pools of it.

But no bodies.

I remembered all the snarling and roaring. Before the licking and rubbing and biting... "Er. What happened to the gang?"

"They had to leave. Something about sending another message to their leaders."

"Uh-huh." All that blood, those gang members didn't leave standing up. So where were the bodies? "Really, Julian. What happened?" Four very big, very bad gang guys. I didn't really think law-book jockey Julian Emerson got all medieval on their heinies, did I?

He didn't respond. While I waited, I watched the scenery go by. The man could walk. And he carried me like I weighed nothing.

I was kind of enjoying it. Except for the not-answering part. I relaxed into Julian's arms. He had nice arms, strong and comfortable. He smelled good, too. The hot battle scent had faded but there was still something tangy and male. Not your basic Brut or Old Spice. "So the gang left."

That he answered. "Yes."

"To take a message to their leaders. To...the Coterie." I studied Julian's profile. Chiseled, very classic. Not so interesting. But he had a nice ear. Looked like it'd be soft and tender under my tongue. His hair made a sexy curve around it. Startled, I realized he'd look absolutely hawt with a diamond earring.

"Something like that."

I had to trace back to my question. The gang leaders. "Uh-huh. So do these mac daddies have names?"

"Pardon me?" Julian frowned. Still no subtitles, I guessed.

"The Chicago Coterie guys. What's their names?"

Julian made a face. "Their leader calls himself Nosferatu."

"Nosferatu? Like a vampire?" I stiffened.

Julian stopped, put me down. His expression was strangely cautious. "*Like* a vampire, yes. If vampires existed."

He was so literal-minded. It brought out the imp in me. "Spoilsport. I bet you don't believe in Santa Claus, either."

"Nixie...what I do or don't believe is immaterial. What counts is that the Coterie is real. And dangerous."

"Uh-huh. And one styles himself a gothy nightmare. Okay. What do the other ones call themselves? Attila the Hun, Michael Jackson, and Dick Cheney?"

He stared at me for the longest time. "That's humor, isn't it?"

I pressed a hand to my heart and gasped. "You recognized it! Julian! There's hope for you yet!"

"I recognize your *attempt* at humor." He grabbed my elbow and steered me north. "But it's misplaced. The Coterie is nothing to laugh about."

"Julian, if grown men are hiding behind daggy aliases like Nosferatu, how can you not laugh?"

"It's not exactly an alias."

"Uh-huh. It's really a family name."

"And that's sarcasm."

"No, that's also humor. Sarcasm is you're a big fucking dodo head if you think I don't know you're not telling me the whole story."

"No, I'm not. Be grateful. It isn't pretty."

I stopped. My fists hit my hips. "Be *grateful?* O thank you Great Legal One, for not burdening poor little Nixie with such terrible truths. What do you think I am, Emerson, a teeny-tiny baby?"

He kept going. "No. I think you're a very small but disproportionately annoying woman."

I raced after. "Who you treat like a kid!"

"In case you hadn't noticed, I wasn't treating you like a child a moment ago."

I had noticed. Grr. "Yeah, well, what do I know? Maybe you're a pedophile."

"And maybe you're a necrophile."

"Huh?"

"I'm fully aware of your adult status, Nixie." After a significant pause Julian added, "At least physically."

I gasped outrage. "Implying I'm being childish?"

"Not implying." His tone was more grouchy than angry. "Why do you have to taste so good?"

"Why do I...huh? I taste good?" A compliment? Backhanded, but it was the last thing I expected. Especially from Julian Emerson.

"Too damned good." He muttered it through barely open lips. Stopped, adjusted his pants. "Go in, Nixie."

For a moment I thought he meant his pants. But no, somehow we were in front of my townhouse. "This isn't over, Emerson." I meant the treating-me-like-a-kid thing. But my body shuddered—it meant the sex thing. The inexplicable, über-hot response my body had for his. I could only hope he didn't notice.

His eyes darkened.

He'd noticed. Fuck.

Which was what I still wanted to do.

"Go in," he repeated. He jammed his hands into his pockets

like he wanted to do something else with them. Like maybe grab me again. His eyes were almost black, his nostrils were flared, and his lips were so tight I thought they'd snap.

I wondered what those lips would feel like between my legs.

And then, cursing my own imbecility, I turned and fled into my townhouse.

Chapter Seven

Julian thought I was a kid. He didn't want me out alone at night. And to top things off, I was dangerously attracted to him. There was only one solution.

Find a guy, take him on a hot date, and bam his bones.

There weren't a lot of single guys in Meiers Corners. There were even fewer that I'd want to date, much less go to bed with. Most were either too old or too young. They were all way too hidebound.

Except for Bruno.

At first glance you'd think Bruno Braun buried the needle on the ultra-conservative meter. He was a big ex-SEAL dripping hair, tattoos, and conspiracy theories. A redneck bear with an *X-Files* fetish. Bruno ran the city's survivalist store, Armageddon 3.

But he was also Meiers Corners's only cross-dresser.

Bruno was just as out of place in Meiers Corners as me. Which was why we got on so well. And which was why, when I wanted to forget Julian Emerson, I called Bruno.

I keyed in Bruno's home phone number. At least I think it was his home phone. Bruno had a land line. Didn't want cell phone satellites GPSing his position. But no one really knew where Bruno lived, not even me. I counted three rings, hung up. After waiting two seconds I hit redial, counted three rings and hung up again. When I redialed another two seconds later, Bruno answered. "Have to make this fast, Nixie." His voice was sort of a low growl. "Can't tie up the line."

"Hey, Bear. What's so urgent?"

"I'm expecting a call. Information about The Coterie." He lowered his voice. "They're trying to take over Meiers Corners, you know."

"So I heard. Annex us to big daddy Chicago."

"If only that was all there was to it."

"Yeah, I heard about the gang problem, too."

There was a short silence. "You know about...the *gang*?"

I was about to pitch out some flip answer when it struck me. The music in his voice when he said *gang*. It was the same music as when Bo said gang. Like gang...was *unnatural*. "I know some. Not everything. Maybe you could tell me more."

"Not over the phone." He whispered it, a tight rasp very unlike the Bear's usual booming roar.

Discussing conspiracies in Meiers Corners. Some hot date. But I was on a mission. "Actually, that's why I'm calling. I thought maybe we could get together tonight. For dinner or a movie or something. And something...after."

"Dinner?" Bruno sounded confused. I forgot he didn't hit the social scene much.

"Yeah, or even just for drinks." Which might help with the after. Wrestling in bed with heavy and hairy suddenly didn't seem near as appealing. At least, not as appealing as lean and legal.

I slapped myself. Brawny and bearish was *exactly* what I needed. "You could give me the 411 on"—I lowered my voice— "the *gang*." I put the same strange emphasis on the word.

"Um, okay. Drinks. Nieman's Bar?"

"Sure. What time?"

"Four?"

"In the morning?!" The only time I was up at four was when I had a gig and was still up from the night before.

"This afternoon."

I breathed a sigh of relief. "Why so early?"

"Before the sun sets," Bruno whispered, and hung up.

I cradled my own handset more slowly. Things weren't adding up. Yeah, okay, Bruno had more conspiracy theories than The Home Shopping Network had "Wait! There's more!" But it wasn't just Bruno who put that odd, unnatural emphasis on *gang*. Bo Strongwell, typically the most normal of men, had, too. And I'd been attacked by unnaturally fast growly guys, not once but twice.

And Julian Emerson had bitten me. Really sank his sharp teeth into my skin.

But when I looked, there were no holes.

If I didn't know better—

My phone rang and I snatched up the handset. "Bruno, can you at least give me a hint about this *gang*?"

"I would, Dietlinde," a booming, jovial voice answered. "But then I'd have to kill you ha-ha!"

"Mayor Meier?" The mayor of the city, calling me? Mayor Meier never called *me*. Oh, not because he's too full of himself. Mayor Meier was the epitome of jolly *Deutsche* friendliness. He's Lawrence Welk in a Santa Claus suit. Throw the cow over the fence some hay, and let's go down by the lake, *ain'a*. "Call me Nixie, Mayor. If I may ask...why are you phoning?"

"*Ach*, Dietlinde! It is warming to my heart to know you are doing the running of the First Annual Meiers Corners International Fun Fair, Sheepshead Tournament, and Polka Festival. Just what we need to bring a little *gemütlichkeit* to our wonderful festival." He pronounced it "just vat ve need" and "vondehful". "*Ach ja*, our own little Dietlinde Schmeling—who I have known since diapers you were wearing!"

The diaper ploy. Emotional blackmail. "Please, Mayor. I prefer Nixie. And thanks, but it's not like I had a choice—"

"*Ja, ja.* There was no one else—no one, you understand? Then, when Twyla Tafel suggested your name, I said, 'Of course! Our *kleine* Dietlinde is perfect, *nicht wahr*?' And then I said—"

"It's nice of you to pick me," I interrupted brightly. Twyla set the dogs of doom on me? I was going to kill her.

No, I wasn't. Killing was too good for the haas. I was going to get *revenge*. "But you know who would really be perfect to run the festival? Someone who runs things for a living. Someone like Twyla!" Revenge this, Twyla.

"Of course, that is who I thought of at first! *Ach, ja,* great minds think alike, little Dietlinde."

And if he said *Dietlinde* one more time I was going to string him up by his *ja*'s and beat him about the genitals with his *ach*'s. "Mayor—call me Nixie, please. So why not go with Twyla now? I'll just return the packet"—of Doom—"and we'll be all set."

"*Ach*, but Dietlinde! You know why Twyla can't do the running of the First Annual Meiers Corners International—"

I took a nano-nap. Tuned back in on "—pregnant."

"Twyla's pregnant?" I screeched.

"*Nein, nein*," Mayor Meier chuckled. "Twyla's *sister* is having the little *liebchen*. But of course *mein gut* Twyla will be out of town to attend the birth."

Mein gut Twyla? My good Twyla, my ass. My friend had not only pointed the finger at me, she'd turned it up in salute! "I thought Twyla was running the beauty pageant!"

"Only the pre-pageant organization, little Diet—"

"Nixie, please!" Sheesh. "What about Heidi? She runs your office...practically runs the city!"

"*Nein, nein*, Dietlinde. The festival must be jolly! Heidi would snap her whip and command merriment. While that is fun in the office, for the tourists—"

I did *not* want to hear about the mayor and Heidi's merry whip. "I get it. It's me or nothing." And my pride would see that I did the job right. I sucked in a resigned breath, let it out on a sigh of acceptance. "Will *anyone* from your office be around to help me?"

"*Ja*, of course. We are not out in the cold leaving you. The alderpersons have all been pressed...er, have volunteered their services."

A bunch of bureaucrats? Oh, great. I knew from experience they'd be no help running things. They'd just argue, table the motion, and go to Nieman's Bar for a couple of drinks.

"Now, I know what you are thinking, Dietlinde. But we have gotten a little new blood on the Common Council since you were the student representative."

"Shh! Don't say that so loud." I flushed. I can't believe I was actually a part of student government. Talk about bad for my hard-ass reputation! Added to the diaper ploy...yeesh.

"*Ja*, well I was just wanting to reassure you. We have that nice young Josiah Moss of the Stark and Moss Mortuary. And Kurt Weiss, manager of the Allrighty-Allnighty. Both are very energetic. Oh, and Detective O'Rourke's sister. Gretchen

Johnson. I remember when she was in diapers." He laughed, all jolly Santa. "I remember when *you* were in diapers."

Sheesh. Did this man have a diaper fetish? "Are Donner and Blitz still on the Board?" Donner and Blitz were two old drunks, perpetuees of Nieman's Bar. I actually kind of liked Donner and Blitz. After the council meetings they were the ones who took me to Nieman's with them. And gave me beers. Don't tell Mom and Dad.

"*Ach, ja.* And bartender Buddy, and the lovely Brunhilde Butt, as well."

I groaned. Lovely was definitely in the eye of the beholder where Brunhilde was concerned. Affectionately known as Granny Butt, Brunhilde moonlighted as an exotic dancer at Nieman's Bar. If you could classify stripping out of a girdle and orthopedic hose as exotic.

"Oh, goodie," I said. "Sounds like a lot of help."

The mayor didn't catch sarcasm quite as well as certain overpriced attorneys (with great hands). No, I didn't think great hands. I was *not* thinking about competent square hands and what they could do sure and strong between my legs. Not...thinking...shit.

"*Ja,* great help. So I just want to thank you. And remind you of the Summerfest playing for the Guns and Roses if we make our target of the five hundred t'ousand dollars. That is vunderful, *nein?*"

Council blackmail, diapers, and the threat of murder by every member of my band if I screwed up this gig op. "Oh yeah. Vunderful."

"Well, that is all, little Dietlinde. Oh, except make sure you have the twenty tickets set aside, *bitte.*"

"Twenty tickets?"

"*Ja,* to the bands. You know my sister is the teacher, *ja?* In Wauwatosa?" He pronounced it Va-va-tosa. "Well, she also does the advising for the Wauwatosa Applied Mathematics Organization."

Great. Now I had to babysit twenty little geeks, on top of everything else.

But the mayor was continuing. "They are interested in the acoustics, *nicht wahr?* So they looking forward to hearing the bands are."

Shit. That reminded me—I had forgotten to reschedule auditions. And this was Thursday night. Unless I set auditions up for tonight, most bands would be unavailable, playing their weekend gigs.

"Twenty tickets. I'll get them to you, Mayor." I hung up and sighed. Then I caught a look at the clock and jumped up. Only two hours to get ready for my date—and worse, to clean my bedroom.

♫ ♫ ♫

I ended up calling the bands with my cell as I walked to Nieman's. I had just finished when I reached the bar. Swiveling the phone and stowing it, I pushed open the door to the old-style corner tap—and immediately went blind.

Oh, yeah. Nieman's keeps its lights *way* low, for when Granny Butt is wiggling on the bar. I mean, how many dewlaps can you see flapping and not lose your fifth boilermaker?

"*Psst*—Nixie. Over here."

Hunkered down—if you could call a mountain trying to crouch hunkering—in the back corner of the bar was Bruno.

I slid onto the barstool next to him, raised two fingers to the barkeep. "Hey, Bear. Come across any good field artillery lately?"

Bruno brightened. "Last week. I sold Elena a replacement for her bazooka. Nice SMAW. Shoulder-launched Multipurpose Assault Weapon."

I blinked. "Elena has a bazooka?"

"Had. For disabling *you-know-whats*."

"I-know-whats?"

"Yeah. Like the *gang* of you-know-whats."

"Oh! The *gang* of I-know-whats. Uh-huh." Okay, usually I was quicker than this. But we were speaking a language that had no known alphabet. I felt a flash of sympathy for Julian Emerson. "Bruno, what the hell are you feening about?"

He straightened, looking offended. "I don't obsess, Nixie. I'm not like those conspiracy nuts, you know. I only deal with truth. Cold hard facts."

The bartender came over with two glasses and a pitcher of bock. I traded him an Abe, which included the tip. If there's one thing I love about Meiers Corners, it's the cheap beer. "I'm sorry Bear." I poured beer for both of us, slid his over to him. "I didn't mean to insult you. So you have cold hard facts about the...*gang*?"

"Yeah. Here's what I found out. There's an organization called the Cook County Indemnity Corporation. They're really a front group for a bunch of fucking operators. They're the ones pushing the Chicago government to annex Meiers Corners."

"Okay." This might be the Coterie Julian referred to. "But what about the *gang*?"

"Well, it's like this. These CCIC guys are not just your usual business fartzecutives. They also run one of the most powerful and most secret *gangs* in the Midwest."

"Uh-huh." Suddenly I was way less convinced. Gosh, Batman. One of the most powerful and secretest of gangs. Run by a bunch of *suits*. Really and truly.

Some of my disbelief must have shown on my face because Bruno scowled at me, his bushy eyebrows going low over his brown eyes. "Don't laugh, Nixie. This gang is dangerous—and they're supernatural."

"Superna—come on, Bruno. You can't expect me to believe that."

He shook his head stubbornly. "There's proof. Strange things going on in Meiers Corners."

Suuure there were. "Like?"

"Like lions and wolves growling in the night. Despite no zoo in Meiers Corners. Like people turning to *mist*." He lowered his voice. "Like blood spatter mysteriously appearing, and just as mysteriously disappearing."

Okay, that rang an alarm too close to home. "All right. Say I believe your 'proof.' The CCIC runs a gang. Does this gang have a name?"

Bruno looked one way, then the other. Then, lowering his face right next to mine, he whispered, "The Lestats."

"The States?" It wasn't unheard of for a gang to name itself after a nation or people. But why states? And why French?

"Not *l'état*," Bruno said. "Lestat, one word. Or rather, a

name."

Lestat. And I remembered Julian saying the leader of the Coterie was a man called Nosferatu. "*Vampires?*"

"Keep your voice down!" Bruno hissed. "*They* have ears everywhere."

"This is why you wanted to meet before sunset," I said in amazement. "You really think these guys are vamp—"

"*Shh.*" Bruno clapped a paw over my mouth. "They may be in their graves during the day. But their human minions are everywhere."

"Everywhere," I said, only it came out "ebbywhir" because his meaty palm sealed my lips pretty well. Bruno removed his hand, looking abashed. "Uh-huh. Human minions everywhere." My tone didn't exactly drip sarcasm, but it was moist.

"*They* are vulnerable during the day. Which is why I've got this." Bruno whipped a huge tube out of the darkness behind him. "This here bazooka used to be Elena's. She took out Dracula with this."

"Of course she did," I said, all the time thinking Bruno had not only broken all his crayons, but had remelted them into one gray blob. "And you'll use that for...?"

He lowered his voice. "Hunting *them*, of course. But only during the day."

"Uh-huh. In *their* graves."

"Well...yes."

"And you know which graves *they* occupy?"

"Well...no."

"Hmm. Well, if you do happen to find an occupied grave, you've at least figured out how you're going to shoot through six feet of soil, right?"

"There do seem to be a few problems with my plan."

"One or two." I was beginning to wonder about my own plan to forget Julian Emerson. Still, nothing ventured, nothing gained. But obviously talking wasn't going to do it. "Put that bazooka down." I wiggled my butt across the stool toward him.

"What?"

"Put that down" was probably not the most seductive line in the world. Pitching my voice like a mellow sax, I said, "Bruno. Let's not talk any more." I touched his shoulder. He had very nice, very broad shoulders. A little beefy, though. Not lean and powerful, like...fuck. "Why don't you put down the bazooka for a moment and we can get...better acquainted."

"What's wrong with you, Nixie?" Bruno eyed me like I had a goldfish stuck between my teeth and it was still whacking its tail.

And I felt...nothing. No connection. No instant fire. Damn.

Still, I persevered. "I'm going to kiss you, Bear. Put down the fucking bazooka."

"Oh." Slowly, he set aside the gargantuan tube. Leaned forward. Puckered up. His lips looked like a red cauliflower planted in a nest of rusty old guitar strings.

There was an image guaranteed to make me hot.

Placing both palms gingerly against his flannel shirt, I leaned forward. Under the shirt Bruno's chest was hard, covered by a mat of springy hair. Nice. My engine started, enough so that I put my mouth naturally against his. He tasted like...beer. Like beer and...hair.

Mentally gritting my teeth, I kissed him. The hair from his mustache poked at my nose. I suppressed a sneeze.

Bruno's mouth opened and his fingers threaded through my curls. He grabbed a little tight, which distracted me. His bear-sized tongue thrust into my mouth, which nearly gagged me.

Then he torqued my head almost sideways to get his tongue deeper down my throat. It nearly threw me off the stool. His mustache got up my nose and I couldn't breathe.

"Bruno," I squeaked, only it came out "ack-ack-ack."

His response was to drag me onto his lap. For a moment I was distracted by the bulge under me. Respectable. Even a couple days ago I would have been very interested.

But Pikes Peak doesn't compare if you've climbed Mount Everest.

I pulled back. Bruno, panting, smiled. "Hey, that was fun. I didn't know you could kiss, Nixie. I always thought of you like my little niece."

"Thanks a lot." I slid back onto my stool.

"So what do you want to do now?"

I shrugged, drained my beer. It was still early, and I didn't have to be at auditions until nine. Might as well finish the plan. "I want you to meet my parents."

Chapter Eight

My mom and dad lived in an old-style bungalow. It was the same house my mother was born in, and her father before her. Because of that, I could officially say I came from Meiers Corners. Oh, my dad's folk, the Schmelings, had been here for two generations. But in the Corners, that was still considered newcomers. My mother's family, the Gutenbergs (no relation to the printing press guy), were here before The Fire. It was even rumored that Great-Grandpa Gutenberg fought in the Civil War, although no one was sure on which side.

My mother rushed out of the house as Bruno and I came up the walk. The smell of cooking meat overlaid with vinegar and onion wafted out behind her. It was Tuesday, which meant sauerbraten.

"Dietlinde!" She trotted down the stairs wiping her hands on her apron. Today's was red-bibbed, trimmed with blue ruffles. Under she wore the ever-present house dress, cut like a parachute and stable in wind tunnels up to a hundred miles an hour.

My mother stopped and frowned at me. "Where is your hat, Dietlinde?"

"Uh...at home?"

"It is thirty-five degrees and you are without your hat? At least tell me you remembered your gloves."

Since I hadn't, immediate distraction was in order. "Mom, this is Bruno."

I was twenty-five and single. Normally Mom greeted any unattached male under the age of fifty with open arms. She glared at Bruno like she was trying to remember where she put the bear trap.

"He owns a store," I added hopefully.

My mother perked up at that. Bruno had passed number one on the Mother Test, Gainfully Employed.

Then Bruno stuck his paw out. "Bruno Braun. Nice to meet you, Mrs. Schmeling."

"Oh," she sniffed. "A Braun." When she took Bruno's hand, it was like she was picking up a dirty washcloth.

My mother has absolutely no color prejudice. She does not judge by race, age, or gender. But Mom went to school with Bella Butt, who used to bite her at recess. That was in first grade, but Meiers Corners folk have long memories. Bella's mother is Brunhilde Butt—nee Braun. Everyone knew the Braun kids were kooks. Troublemakers. Class clowns.

Bruno, I could see, had failed Mom's Test number two: Good Family.

I was a troublemaker and a kook too, but I came from a "good" family. Apparently that made everything okay. I snorted to myself. And Julian Emerson had trouble understanding *me*? No, no. *Not* thinking about him. "Bruno's my date. I brought him home for supper."

My mother's lips thinned in displeasure. But she knew her duty as a Meiers Corners hostess. She would be hospitable, even to a Braun, if it killed her.

Half an hour later, after the fastest supper on record, Bruno pushed back his chair, dabbing genteelly at his beard with a paper napkin. "That was awesome sauerbraten, Mrs. Schmeling. I haven't had food like that since my Granny Butt took us to the parish Sheepshead Tournament and Sauerbraten Smorgasbord."

"The parish? You aren't...Roman, are you, Bruno?"

"Me? Naw, I go to Our Savior. Every Sunday, regular as clockwork."

This was good. My mother was a charter member of the Lutheran Ladies Auxiliary Mothers Association, and church was very important.

She nodded, and I breathed a sigh of relief. Bruno had passed number three (Good Lutheran) on the Mother Test. We were two for three. "Will you be seeing Dietlinde again, Bruno?"

"Dietlinde?" Bruno asked, looking confused. "I don't think so." He gave me a "Who's Dietlinde" look and I discreetly pointed at myself and mouthed, "Daggy name."

But it was too late. Bruno had failed both number four (Thoroughly Enthralled by My Daughter) and number five (Has a Brain).

To be honest, Bruno had failed the last on my own private test, too. Not that Bruno was dumb—he wasn't. But he was smart only about certain things. And I simply wasn't into any of the things he was smart about. Like conspiracies, or guns, or hand grenades—or even stiletto heels.

Julian Emerson is smart, a little voice in my head whispered. *Very smart.*

Shut up, I whispered back.

He's so smart, the voice whispered, *he can read your desires in your eyes.*

Yeah, my pussy murmured in agreement.

Both of you shut up, I hissed mentally.

"Nixie—is something wrong?"

I blinked. Bruno and both my parents were staring at me with some concern. "Uh, no." I sprang up. "I'll just go start the dishes." I grabbed up plates and utensils and sped off to the kitchen.

Bruno did not follow. Too bad. He failed the most important test, one both my mother and I had. Number six: Helps With The Housework.

By the time I finished rinsing dishes and loading the dishwasher, Bruno had gone. To be fair, he had his store to run. To be catty, Bruno had no regular hours and could have opened at nine as well as eight.

But it left more dessert—German chocolate cake with to-die-for homemade cooked coconut frosting—for me. We sat at the table, my mother, my father, and I, and savored cake. It was the one part of the meal where no one talked. Like being in church. You don't chat in the presence of the Holy.

"Well," my mother said after we'd finished the last crumb. "That was an—interesting—young man."

"Bruno's a nice guy," I said. "More of a friend, though."

My father, who had not said a single word during the whole

meal, put down his coffee cup. Patted his lips with his napkin. Folded it neatly and set it on the table.

From living with him so long, I didn't need subtitles. My father's words were in his actions. He was relieved.

So was my mother. Enough to try to set up Bruno's replacement. "You'll never guess who I ran into at the deli today. Denny Crane! And guess what? He's taken on a new partner in his law firm. Just out of school. Graduated top of his class at the East of Chicago University."

I didn't point out that east of Chicago meant Lake Michigan.

"Bart is his name. Isn't that nice? Bart just moved to Meiers Corners."

I grimaced. Oh, no, I thought. Here it comes.

"Mr. Crane says Bart doesn't know anyone here. I bet he's lonely."

"Uh-huh."

"Lonely. And probably bored, too, after the hustle-bustle of the big city. I bet a nice law school graduate would like some company. Don't you think so, Helmut?"

My father was reading the paper. Smart.

"I bet a nice law school graduate would like the company of a sophisticated young lady."

I felt my eyes roll, slapped my hand over them. "And *I* bet a grown man can find something to entertain himself, even in Meiers Corners."

My mother *humphed*. "Mr. Crane agreed with *me*. He thought Bart would like a little companionship."

Danger, danger, Will Robinson. "Mother, what have you done?"

"It's only one meal, Dietlinde. Not even a date."

"Mother—"

"Friday night. Dinner here at the house. We'll have chicken and dumplings."

I gritted my teeth. "Mother, I can't."

"Saturday, then. We'll have pot roast."

"Mother, I work weekends!"

"That *band*?" my dear, sweet mother scoffed. "That is not

work, Dietlinde. That is a hobby."

We'd been having some variation of this conversation since I was thirteen. Arguing was just a waste of breath. I rolled my eyes and didn't cover it this time. "Yes, Mother."

"What kind of paycheck does playing in a rock-and-roll band bring home? You can barely live, much less raise children."

She'd have an even bigger fit if she knew I sometimes only got paid in pitchers of beer. "Yes, Mother."

But she was just getting started. "And how can you interest any kind of decent husband if you will not be home weekends to take care of his *needs*? You mark my words. A man won't stay with the cow if she doesn't give him any milk."

Gosh, and other girls got lectured about giving the milk away for free. I should consider myself lucky. "Yes, Mother."

"And who was that young man you were seen with at the mayor's office?"

"Yes, moth...*what*?"

"Alba Gruen heard it from Kristin Fenster who was at Dolly Barton's Curl Up and Dye today getting her roots touched up."

Oh, great. I was featured gossip at Dolly Barton's, Meiers Corners's gigabit rumor router. "Um, I wasn't with anybody. You done with that?" I sprang up, grabbed the desert plates and escaped into the kitchen. There, I took my time rinsing them and putting them in the dishwasher. As I added soap and started the cycle I wondered if all the uncomfortable questions were a secret mother ploy just to get me to do the dishes.

I left my parents' house and headed southwest. It was still too early to go to band auditions. I got the bright idea that I should go walk around the festival area. Then I could decide if I needed a shuttle, or if the drunk people could just stumble from one event to the next.

My parents lived on Fourth and Roosevelt, on the upper east side. The official festival parking lot was at Nieman's Bar, where we'd also be holding the Sheepshead Tournament. That was on West Fifth and Main. I humped the mile over.

It took me about fifteen minutes. I still had an hour or so to kill until auditions. So I walked north on Fifth, then ambled around the area.

The beer tent would go nicely in the Good Shepherd parking lot, one block north of Nieman's. The midway (sans rides) would be set up in the church basement. I kept going.

The whole next block was tourist central. Fudge shoppe (The Fudgy Delight), pastry/bakery store (The Pie Delight), deli (you guessed it, the Deli Delight), and the Caffeine Café. The deli would host the cheese tasting, the pastry/bakery was doing the cake contest. The beauty pageant, perversely enough, was being held at the Fudgy Delight. That had been a dance hall in the forties and had a small platform stage and twenty tables with chairs. Chairs, of course, were the rarest commodity. So far, so good.

The biggest problem was finding someplace large enough to house the bands. It was bad enough trying to find a place to audition them. Having a crowd listening and dancing added a whole new level of logistic and equipment nightmares. Dentist office, nope. Dolly Barton's salon, nope. Blood Center, double-nope with a dollop of ick.

Sighing, I walked back to the fudge shoppe. Not enough room for performance, but it would do for tonight's auditions. Cary Grant still hadn't paid his electric bill and The Fudgy Delight was the only place big enough that wasn't full of customers on a Thursday night. I stopped in, to double-checked the arrangements.

To my surprise, an auditionee was already there, setting up a karaoke machine. The comfortable, baggy clothes and haphazard chestnut hair clued me to her identity even before I saw her face. Rocky Hrbek, the flute player in our orchestra.

I knew Rocky from high school. As a gawkward teenager, Rocky was overweight and plagued with acne and greasy hair. Her best friend was her flute. I sort of empathized with her, since mine was my guitar Oscar. I never knew what she called hers.

High school was not forever, thank heavens. After college Rocky came back to Meiers Corners slimmed down and cleared up. She was now incredibly hot.

She didn't know it. Not a clue. In some ways that made her hotter. Guys...and even some gals...made passes at her, but Rocky just didn't get it. She dressed like a frump, cut her own hair, and never wore makeup. She was hot, but I think she still *felt* like a high school misfit. I really sympathized with that.

The door of the Fudgy Delight jingled when I entered. Rocky turned. Seeing me, she gave me her stunning smile. Stunning, as in I had to pick my jaw up from the floor. "Hey, Nixie." She had a smooth contralto that sounded like honey.

I cleared my throat, to give me time to recover my composure. "Hey yourself. Um...what are you doing here?"

"Auditioning," Rocky said, as if it were the most natural assumption in the world. "I came early so I could warm up."

I stared at her. Rocky was classically trained, more comfortable with Dvorak than DragonForce. "This is for rock bands."

"Yes, I know." She patted the machine. "That's why I brought this."

"You're...singing?"

"Of course not, Nixie." Rocky laughed, a bell-like sound that made you want to amuse her forever just to hear it. "I'm playing my flute. The Mozart Concerto in G."

"But—" How did I phrase this? "Isn't that classical?"

"Sure. But I rearranged it. Flute and garage band. I thought it'd make a nice alternative to sappy pop charts everyone else will be doing."

I was speechless but tried anyway. "Uh...but..."

"I based my arrangement on Weird Al's sound. I like what he does with accordion."

I didn't bother to point out that Weird Al does parodies. Flute and garage band was already disastrous enough. But sarcastic flute and garage band? Yikes. I was trying to work out what I could possibly say when my cell phone tweedled "Flight of the Bumblebee".

My phone is set with a different ring tone for each of my family and friends. My parents are "Home on the Range". Elena is the theme from *Cops*. You get the picture.

"Flight of the Bumblebee" meant Unknown Number. I pulled out my phone and stared at the display. Blocked call.

Interesting. And fortunate. "I've got to take this. Um, see you in thirty, Rocky." Maybe I would think of something to say by then. As Rocky waved a cheerful goodbye I slipped out the door and spun open my Juke. "Talk to me."

A slight pause. Then a harsh, deep voice rasped, "Dietlinde Schmeling."

There was something creepy about the voice. It sounded hollow. Too hollow. Spooky-hollow, like there was no person behind it. It had to be machine-enhanced because no human vocal cords could have produced that voice.

The best defense against spooky is Attitude. I reached in my pocket for some chewing gum. As I popped it out of the blister-pack I stuck the phone between shoulder and jaw. Using my best punk tone I said, "What'cha want?"

"Dietlinde Schmeling. You will resign."

He kept repeating my daggy legal name. No matter how creepy, that was plain annoying. "Resign what, Deep Throat?"

"You will resign as head of the fundraiser, Dietlinde Schmeling."

He'd done it again. *Dietlinde*. It was like a hit between the shoulder blades. "That don't make no sense, Deep Whoever-you-are. Why should I?"

"Because if you don't"—ominous pause—"something *bad* will happen."

"Something bad, uh-huh. Is that something *bad* or something *Bad*? Or something *B-A-D*? And who the hell are you, anyway?"

"This is no joke, Dietlinde Schmeling. If you do not resign immediately, you *will* regret it. Do *not* cross Lord Ruthven." He hung up.

I stared at my phone a moment before swinging it shut. That was just psycho. Especially that "Lord Ruthven" shit. Who'd he think he was, Bob Dole? I began to wonder if maybe Bruno wasn't on to something with all his woo-woo theories.

I shook the thought away. I still had to find a place for the bands to perform.

So, trying to put that double-weird conversation out of my mind, I walked one block east, to Fourth and Jefferson.

And saw it.

Heavenly angels sang, fairies danced, and fireworks lit the night sky. It was the Perfect Place.

Kalten's Roller Skating Rink had been a hopping spot in the

heyday of roller blades. Now it did more weddings and parties than skating. But it was big, it had chairs, and it was near enough to the other venues for people to walk (or stumble, if they were drunk, or drag themselves there with their lips). A convenient little sign in the door gave me a number to call for party reservations. I pulled out my cell phone, punched it in. I got an answering machine, but I left my name and number and slipped my phone away, feeling tons lighter.

"Well, well. What have we here? It's Emerson's little blood-chick."

I jerked around. A man emerged from the shadows. A man in a suit. He looked like—no, that was impossible.

This was even creepier than the voice. The guy emerging from the shadows looked like the suit from the gang. The *first* suit. The Der Arnold guy—Cutter. Who had possibly been a headless body the last time I saw him.

He was remarkably recovered now.

I kicked my breastbone up. My shoulders automatically squared, my spine straightened. I was scared, but at least it didn't show. "What do you want?"

"Where's your protector, chickadee?" Cutter murmured, coming closer. "Are you all alone? Mine for the taking?" He reached out, skimmed fingers along my jaw. I jerked back.

He smiled at my reaction. It revealed long canines. Really long. Almost like—fangs.

I didn't stop to think. I whipped my keys out of my pocket, fanned like claws between the fingers of my fist. Putting my body behind it, I slashed them up into his face.

Cutter *howled*, covered his face with his hands. Blood dripped from behind.

I ran.

Straight into one of the long coats. "Where do you think you're going, blood bitch?" Long fingers tightened cruelly around my upper arms, pricked into my skin. I glanced down in panic. They were—real claws.

Chapter Nine

"Let me go!" I shrieked, struggling like a maniac.

It was like I did *nothing*. The guy's strength was immense.

Until square, competent fingers wrapped around the claws. Square, bronzed fingers which pulled the claws away with startling ease.

The gang guy's strength was immense, but Julian Emerson was stronger by far.

I expected one of those blasé comments of his. About this being particularly ill-considered, or believing the fellow was out of line.

Instead, Julian *growled*. "Let the *fuck* go of her."

With a grimace of pain, the coat taunted, "Why? She your chew toy, Emerson? Oh, that's right. You and your kind call them *donors*."

Time out here. I *did* note all the blood references. But in my defense, I thought it was only a gang thing. A code for how dangerous they were, like tattoos or signs.

Of course, that didn't explain how I missed the other glaring inconsistencies, like what a big Chicago gang really wanted with tiny Meiers Corners (our two-hundred-fifty-dollars-per-year drug money? The joy of knocking over our one-man convenience store?). Maybe I just didn't want to notice.

I preferred to think I was distracted by Julian Emerson's rampant masculinity.

Speaking of which...at the gang guy's taunt, Julian's eyes turned hard as rubies. Through tightly closed lips he said, "You are an unprincipled savage." Then he seized the gang guy and tossed him twenty yards like a pitcher nailing home plate.

My jaw dropped. Julian had flung a two-hundred-pound man like a baseball. And a man who had come back from the dead had honest-to-gosh, real-live mastiff-sized fangs. Glinting in the moonlight, not plastic, not imaginary. Not anything but *scary*.

Obviously we had left the Topeka airport, Toto, and were circling over Sunnydale.

Cutter sprang forward. He bared fangs at Julian and hissed. Not a human hiss, but the low, deadly warning of a beast. The hairs raised on the back of my neck.

Cutter's face was completely unmarked, which unnerved me even more. I had raked keys over that face. I had seen blood dripping from between his fingers. Yet now he could be a Coverboy makeup model.

I was unnerved, but Julian wasn't even fazed. He stalked toward Cutter, so big and menacing that *I* shivered. "You and your gang will get one thing straight, Cutter. If even a single child or female complains of so much as a pinprick, I am coming after you. And I will *shred* you. I will feed you strip by strip into the furnace of the sun."

It sounded gruesome. And strangely, I didn't get the feeling Julian thought he was exaggerating.

"But if you or *any* of your gang even *touch* Nixie"—and here Julian emitted a growl that sounded like it came from a twelve-foot tiger—"I will personally disembowel each and every one of you and toss your guts to the crows while you watch. And that's just to start."

In response, Cutter and his hench mutant squeaked. Backing away, they faded silently into the night.

Well. Apparently civilized suit Julian Emerson had a savage side. It made me...hot.

Until he turned his fierce expression on me. "What the hell were you doing? Didn't I tell you *not* to go out alone at night?"

Relief evaporated. I drew myself up to my full height and glared back. "What was I supposed to do?" I returned, fists hitting hips. "Call on you, O Great Protector? Oh, wait, I can't. You never gave me your phone number."

"I'm staying at Strongwell's. You know that number, yes?"

Okay, that explained why he'd been working out half-naked there. In my own defense, I'd been a little distracted by pumped pecs and sleek bronzed skin and...yeah.

"But to remove even that excuse—here." Julian whipped out a card, so fast that if it had been a knife it would have sliced the night in two. "My cell phone. Next time, *call*."

"Gee, thanks, SuperLegal." I stuck the card in my jeans pocket without a glance. "Don't you have more important things to do, Emerson? Like drawing up torts or researching precedent or something? The things we're paying your five-fucking-C fee for?"

His fingers went around my upper arms. His eyes flared almost red in the streetlight. He looked like he wanted to shake me. "Stopping the courts is worthless if I can't stop the gang."

Well, that was just laughable, so I laughed. "You? You personally are going to stop a *gang*? How? By throwing your law books at them? By *talking* them to death?"

"No. I'll speak the only language they understand. The language of tooth and claw." He released me. Just before he turned away I caught the glint of two very sharp teeth.

"Yeah, yeah. I get the animal metaphor, Emerson. But it's a metaphor. This gang is real. And dangerous."

"So am I."

"I'm sure you are, in a courtroom," I cried, exasperated. "But not against these playas! They're big, strong, and there are a whole big city of them! There's one of you. They'll completely pwn you, Emerson!"

The puzzled tilt to Julian's head clued me that his slang dictionary still wasn't online.

"*Pwn* you, Emerson!" Like yelling it would make him understand the crushing, devastating pwningness of it all. "And I'm worried—" I cut off, suddenly realizing what I'd almost blurted. *I'm worried about you, Julian. Scared for you. I care about what happens to you. I care—about you.*

He slewed me a look over his shoulder. Slowly, his lips curved. He knew. Even though I hadn't said the words, he'd heard them loud and clear anyway.

"Shit, there's such a thing as being too quick." I jammed my hands in my pockets and turned red.

"Is there?" He came to me and gently pushed a strand of hair away from my eyes.

"What is it with you, anyway? Do you read minds, or are you just that smart?"

His thumb feathered over my cheek. "Mostly I read your face. Listen to your voice. But I can smell, too, you know. Smell when you're afraid. Smell when you're concerned. Smell when you're aroused." He almost purred the last.

I watched his eyes darken. "We're outside, you know. In public."

"Really?" He unbuttoned my jean jacket. Unzipped the Garfield hoodie underneath. "Does that bother you?"

I looked down. He'd exposed a strip of skin from my neck to my belly button. Including a quarter-moon of breast on each side. I hadn't worn a bra tonight, thinking I was going to get laid. Maybe, I thought hopefully, I still was. "It doesn't bother me." My voice emerged thick and husky. "I thought it'd bother you."

"Not in this lifetime." He opened his hand and slid it onto my exposed skin. His square, competent hand slid up the swell of my breast. Under my hoodie.

Directly onto my nipple.

I arched into his hand, feeling his skin abrade my breast. My nipple filled and tightened, tingled and clamored for more.

"What is it about you, Nixie?" Julian's voice was accompanied by a rhythmic rumble, like a cat opening its mouth on a purr. "Your smell, your taste, the feel of your skin...hell, everything about you arouses me."

"Sorry." I closed my eyes and leaned into him. Not sorry at all. "Don't you have two hands, Emerson?"

"Yes." He cupped both breasts and thumbed my nipples. Little shivery jags of lightning arced through me in response. "And," he added hoarsely, "a tongue."

"Oh, fuck," I said as he bent from his great height and his mouth opened on mine. It was the last thing I said for quite a while.

As his lips played over my skin, his tongue touched here, there. The corners of my mouth. The tip of my earlobe. My throbbing pulse.

His fingers pinched my nipples, erotically beating out an *S-O-S*—or an *O-M-G*. One arm wrapped around my back, his hand splaying under my jeans. I hadn't worn a thong tonight, either. As his hand moved in and encountered only naked skin, he growled. He pulled my hips into his, hard. The rumbling purr grew so loud I could practically feel it thrumming against my chest. Against my belly. Against my pussy, pressed into his hard heat.

His hand found and cupped my butt. Slid down it, squeezing gently. One finger tickled the edge of my pubic hair.

I tried to tell him, yes, further, *now*! But all that emerged from my throat was a gut-deep moan.

I had forgotten this was Julian, the man who could read my desires in my scent. The finger pressed forward. Slid into thick moisture. Julian voiced a strangled groan, pushed his hips into me. His hard cock dug a hot hole in my belly. His breath was coming in short, sharp gasps. "You're hotter than the sun, Nixie. So silky and wet for me. Open up, sweetheart. I'm going to make you come."

And his finger stabbed home.

I shrieked. Yes, yes, yes! I screamed. Only it came out a muffled moan, because somehow I had latched onto his earlobe and was suckling.

"Ride me," he whispered. "Ride my finger." He slid his other hand between us. Slid it down the front of my pants. Opened his palm, cupping my pussy. From behind, his finger continued to slide in and out.

My hips started moving, almost with a mind of their own. His finger was so hot it burned. If he'd made it any hotter, it would've been a candle. I rode that hot, hard finger, my breath rasping faster.

His cupping hand flexed. A *second* finger slid in from the front. Caught, I rocked between the two, the hand cupping my pussy and the one pressing against my butt. I gasped at the feel of two thick fingers thrusting. I wept at the scrape of teeth against my cheek, down my jaw.

All around us the night watched. This was not dark bedroom under-the-covers missionary position vaginal sex. This was hot, steamy, nasty fucking, and I loved it. My fingers tangled in Julian's black hair and I pressed his mouth closer. Reveled in the feel of his hands thrusting hard into my pants. He may have been a stodgy old lawyer but he was a wonderfully dirty stodgy old lawyer.

And then his back hand moved and a wet, slippery finger slid into my ass. And I realized there was nothing stodgy about Julian's sexuality at all.

Both fingers thrust into me and I screamed. Gasped as they slid out. Screamed as they banged home again. "Oh my...oh my..." I was going to come. Just on two of Julian Emerson's fingers, I was going to come.

His mouth opened on my neck, forcing my head back. Teeth pressed into my pulse. Breath fanned hot on my skin. Fingers cocked back like pinball plungers. Purring rumbled in my ears, over my skin, all around me.

With a bone-shattering growl Julian Emerson drove into my body. His fingers thrust into me, his teeth pierced my throat. His tongue pressed into the gush of hot liquid pulsing from my neck. His fingers slid in and out in a frenzy.

I climaxed like a booster rocket. My orgasm hit me so hard my body folded in two. The rictus of pleasure slamming through me was so bright it was almost painful.

Through it all Julian lapped up blood and churned come.

I went over the edge into darkness.

♫ ♫ ♫

I woke in my own bed feeling lightheaded and curiously at peace. A glance at my alarm showed it was almost nine in the morning. I had slept a solid twelve hours.

I *never* sleep that long. I sat up, immediately swaying. Woozy. Grabbing my head I held it until it stopped spinning. When I could see more clearly I noticed a glass and some cookies on my nightstand, within easy reach. Gingerly I lay back against my headboard and picked up the glass. I drank. It was some sort of juice, tangy and sweet. I drank it all.

It was only as I scarfed the fourth cookie that I thought to wonder how they'd gotten there. I don't buy juice. And I can't keep cookies in the house, not for more than an hour anyway.

Then I remembered Julian and the orgasm from beyond the galactic rim, and wondered how *I'd* gotten here.

Surely desk-jockey Emerson hadn't carried me all the way

home to my townhouse.

Only I had to stop thinking of him as a mere desk jockey. His body, which I'd seen at Elena's, was primo, lean and muscular. He'd fought big, tough gang guys. He moved like a hunter. He made love like a porn star.

He bit like a v...

Oh, no. So not going there. I liked horror stories as much as the next guy. But weird, wacko explanations were Bruno's department, not mine.

Still, if the Lestat gang really was a bunch of v-v-v...well, it only made sense to counter them with another v-v-v...

No, no, no. This was ridiculous. Julian Emerson was an attorney. A bloodsucker, to be sure. But not *literally*. He didn't have any of the other qualifications, like wearing a silk-lined black cape, or speaking with a Transylvanian accent, or sleeping in a buried coffin during the day—

Of course! I could prove Julian wasn't a...wasn't a... I could prove it. He was staying with Bo and Elena. All I had to do was call them. Ask for Julian. If he came to the phone, I knew he wasn't sleeping in a...yeah.

I sat up, felt something dig in my jeans pocket. Julian's card. Extracting it, I realized I could call him direct on his cell phone. If he answered, it would prove he wasn't sleeping in a...no, actually it wouldn't. It would prove he wasn't sleeping. It wouldn't prove he wasn't in a buried cof...yeesh. This was getting complicated.

So I reached over for the phone, dialed Elena's before I could think myself into a black hole. She answered on the tenth ring, just as I was about to hang up. "Strongwells," her voice came sleepily.

Reminding me not only toothy monsters-that-didn't-exist slept during the day. "Sorry to wake you, Elena. But, um...can I speak with Emerson, please?"

"Julian?" Her tone was definitely more awake. "Why Julian?"

"I just wanted to, um, ask him something. I saw him last night but forgot to...um."

"Nixie—you sound kind of strange. You're not thinking anything...weird, are you?"

"Weird? No way. I'm not thinking weird in the least." I gave a hearty laugh to prove it. "Certainly not about Julian Emerson, Mr. Boris Normalsky."

"Oh, good," she said, but her tone was doubting. "Because—well, you know I'd never let anything happen to you, right?"

"Right," I said, wondering where that came from.

"Nothing—weird, I mean."

"Sure," I said. "But can I talk to Emerson...?" And of course, that was the question. Could I talk to Julian? Or was he somewhere he couldn't talk? And I didn't mean the potty.

"You'll have to wait while I get him. Unless you want me to have him call you back?" I don't think I imagined the hopeful note to her voice.

"I'll wait," I said as cheerfully as possible. I even started humming the "Beer Barrel Polka" to show how unconcerned I was.

"Okay. I'm going to get Julian now."

As I said, I get a lot of info listening. I heard a door open. That was Elena leaving her and Bo's bedroom. Then silence, but that was consistent with padding barefoot down a hallway. No creak, so I know she didn't go up or down stairs. And then a knock. "Julian?" Elena said. "Nixie's on the phone for you. Sorry to wake you up, but can you come talk to her?"

And then to my great relief, I heard the click of a door opening and the sound of the phone changing hands. When the deep, elegant tones came, I'd never been so happy to hear them.

"Nixie. What the hell are you doing, calling so early?"

Deep, elegant—and grouchy, I amended. But I was still happy to hear him. "I just wanted to, um, thank you for the juice. And cookies. That was you, right?"

"Yes," he said, his tone a little less surly. The sound of the door closing came and he added, "I thought you could use a little refreshment when you woke. You were sleeping pretty hard."

Hard. I'd *come* pretty hard.

Leaving him, I realized for the first time, with a pretty big hard-on. Which could account for the grouchiness. "Um, yeah. Sorry about dipping on you like that. Before you, um, you know."

"That's all right. I enjoyed watching you."

I'm not shy about sex. But thinking about Julian watching me while I shuddered and spasmed and folded in two...my face heated. "Uh, yeah. Hey, why don't I return the favor? In fact— why don't I come over right now!"

Julian only chuckled. "I don't think you'd like the accommodations here. My room is in the basement. No windows."

I sucked in a breath, earlier fears rising. Coffins.

As if he heard my thoughts, Julian said, "Don't get me wrong. It's quite spacious. But it's a bachelor's pad. A little dark."

I let out the breath. "That's okay. What I have in mind involves Braille."

"Nixie," he said, his voice all tight and growly. I decided I really liked Julian Emerson's voice that way. "I'd love for you to..."

My phone beeped. I lost the rest of Julian's words. "What? What did you say?"

"I said I'd love..."

My phone beeped again. "Oh, hell. Someone's calling. Julian...uh, can you hold?"

"I don't know." His tone was pure seduction. "Can you?"

Oh, double-hell. "Uh, yeah. Just a minute." I clicked over. "Hello?"

"Nixie? It's Mom. Can you come to supper Friday?"

This was beyond what a woman should have to take. "Mother, I already told you—"

"It'll be early. Five, five thirty. You'll have plenty of time to get to your...music."

Of course my mother couldn't call it a job. "Mom. If you're having company"—euphemism for "forced date"—"I'd need to stay."

"No company," she said quickly. "Just family. Your father and I hardly ever see you anymore."

"You just saw me last night!"

"That doesn't count. You were with that Braun boy. And

93

besides, you spent half the time in the kitchen."

Because of *her*. But..."All right, Mom. I'll try to make it."

"Good. See you at five thirty. And Saturday brunch at two o'clock." She hung up.

"What...?" But she had already gone. That bit about brunch was slipped in so fast it was sure to be a set-up. But fighting a determined German mother (and specifically *my* determined German mother) was as productive as playing Find the Matching Snowflakes. So I clicked back over. "Julian?"

"Nixie, sweetheart." That was a relief. His voice was still on "vibrator".

Unfortunately, I was now set on "mother". "About coming over—"

"It's all right." His voice smoothed back to rich and dark. "I probably should get some sleep anyway. That was your mother?"

Was the man psychic? "How did you know? And don't say you *smelled* it. Not even your nose is good over a mile away."

He laughed. Julian had a very nice laugh, sort of a chocolate-silk chuckle. "Before you took that call you were hotter than a furnace. Less than a minute later you're reluctant as a nun. Not even an ice bath can cool passion as fast as a mother."

"Yeah."

"What did she want?"

"Oh, just to strong-arm me into supper tomorrow. Oh, hey." The bright idea bulb lit over my head. "Want to come?"

"I'd love to, but," Julian said.

The bulb burst. "Yeah, I thought there'd be a 'but'."

"I have evening meetings. I can't get out of them."

"Dinner's going to be early," I said hopefully. "Five, five thirty. So I can make it to my gig."

"You're playing Friday night?"

"Just locally. Nieman's Bar. So about supper...?"

"Nixie, I can't. Some other time, though."

"Yeah." I hung up, disappointed. I didn't have to have Suity subtitles to know what that meant. Some other time—like never.

I didn't think I could feel any worse—until I remembered the auditions. The auditions that were scheduled for last night, which I had totally missed. I whacked myself in the head. That started it whirling again so I went to my kitchen where I found the rest of the juice and cookies, and polished them off.

Then I sat down to make phone calls. With my back against the wall, there was only one day and one place to schedule them. And only one time. I shuddered.

I was going to have to get up early Monday morning.

Chapter Ten

I had forgotten about insurance for the festival, as well. Though I could have blamed it on all the stuff going on, I knew exactly why it had "slipped my mind".

It would kill me.

Not literally, although I did get short of breath just thinking about it. But there was a chain of events in every person's life. Birth. Diapers. Sippy Cups and Potty Training. School. Learning to Drive. First Job and Introduction to the IRS. Career. First Major Purchase and Credit. Buying Insurance. Death.

And it wasn't just being the step-before-death thing that was bothering me.

If I bought insurance, what would happen to me? Who would I be?

We all had heroes. Not just the bigger-than-life Superdudes of our imagination. But real people we loved and wanted to be like. Real people who were bigger-than-life in our hearts.

My first hero was my older sister Giselle. Giselle helped me the first time I escaped from my crib. She showed me how to get my own cereal Saturday mornings. How to turn on the TV myself.

Giselle taught me to be free. She gave me my soul.

My second hero was my Aunt Nixie. Christmas and birthdays I got pink socks and underwear—except from Aunt Nixie. She bought me magic sets and toy guitars. My parents sent me to summer school. Aunt Nixie took me to her summer home on the lake. My other aunt, Aunt Dietlinde, gave me sewing lessons. Aunt Nixie taught me to ride horseback.

Aunt Nixie fired my imagination. She gave me my mind.

My third hero wasn't a person. It was music. Music transported me out of my gray world into millions of colors. It was my drug of choice, even better than beer. It was what I could do that made other people happy.

Music gave me my heart.

Don't get me wrong. I loved my parents, and Meiers Corners. I even loved Aunt Dietlinde the Drab. I didn't like emo so much, but not even emos liked emo.

But I didn't want to be like them. I didn't want to be beaten down by responsibility and respectability. Beaten down year after year until I was flat and gray. Until I was dead but didn't know it. Or worse yet, didn't care.

I had to grow up some. Even I knew that. I couldn't do band gigs without driving. I couldn't ignore April 15. I didn't want to wear diapers again until I was a hundred and five.

But buying insurance? I'd never forget that's the last gray step before death.

♫ ♫ ♫

Friday night I spent most of my time hiding in the kitchen...I mean doing the dishes. Mother had met Mr. Crane's new law partner, and couldn't stop singing Bart Bleistift's praises. I hadn't even met St. Barty but if I were singing his praises, my songs would rhyme Barty with farty and Bleistift with...well, that didn't rhyme with anything but it sounded like booger to me.

As I stacked dishes, I thought maybe it was a good thing Julian had declined supper. How could he possibly compete in the Mother Race with St. Bart?

Except Julian wasn't competing in the Mother Race. The prize apparently wasn't worth his effort. And I got mad/hurt at him dipping out on supper all over again. Unfairly, but there it was.

I had to come out of the kitchen some time. And even St. Farty Booger couldn't spoil chocolate chip cake with fudge frosting.

As soon as supper was done, though, I fled...I mean, left. I had to get ready for my gig. We didn't start playing until nine but it took us about an hour to set up. Before that I needed to change and put on makeup.

Guns and Polkas was a five-piece band. Lob, Rob, Cob, me, and Durango. Lob was on drum, Rob did bass (doubling on accordion). Cob was the singer, and I was rhythm guitar (I doubled on clarinet). Durango was lead guitar. We had a sound that crossed Weird Al with Nirvana, with a little Flogging Molly thrown in. Topped off by Elvis. Our sound was...unique.

Tonight my mind was less on my costume and more on my problems (how was I going to avoid my mother's latest attempt at Chaining Miss Nixie, and how the hell was I going to get Julian Emerson out from under my skin now that he'd given me the best orgasm of my life?).

So I threw on the first thing that came to hand. A black spandex microskirt with thigh-high leather boots and red nylon see-through tank under a tiny black suede vest. No bra under the tank.

No thong under the skirt, either. Julian had turned down the pleasure of my company but hope springs eternal.

Or maybe some other handsome dark stranger would pop up in Meiers Corners. Maybe he'd wear leather and ride a Harley and smell like sex.

And maybe I ought to smack myself senseless with my Fender Strat. Two days ago I was perfectly happy with my life. Now I had sex on the brain.

I had better things to think about. Like my makeup.

The great thing about being a rock musician was you could wear the gaudiest makeup in the world and get away with it. Tonight I colored my eyelids a rich metallic teal. Used eyeliner so thick even Pharaoh would have looked slutty. I painted my lips crimson red, then slicked an inch of gloss on over. My mile-long fake eyelashes danced with glitter. Brushing a sparkly bronzer on my cheeks, I was ready.

Anyone else would have looked like a hooker. As small as I was, I looked like an overdone fashion doll. Either way, in normal light it was garish.

Under stage lighting I would look amazing.

I shouldered my Pro Tec clarinet gig bag and picked up Oscar, my Strat (but I only call him that when no one's around). In the other hand I had my small amp. Lob the drummer would bring the larger amps and mixer that the whole band plugged into, but I liked having mine just in case.

We met in the parking lot east of Nieman's Bar. Our lead guitar Durango was just finishing up getting a blow job from Drusilla. Dru was the Corners's only full-time hooker. She was also the only woman I knew with natural double-D boobs. I waved. Drusilla waved back. Only one of us had her chest join in.

The band's first set was par for the course. A couple drunks got up to dance, Granny Butt stripped on the bar. After break, I was tuning my guitar when I glanced up and saw Julian wander in.

My nipples immediately popped up to say hi. Almost as quickly, they shrank back out of sight.

Right behind Julian were Drusilla's DDs.

I gave my high E string a crank. The tuning machine was bent, and it turned hard. Fine. Suited my mood. Now I knew who Julian's important "meeting" was with.

Fucking unfaithful attorney. How insensitive was he, parading his new girlfriend in front of me? It was like Spiderman 3—but without Tobey Maguire's cuteness.

Intuition always told me not to trust suits. I should have listened. I gave the key another hard twist.

If I had any doubts that Julian and DD-Dru were together, they were killed when Julian ordered. The bartender handed him two drinks. Julian passed one to *her.*

I cranked so hard my E string broke. Fuck.

Luckily I carry spares, and the exercise of changing the string calmed me somewhat. By the time I was ready to play I had almost forgotten about the Insensitive Jerk Attorney.

The door opened again. Good. Mr. I-Didn't-Go-Thongless-For-Him was leaving.

Only Julian was still sitting there, Double-D Drusilla next to him. Great. So who had left?

Or who had come in?

Oh, no. Please, no.

A goofy grin on his face, an instrument case in his hand, Dirk Ruffles trotted up. "Hey, Nixie. I finally thought of what I can do for the festival fundraiser."

"Dirk, now's not a good time—"

"I can help audition bands," he said brightly.

My mouth kept flapping but nothing came out. Finally I squeaked, "But...but you're not a musician."

"But I am." His face glowed with pride. "Saxophone. First at State three years in row."

"Uh, yeah. Dirk, I'm glad you played in high school, but—"

"That was junior high." He slid his case onto the bar and with smooth efficiency, put mouthpiece on horn. Wet his reed and slipped it on, tightening the ligature with a few expert twirls. Took an experimental blow, noodled a few notes. A few more. Then Dirk Ruffles, clueless Dirkenstein, played "Take Five" from memory, including a killer improv.

My jaw dropped. He was *good*.

He pulled a stool over. "I thought I could sit in for a few numbers. If that's okay."

"Yeah," I said, taking a quick check of the band's nodding heads. "Sure."

That set was magic. Music flowed from my fingertips like fairy dust. The slow songs blended like cream. The fast songs popped with manic energy. It was like we just couldn't miss. The whole bar was dancing or clapping along.

The only downer was when Drusilla pulled Julian toward the dancers. But even that was magic—he shook his head. She ended up dragging out Donner, one of the bar regulars (who Elena described as a collie with a horse's teeth). They looked like Elvira moshing with Scooby Doo. As Drusilla danced, her DDs swayed pertly, drawing the gaze of every male in the bar.

Except Julian. He caught my eye and tipped his glass at me. I flushed and looked away. He knew I had been watching him and Drusilla. Maybe he even thought I was jealous. Which I certainly was not. My jaw kicked up and I started a furious six-string slash, a la DragonForce. I was *not* jealous. My fingers scrubbed over the strings hard and fast.

The new E string snapped.

That, of course, ended the second set. As I replaced the string with my last spare, a pair of wingtips appeared before me.

"What do *you* want?" I was not in a good mood.

"Nice playing." Julian's voice was oh-so-reasonable.

"Thanks." I shot him a dirty look.

"You have a bent tuning machine."

My head snapped up. "I suppose you're a musician, too. Everyone's a fucking musician tonight."

Julian shrugged. "I am. But I haven't played in a while."

"Yeah? What's your instrument?"

"A little of this, a little of that." His eyes glinted with humor. I was mad and he was teasing, which made me all the madder.

I gritted my teeth. "I don't suppose you'd care to be more specific."

"Some piano. A little flute. My main instrument is viol."

"Viol? You mean violin, George?"

"Julian," he corrected. "Actually, I meant viola da gamba."

Oh, great. Just fucking great. Suitguy played an instrument that hadn't been popular since the sixteenth century. "I know your name is Julian, you nook-yoo-ler schmuck!"

"Ah," Julian said wisely. "Earth humor."

I tuned the new E string. It was a quarter tone off, sounding like a lemon hitting an open wound. "Why're you here, anyway? Trying to impress your girlfriend?"

"Actually, yes."

He admitted it! My eyes flew up. Julian was smiling wickedly. I wanted to whack that grin off his face with my amp. No, with Lob's amp. And then maybe I'd ram my clarinet reedy-end first up Julian's tight ass.

"Are you?" Julian asked.

My mad hit a wall of confusion and stumbled. "Huh?"

"Are you impressed? That I came to hear you?"

Julian Emerson had come to hear...me?

No way. He had to be lying. Maybe he was trying to butter me up for some reason. Hell, he was a lawyer. Maybe he was lying just to keep in practice. I gave him a challenging glare. "I meant Drusilla, Nimrod."

"I know." His expression gentled. "You have nothing to worry about. Dru and I are just friends."

Yeah, sure. And Romeo just had a casual relationship with

Juliet. "I thought you had meetings all night."

"I did. I do. I had a break, and thought I'd come listen to you play. I have to go back soon."

"And what about Drusilla?" I could have slapped myself to be so transparent.

He shrugged. "We met in the parking lot. She had a break too, so I said I'd buy her a drink. What time do you get done?"

"Nice try changing the subject, Emerson."

"I like it better when you call me Julian. Oh, well. At least I've improved from Nimrod."

That sidetracked me. "You get that without subtitles?"

"I recognize the Biblical reference. By the way, Nimrod was a mighty warrior, not an idiot. But I wasn't trying to change the subject. I was trying to find out what time you're done playing."

"Why, so you can walk me home?"

"Yes." Before I could squawk that I wasn't a damn kid who needed to be walked home from school, he added, "And maybe stop by your place after. If you want me to."

My stomach fell through my belly and hit my pussy with a splat. I squirmed on my stool, leaving a very wet streak. There were disadvantages to not wearing underwear.

Julian, damn him, saw. His eyes got very dark. "What time," he said, and this time his vocal cords were as tight as my E string.

"Um...two. I should be packed up by two thirty."

"I'll be here." His eyes were glued to my stool. "Don't change clothes."

"I...I won't." My mouth was suddenly dry.

"Good." He spun and strode out the door.

I sat and stared at that door for the whole break. Fantasizing. When the next set came, I played the entire thing with the E string a quarter tone sharp—and never noticed.

Chapter Eleven

Julian didn't show by the time we finished. Two thirty came and went. I changed all the rest of my strings. No Julian. I was super-slow packing up. Julian still hadn't come.

The band was gone. The customers were gone. It was just me and the bartender when Drusilla came sauntering back in. I hoped she was here to see Buddy.

"Hi, Nixie," she said in her smoky alto, killing that hope. Dru was everything I'm not—tall, stacked, and dripping sex appeal. I'd never been jealous of her before. It wasn't a comfortable feeling.

"We're just friends, you know." She perched her perfect ass on a stool next to me. "Julian and I."

"None of my business," I mumbled.

"No, really. You don't have to worry."

"Worry? Why should I worry?" I gave her a perfectly cool and unconcerned and definitely non-jealous look. "Nothing to worry about. I'm not interested in a stodgy old suit. Not me. I'm Nixie the Pixie. He's Mr. Straight N. Narrow. We have nothing in common. If we were all elementals, you'd be earth, I'd be air, and Julian'd be concrete."

"There's a reason for Julian's self-control." Dru leaned toward me, her double-Ds surging forward like a tsunami. I jerked back before I drowned. Good thing, because one jumped out—it would have KOed me if I'd still been in range. "Rumor has it he fell in with a wild crowd," she went on as she nonchalantly tucked her boob back in. "I guess he did some damage before he came to his senses. It made him vow not to be so reckless."

"Reckless? Are we talking about the same man?" I snorted. I hoped she would tell me the full story, but would have pushed pencils up my nostrils before admitting it. "Emerson is so old-school he still uses Betamax. He probably plays CDs on a turntable. He's so uptight he breaks rubber bands by just looking at them."

"Maybe." Dru shrugged one round white shoulder. "But I heard he used to be a lot more fun in the old days. Well, I just wanted to reassure you that there was nothing going on between him and me." She slid her fanny off the stool and sauntered out.

After that, waiting only got harder. I unpacked, cleaned my clarinet, and packed up again. I unpacked, wiped down my strings, and packed up again. Where the hell was he?

Julian hadn't come by three. The bartender was starting to yawn in my face. It was time. It was past time. Like it or not, I'd been stood up.

Where the hell was he?

It pissed me off. I mean, what good was a steady, reliable suit if he wasn't steady and reliable? All right, that was two-faced of me. I complained that he was too serious and stodgy but then complained when he *wasn't*.

The problem was I'd had too much time to stew. About Julian and Drusilla, of course. But really. Dru's reassurances only served to make me more suspicious. Just *friends*? How did Boston attorney Julian Emerson become *friends* with Meiers Corners hooker Drusilla? How would they even meet? Touring the law schools in Chicago? At a prostitute convention in New York? A cruise of the Bahamas, she with her sugar daddy and he with his law books? I mean, come on. What did they have in common besides him having a cock and her a place to put it?

"Sorry I'm late," came a deep Boston Brahmin voice. Julian strode through the door, nodding to the bartender as he passed. "Hello, Buddy." Julian had on coat and suit, both casually unbuttoned.

I was so relieved to see him...the fucker. "Where the *hell* have you been?"

"I love you too," Julian said lightly, brushing a kiss across my lacquered lips.

I love you. He didn't mean it but my innards did a little

thrill. "Answer me, Emerson. You can't just waltz in here an hour late—"

"I had a spot of trouble on the way. Shall we go?" He picked up my amp and guitar.

"Just like that," I fumed. "You had a 'spot of trouble' and everything's okay. Well, it's *not* okay! I want an explanation. You'd better have hit a fucking iceberg to be an hour late!"

Julian stared at me, intently, like he was reading my brain. "I'm sorry, were you worried?"

About to cut each of his shiny vest buttons into a shiny new ass hole, I stopped. Deflated. Realized I *had* been worried about him. "No, of course not."

Julian, damn him, didn't even blink. "That's sweet." He gave my lips a longer, deeper kiss.

"I was not worried," I muttered against his mouth.

"Of course not." He put down my amp and guitar and pulled me in for a soul-searing kiss.

The sound of a throat emphatically clearing brought us both around. The bartender stood there, tapping his foot, pointing at his watch. "Find a bedroom."

"My apologies." Julian picked up my amp and guitar. "Nixie?"

As I slung my clarinet over my shoulder and followed Julian out, I hoped the bedroom he had in mind was mine. Then I was distracted by his ass. Nice, I thought. I wondered what it would look like without the coat covering it...or the pants. Maybe I would get to see tonight.

I followed him, fantasizing the whole time. I live a little under a mile from Nieman's Bar. That's a lot of fantasizing, especially with an ass as dreamy as Julian Emerson's. I think my thighs were squeaking as I walked.

We made it about four blocks before Julian dropped amp and guitar case and turned, growling.

"What's wrong?" I dropped my own freight, cast frantically around me for danger.

To my utter shock, Julian grabbed me. "*You.* Your arousal is driving me mad!" He yanked me in by my hips. His hands slid under my skirtlet and encountered naked butt.

It was instant explosion. Julian's mouth came down on

mine like a jackhammer. His strong, hot fingers bit into my ass. His mouth was on fire. My ass and mouth were searing. I felt like a candle burning at both ends. No, that's too tame. Like a firecracker belching double flames.

I jacked my hips up and back. Obligingly, Julian's fingers shifted down, rasped across my vulva. "Bedroom," I panted into his mouth.

"Too far," he said, stabbing fingers into me. He hoisted me into the air, settling me against his waist. As one hand continued to plunge into me, I heard the distinctive sound of a zipper being pulled down.

Smooth male flesh teased my pussy. Pressed against my swollen lips. Smooth and huge—damn! Julian's head was as big as my whole vulva. How would that monster feel going in? I shuddered with anticipation.

"Where are they?" a masculine voice shouted.

And a woman. "Don't try anything! I'm armed!"

Julian groaned. The zipper sounded again. *I* groaned.

"Where are who, Strongwell?" Julian called, setting me down. His voice was my favorite tight and growly and I groaned even deeper.

It was Elena who answered, in clipped cop mode. "Someone phoned. We got a tip. About where the bad guys...what have you two been doing?"

I peeked around Julian's bulk. Elena was staring at me like I'd gone crazy. And maybe I had. Tiny punk musician and skyscraper stodgy suit? Elena was right to stare. "Nothing," I squeaked.

"Nothing," Julian agreed. "Unfortunately."

"Doesn't smell like nothing." Bo's smile looked suspiciously like a trouble-making grin. "Smells like se—"

"Serious stuff, yes I know, Strongwell." Julian gave him a dirty look. "Why are you here?"

"We got a tip," Elena repeated, stowing something that looked like a bassoon on her back—if the military made bassoons.

"A tip? About the Coterie? Or this gang we've been dealing with?"

"The gang," Elena replied. "About where they sleep."

That's how she said it. Not "where their headquarters are", or "where they're holing up". Where they *sleep*.

"We got a phone call." Bo flashed a strange, warning-sort of look at Elena. "Tipped us the gang was *staying* here."

"Here?"

"At the abandoned Roller-Blayd Factory."

Sure enough, we were a block away from the old boarded-up building. I hadn't noticed, too taken with Julian's own, er, stiff plank.

"A phone call. We'd better check it out, then." Julian didn't sound too enthusiastic.

Remembering my own threatening call, I asked, "What did the voice on the phone sound like?"

"Weird." Elena shivered. "Raspy, but hollow. Like a cheap radio with the bass off and the treble cranked all the way up."

Julian frowned.

"Yeah, sketchy." I remembered annoying Deep Throat boy. "I may have spoken with your guy."

"When?" Elena sounded curious.

"When?" Bo sounded alarmed.

"When!?" Julian shouted above them both. He sounded plain furious. "And why the hell didn't you tell me?"

"Language, Julian." I waved him down.

He didn't look soothed. "You will tell me when this call occurred. You will tell me right now!"

I blinked. Deep Throat boy was weird, but no weirder than Headless Horseman Cutter. Why was Julian so upset? "Don't get your undies in a bundle, Emerson."

"Nixie, so help me, if you do not tell me right this minute, I will personally make you sit through reruns of Spanish soaps."

Ooh. Julian was learning all my weak points. "Fine! Some daggy guy rang me on my Juke last night. Kept calling me *Dietlinde*. What a Nimr...I mean faphead."

"What did he want?" Bo asked before Julian could verbally manhandle me any more.

"He told me to drop the fundraiser."

"What?! You can't!" Surprisingly, it was not Julian who said this, but Bo.

"Nixie." Julian took me by the shoulders. "Did this male say what would happen if you didn't?"

"Yeah. Something 'bad'. How fuzznucked up can you get?"

Julian's frown turned from anger to confusion. "Fuzznucked?"

"Fuzznucked up," Elena corrected helpfully.

"No subtitles," I told her.

"Poor Julian," she said.

"Poor Julian," I agreed.

"Nixie! Spanish soaps!" Julian snapped his fingers in front of my eyes. I have to admit it was effective in regaining my attention. "What do you mean, 'bad'?"

"He just said 'bad', Julian. Okay? He didn't explain it, didn't expand, expound or expatiate. He said bad, and that he wasn't joking. I just blew it off at the time. This Ruthven guy was a bit woo-woo, if you know what I mean."

"Ruthven." Julian exchanged a look with Bo that I could only call tense. "We'd better get them home."

So *I* traded looks with Elena. I had a feeling about who 'them' were.

She spoke for both of us. "No. No way. We've got as much at stake in this as you do, gentlemen." Under her breath she added, "Maybe more." Turning to Bo she said, "We came here to investigate the warehouse, Bo. Let's do it."

"Elena," Bo said. "This may be more dangerous than we thought."

"Bo," she returned with that warning tone of voice only married people can do. "We came here to investigate. I'm investigating."

Even I could hear the unspoken, *Whether you like it or not.*

Elena shouldered her bassoon grenade launcher (which I figured from my conversation with Bruno must be an SMAW) and stalked toward the warehouse.

Bo ran after.

Julian sighed. "I should stay with them. In case they need help."

I picked up my clarinet. "Let's go."

"Nixie—oh, never mind. You'll be safer with me anyway." He

took guitar and amp and followed Bo and Elena at a smooth glide.

I trotted alongside. "Julian...do you know this Ruthven guy?" And then, because I was coming to trust him, I added, "Do you think he sounds kind of...inhuman?"

To his everlasting credit, Julian did not laugh at me. "Yes, I've met him. And yes, I find him a bit odd."

"Woo-woo odd, or creepy odd?"

Julian shrugged. "Ruthven tends to be melodramatic. Who else would style himself 'Lord'? But that doesn't mean he isn't dangerous."

"Is he part of the Ichabod Crane gang?"

Julian eyed me strangely. "The what?"

"Ichabod Crane. You know, Legend of Sleepy Hollow? Headless Horseman?"

"Yes, I get the Washington Irving reference. How does it relate to a gang—" Julian actually stopped speaking, almost impossible for a lawyer or politician. Ground to a halt. "You don't think Cutter was decapitated, do you? And somehow had his head reattached?"

I pulled up next to him, and smiled sweetly into his face. "That's impossible."

"It *is* impossible."

"So is he? Is this Ruthven guy one of the Lestats?" I threw out the name to see if I could get a reaction.

Julian didn't startle or stutter. But his eyes narrowed suddenly on mine. "Cutter works for the Coterie. Ruthven is second-in-command of the Coterie. Who are the Lestats?"

"Oops, sorry, my mistake." I traipsed off toward the warehouse.

Julian spun me back. "Where did you hear that name? The Lestats?"

"Somewhere. I don't remember."

"Nixie. Don't. This is far more dangerous than you know."

"Is it?" I finally lost my temper. "That's what people keep telling me, but I wouldn't know, would I? Because no one will *tell* me anything, not really. Oh, they say something *bad* will happen. Or that it's *dangerous.* But they don't give me details. They don't tell me why." I grabbed Julian by his cashmere lapels and looked up pleadingly into his eyes. "Why, Julian? What's so dangerous about this gang? What's so bad? And why do people say 'gang' like it's something *unnatural?*"

"Nixie—"

"*Don't*, Julian." He was going to say that I wasn't prepared for the truth. Or, worse, that I was imagining things. "Don't lie to me and don't treat me like a kid."

He set down my amp, brushed back my curls from my face. "I'll try not to. But it isn't easy to explain. And isn't safe to speak about it in public."

"Public? We're outside an abandoned warehouse—"

"Which is rumored to hold the very gang we're talking about. Nixie, I'll tell you, I swear. But not now. Okay?"

I gazed up into his eyes, wanting to believe him. Wanting to believe he trusted me enough to not treat me like a kid. Wanting to believe he cared enough not to lie to me. "All right, Julian. I'll wait. But not forever."

Chapter Twelve

Boards covered the warehouse windows, high overhead. Boards had also been nailed over the door, but one was askew, revealing a child-sized hole. Julian pushed my guitar and amp through. Then he folded his big frame and slid deftly in.

Julian's big, hard body fitting small holes made me pause for a moment and fan myself. Whew. I ducked in after.

As Julian straightened, all points alert, I looked around with interest. The lights were on. Maybe that meant someone was home. Maybe the mystery wouldn't have to wait for Julian to explain. Maybe I'd see the gang "where they slept" right now.

I trotted forward. Julian picked up my equipment and glided after me. The concrete floor was disappointingly empty. Not even sleeping bags. About midway a set of spiral stairs led up to a platform.

Bo and Elena were just disappearing into a single-room office on the platform. We had crossed halfway there when they came back out. "Nothing here," Bo called down.

"No," Julian said. "I would have smelled them."

I found that a little hard to believe. "Smelled them? Is this the BO gang? Haven't showered since 1852?"

"They're a bit younger than that," Julian said with a smile. He seemed more relaxed. "This was a false alarm. We can go home after all."

Home? With Julian? I was just absorbing the possibilities when a scream shattered the night.

Bo streaked down the stairs. "Outside." He went almost supernaturally fast, Elena clumping behind.

"Stay here." Julian dropped my amp and guitar and

streaked after.

Julian dropped my baby! I immediately fell to my knees to throw open the latches and check on poor Oscar. Thankfully my Strat was okay.

I was relatching the case when Elena reached me. "We're supposed to stay here," I said, rising.

"The hell with that." She unshouldered her SMAW. "Samuel and I have work to do." She patted the large tube.

Samuel? Elena had *named* her bazooka?

But if she was going, I was going. "Okay, let's kick some gang butt."

Elena flashed me worried eyes. "Nixie...you're not armed."

"Oh, not you too. I'm *not* a kid, and I'm *not* helpless! I know what I'm doing, Elena. I study Taekwondo with Mr. Miyagi three times a week!" Yeah, really. Mr. Miyagi Park, actually, but he even looked like Pat Morita from *The Karate Kid*.

"But Nixie...this gang is, well, monstrous. It takes more than guts and hand-to-hand technique to stop them."

"We can stand here all day arguing, or we can go Bruce Lee some Lestats. Which is it, Elena?"

The worried look turned to shock as she stared at me. "You know about the Lestats? You *know*, and you're going into combat *unarmed?*"

The incredulity in her voice should have clued me in. But I was too mad at everyone treating me like a kid.

At that moment, I was a kid, and a stupid one at that. "Enough fapping, Elena. Are we women or are we wimps?"

Elena stared at me a moment longer. "All right," she said finally. Let's go.

I climbed through the hole in the door, into the end of the world.

Chaos. Violence. Screams.

Gaunt, fiery-eyed men rampaged outside. Skull-headed, unnaturally fluid men with teeth like jagged glass. Evil-looking men, seemingly hundreds of them. A knot of red fire and flashing knives, surrounding...shit.

Surrounding Julian and Bo.

Bo held a limp bundle in one arm. The bundle had two blonde heads. I realized it was two people, one a child. They seemed unconscious...or dead.

Bo fought ferociously with one hand. He wielded what looked like a long knife, or a sword. The blade whistled through the air, forcing the gaunt men back.

One man dove forward, under Bo's blade. The man came up swinging a wicked-looking knife.

Bo dodged and spit him on the sword like a pig.

I shuddered.

Julian fought by Bo's side. Like Bo, he slashed at the masses with a long blade, spinning with deadly grace and speed. Lightning fast, almost savage.

I almost didn't recognize lawboy Julian. His face was sharp and hard, skin like bladed armor. His eyes glowed red. His mouth opened in a horrific roar. Revealing—revealing—

Fangs.

Foot-long fangs, or so they seemed to me. Like a sabertooth tiger's. Roaring through those monster fangs, Julian whirled his lethal blade—and sliced through an attacker's throat.

Geysers of blood sprayed from the gaunt man's severed neck. So much blood. Fountains, that became rivulets and finally stopped. That was actually worse. He had to be dead.

But that wasn't the end of it. Instead of dropping the body, Julian grabbed the man by the hair. Yanked him in. The head flopped like a rag doll.

Foreboding lanced me. Julian seized the man in the crook of his sword arm. He slapped a palm on the man's head. Pushed...twisted.

To my horror I heard a series of wet pops. Like ripping off a turkey leg. Through the roars I could actually hear the *chock* of broken vertebrae as the man's neck snapped.

Julian lifted the man by the hair, body dangling limply. He raised his sword.

I wanted to shout *wait, stop!* But my throat wouldn't obey.

With a fierce, inhumanly powerful stroke, Julian sliced the man's head completely off.

I spun away, dizzy. Julian Emerson was chopping off heads. I fell to my knees and was violently ill next to a broken board.

It seemed like that nightmare took forever, but in fact it was only a few moments. Elena was just emerging behind me from the Roller-Blayd factory. She stopped. Screamed, "Gretchen! Stella!"

Dripping spit, I pulled my head up. The limp bundle in Bo's arm—the blonde heads. Bo held Elena's sister, Gretchen. And her five-year-old niece, Estella.

Elena ran into the fray, her SMAW blazing. She stopped for an instant and turned sideways as she shot. If I had been in my right mind I would have wondered why. As it was I saw the reason. The payload exploded in front, the recoil blasted behind. Swaths of men flew in both directions. Bodies exploded, burned.

Elena cut a path through the attackers. A path of exploding death.

I didn't understand the wholesale destruction Elena was delivering. Oh, I understood her anger, her fear. The gaunt men were attacking her husband, her sister. Her small niece.

But it seemed extreme. Elena blew great burning holes in skeletal torsos. Bo stabbed and hacked, ripping open bellies and throats. Julian slashed and sliced, severing throats and even limbs.

None of my friends seemed to care that they were slaughtering *people*.

It was not over quickly. Later I knew there weren't that many attackers. But it seemed for every creature who fell at Bo's hand, for every one who crumpled at Julian's feet, ten more came to replace them. The attackers boiled up around Bo and Julian like a monstrous football huddle.

No matter how many were killed, the circle of gaunt men rose up again. Undeterred. Jumping over the corpses of their fallen.

Sheer numbers must bring my friends down.

I shuddered, wondering what I should do. What I *could* do, unarmed as I was.

As I knelt there, undecided, one of the gaunt men stumbled from the pack toward me. His hands were pressed to his neck. Blood soaked his shirt.

He fell to his knees just a few feet from me. Collapsed to the ground with a *whump*.

I crawled over to the man. His head was canted at an unnatural angle. His hands fell away from his neck.

His throat was almost completely severed.

I shuddered, covering my mouth. A scream rang in my head but all that came from my mouth was a terrified little hiss.

And then—the unthinkable happened.

The head *moved*. The neck started to straighten.

The throat...started to close.

Before my eyes, the muscle and gristle knit. Became whole. Over it, the seam of skin fused. Like clay smoothed shut.

Soon not even a scar marked where the man's throat had been cut.

The body *sat up*. The body...man...corpse...God, I don't know what he was...he cricked his neck with a loud pop. Grinned and rose to his feet. Joined again in the attack.

I freaked. All my cocky self-confidence vanished. This wasn't kind-of-weird-but-sexy Julian biting me. This wasn't sitting in a bar with Bruno whispering conspiracy theories.

This was blood-splashing *horror*. This was shambling hordes that kept coming and coming. This was fighting the battle over and over until you just gave up and lay down and died.

I ran back into the warehouse. Grabbing my guitar case to my chest I huddled, eyes tightly closed. Shivering. Wanting to throw up but only choking on dry heaves. "Shit, Oscar. It's real. V-v-v...they're real. Hordes of vam...vampires...they're out there. I'm dead. We're all dead." In his case, Oscar hummed a scary little threnody.

I don't know how long I stayed like that. I know at some point I cried because when Julian came, Oscar's case was wet.

Julian didn't say a word, only knelt and gently wiped my face. Put his arms around me. Held me and rocked me. Eventually I felt safe enough to open my eyes. I wouldn't let go of Oscar. Julian seemed to understand, simply lifted us both into his arms. He must have picked up my clarinet and amp, too.

He took me home. Undressed me like a child and put me to

bed. Settled Oscar in bed next to me. Found my stuffed Jimi bear and put it in bed on my other side. Only then did he leave me, and then only long enough to get some cocoa.

He brought the hot cup to me and made me drink. He had to hold the cup because I was still trembling.

After I finished all of it, he set the cup on my night stand. Sitting next to me, he brushed my hair back from my face. "Do you want to talk about it?" It was the first thing he'd said since telling me to stay put.

"Were those...were those what I think?" My voice was thick and the words garbled, but Julian understood and nodded. I blinked back tears. "But there were hundreds of them! How did you survive?"

"Not hundreds. Maybe thirty." He took a deep breath. "And we survived because we're the same as them, Bo and I." Julian watched me carefully, as if judging my reaction. "But you knew that."

"No," I whispered. I hugged my Jimi bear tight. "I thought maybe...I suspected...but not really." I had thought v-thoughts. But my picture was Count Chocula. Dapper and pointy and part of this complete breakfast. Not even light-years close to reality. I looked into Julian's face for the first time. Seeing his blue eyes soften, I said, "Will I...will I become one now?"

"Oh, Nixie. Of course not." His fingers brushed gently over my cheek. "Only dead people can turn. You're very much alive, sweetheart."

"Then...what are you going to do to me? Now that I know?"

Julian took in another deep breath, let it out. Giving him time to think, or maybe giving me time to adjust to the worst. "Nixie...we can induce a certain forgetfulness. But only in cases of brief exposure. And only when the memory isn't set. The trauma works in your favor, but..." His eyes shifted away from me.

Meaning the worst. "But Elena knows. She does, doesn't she? That's why the bazooka."

"Yes. Elena is part of our world, now."

"Meaning what? That she's Bo's slave?" I could have slapped myself for being such a blind idiot. "She is, isn't she? Bo's blood slave."

"She's Bo's *wife*," Julian said gently. "She gives Bo blood, but it's voluntary. All Bo's donors give by choice."

"Donors." A shudder went through me. "A damn blood bank. People are a blood bank to you. No, it's worse. We're food, aren't we? Like a smorgasbord." I pictured rows of steam tables, but with people under the gleaming silver lids.

"I said donors and I meant it." Julian paused. "Would you like me to explain?"

No, my mind screamed. "Yes," I whispered.

"Vampires can't make their own blood." Julian caressed my hair. "Like people whose bone marrow fails. So we need transfusions."

"You don't...drink...blood?"

"We take transfusions by mouth. But it goes directly into the bloodstream. Not the stomach."

"Not food?"

"No."

It sounded like the truth, but I needed to be sure. I looked deep into Julian's penetrating eyes. That was probably dangerous, given the whole vampire/minion thing. But I had to know. I saw only honesty and a tender compassion. "So once your bloodstream's full...that's it? No more biting?"

Slowly, he shook his head. "Red blood cells die, Nixie. We need fresh blood about three times a month."

"Cows?" I asked hopefully.

"Only humans can make human blood, sweetheart. We need to drink from them."

"And the...the 'humans'." My shivering increased. Julian was *not human.* "They're all *volunteers.*"

"Yes. For us," Julian said. "For Bo and myself, and those like us."

I hugged my Jimi bear to my chest. My fingers stole to my neck, where Julian had bitten me, not once, but twice. "What are you going to do about it?" I repeated. "Now that I know. Are you going to kill me?"

"No! We don't kill people, Nixie."

If I hadn't been so numb I would have been incredulous. "What about the warehouse? You *killed* dozens of people there. Slaughtered them."

"Not people. And we didn't kill them."

"Oh, no. You only sliced and diced them—" I stopped, flashing back. The body that fell near me. A vivid picture hit me, the body's severed neck, *rejoining*. I shivered and clutched Jimi harder. "Why did you do that? Why so much...destruction?"

"Vampires are incredibly resilient, sweetheart. Wounds heal almost immediately. The only way to stop a vampire is to remove the heart."

"Without a heart, a vampire is dead?"

"Without blood flow, the vampire can't move. But he's not dead. Put a heart in, any heart, and he heals. Even without intervention, the heart eventually regenerates."

"They never die?" I said, horrified.

"We can die. Burning destroys us. A crematorium, or if we're out too long in the sun. Beheading is almost as good. Then the body has no direction. And a head can't move by itself."

"That's why you cut off...sliced...yeah." I tried to swallow, felt like a baseball was in my throat.

"We had to disable the rogues, enough to get you and Gretchen and Stella out alive. But they'll put each other back together before morning."

"Fuck."

"Yes." Julian paused. "Before the fight...you asked me not to treat you like a child. Not to lie to you. Did you mean that?"

"Yes," I said in a very small voice.

"Do you still mean it?"

I had to think about that. "Probably," was the best I could come up with.

Julian put his hand over mine. "I have to leave soon, Nixie."

"No!" I dropped Jimi and clutched Julian instead. "There's still hours until dawn. You don't have to go until dawn, do you? Oh, please don't go!"

"I'm sorry, sweetheart. Remember what I said about those rogues putting each other back together before morning?"

"You said...it's because you didn't kill them."

"Yes. But we did spill a lot of blood."

"Can't you get someone else to clean that up?" I asked hopefully.

"That's not it. Nixie, the rogues will go to ground and heal. And when they rise tomorrow night, they'll need to replenish. Which means blood, and lots of it. Fresh, hot, human blood."

That cut through my numbness. I gaped at him. "Shit."

"Exactly." Julian rose. "Don't worry. You'll be safe here." He leaned down, brushed a kiss across my forehead.

"Wait. Julian. What will you do?"

He was already at the bedroom door. When he turned, his face was in shadows but his eyes glowed unnaturally red. "Try to find an alternate source."

"And if you can't?"

"Then Bo and I will need to destroy the rogues. Permanently."

♫ ♫ ♫

I eventually got to sleep. When I woke it was with a kink in my back from snuggling up to Oscar. It's hard to spoon naturally into a Fender case.

They say sleep is the great rejuvenator, and that's true. My natural optimism had been partially restored.

Yes, I had failed utterly in a pinch. But I had been unprepared. Guessing vampire wasn't the same as seeing one. Reality was, it would take as much training to learn to beat a supernatural foe as it did to get a martial arts black belt in the first place.

If it was only a matter of training. I now knew more than I had yesterday, but not enough. I still had a bunch of questions. As I dressed, sunlight streamed through the window. If lore was correct, Julian would be unavailable until nightfall.

But it seemed Elena knew the answers, too.

I trotted over in less than twenty minutes. When I got to the Strongwell apartment Elena was out. To my surprise, Daniel Butler answered the door.

Everybody knew everybody in Meiers Corners. Butler's wife Joan was my third-grade teacher. Daniel Butler drove the bus on all our field trips. I remembered him as the little silver-haired guy in blue jeans who handed out the juice boxes.

Today Daniel Butler was all dapper in black cutaway coat, wing collar, and silk tie. Like the understudy for Tim Curry in *Clue* or Chris Barrie in *Lara Croft*. Like he took his name one step too seriously. "Hey, Mr. Butler. Going to a costume party?"

To my surprise, he blushed. "Not exactly. I just, um, well..."

"And how'd you end up with door duty for an apartment building?"

"Joan and I have the first unit. It's, ah, easier for me to answer the door. When the doorbell rings. Since there's no way to buzz visitors in."

"Uh-huh." That rang as true as plastic wind chimes. But none of my business. "Is Elena in?"

"The mistr...Mrs. Elena is doing some shopping, I believe."

"Shopping?" I echoed. "For what?"

To my surprise, Mr. Butler got all red and stuttery. "I can't say...I mean, I'm not sure. Maybe groceries. I think. Or shoes. Yes, that's it. Miss Stella grew out of another pair of school shoes."

Intuition whacked a mallet on a really big gong. "And how is Stella and her mom? After last night's...events?"

Butler's eyes got big. "You know about that? About...them?" He glanced up and down the street, then grabbed me by the elbow and dragged me inside. "You can't say anything."

"I'm not planning to. But a) you can tell me where Elena really is and b) you can tell me how Gretchen and Stella are really doing."

Butler's face went glum. "Miss Stella and Mrs. Johnson are doing about as well as you'd expect. Not well at all."

"Why were they at the warehouse, anyway?"

"After Mr. and Mrs. Strongwell left, Mrs. Johnson took a call, then raced out after them. Apparently Miss Stella followed her mother, though no one knew it at the time."

"Gretchen left Stella alone?" That was unheard of. Gretchen was the best mom since June Cleaver.

"No, Mrs. Johnson left Miss Stella with a young lady who was supposed to be watching her, and was instead talking on the phone. The young lady has been severely chastised, not the least by Mr. Strongwell."

"And Elena? Where is she?"

"The mistress has gone to find any spare blood in the city. For the rogues when they rise. I wish Mr. Strongwell would just kill them. In a way, he is too civilized."

Too civilized. Something I never would have applied to Bo Strongwell before. Just like I'd never considered Julian Suitguy the type to slice off heads. My perspective was certainly changing. "So Elena went to the Blood Center?"

Daniel Butler eyed me strangely. "No, of course not! That blood is strictly off-limits."

"It is?"

"Well, of course it is. That's one of Mr. Strongwell's duties, isn't it? Protecting the distribution center. Especially now that the *gang* has come."

I frowned. The whole Bo and Lestat thing obviously had unknown depths. I would have to ask Elena about that, too. "Where would Elena have gone, then?"

"The Stark and Moss Mortuary, for one. Nieman's Bar, for another."

"Nieman's Bar has *blood*?"

"My twin works there," Daniel Butler said, sounding a little smug. "Who do you think came up with the recipe for the Red Special?"

The bartender at Nieman's. Buddy. Did everyone in this town know about vampires except me?

"If the mistress isn't at the funeral home or Nieman's Bar, you could try the police station."

"The police station has blood?" That made even less sense than the bar.

"No, of course not. Because of Miss Drusilla."

At that, my brain slipped out of gear. I had to work to grind it back into low. Drusilla was a hooker. Meiers Corners's only full-timer. What did she have to do with the cop shop? And what did either of them have to do with blood?

Then I remembered Dirk saying Police Captain Titus was a pimp. At the time I thought it was a metaphor, like me saying Julian the Lawyer was a bloodsucking vampire. But my metaphor had turned out to be reality. Maybe the pimp-thing was, too. Come to think of it, why had I ever believed clueless

Dirk capable of a metaphor?

So that was the link from DD-Drusilla to the cop shop. But where was the link with blood? Unless...oh, no. It couldn't be. Not another vampire.

Except if Drusilla was a vampire, it would explain how Julian knew her. Suddenly I wanted it to be true. It would explain what they had in common—besides Tab A and Slot B.

Optimism fully back online, I turned to go. "Thanks, Mr. Butler. You've been a big help."

"Pleased to be of service," he said. "Oh, Miss Nixie, one thing."

I stopped at the door. "Yes?"

"If you do run across mistress Elena, could you ask her to pick up some shallots? We're having guests for dinner and Cook is out of them. In fact, perhaps you would like to join us?"

"I'd love to, but—" I had nearly forgotten The Mating Game at my parents. "My mom's doing a thing. Hey, Mr. Butler. Do you know Denny Crane's new partner? Bart Blei-something?"

"I have heard of him, of course."

"Is he a you-know?" Meaning vampire.

"Certainly not." Mr. Butler sniffed as if he was affronted.

"Great!" I pushed out the door.

As the door swung shut, I seemed to hear Daniel Butler say, "But Mr. Bleistift *is* a—"

But I might have been hearing things.

Chapter Thirteen

I checked Stark and Moss Mortuary, Nieman's Bar, and the cop shop. Just for kicks I strolled by the Blood Center, but beyond learning there was a big shipment going through in a few days, I got zip. Elena wasn't at any of the places I checked.

By then it was one fifteen and I didn't have any more time to look. I barely had time to shower and change.

Even so, I managed to show up at my ancestral home bang on the dot of two. Which of course had my mother flinging open the door and shouting, "You're late! Get in here and set the good china! And would it have hurt to dress up a little?"

"I changed my shirt." I looked down. My original tee had a yellow triangular caution sign emblazoned with the tasteful slogan "Slippery When Wet" and an arrow pointing toward my crotch. This shirt read, "I'm Up, I'm Dressed, What More Do You Want?" Apparently my mother wanted a lot more. I sighed and followed her in.

Today's apron was white eyelet. And my mother had done a full makeup, complete with lipstick and blush. *And* she was wearing heels.

This was trouble.

"I thought brunch was at two." I edged out of my jacket. "And what's with the good china?"

"I said to *be* here at two. Bart's coming at two thirty. I thought that would give us enough time to get ready. But no! You have to be late."

Late by Meiers Corners's standards, where you were expected to show up twenty minutes early. Where two o'clock was one forty, and two thirty was ten minutes after two. "Sorry,

Mother."

"Well, it can't be helped now. You set the table, I've got to check on the ham."

"Ham? We're having ham?"

"Spiral cut. Brown sugar and brandy glaze."

It was worse than I thought. Similar to the Mother Test, my mother has a Food Scale. An ordinary family meal was sauerbraten or pot roast. Special occasions like birthdays got stuffed pork chops. Holidays with guests were turkey or Cornish hens.

Only God got spiral-cut ham.

To top it all off, my mother had the silver flatware and the Bohemian crystal out. As I set the table, I felt like I was decorating for my own wake. St. Bart was coming, and he got ham and the best china. In her mind, my mother probably had us married already. I would be lucky if she wasn't knitting little booties.

Something about dread speeds up time. It seemed like only ten minutes had passed before the doorbell rang.

Or maybe St. Bart was on Meiers Corners time.

"There he is!" My mother tore through the dining room like a tornado. "Get the hors d'oeuvres, Dietlinde."

My mother had made hors d'oeuvres. Please. Just barbeque me. It'd be less painful.

Dutifully I went to the kitchen and brought out the silver tray of mini-sandwiches and artistically decorated crackers. Not even cheezwhiz and Ritz. I said a quick prayer that we weren't having champagne.

I heard voices as I brought out the tray. My mother, cooing, for heaven's sake. My father, actually saying "Hello". And St. Bart...who had a very nice baritone.

"Thank you for inviting me over, Mrs. Schmeling. I've been a little cooped up since moving to Meiers Corners."

"We must seem tiny after the Big City." My mother, normally the staunchest defender of the Corners.

Surprisingly St. Bart replied, "Not at all. But my apartment and the law office are a bit cramped. And I don't get out much. Once it snows I can do some cross-country skiing, but until then it's just cold."

"In the old days we would have had a foot of snow by now." My mother again, apologizing for the weather. St. Bart must really be something. I took a deep breath and rounded the corner.

And stopped, and stared. Hanging up his black wool overcoat was a slim, dark-haired young man in ivory cable sweater and jeans. His hair was thick and wavy, his butt nice and trim. His shoulders were good and solid. Not as broad as Julian's. Then again Julian had a supernatural advantage...or so I guessed.

The young man turned. His face was open and boyish, with a light dusting of freckles. His blue eyes lit when he saw me and his generous mouth turned up in a smile. "You must be Dietlinde. Hi. I'm Bart." He stuck out his hand.

Bart had the slim, artistic fingers I'd expected Julian to have. I met his handshake, appreciatingly firm but not tight. "Call me Nixie."

"Nixie?" Bart kept smiling, looking questioningly between my mother and me.

I took pity on him. "Nixie's my middle name."

"*Ach*, that *dumm* name," my mother said. "I don't know why you use it when Dietlinde is so much prettier."

"I kind of like it. Nixie," Bart said again, getting a smile out of me. "Has an impish sort of ring. Like pixie."

"Exactly my point," my mother said.

Taking a cracker off the tray, Bart gave me a wink. "If you don't like it, Mrs. Schmeling, why'd you give it to your daughter?"

"The aunts." My mother's mouth set as if tasting a twist of lemon. "We named Dietlinde after my two sisters. Older and younger."

"That's a nice tradition. My sister's named after my grandmothers."

That dropped into a sudden silence. Bart munched cracker. Sucked some creamed chicken liver off one finger. He pretended there was no awkward gap, but I knew he'd noticed it because he shot me a questioning look.

My grandmothers were named Eva...and Giselle.

I shrugged and gave Bart an eye-roll. Signaling no biggie,

although, of course, it was.

We all sat in the front room. My dad spoke. "Beer?" He looked at Bart.

"Yes, please, Mr. Schmeling. Just one."

That earned a look of approval from my father *and* my mother, although for different reasons. "So, Bart," my mother said as my father escaped...er, left for the kitchen. "You are a lawyer? How do you like that?"

"Very much, Mrs. Schmeling. I'm learning a lot from Mr. Crane. My goal is to practice in Chicago some day. Become a partner in a high-powered firm."

"And that pays well?" My mother is nothing if not transparent.

But Bart didn't seem to mind. "Oh, yes. Even in Meiers Corners it's quite profitable. But in Chicago, well, the sky's the limit."

The Saint had passed number one, Gainfully Employed, with disgusting ease. I plucked a small sandwich off the tray and chomped.

"And you grew up in Chicago? I know some people in Chicago. The Schwartzes. Maybe you've heard of them?"

Trying to ascertain how he scored on number two, Good Family.

"Mother, there are three million people living in Chicago. Almost ten million in the metro area! It's highly unlikely that Bart has met—"

"You mean Hans and Gretel Schwartz?" Bart's face lit with pleasure. "They were our neighbors for ten years. Their oldest daughter Caroline babysat me when I was a kid."

My mother actually clapped her hands in delight. "You heard Caroline has had her first baby, yes?"

"Heard? I'm the godfather!"

After that it was old home week. The baby had been baptized at Good Shepherd Lutheran church, which put Bart over the top on three, Good Lutheran. I got bored within ten seconds. They yakked so enthusiastically I thought my mother totally forgot four—Enthralled by My Daughter. Or maybe she replaced it with Form 4EZ—Enchanted by Mom.

Finally she moved on. "So is lawyering hard work, Bart?"

Looking for five, Has a Brain.

"I'd say fascinating." Bart spread his artistic fingers in a gesture of eye-opening delight. "The intricacies of the law, the research and the fire of discovery...it has a sort of poetry, Mrs. Schmeling."

Well, wasn't that guaranteed to make my mother swoon.

My dad returned with the beers, apparently hiding out in the kitchen until all the tests had been administered and the results tabulated. We hadn't done number six, Helps with the Housework, but I got the impression with St. Bart, my mother would cut a little slack.

At dinner, talk turned to music. Bart played a little trumpet in junior high but hadn't touched it in years, which was frankly somewhat refreshing. And he was cute, in an open and boyish sort of way.

Maybe cute, open, and boyish was just the thing I needed to forget about dark, dangerous, and bitey. "Hey, Bart," I said as we gathered up the dessert dishes. (He passed six, too.) "My band is playing tonight. Want to come?"

"Sure!" Bart smiled his Opie smile.

I smiled back and waited. A little quiver of interest fluttered in my tummy. Okay, not the hot rush of lust Julian inspired, but I was willing to work with it. "We're at the Alpine Retreat and Bar. On the edge of town. First set's at nine."

"Great! I'll be there."

♫ ♫ ♫

That night I dressed with care. My mother liked Bart, my father liked Bart, and even I liked Bart some. After all, he called me Nixie. I owed him a decent chance.

And Julian, while the best sex I'd ever had (without even screwing), wasn't going to stick around forever. He'd come to Meiers Corners to deal with the Chicago thing. When that was done, he'd go back. And he was hardly likely to ask me to come with him and meet his holy Boston Brahmin friends.

Besides, where did a vampire score on the Mother Test?

So I dressed in something that would be sexy without scaring Bart off. Something interesting and provocative, not too far off my punk personality, but with the sharp edges filed down a little.

Which meant trying on every combination of underwear and clothes I owned.

I finally opted for stretchy pink lace boy-cut panties and pink lace bra. Over that went a pink camisole—and black leather pants and boots. I mean, fun's fun and all, but girly was just not me. Then I pinched up my curls in tiny butterfly clips and slicked on strawberry lip gloss.

Okay, maybe I'm a *little* girly.

I half-expected Julian to show up all the time I was dressing. After all, we had been apartmentus-interruptus last night. Weren't staid suitguys taught to always finish what they started?

Oscar was lying on my bed where he'd been since the incident at the warehouse. I opened the case and checked him over. As I started to put him away, I was caught by the bent tuning machine.

It got bent when Oscar was practically brand-new. He was my first purchase with my own money. I made the mistake of laying him on the floor during practice. My sister Giselle ran in, not looking where she was going as usual. A force of nature, Giselle was.

She stepped on baby Oscar. Bent the tuning machine. I was angry about it at the time, yelled things I don't like to remember. She promised to get it repaired, but Giselle never had money. Too generous, with her own cash and everyone else's.

Two weeks later she was dead.

I never got that tuning key repaired. It reminded me of Giselle. That life was short, sometimes way too short.

It reminded me to always, *always* seize the day.

I wanted to seize Julian. Where the hell was he? Maybe he thought I was still reeling from the trauma of seeing hordes of guys dismembered. Maybe he was waiting for me to call him.

Or maybe he had more *meetings*. His fucking job. His fucking *responsibility*. That made me angry, until I remembered his other job. The one where he had to worry about dismembered guys rising again. Hordes of dismembered guys, thirsty for blood.

What if Elena hadn't found any blood for them? What if she hadn't found enough?

Maybe Julian wasn't ignoring me. Maybe Julian was out finishing—the job.

As I picked up Oscar I put that gruesome little thought firmly out of mind. Tonight, I wasn't going to think about supernatural beings. I was definitely not going to think about supernaturally erotic beings whose bites were orgasmic—no. Not thinking about that at all.

Which of course made me think about *only* that. It was worse than an earworm, that little tune that gets stuck in your head and eats out your brains. With great deliberation I put Julian and his dark sizzling sex firmly out of my mind. As I backed out of the garage I was so *not* thinking about orgasmic bites that I nearly sheared the mirror off the side of the car.

We started our first set at nine fifteen. Bart showed up about half an hour later. He bought himself a single beer at the bar and found a table. Tipped his beer toward me and smiled. I had to admit he was very cute. His smile warmed my belly and tickled my twinkle lips. And *this* lawyer didn't saunter in with any hookers on his arm.

Although wouldn't that give my mother a fit?

After we finished the set, Bart wandered over. I put Oscar in his case and rose to meet him—Bart, I mean. Standing on tip-toes, I brushed my lips across his. He waited a split second before returning the favor, lingering a little longer than I had. He had nice technique. We kissed once more before I dropped off my toes.

"Buy you another?" I indicated his almost-empty glass.

"Oh, no. Thanks, but I never have more than one an hour. That's how long it takes to metabolize one drink, you know. One hour."

"No, I didn't know." Well, now was the hard part. Making conversation. What to say, what to say? With Julian it was easy. We were always fighting. When he wasn't comforting me. Or arousing me. Or biting...no, not thinking about that. Shuddering about that, but not thinking about it. "So. Um, did you have any trouble finding the place?"

"Nope. Your mom gave me directions after you left."

"My *mom*? She knew directions to the Alpine?" Whoa. My

mother—in a bar?

"Caroline Schwartz got married here. Isn't that amazing? You and I could have met two years ago."

"I didn't come," I said. "I had a gig that night. A paying gig."

"Oh." Bart shrugged. "Well, I suppose you have your priorities."

"Yeah. Paying my bills has always been kind of important to me."

Bart appeared to think that over. "Did you ever think of getting married, Nixie? That would help pay the bills."

"Oh, *su-ure*. That's the only reason I'd get married. To pay the bills. Sex and love wouldn't enter into it at all."

There was a pause. Bart's eyes glazed over, sort of like Julian's when he needed a translation. "I'm just saying. Two incomes and all." Okay, so he was like Julian, but not. Julian knew sarcasm when he heard it. And he at least *looked* for a translation. Bart apparently didn't.

That topic exhausted, I moved on. "So, what did you think of the band?"

Bart came back from coma land. "Great electric bass. Real driving force."

"Rob's got chops," I agreed.

"And I liked your clarinet work. I've never heard the "Beer Barrel Polka" in a sixteen beat before."

Bart knew something about music. Bruno hadn't worked out, but maybe Bart could. Time to implement Phase II, bone-bamming. "Thanks. Hey—I get done at two. Want to come over?" I didn't have any etchings, but I could play Oscar to impress him.

Bart's smile faltered. "Oh, wow, I'd like to, but...I can't. I've got to work tomorrow."

He had to go to work on a Sunday? Weird, but I minded my manners. "Oh, well. Doesn't break my crayons. I was just going to floss my Strat." Subtitled, it meant I wasn't upset, that I was only going to show off on my guitar.

But Bart didn't even seem to notice I'd said anything. Without a hitch he went on. "Love to come by, but I have a bunch of meetings, first thing in the morning. Can't get out of them. So I have to get a good night's sleep. I have to be alert for work!"

Apparently what Bart didn't understand, Bart ignored. That time he didn't even try to process what I said. "Alert for work! Absolutely essential!" I agreed heartily. My tone was so jolly Julian would have heard the acid in an instant. I was laying it on so thick even my mother might have noticed.

Not a ping on the Bart meter. "Absolutely, Nixie. A good night's sleep is vital."

It was sort of sad. Still, sex didn't require understanding—just friction. "If not tonight, maybe tomorrow?"

"Sure. I'll walk you home after dinner."

"Dinner?" Had Bart asked me out and I missed it?

"Sauerbraten. I gave your mother my family's recipe. She's going to try it out. Six o'clock."

"Um, Bart? I don't go to my parents every night—"

"Maybe you'd better make it five forty. Your mother was a little upset you were late today."

"I *wasn't* late—"

"I'm just saying." He gave me a quick kiss. Nice, but hurried. "See you!"

And, polishing off his one beer, Bart left.

I got Oscar out of the case, tuned for the next set. Well, that was certainly anticlimactic—in more ways than one. That night I went home alone, and slept with Oscar.

Chapter Fourteen

I didn't see either Julian or Bart the next day. No way I was going to martyr myself on the maternal stake (or steak, knowing my mother) for St. Bart. And Julian had to *work.* I spent Sunday with Oscar and a couple music mags, neither of which cared I was grumpy. I turned in early, to be awake for auditions. I tossed and turned for two hours before falling asleep at the regular time.

The next morning was band auditions for the festival. Monday morning's not the best for musicians of any kind, but I figured at least they'd had the whole weekend to warm up.

Besides, this was the third time auditions had been scheduled. More importantly, there was less than one week until show time. And too many things had interfered already.

I *had* to hear the bands this morning. Or else.

I commandeered the council chambers for the auditions. The room had been restored to its 1872 glory (after The Fire). All around me head-high wainscoting and hardwood floors gleamed. Since there was nothing but bare wood and chairs, the reverberation alone would break eardrums. I'm used to it, though.

As the first band set up, I settled into a chair in the back of the room. Dirk Ruffles rushed in a few moments later, prattling breathlessly. "Sorry I'm late, Nixie. Have I missed anything? Or have I missed everything? Am I too late, or only Meiers Corners late?"

"Don't stress. We're just starting."

The first band was three high school kids who'd obviously never played anywhere but their parents' basements. The singer was screaming but I could barely hear him because he'd forgotten to turn on the mic. The guitar solo was punctuated by squeals of feedback.

Since it was probably their first public appearance, I let the kids jump and jangle for almost ten minutes before I stopped them. "Thank you."

They came slouching back, trying not to look too eager. The singer said, "So, like, can we play?"

"I'm scheduling you for two a.m." By then the beer tent should have done its work.

"All right!" Echoes of congratulations and body slams escorted them out. As the next band set up Dirk leaned over to me. "That was nice of you, Nixie."

"Yeah. I'm a softie. Don't let it get around."

"Too late." The deep, cultured voice came from behind me.

"Julian?" I spun. Sure enough, there he stood, tall, dark, and luscious. Instant bootie burn. I shot up from my seat. Almost fanned my crotch.

He smiled slightly. "We're glad to see you, too."

We? Him and who...oh. I glanced down at his hips. But if Mr. Big Gavel was waving hi, I couldn't see it under the worsted. Stupid suit.

Julian took the chair on the other side of me. "How are things going?" Said with obvious concern, he was asking if I had recovered from the up-chuck and run from Friday night.

"Fine." Dirk was listening in and I didn't want any awkward questions, so I added, "I finished locking down all the committee chairs and backups, and yesterday I confirmed the venues. Today Dirk and I are auditioning bands."

"Ah." Julian flashed a look at Dirk. Message received. "How long will that take?"

I skimmed over my list. Twelve bands. "If everyone does preset before they come in? Three, maybe four hours."

"Mind if I watch?"

Did I mind? Did I mind that Julian was sitting so close I could feel his sexual heat beating like radioactive fallout through my body? Hell, yes, I minded. I leaned in. "I don't know if I'll get any work done that way. Don't you have meetings, or something?"

"Not right now. The opposition is conferring. I'm all yours for the next four hours." Julian bent in close too, so close his lips were a breath away from mine. "Any way you want me."

Whoo-hoo. Fan me with a bellows. Any way I wanted? I could think of a lot of ways...if there were a bed nearby, which there wasn't. Not that no bed would stop Julian. I remembered a couple incidents while standing... Did I say bellows? Fan me with a jet engine. "Working," I managed to grit out.

"No problem." Julian sat back, casually stretched one arm around my chair. His arm was hot as coals. When his fingers began to trace curlicues on my neck, I nearly shot into orbit.

"Working," I reminded him with a squeak.

"You're not actually working right now, Nixie," Dirk pointed out oh-so-helpfully from my other side. "You're waiting for the next band to start."

"*Thanks,* Dirk." Couldn't they tune any faster?

In fact, Julian had drawn the Mona Lisa on my neck before the band was ready to play. His fingers obligingly dropped away on the first beat. Perversely, I missed them.

Just as the band finished I felt a really warm hand slide under the bottom of my hoodie. Fingers landed unerringly on the naked skin between my top and my low-cut jeans. "Julian."

"What?" He was all innocent-like. The fingers caressed lightly along my spine, down to the dimples in my hips. I squirmed. They stroked down under the band of my low-riders. When they started rubbing my tailbone I nearly shrieked.

"Hey, Nixie! What's up?" a honeyed contralto said.

"Rocky!" I jumped. Not all of it was surprise at seeing her. Julian's hand took advantage of my momentary rise to slip between the cheeks. "*Argh!*"

"Nice makeup." Rocky took off her glasses and polished them. "Is that a new shade of blusher?"

"Uh, maybe."

"Well, it's really a good color for you." She put her glasses back on, adjusted them some. "Looks real natural." She stopped, and frowned. Her eyes followed the curve of Julian's arm around my shoulders. Went down. Stopped.

"OMG." She turned bright red. "OMG." She covered her mouth. "OMG," she said again, sort of muffled.

"Rocky, it's not what you think."

"Yes it is," Julian said.

"OMG," Rocky squeaked, turning flame red. I felt just as red. As I extracted Julian's hand from my posterior, Rocky spun away. She fled to the other end of the room, where the second band was packing up. She was bright red as she hooked up her karaoke machine. Bright red as she played what thankfully turned out to be decent rock and roll, although it was kind of weird hearing the Mozart Concerto in G for flute and garage band. And as she packed up and left, I thought I heard her say "OMG" another four or five times.

Seven more bands followed in the next three hours. They ranged from okay to pretty good to absolutely top of the food chain. I was relieved not to have to turn any of them down. Most I gave the standard contract—$500, free food and beer, and all the CDs they could sell. Two I gave $1000, and I was still under budget.

In between each band Julian caressed some portion of my anatomy. After the scare with Rocky he started back at the top. But he was an industrious boy and he busily worked his way back down. By the second-to-last group he'd snuck his hand into the sweet spot of my low-rider jeans. After three hours of foreplay I was practically crawling the ceiling.

The second-to-last group took the stage while my eyes were screwed shut and I was concentrating really really hard on not rocking my hips in time to Julian's fingers in my slit. Dirk was normally clueless, but even *he* would notice me having an orgasm right next to him. Probably.

So I didn't see the band until the first dirgy downbeat. My eyes snapped open. At first I thought my eyelids were still closed because I saw nothing but black. Black instruments, black horned glasses, cascades of black hair, black eyeshadow and jewelry. Then the black resolved into five metrosexual morticians.

Moaning about the futility of love, life, and the universe.

Ugh. Emo.

I hate emo. They're at the opposite end of the spectrum from Guns and Polkas. We sing about the *stupidity* of love, life, and the universe. Totally different.

Dirk leaned over. "They're kind of depressing."

135

"They're emo. That's their thing."

"Emo?" Julian asked.

"Yeah. Emotive Hardcore. Though these kids are going for the EZ-bake version—a mushy sort of goth. Depressing, really. Real drama llamas." I watched them shuffle around, all pale and drawn. White faces, black clothes. Red lipstick. "How vampirey," I said without thinking.

Julian bent his head, skimmed just the tip of a fang along my neck. "Not really."

I shuddered with instant lust. Fueled by three hours of intimate touching, but hey. Spark to dry tinder. Enough was enough. I shouted, "Okay, thank you!" The moaning faltered. "Thank you very much."

Jangled chords petered out. "But..." The lead moaner (or I guess singer) looked at his mates in confusion. Focused on me. "We just started."

"And I could tell instantly your band is *just* what we need. Here's your contract, sign and return." One more band. One more band to go, and only three of Julian's four free hours had passed. One more band and I'd have an hour with Julian. With what he could do in five minutes, I wondered if I'd survive a whole hour.

Pachelbel's *Canon* sounded discreetly to my right. Julian slid a slim flip phone out of his breast pocket. "Emerson. Yes. Yes, I understand." He shut the phone. "Nixie. I have to go."

"I thought you had four hours!"

"They got done early. I'm sorry." He stood.

I leaped to my feet too, practically threw the paperwork at the band. "Julian, I've only got one more group. Can't you wait a few minutes?" At the front of the room the last band started tuning up. One part of my mind heard the guitarist match the fifth-fret E-string to low A...and miss by about twenty yards. "It won't take long."

"Believe me, I wish I could." He bent and kissed me, all tongue and heat and liquid desire with just the hint of fang. "But Nosferatu himself is there. Negotiations have reached a critical stage."

"Uh, yeah." Just Julian's kiss made me dizzy. Dizzy like he'd shorted me out. "Maybe I can come along?" After all, it was a meeting. If he could rub me to near orgasm while I auditioned bands, maybe I could do a Police Academy on him and blow him under the table.

"Nixie." Julian grabbed me and kissed me harder. "I'd love for you to come along."

Oh, yeah. "Dirk, gotta go. Take the last band, will you?"

"But Nixie..." Dirk winced as the group struck their first chord—G major with overtones of F-sharp, B-flat, and the kitchen sink. "I don't know if I'm qualified."

"Just give them the last time slot. 2:30 a.m." I cringed as the band oozed into the next chord. If notes were cars, I think there was a D major under the wreckage. They were worse than the high-school garage band. It sounded like they had only started playing their instruments two days ago. "Maybe 3:00 a.m. would be better."

"I don't know, Nixie. I'm not sure they're what we want."

I wasn't sure either, but I was thinking with only one of my wet parts, and it wasn't my brain. "It'll be fine. Just give them the standard contract." The singer started. He sounded like a cat or dog, if they were frozen and cut with a band saw. "On second thought, the minimum will be fine."

Pachelbel started firing again. "Emerson. Yes, I'm on my way." Julian flipped his phone shut and slid it into his breast pocket. "Nixie, I've got to go."

"I'm coming!" I tossed my file at Dirk, who for once was speechless.

As Julian and I got to the outer door a smoky-glassed limo slid to the curb. My hackles raised at the in-your-face wealth until I remembered Julian was a sun-shy vampire. Then the opaque ride became an Opportunity. "How far do we have to drive to this meeting?"

Julian turned to me, his eyes lit with interest. "How far do you need?"

"With this morning's foreplay? About three minutes."

"I think we'll have three minutes."

To my surprise, Daniel Butler got out of the driver's seat of the limo. Still dressed in his butler costume, but with a jaunty little cap perched on his silver head. Huh. Maybe he worked as a driver for living. It would explain why he'd done bus-duty on our field trips.

As Daniel opened the limo's passenger door, Julian smiled at me. "Here we go." He flowed down the stairs and into the car almost too fast for me to see.

I followed at a clumping run and hopped in after him. "Whew! That was fun." I glanced at Julian, was surprised to see him slumped in his seat. Intense pain seared his face. "Julian, what's...wrong?"

I sniffed. Something smelled funny. Smoky, like Sunday grilling out...and I remembered Julian telling me about vampires burning—dying—if they were out too long in the sun. And though it was November, today's sun was bright and direct.

I swore. "Julian! Are you okay?"

"I...will be. In...a minute." He passed a hand over his face. He was sweating profusely, and looked sick.

Without thinking, I reached up to touch his face. Instantly I pulled back my fingers. Julian's skin was hot, almost burning. And not a hundred-and-four-degree fever burning. *Burning* burning, like an oven. I swore again. "Why didn't you tell me noon sun would make you burst into flames?!"

"Not...sun. You." And shockingly, Julian reached for me.

I pulled back. "WTF, Julian! You're badly injured! I can wait until tonight."

"May...be...still meeting...then." Julian spoke slowly, his voice cracking. "May be now...or never." His fingers closed over my breast.

"Stop that! Sex isn't important enough to die for, Julian!"

The ghost of a smile crossed his face. "Already...dead. And not flaming. Don't flame for...ten, fifteen minutes." His voice was gaining strength.

The squeezing fingers sent little shocks of need through me. "Shit. You're a pain in the ass, you know that?"

"Just...stubborn. Like you."

"Not. Stop that, I said! We've got three minutes before we get to the meeting place. Concentrate on healing, not sex."

He leaned over, began to kiss along my ear. "I recover...fast."

"Yeah? Fast enough to take another serious hit of sun when we get there?" I closed my eyes and without meaning to, leaned into his lips. "I'm guessing those fifteen minutes before you burst into flame include a few minutes of unconsciousness." I pulled back, although it wasn't easy. Glared at him. "What if you get halfway to the door and faint? How'm I gonna drag your giant carcass the rest of the way?"

That faint smile. "Butler will help."

"Oh, goody. I hope he's brought the asbestos gloves."

"Asbestos is a...carcinogen. The gloves are canvas."

I stared at Julian. "Mr. Butler really has a pair of fireproof gloves in the car?"

"No, of course not. Just teasing. No gloves." Julian pushed himself straighter in his seat. "In the car, that is."

Meaning Butler did have gloves at home? "You're a lawyer. You *can't* joke." Especially not about something as serious as bursting into flames.

"At least...the sex will be hot."

My eyes opened wide. "Another joke? Did the sun fry your brain, Emerson?"

"Maybe," he murmured, and leaned over to kiss me on the mouth.

His lips were still too hot to be human. They seared me, set me instantly on fire. His tongue pushed into me like a flame. His hand cupped my head, and his palm felt like a fireplace does after you've been shoveling snow.

"Julian, this isn't the best—"

"Quiet now, Nixie," he muttered against my mouth. His tongue swept lightly over my lips. His hand drifted down to my neckline. He unzipped and unbuttoned until my bra was exposed. It was unlined, softcup. Julian kissed his way to the tip of one breast, where he suckled the nipple through the thin nylon. Hot mouth tugging, I nearly shot into orbit.

I guess he really did recover fast.

A tinny speaker crackled. "We're almost there, sir."

"I'm not quite ready, Butler," Julian said between suckles. "Drive around the block a few times, would you?"

"Yes, sir."

Kneeling in the seat well, Julian swept away the bra cup and began feast. His tongue brushed my skin until it was on fire. His fangs bit shocks of electricity. It drove me wild. I clutched his shoulders, my hands grabbing worsted wool.

Damn. I wanted to feel him, not his fricking suit.

I plunged under with both hands. Tore back the lapels. His overcoat was open but his suit coat wasn't. Buttons popped. Neither of us cared.

His mouth returned to mine. His hands were undressing me almost too quickly for me to follow. I shrieked, "You too!" and scrabbled at his shirt.

He fizzed under my frantic hands. It was like the first night when we were attacked. He was solid, then misty, then...OMG, he was beautifully made.

My hands roved over naked skin smooth as butter. Rich as cream, if cream coated steel. I swept my palms over his chest. Big slabs of pectoral. Down went my hands. Rippling abs, feathered with short, fine hairs. Down, down...I slid my fingers through a tangle of silky hair, and grabbed...his forearm?

I pulled away, and gasped. At least part of him was *fully* recovered.

Julian pushed me back onto the seat. He grabbed the cloth at my hips and yanked. Jeans, spandex shorts, and lacy boy pants (red this time) came in one pull. Julian's eyes homed like a violet laser on my pussy. His nostrils flared, his cock jerked in my hand.

He lifted my leg over his shoulder and went down on me.

Julian's mouth was burning, this time with sexual heat. His tongue licked flames. His fingers played and pressed and thrust. And something long and smooth rubbed deep between my labia—something that felt suspiciously like a fang.

A rumbling filled the car, a thrum of arousal. A male lion's purr. Only there was no lion, there was only Julian. His eyes flicked up, collided with mine. His pupils, completely dilated, were blood red. Like two hot coals. Like glowing rubies.

Seeing those burning red eyes between my legs, I shrieked and went over. Climaxed in bursts of heat and light. It was powerful, the best I'd had.

Until Julian sank his fangs into my mons.

I screamed. My hips jerked up, thrusting the sharp tips deep. They burned into me like live wires. Julian's mouth opened, his tongue flaming along my clit. He started licking me like a thirsty dog. Lapping, growling. His hands opened on my hips, fingers digging deep as he held me still for his assault. I jerked in his grasp as wave after wave of contractions hit. It went on and on.

When I finally came to myself, I felt a little dizzy. Julian was licking gently over my mons, tickling the ends of my pubic hair with his tongue. His erection was still hard and pulsing, but his eyes were a soft blue.

"That was..." My voice didn't work quite right. I tried again. "Where did you learn to...shit. I can't think straight, much less talk right."

"Then let me say it for you." Julian's voice was dark and growly, just the way I liked it best. "That was terrific, because you taste wonderful. And that wasn't learning on my part, dear heart. That was inspiration."

Shit. With sweet-talk like that, how could I resist? "I heard you guys have to be invited over the threshold." I spread my thighs and patted my pussy. "C'mon in."

Julian inhaled so sharply I thought he'd choke. His eyes went instantly from cool blue to burning red. His fangs jumped to attention. So did his cock, standing a rigid forty-five degrees from his belly. His balls looked tight enough to burst.

I put my fingers on my labia and spread.

Julian choked. Vaulting onto the seat he grabbed his cock and stuffed the head into me.

The intercom buzzed. "I've gone around the block three times, sir. Shall I park now?"

"No!" Julian's cock pulsed violently in the vestibule of my pussy. "Drive around it again. Drive around the whole fucking city!"

"But sir...the meeting—"

"Fuck the meeting," Julian snarled, and drove himself into me.

He stuffed me *full.* I shrieked, and the intercom clicked off with a little squeak.

Between my legs, Julian was sweating. His teeth gritted, he retreated slightly. He thrust again. My eyes popped when he went *deeper.* He withdrew, and did it again. He hit my womb. I jerked with the twang of pain.

"Fuck, Nixie," he growled. "You're so small...so tight. I don't want to hurt you, sweetheart. Put your hands around me." He

141

pulled my hands down, against his cock. My fingers wrapped automatically around the tree-trunk width of him.

He was panting now. Sweat rolled off his forehead as he strained into me. He slid himself in as gently as he could, but he was so big he stretched me like a baby's head. I squeezed his cock with my hands, was rewarded with a groan so deep it could have come from the Grand Canyon. "Ride me, Julian," I urged him. "I'll hold on. Ride me hard."

Julian took one disbelieving look at me. What he saw must have reassured him—or turned him on unbearably. Because his eyes glowed and his fangs grew even longer and he started slowly but worked up to pummeling into me like a steed in full gallop. It was like a wild stallion turned loose between my legs. I could barely hang on, his thick cock pistoning through my fingers. Even with the extra inches of my clenched hands, he filled me completely and deeply on every thrust. He pounded me into the seat, so hard I bounced.

And then he slowed, and his balls tightened up like wire strings.

I squeezed the hell out of his cock the same moment he bit into my neck.

We both screamed. My legs locked around his hips, grinding us together like granite wheels. His mouth scalded my throat. My hands and pussy pumped him dry.

He collapsed on me. We lay in a sweaty heap on the leather cushions. The compartment smelled of sex. If this was Bo's limo, Julian was going to have to pay to have it detailed.

A good use of his five hundred an hour.

The intercom buzzed. Hesitantly, Butler said, "I circled the city, sir. Should I...should I continue driving?"

"A moment...longer, Butler." Julian's voice had smoothed out some, but was still croaky.

We took that moment to find clothes. It took a little longer to put them back on. Julian helped me out when my bra twisted. I thought that was nice. He gave my strap a pat, then handed me my top. It was kind of domestic.

Nice? *Domestic?* What was I thinking? I'd just had bloody sex with a vampire. How did I equate that with domestic? Did I think I could tame a vampire? An undead creature of the night?

Did I even want to? After all, I was the adventurous one.

Always trying to be bold, risk-taking. Why would I want to domesticate a vampire?

Although it would be nice for my mother.

That woke me out of my sensuous haze, fast.

"Something wrong?" Julian asked, lacing up his wingtips.

"No. Yes. I don't know." I *couldn't* want to bring a vampire home to meet the folks, could I? Hello Mom, Dad. No, we won't have ham or beer or hors d'oeuvres. A glass of blood, maybe. Or blood sausage. After all, this was Meiers Corners.

I backed away from those thoughts, fast. "So what happened the other night? With all the dismembered vamps?"

Julian eyed me strangely but answered readily enough. "We were able to pull together enough blood to satisfy most of them."

"Most of them?"

"I had to take a few apart again. Bo sent for extra blood from the Ancient One in Iowa, but it didn't arrive until the next night."

"You didn't finish them off? Julian, they tried to destroy you and Bo. They tried to *kill* Gretchen and Stella."

"I couldn't risk it. I don't want to undermine the negotiations with Nosferatu. Speaking of which, we're here." The limo pulled to a halt. Julian ran a hand through his hair, neatening it.

I helped him. "What are you negotiating for, anyway? I thought this was all going to be settled in court."

Julian gave me a gentle, pitying look. "Few cases actually go to trial, Nixie. And you'd better hope this one doesn't." At that moment Daniel Butler opened the limo door. Bright sunlight warmed my back.

I slid a hand onto Julian's cotton-clad chest. "You'd win in court, Julian. I know you would."

He smiled slightly. "Thanks for that vote of confidence. I know how much you trust lawyers."

"But if you could stop the annexation in court, why go through negotiations?"

"There's more at stake than the annexation."

"There is? What could be worse than a bunch of money-grubbing politicians getting control of Meiers Corners?"

143

"A bunch of blood-grubbing *vampires* getting control of Meiers Corners. If Nosferatu and the Coterie take over here, it would be disastrous. And nothing Bo or I or even the Ancient One could do would help. Nixie, I'm sorry. I've got to go." Julian slipped fluidly over me and was gone.

"But—" I stared at his receding back. He was traveling so fast his open coat flapped like a flag on a windy day. Oh, yeah. I'd torn off the buttons. Little wisps of smoke followed in his wake.

Apparently what Julian was doing was more important than I thought. I wondered what the Coterie really intended for Meiers Corners, if it would be so disastrous. I guess I hadn't imagined much beyond higher taxes. Julian made it sound a whole hell of a lot more serious.

What was up, I didn't know. I couldn't ask Julian, not while he was head-deep in negotiations.

But then I remembered Elena, and that I was not alone in the land of fangy weirdness.

I had originally meant to accompany Julian into his meeting. But that was only because I'd been so excruciatingly horny. Now I was pleasantly sated. And if Julian was doing his Super Suit lawyer thing, I'd be bored to death. If he was doing some chest-beating vampire thing, death might take another guise.

Besides, Elena owed me mega-explanations. She'd lied to me to keep me in the dark. No blood on the sidewalk, hah. She knew all along about the dentally endowed. About Julian, the Coterie, and the Lestats. Heck, that SMAW wasn't to take out chipmunks.

So, physical stimulation completed for now, I decided to pursue the intellectual stimulation of cross-examining a cop.

Chapter Fifteen

When I got to the Strongwell apartment building a little after noon, chaos greeted me.

The front door was wide open. Various pieces of furniture and household goods were arrayed on the lawn. As I approached, Elena tromped out with a floor lamp.

"Elena!" I ran toward her. "I have some questions for you, girlfriend. And you owe me some answers!"

She scowled at me. Snapped, "You're going to have to wait." Brushing by me, she plunked the lamp down next to a rolled-up Persian carpet.

I gaped. Elena, surly? "What's going on?" Shaking loose of my paralysis, I trotted after her. The sharp, acrid smell of smoke assaulted me. "What the...? What happened here?"

"What do you think happened? We had a fire."

"Oh, no! Is everyone okay?"

Elena passed a hand through her long curly hair, making it a wild mess. She sighed. "Yeah. Thanks for asking."

"So what are you doing?" As I spoke, her sister Gretchen and Daniel Butler's wife Joan stumbled out, laboring under another rolled-up carpet. Elena saw them falter, ran to help.

The three of them, gasping and floundering, lugged the carpet to the growing pile on the lawn. Heaving it into place, Elena stood for a moment, breathing heavily. "We're clearing the room. For the safety inspector. We'll sort out what's burned and what's not once we get everything out."

"The fire was limited to one room?"

"Fortunately. The parlor." Elena raised her brows significantly.

"Someone put too much wood in the fireplace?"

"No. Help me with the next load." She used her eyes to indicate I should follow her inside.

The parlor was a mess. Charred wallpaper and half-burned furniture had apparently been both hosed and foamed. A space near the window was completely black. "What happened?" I asked again.

"Bo and I were working on the beauty pageant last night. Fun way to spend a Sunday." Elena gave me a grouchy look and I apologized with a shrug. "We went to bed around six a.m. and left the paperwork on the table."

The parlor table was where Elena and I had pow-wowed the first night I met Julian. It had been...near the window. Right where the black char was worst. "You mean the *paperwork* started the fire?"

"I mean the fire started *in* the paperwork. And not spontaneously." Elena waited, watched me while I absorbed the implications.

"Someone burned the paperwork for the beauty pageant? But why? A guerilla feminist?"

Elena stared at the blackened wallpaper. Picked off a bit. "Thank goodness we have insurance." I thought she was ignoring my question until she went on, "Have you managed to get insurance for the festival?"

"Well, no, but..." Connections whirred in my brain. "You mean you think someone is trying to sabotage the festival?"

Elena wore her cop-face, unreadable and hard. "Have you had problems lately? Anything interfering with or delaying you?"

"Aside from vampires attacking all the time and daggy über-vamps phoning me? Gee, let me think."

"Is that a yes?"

The problem with Elena in cop mode was that she had no sense of humor. "Well, I almost didn't get bands auditioned. But that was natural causes." Cary Grant's stinginess in the first case and my own horniness in the second. "But why are you asking if I've had trouble?"

Elena glanced out the window like she was checking for eavesdroppers. She lowered her voice. "The Coterie was using the Lestat gang to distract us. Now they've advanced to committing actual crimes."

"But...but why?"

"To make it impossible for us to raise the money we need to keep them out of Meiers Corners."

I had just heard from Julian how important it was to keep the Coterie out (even though he hadn't told me *why*). "But even if the festival is stopped...maybe we can talk Julian into accepting a reduced fee—or maybe waiving his fee altogether."

Elena spun from the window. "It isn't that, Nixie! Julian's not getting a dime as it is."

"*What*? Then who is the money for?"

"Judges. People with political clout. The Coterie has huge political influence, not just in Chicago, but across the U.S. And they're not always ethical in how they use it."

"We're raising money for *bribes*?" I put fists on hips and frowned. "Hell, Elena. How low do we go? Selling our souls? Meiers Corners isn't that important. Not if it means paying bribes and getting people's houses burnt. Let's just let Chicago annex us and have done with it."

"It isn't that simple."

"Oh, for heaven's sake—of course it's that simple! What is it with you? You, and Julian, and—"

"They want the Blood Center."

My lips kept going but no sound followed. The Blood Center? Why should a bunch of *suits* want a small-town blood center?

Then I remembered this particular bunch of suits were vampires, but it still didn't make sense. Surely there was blood and blood aplenty in Chicago. Three million mobile bags of it, to be precise. Why would they want our little operation? "But we're just part of the Hemoglobin Society's distribution network. It's not like we're Red Cross, or anything major."

"We still pass over a thousand units through weekly. In fact, a shipment of three thousand units is going out this Saturday."

"Three *thousand*? That's a...a lot of blood." Several hundred gallons, if I was figuring right. "But controlling the city won't give the Coterie access to the blood."

"No, but it will let them write laws. And if the laws don't loosen the proverbial purse strings, think of the political and economic clout they'll have. And they're vampires on top of it. No one will be able to oppose them."

"No one? What about Bo? What about Julian?"

"You can't think they'll let Bo stay here if they take over. And Julian has to go home sometime."

"Shit," I said. "So what do we do?"

Elena picked up another lamp. "Everything we *can* do to see the festival goes off well. The money we raise will curb the Coterie."

"And the Lestats?" I found a small table, hoisted it, and followed her toward the door.

"Ah, yes. The Coterie's terrorist gang. We need to keep them from terrorizing us."

"That's a plan. Do you think Bruno can get me another bazooka?"

Elena smiled slightly. "Maybe he can lend you my old one."

That reminded me. "I was going to ask you how to stake vampires anyway. After the attack at the Roller-Blayd factory."

Elena surprised me by blushing. "Oh. It's um, a little more complicated than you might think."

"I didn't think anything, yet."

"Well, of course not! Still...I'd better have Bo explain. He's the expert."

It was an odd reaction. Maybe Elena thought you killed vampires like on TV? As soon as this thought entered my head, I rejected it. Not Elena. Not Ms. Show-me-the-facts Cop.

Elena pushed a hand through her curls. "And I suppose you have other questions, too. After the assault."

"Well, yeah. But considering what happened...I suppose they can wait."

"Knowing you, not long." Elena led me to the kitchen, where her cook was making a batch of cinnamon rolls. "Wait here. I'll go get Bo."

I sat and watched the cook work the dough. The repetitive kneading soothed me. Moments later the back door opened and Elena returned with Bo. She pulled out a chair and leaned it against the wall in one corner.

Bo pulled out another, reversed it, and straddled it like a horse. "I understand you want to know how to stake a vampire," he said to me.

Beyond him the cook continued her methodical kneading, undisturbed.

Apparently not a weird conversation for this household. "Yeah. Elena says there's a trick to it."

He smiled slightly, gave Elena one of those married people looks that's impossible for outsiders to decipher. "Not so much a trick. You need to drive a stake through the heart."

I considered it. I was pretty sure ribs and the breastbone were in the way. I was strong, but even my muscles couldn't poke a stake through bone. "With a mallet?"

He beamed at me, like I was a particularly bright pupil. "That might work, assuming the stake was big enough. And assuming the vampire held still long enough."

"How big a stake?"

Elena held up her forearm. "About this thick."

Bo nodded. "Thick enough to punch out the heart. You can also go up through the belly. But then you have to pierce the diaphragm."

Elena said, "The diaphragm is the sheet of muscle under the lungs. It's what you use to breathe."

"I'm a clarinet player, Elena," I said a little dryly. "I think I've heard of a diaphragm."

"Oh. Sorry."

I asked Bo, "What did you mean about the vampire holding still long enough?"

"Vampires are much faster than humans. If one sees you coming, he'd retaliate or run long before you could stake him."

Having seen Julian run, I could attest to that. "Then staking is virtually useless."

"Not quite. It works if the vampire is asleep. Or if you're staking a youngling who doesn't know enough to pull the stake out."

"Oh, great. They can pull it out?"

"Yes. And if the stake isn't thick enough, the heart heals around it and goes on pumping. Oh...and you need to remember the stake doesn't destroy the vampire. It only

149

immobilizes it."

"Lovely. Anything else?"

Elena said, "Older vampires can mist. The stake just drops out."

"I thought all vamps could mist."

"No," Bo said. "That power doesn't develop until the vampire's about a hundred."

"So basically, I can only stake a young, sleeping vampire."

"And then run away very fast," Bo agreed. "Because even an immobilized vampire will go for your throat if you get too close."

"Okay," I said. "I think I'll stick with the bazooka."

♫ ♫ ♫

Elena's apartment fire made me realize I couldn't put it off any longer. If the Lestats were actively undermining the festival, I needed—gasp—insurance.

Elena's agent didn't do commercial policies. She put me in touch with a company in Chicago. CIC Mutual. Stomach churning, I punched in the number.

"CIC Mutual!" a girlish voice chirped. "Safe and Secure for You and Your Family! How may I direct your call?"

I had to shake off the saccharine buzz. "Uh...I want to buy some insurance."

"You've reached the right place, ma'am! CIC Mutual, Insurance for Every Need!"

"Yeah. That's why I called an insurance company. Look, could you connect me to an agent or something?"

"Our Professional Agents are Available to Serve You Twenty-Four Hours a Day!"

"Good, good!" I gritted my teeth. "Can I speak to one?" One who hopefully didn't chirp.

"Our Agents are in the Phone Book! Thank you for calling, and have a great day!"

And she hung up on me.

"No wait! Fuck."

Grumbling, I redialed.

"CIC Mutual! Safe and Secure—"

"Give-me-the-name-of-an-agent!" I spoke as loud and fast as I could, hoping to knife through her spiel.

"Our Professional Agents—"

"Just a name!"

"Have a great day!"

And she hung up again.

"Double fuck." I dialed four-one-one.

"What city ple-uz?" Not so chirpy, but still a bit sing-song.

"Chicago. CIC Mutual Insurance A—"

"Thenk-yew."

"No, wait! I want the agency—"

A click. Then came Eve, the first woman of voicemail and automated systems everywhere. "The number is area code six. Oh. Six." And she gave the exact same number as the one I already had.

"Fuck." It looked like I would have to do this the old fashioned way.

I called my mother.

"You are buying insurance, Dietlinde? I am so proud of you!"

My mother's obvious delight made me wince. "It's for the festival, Mom."

"I heard *you* are running that!" my mother enthused. "My little Dietlinde, responsible for the organization of the mayor's festival. As a child, Dietlinde, sometimes you broke my heart. But this all makes up for it! I'm proud of you. Your father is proud of you. All of Meiers Corners is proud of you!"

Ow! KOed in my guilt gland. "Yeah, Mom. About the insurance?"

"Yes, yes. You must call CIC Mutual."

"I tried that, Mom. All I get is the receptionist from he...heck."

"No, no. You do not dial the main number. You dial the customer service representative of the direct sales department."

That just made my head ache. "Could you just give me the number?"

"Don't you have a phone book? Honestly, you should move

151

back home. Would it hurt for you to keep your father and me some company in our waning years?"

Move home. Oh sure. And never get laid again. Not in this lifetime. "The number, please, Mom?"

"Oh, very well."

"Thanks." After taking down the number, I got off the phone as quickly as I could, which in this case was after twenty more minutes of guilting. Then I called the insurance company.

This time I got a reassuringly depressed person. I explained what I wanted to him.

"You're looking at a comprehensive business policy." Some clacking and whirring in the background sounded like a calculator. "And an umbrella liability policy." More numbers punched, followed by more whirring. I didn't like how long the whirring went on. "And an umbrella comprehensive policy. Did you want to insure the buildings?"

"Um...I guess so."

"Basic fire and damage. What deductible?"

"Well...what's available?"

"We have five hundred, a thousand, twenty-five hundred, five thousand—"

"The thousand," I cut in. I was developing a dull headache.

"Did you want to insure the contents of the buildings?"

"Wait a minute. The first thing you said was comprehensive business policy. I thought that 'comprehensive' meant 'all'."

"Sure. All liability. Do you want to insure the contents—"

"Yes, of course." This was way too complex. I just wanted insurance. What was it with all the comprehensive umbrella liability fire damage?

"Did you want to insure against acts of God?"

"No!" Enough was enough. "Look, what's the bottom line?"

More clicking and whirring. "That'll be...a hundred twenty."

Car insurance was more. But this was only for three days. "A hundred twenty dollars? Okay. Did you want cash or a check?"

There was an unexpected snort from the other end of the line. "Not a hundred twenty dollars. A hundred twenty *thousand* dollars."

My breath rushed in, flipped around my tonsils, and ran out my nose so fast it tied a knot in my throat. I choked. "A hundred...th...*thousand*? But it's just three days!" My whole festival budget was less than half that.

"Ten buildings and contents. An estimated five thousand attendees?"

"Well, yes, but—"

More clicking and number crunching. "That's fifty thousand for physical property and fifty thousand for liability. And twenty thousand for the umbrella."

"Do I need an umbrella?" It was November. Snow was much more likely than rain.

"We-ell," he said slowly, "I recommend it. Unless you want to cap coverage at fifty thousand per incident. Most lawsuits start at fifty. And if there's hospital bills..."

My head was spinning. "All right. Keep the umbrella. What about just basic fire and liability. Does that reduce things?"

"Sure." Click-click-whirr-whirr. "Eighty."

Eighty thousand..."Thanks. I, um, have to think about this." I hung up.

I tried five other companies. Though I'm not sure I was comparing apples to apples, the numbers were still way too big to be dollar figures.

So I called back CIC Mutual. "Isn't there some other way?" I asked after identifying myself. "Something cheaper?"

"Well...there *is* the employee discount."

"What's that?"

"It's a great benefit." The morose voice warmed for the first time. "Not many companies have it. Employees get a fifty percent discount on all products. We have an opening, you know. In records administration."

"Records?" I could hope he meant vinyl.

"File Clerk I. You'd have to commit to a full year. But it would reduce the insurance for your festival to"—clink clunk whirr—"forty thousand dollars."

Forty thousand. Still high. But at least it wouldn't wipe out my *entire* budget.

But I would have to work at an insurance company to do it. Just rip out my heart and donate my brain to science.

"Well...I...I'll have to think about it."

Think about it, right. What other choice was there? I tried to console myself that it was only a year. I could be responsible for a year, couldn't I? For 365 days...or 366 if next year was a leap year. Rip out my heart? Tear out all my organs and sell them on the black market. Bend me over and poke me repeatedly with a fish fork.

But the stakes had risen. It wasn't just the band getting a juicy gig out of this. Meiers Corners needed this money to keep vampires out. And according to half the world, I was the only one who could run the festival. The mayor believed in me, the city believed in me.

And, as the final nail in the coffin, my mother was *proud* of me.

Unless a miracle intervened, I'd have to do it.

I hung up the phone and cried.

Chapter Sixteen

With a one o'clock meeting, I couldn't shake my blues in the usual ways. No time for an hour strumming my boyfriend Oscar, or even ten minutes with my vibrator Viggo. So I decided on the next best thing: a fantasy starring me and Julian.

As I walked to City Hall, I remembered the limo ride earlier. Julian's supernaturally hot hands running over my naked flesh. Breath like fire, a dragon snacking on my pussy. A thick, sleek cock, pistoning between my clenched fingers, hammering into me. If Julian could package body parts, he'd outsell Mattel.

And that mist thing! Oh, the possibilities! I imagined lying in bed, stripped bare. I imagined Julian's mist, flowing over my skin. Cool, smooth, leaving goosebumps of need in its flowing wake. Julian's mist running like water over my belly. Pouring down my vulva. Pooling between my thighs. Ooh.

And his fangs, *mmm.* Sliding between inner and outer lip, a smooth, hard finger. Perfect counterpoint to hot, soft breath. And when Julian bit my mons...oh, yeah. Even the memory of the sharp need lancing through me made my nipples erect.

At one o'clock I stood at the head of the council conference table, in a much better mood. Almost too good a mood. While I squared my notes on the small tabletop podium in front of me, I had to furtively clench my overheated thighs. I hoped my nipples weren't visible. For the first time I wished my bra was padded. I wanted my secret fantasies to stay totally secret.

After discreetly checking my chest (nipples thankfully down) I cleared my throat. "Thank you all for coming today."

People kept jabbering all around the table. I barely heard myself above the conversational din. Ah, yes. The Meiers

Corners Common Council, just as I remembered it. Argue, don't decide anything, and go out for drinks.

"Please, let me speak." No effect. My fantasies faded. "I want to start the meeting." Yak-yak-yak. My good mood evaporated. "Come to order!" If anything, they got louder.

I was going to have to sell body and soul to an insurance company for this festival, and I couldn't even get some basic respect. Fuck that.

"*This meeting will come to order!*" I didn't have a gavel (which made me think of Julian's gavel, which made me hot) so I pounded my fist on the podium. It cracked in two. All around me startled faces blinked in sudden silence. Though I hadn't meant to break the podium, it worked, so okay. I wasn't as surprised as they were. I'm small, but I pack a mean punch.

Plus, it made me feel even better. The Lestats and the Coterie and insurance might be totally out of control. But I could still run this meeting.

I picked up my notes. "Let's get started. As you know, the festival begins Friday. That's four days from now. You each have in front of you a list of events, who's running what, where, and when."

"Then everything's done!" Dieter Donner said brightly. He smiled like Donkey, wide and toothy. "Let's go drink!"

There was a general murmur of assent. People started rising.

"Sit down!" I glared at the assemblage one by one. Josiah Moss, the somber partner in Stark and Moss Mortuary. Kurt Weiss, the curly-haired, nervous manager of the Allrighty-Allnighty convenience store. Gretchen Johnson, Elena's younger sister. Buddy, the bartender at Nieman's Bar. Dieter Donner and his partner Franz Blitz, the horse and carriage of the bar. And Brunhilde Butt, Granny to Bruno Braun and a wilted Gypsy Rose Lee to the rest of the city. The Meiers Corners Common Council. "Ladies and gentlemen. We are nowhere *near* done."

"We aren't?" Josiah Moss asked in a mellow, non-sectarian voice. Considering where he worked, I guessed sounding vanilla-bland was an asset.

"No we aren't," I barked, very non-vanilla. "Except for Buddy, who's running the Sheepshead Tournament, none of you have duties."

"And we thank you for that, Miss Schmeling." Blitz rose and bowed. "Shall we adjourn for a drink, as we used to when you were a student member of the...?"

"None of you has duties—yet," I broke in frantically. "I'm going to take care of that right now."

"Surely you don't need us. Not if all the events have chairpersons. You don't need us." Kurt was so anxious, he almost yipped it. Kurt played MMO games. His nom de guerre was Poodle Boy, and it fit.

"I want to be absolutely sure everything goes off as smoothly as possible. So I want all the events double-teamed."

"I don't understand. You want us to run things?" Granny Butt reached into her blouse and adjusted a bra strap. I got a whole eyeful of yellowed, stretched-out elastic.

I rubbed my eyes. Nope. Didn't scrub the sight away. "Each event already has someone to run it. I want you to help that person. Like a producer in a movie. It's your job to see that everything they need is there, that things go off on time...stuff like that." I passed out another paper. "Here are your assignments. You'll see some of you have two. Mrs. Butt will be helping out with the cheese ball tasting and the cheese contest at the Deli Delight. Brunhilde, please note we're opening the cheese ball tasting before the official festival opening time. It's the only one scheduled before 4:30."

"Why is that?" Granny asked.

"We're going to try to give people a buffer for the beer. Now, Josiah Moss will be handling both the bands and—"

A duck-like muddy rasp interrupted me. "Hi, Nixie, sorry I'm late! But I had a shoelace break and when I went to the store to buy a replacement I saw Mayor Meier—oh, he says 'hi' and thanks again for running the First Annual Meiers Corners International Fun Fair, Sheepshead Tournament, and Polka Festival and—" It was Dirk Ruffles, the most male person I knew (because he had exclamation points and commas, but he never had a period).

Josiah Moss went an odd shade of ashen gray. In a choked voice he said, "What...what is *he* doing here?"

Dirk perked up at the voice. "Mr. Moss! Fancy seeing you here! Are you helping with the festival?" He started over with his lumbering stride, his hand stuck out for a shake.

Moss half-rose from his chair and started backing away. "No...no...keep away!"

Like the Battery Bunny, Dirk just kept on going. "Mr. Moss, what's wrong? Why are you bent over that way? Does your tummy hurt? Can I help?"

"No!" Moss spun on his heel to run.

"But I know just what cures a tummy-ache, Mr. Moss! My mother always said a nice pink pill will settle you, and I have one here—although I didn't used to carry medicine, but since the time that vam-peer guy in the cape had pinkeye, I put pinkeye medicine in my fanny pack and I thought what the heck, I'll put in the other medicines too! All my mother's remedies are here—Mr. Moss?"

Dirk was clumsy but long-legged, and before Moss could take even a couple steps, Dirk caught him by the wrist. Moss flailed at him, mouth agape in fear. Dirk, who wouldn't know fear if it ran cold fingers down his spine or even shoved ice up his butt, simply popped a small pill into Moss's open mouth.

Moss gasped, coughed, and gulped. There was a moment of pure terror on his face when he realized he had swallowed Dirk's pill. "What—" Moss croaked. "What...was that?"

"Just a tummy pill, Mr. Moss. See, I have a whole fanny pack full of medicine. Well, it's not really a fanny pack because I wear it over my stomach, so I guess that makes it a stomach pack—"

"*What was that pill?*" Moss shouted, no longer gray and somber, but red and very upset.

Dirk pulled the mouth of his pack wide. "You can see. Drops for pinkeye and lozenges for sore throats. White pills for headaches and pink pills for tummy-aches and blue pills for...oh-oh."

Moss went white. "Oh-oh? What do you mean, oh-oh? What, oh-oh!?"

"I put in three of each color pill. Three white pills and three pink pills and three blue pills." Dirk sounded mildly annoyed.

"But...?"

"Well, now there's still three white pills and three pink pills. But there's only two blue pills. Huh. I must have gotten it wrong. I must have put in three white pills and four pink pills and—"

Two blue pills instead of the expected three. I had a horrible suspicion. "Dirk?" I interrupted. "What are the blue pills?"

"Huh?" He blinked muddy eyes at me.

"The blue pills. What are they for?"

"Constipation, of course. Really good, too. My mother would give me one of these and within minutes I was like a brown geyser—"

Moss turned green. Then blue, then pink, then red. Then, without another word, he raced from the room.

"Well," I said, watching him go.

"Well," Dirk said, for once at a loss for words.

I picked up my notes. "I guess *now* we're done. Let's go get those beers."

♫ ♫ ♫

I blamed the fourth beer for what happened next.

The Common Council meeting had started at one. We made our way to Nieman's bar at one fifteen. I had four beers in four hours, which according to St. Bart should have meant the alcohol was out of my system when I left at five.

Except three of those beers were after four, when Granny Butt started stripping. When I was a high-schooler, Granny's skin had fit her like elephant socks, and she hadn't gotten any firmer over the years. I *had* to drink, or dig my eyeballs out with teaspoons.

So I was traipsing down the sidewalk a little crookedly when the streetlights flared to life. I stopped. Stared. Checked my watch. The big hand was on the nine and the little hand was almost on the five. I was a bit fogged on what time that was. But I was crystal clear that I would soon have company.

"Just what are you doing here? Out, *alone*, at night?"

I knew that grouchy voice anywhere. My favorite vampire had come to protect me. Beer bubbled happily in my blood. "I thought you had negoatee—negushiat—negotiations." As I said, three beers in one hour. My tongue was pleasantly numb.

Julian was anything but pleasant, or numb. He grabbed me by the arms and turned me. "I thought I told you to stay...have you been drinking?"

"Got it in one, Feeny Todd. Blood alcohol level at least .11. Hey—does that mean if you bite me now you'll get drunk?" I smiled up at him (and up), trying to picture a drunk Julian. Drunk sex was usually sloppy wet sex, but I had a hard time imaging Julian's sex even more sloppy and wet. Or maybe not. It would be slidey, slippy, in-out gushy. Water slide tangly.

Julian's beautiful nostrils flared. No doubt he smelled my red carpet being rolled out. But he just grabbed my elbow and pulled. "Come on. I'm taking you home. And it's Sweeney Todd."

"Not with you feening about me missing curfew. So what happened to the negushee—meeting?"

Julian shot me an annoyed look. "Negotiations...broke down."

"Why?"

"You don't want to know."

I *did* want to know. I tried to stop him. No go. I tried to break away from him. I had as much success as if I'd been superglued to a bullet train. So I did the next best thing. I launched myself at him, catching my arms around his neck and wrapping my legs around his lean waist. "Why?" I asked again, dropping little kisses on his smooth, good-smelling jaw.

"Nixie—" Julian said dangerously.

Oooh! It was my favorite growly voice. "Why did the nego...they break down?" I slipped my tongue into the corner of his mouth. Pumped my hips lightly against his waist. His hands slid over my butt, fingers clamped tight. He turned his mouth into mine, tongue first. To take me in a soul-searing kiss, I was sure. But I wanted answers, not oblivion. I turned my face away. "Why?"

"You are the most frustrating...infuriating..." He pulled my hips into his. Whoa. That was some hard-shell briefcase.

I wriggled against it. Bright little sparks zapped between us. "You might as well tell me. I'll find out anyway, from Elena."

"Damn it, Nixie. Nosferatu was angry at me and negotiations broke down. That's it." He rubbed himself against me, playing the hardest part of Mr. Briefcase right down the center, where I was hottest and wettest. "Satisfied?"

"Not nearly." My hips pumped in rhythm. "Why was he angry?"

Julian's tongue came out, swirled up my neck to my ear. Between gentle sucks on the lobe he said, "Because he was. Drop it, Nixie."

I twisted out of his sensual wrestling hold, put the hold on him. Sucked not so gently on his earlobe. When he closed his eyes in pleasure I lowered myself slightly, enough to open his vest and suck his nipple right through two layers of crisp cotton.

Even that didn't bring cleansing confession. So I drove my hand between us, down into his pants. What met me there overfilled my palm. Opening my fingers I rubbed the flat of my hand over him, fast, like sandpaper.

"Fuck, Nixie! I'm going to *rupture*."

I palmed Julian to within an inch of orgasm. His eyes clamped tight and his head threw back in extreme need. Suddenly I stopped rubbing. "Why?" I said sweetly.

Any other man might have roared with pain. Julian's throttled groan was somehow five times as raw. "Nixie...oh, damn." Eyes still closed, he set me down, gently, almost reverently. His lips were split by long fangs, and he was breathing hard through distended nostrils. "I was late. Nosferatu took that as an insult." He opened his eyes just in time to see it hit me.

Julian was late because of our sex in the limo. "I haased the meeting? *Me*?" I was cold at the realization.

"If haas means something bad, no, Nixie, you didn't. I did. It was my responsibility to get there on time, my responsibility to successfully conclude the negotiations."

Fuck. Responsibility again, rearing its ugly phiz. But in this case it was my lack of same that haased things. My lack of control that made keeping nasty vampires out of Meiers Corners just a little harder. "But you didn't—because of *me*." I was ice to my core.

"No, Nixie. I didn't because of *me*. Because I let desire interfere with duty. Because I let impulse overrule self-control."

He took my face in both hands. His eyes flared bright red.

161

"I didn't because I wanted to fuck you so bad I thought I'd *explode.*"

"Oh." I'm not a prude but that made my cheeks heat.

"So you see, it's my fault, not yours."

Nice of him. "But I'm part of the problem." A big part. Julian had broken his rigid self-discipline for me, with catastrophic results. I had led him astray.

Like that first rumored wild crowd. I remembered Dru telling me about the damage Julian had wreaked in his recklessness. How it had changed him, made him the stodgy suit he was today.

Surely this was just as bad. I wondered if he would now get even more puritanically proper.

Was this a replay? And had it been a woman the first time, too?

Red eyes narrowed. "What's going on in that devious little head of yours?"

"Devious?" I widened my eyes to maximum innocence. My eyes were so big I felt like a damn anime girl.

"Try again." He lifted my hips until I was pressed directly against the big briefcase in his slacks, enlarged now to carry-on luggage. "How are you blaming yourself?"

Heat seared my crotch. "I'm not, exactly. Dru sort of said you used to be a lot more fun, but then something happened. I was sort of wondering if it was, you know. Like this." I rotated against him, a little shiver running through me at the feel of his cock straining for me.

"No, Nixie. It wasn't anything like this. Nobody but you excites me so much that I forget my responsibilities. That I not only forget my responsibilities, I don't even care."

He gave me a deep, hungry kiss. "You make throwing away my self-control not only right, but a joy."

That melted through the guilt and the cold. "So...um. No negosh...meetings. Does that mean you have the night free?"

I didn't think it was possible, but Julian's eyes turned redder. His fangs, which had been retracting, burst full-length. "Yeah," proper, staid Julian Emerson said. "Oh, fuck, yeah."

"Well, then." I ground my pelvis into him. "Why don't we—" I was interrupted by *Home on the Range.*

My cell phone. My parents.

A dip in Lake Michigan would have been less freezing.

Abruptly sober, I automatically flipped out the phone. Automatically said, "Hi, Mom." Automatically braced myself for a lecture.

Julian's fangs disappeared like a retractable tape measure. His eyes went from crimson to slate in two seconds flat. Maybe he was bracing himself for a lecture, too. Gently, he set me down.

"That Braun boy was here," my mother said without preamble. "He dropped something off for you."

Terror gave way to relief gave way to curiosity. "Bruno left something for me there? Why not my townhouse...? Oh, yeah." I'd only been living in Elena's old place a few months. Bruno apparently wasn't aware I'd moved out of the ancestral home. "What is it?"

"I don't know, I'm sure. It looks like some sort of musical instrument."

"It looks like a *what*?" If the Bear played anything, it was the kazoo. So not his instrument, then.

I started pacing the sidewalk. The next obvious question was, what kind of musical instrument. Except, to my mother, everything is either a flute, a guitar, or a drum. A tuba is a big flute, a violin is a small guitar. A clarinet is a black flute, even though I'd played one for over a decade. "What size? Big or small?"

"Big," she said. "A big flute." See?

So I imagined a bass flute. Bruno carries a variety of weapons and supplies, but nothing like a bass flute. So I thought bigger. Longer, wider...like a bass clarinet...or bassoon...oh, shit.

Bruno had given my mother the bazooka.

I muted the phone, turned to Julian. "I've got to dip out. The Bear hustled a burner on my mom, and I gotta turbo myself to the ancestral palace before she caps her ass."

There was a moment's silence. Then Julian said in a mournful tone, "Will I ever understand you?"

"I don't know, Helen Keller. Will you?" I started off at a fast clip. Punched off the mute. "Mom? Don't do anything with the, ah, flute. Don't even touch it."

Julian followed right behind. "Is your mother all right? Where are we going?"

With an irritated poke, I muted the phone again. "*You* aren't going anywhere. *I'm* going home." Punching the mute off, I said, "I'll be there shortly." I swiveled the phone shut and stored it.

"Nixie." Julian grabbed my elbow and spun me to face him. "You're not going anywhere without me. Nighttime was already dangerous, and now Nosferatu is angry. If he orders the Lestat gang—"

"For heaven's sake, Julian! You don't need to walk me everywhere."

"I think I do."

I shook off his hand and trotted away. "Fine. But don't say I didn't warn you."

"I beg your pardon?" Julian followed.

"You want to walk me home? Fine. Because, guess what, Horatio. You get to meet my parents."

Chapter Seventeen

That shut him up. We started racing to my parents'—well, I raced and Julian sort of flowed—in silence. I have to hand it to him, though. He stayed with me like a second skin, despite the warning. Although, as fast as Julian moved, I guessed he was going to dip out as soon as I was safely inside Mom and Dad's house.

But once underway he started the old familiar refrain. "Nixie. About Nosferatu—"

The last thing I wanted was another earworm, especially not one tinged with guilt. Time for major distraction. "Dru told me you and she are just friends."

"We are. But Nosfer—"

"Yeah, Nosy's angry, stay in at night, lock all the doors and use garlic deodorant. I get that. I'm more interested in what made you the Betamax Stuffy-lupagus you are today. Since it wasn't a woman?"

Julian blinked. "You're asking what made me decide to eschew puerile behavior?"

"Uh...yeah. I guess." Sometimes I got the feeling we both needed a permanent link to Babel Fish. "What happened?"

He was silent for several seconds. Finally he said, "I'm not proud of it."

"Tell me more," I said in my best Suitglish.

His jaw worked, like he was chewing something rancid. "Fine. I'll tell you. Since you'll just torment me until I do."

"*Torment?* No way. Coax, maybe, or urge—"

"Do you want to hear this or not?"

"Um...yes." And because his eyes were shading violet, I added, "Please?"

Julian took a deep breath. "In the early eighteen hundreds I got caught up in the Romantic movement. I fancied myself a poet."

"Byron and those guys?"

"At first. At first all I did was hang around coffee shops wearing a big shirt, trying to get laid."

I snorted. "Sounds like the beatnik era, minus the goatees."

"There are cycles. Anyway, I got restless. I don't know, maybe it was some sort of middle-age crisis. A poet acquaintance had made the transition to vampire. He said my poetry was garbage. That I was not a 'real' artist. William said 'real' art was in throwing away boundaries."

"Who?"

"William the Bloody. You wouldn't know him. I can't believe I let him get under my skin. Well, one night I got drunk with him and his cronies. Turned out his brand of artistic freedom and 'real' art translated into slash and burn. Later I found out one of the buildings I burned had occupants."

"Oh, Julian." What began as an exercise in distraction now sent an arrow of sympathy straight through my heart.

Julian gave a laugh colored with self-disgust. "Fortunately for me, they were dead before I set the fire. Unfortunately for them, William and company also practiced the artistic 'freedom' of torture."

I could see why Julian hated the non-conventional. I would have to rethink my view of him.

"I haven't thought of that incident in years." He shook his head, as if shaking the memory away. "Is that your parents' home?"

I looked up. Sure enough, I saw the familiar bungalow. We'd have to talk more later.

Mounting my parents' stoop, I turned to face Julian. "Well. Thanks for the ride."

A slight smile broke through Julian's grim expression. "It was the least I could do." I thought he'd missed the sarcasm, but he bumped his hips and flashed me a hint of fang. Oh, man. I'd forgotten about the *limo* ride. Sobering, he said, "You'll stay inside the rest of the night?"

"Do I have to?" I thought we'd passed the stage where Daddy had to lay down the law for the little girly-girl.

"I worry," Julian said, and I felt my mad drain away.

"Yeah, okay." I shuffled awkwardly, wondering if I should give him a kiss or not. Wondering if I *could* give him a kiss without having a whole fap-fest on my parents' stoop. "Well. Uh, bye."

"Sweet dreams, Nixie." Julian bent to give me a gentle brush on the lips.

That was when the door banged open.

"Helmut! Dietlinde's home!" My mother reached through the door and yanked me inside. "And she has brought home a *friend*." The word had as much warmth as if she'd said "worm". She inspected Julian as closely as a drill sergeant. "Who are you?"

Ever-suave, Julian straightened and held out his hand. "My name is Julian Emerson, Mrs. Schmeling."

My mother eyed him with mistrust. "You're not one of those punky rock groupers, are you?"

"No, Mrs. Schmeling. I am an attorney at law."

My mother's whole demeanor changed. She grabbed Julian's outstretched hand and tried to tug him in, too. "Oh, well, that's different, now, isn't it? Come in Mr. Emerson. Come right in."

To his everlasting credit, Julian looked to me for permission. Not the vampire-over-the-threshold permission. But my actual approval for him to meet the folks. Struck speechless, I could only nod.

My mother's pretty strong but Julian entered under his own steam. He gave the place a cursory glance. I pictured my childhood home from his perspective. Nubbly, fifties-style beige couch. Cheap nylon carpet. Doilies straight out of the nineteenth century. No upscale seaboard manor this. He would be superior, maybe even disdainful.

As if he could hear my thoughts, Julian slewed me a look. "You have a lovely home, Mrs. Schmeling." His tone was entirely sincere.

"Why, thank you, Mr. Emerson." A delighted smile crossed

my mother's face. She took Julian by the arm and led him into the front room. "Sit, Mr. Emerson. Dietlinde, I made a fresh pot of coffee. Go get Mr. Emerson a cup." I could see the gleam enter her eye. The predatory gleam of a mother in full husband-hunting mode. Maybe St. Bart hadn't won the race yet.

Mother practically pushed Julian onto the couch. Julian, though he didn't realize it, was just so much fresh meat. I hesitated. "Jul...Mr. Emerson was kind enough to escort me home. But he can't stay—"

"Nonsense. Have you had dinner, Mr. Emerson? We have ham in the fridge. A man's got to eat, *nicht wahr?*"

"A man must eat," Julian murmured in agreement.

"So go, Dietlinde." My mother shooed me off. As I hesitated she turned to loom over Julian like the Phantom of the Opera, complete with hover-cape.

Shizzle. Julian was dead. And did vampires even eat ham? "Um...isn't it kind of late for supper, Mom?"

"Late?" My mother said indignantly. "Late? It is not even six p.m. Practically the whole day is left. In the old days your grandfather would have worked the fields another five hours by moonlight."

"And Großmutter would have sewn a dozen dresses for the Lutheran Ladies Aid & Relief Group with only a single candle. Yes, Mother." I tried one last time to derail this disaster. "But Julian can't stay. Julian—"

The gleam returned. "It's *Julian,* is it? Julian, not Mr. Emerson?" She attacked Julian. "Just how long have you known my daughter, Mr. Emerson?"

Thankfully, Julian was unfazed. "We met at the mayor's office last week, Mrs. Schmeling. We're both involved in the annexation matter." Implying we met under highly official and impeccable circumstances. For the first time I blessed his cool control.

"Really? Tell me more, Mr. Emerson." All man-trapping systems now fully engaged, Mother took the chair opposite him. "Dietlinde, where is that ham?"

Julian said, "Coffee will be fine, Mrs. Schmeling."

"You heard the man, Dietlinde. Go get the coffee!"

I gave up. Hopefully, if Julian could hold his own against

vampires and mobsters, he could take on one German mother. I went to get coffee.

When I returned my mother was cooing. "The *Boston* Emersons? Then you can trace your family back to England?"

"Yes, Mrs. Schmeling. In fact, one of my relations served in the court of Elizabeth I."

"How thrilling, Mr. Emerson."

I breathed a sigh of relief. So far so good. I advanced into the room.

I was setting the coffee down when she hit him with, "So when did your family give up the Episcopal Church?"

Red alert, Mr. Spock. I tried to catch Julian's eye to warn him. When that didn't work I flailed my hands silently like a berserk puppet.

Julian was either criminally insane or stupid, because he ignored me. "The Church of England, actually, and we didn't give it up."

My mother sat straight in her chair. Her eyebrows snapped together in a frown. Red eyes and fangs would not have been unexpected.

I covered my face with my hands and sank onto the sofa. Couldn't he have lied? Just a little?

My parents are old-school Missouri Synod Lutherans. I could just guess what my mother was thinking. Anglican?! Heathen! Julian was surely toast now. Mother would never stand for a mixed marriage.

Mixed *marriage*? Abruptly I uncovered my face. Where the hell had that thought come from?

I soothed myself. Surely it came from my mother. Mom was thinking marriage so I thought marriage. *I* certainly wasn't dreaming about wedding cakes and happily ever after. Especially not co-starring Julian Emerson, Suitguy Deluxe. Although his wedding tackle was certainly deluxe...no, no, no!

Julian spoke, distracting me. "Tell me more about *your* family, Mrs. Schmeling."

It was the only thing he could have possibly said to redeem himself with my mother. Family stories and secrets were her lifeblood. She could yak half the night away.

Of course I'd heard all the stories before. So many times, in fact, that the entertainment had been leached out of them. Now on the big screen, Nixie's Family! in tedious technogray.

But Julian asked questions so skillfully I found myself listening to *new* stories. Things I'd never heard before. Things I'd never known before.

For example, I knew I was named after my aunts, my mother's sisters. But...

"Dietlinde is your older sister, Mrs. Schmeling?"

"Yes. And Nixie my younger sister."

"Three girls and one bathroom? How did you get along?"

My mother laughed, but then got quiet. "The bathroom wasn't a problem."

"No?" Julian prompted gently.

My mother took a deep breath, like she was gathering strength. "No. Our parents died. When I was fifteen and my sister Nixie was twelve. Dietlinde raised us. She was only eighteen. But she took two jobs and kept us together. Kept a roof over our heads and food on the table. To me, she was a hero. Nixie—my younger sister, that is—never appreciated how hard Dietlinde worked. Nixie thought Dietlinde was dull and stodgy."

"Aunt Nixie is just a free spirit," I said. I always liked her best. She gave me dolls and bikes and magic sets. Aunt Dietlinde gave me—socks. Aunt Nixie took me for rides in her motorboat and on her horse at her summer cottage. Aunt Dietlinde took me to knitting classes.

I always felt like a changeling in my own home. A splinter in my own family tree. Aunt Nixie was the only person who seemed to understand.

My mother sniffed. "Aunt Nixie was a troublemaker and a spoiled brat. She spent money like water, and never stopped to think where it came from. I can't count the times, even now, that she borrows money from Dietlinde. Bah."

Aunt Nixie borrowed money from Aunt Dietlinde? But...Aunt Nixie had all sorts of things, nice things. Aunt Dietlinde had next to nothing. It wasn't fair for Aunt Nixie to take money from Aunt Dietlinde. I felt my brow furrow in a frown. I would have to rethink some more things, apparently.

"And your older daughter, Mrs. Schmeling? Will I get to

meet her?"

"My older...where did you hear about Giselle?" My mother's face went stark blank.

"You have pictures." Julian indicated a shelf full in the next room, just visible through the doorway. Damn, he had good eyesight. He looked at my mother and his expression changed. "I'm sorry. I didn't realize she had passed away."

I felt my jaw drop. Julian had a good brain, too, if he read *that* from my mother's blank face.

"Oh. Well. It was a long time ago."

Gently, Julian took my mother's hands in his. "That makes it harder, not easier."

"You're right." My mother blinked rapidly, as if against tears.

"Please tell me," Julian said, his voice warm with compassion.

It was a nice try, but I knew *that* was doomed. My mother *never* talked about my older sister's death. I had asked, many, many times over the years. Mom never said a word, other than Giselle was a wild girl who had died of a drug overdose—and if I *ever* touched even a cigarette I would be grounded for the rest of my life.

My mother was just a tad overprotective of me.

"Giselle was sixteen."

I stared at my mother in shock. But that really was her mouth moving. Really was my mother, talking...about my older sister.

"Only sixteen. And such a hellion." Mother paused. Added, almost reluctantly, "So independent. Such an original."

"How did she die?" Julian asked. It was less a question and more a breath; a whisper of acceptance and encouragement.

"She had an accident." My mother's reply was just as soft. "Giselle used to go joyriding, though I told her not to. Such an adventure, she would say. So exciting."

"A car crash?"

"No. A boy took her up on his motorcycle. They were going too fast down a country lane and...and Giselle was not wearing a helmet. Neither of them were. But only my Giselle died."

My jaw dropped. "Mom! You said she died of a drug

overdose!"

My mother turned on me, her expression angry but her eyes suspiciously shiny. "I did not want you idolizing your sister! I did not want you taking off higgledy-piggledy with some man and dying...too..." My mother covered her mouth, realizing what she'd revealed.

All my life, my mother had swept Giselle under the rug. I thought it was because she hated Giselle's independence.

Now I saw it hurt Mom too much. That she didn't want me to end up the same way.

Wow. I would have to rethink more than a few things.

A small sob came from my mother's chair. Any thinking or rethinking stuttered to a halt.

Oh, fizzle-shizzle! Mothers weren't supposed to cry. Especially not *my* mother, stalwart, stifling, and never, ever sloppy. I tried frantically to think of something to keep her from going off the deep end.

I just didn't know how to deal with Mom being vulnerable.

Julian came to the rescue. "Would you pour me some coffee, Mrs. Schmeling?" He picked up cup and saucer and held them out, matter-of-fact. So nice and normal.

It was the only thing that could have pulled Mom back from that scary emotional brink. "Why...yes. Yes, of course, Mr. Emerson." My mother picked up the coffeepot, which clinked once against the tray. Then she had it under control and smoothly poured him coffee. Julian took a small, appreciative sip.

"Excellent coffee, Mrs. Schmeling."

"Do you like it?" She set down the pot and wiped discreetly under her eyes. "It's some of the fancy roast from the grocers," she continued in a more normal tone. "Usually I don't go in for those Vee-and-ease fancy-schmancy coffees, but..." And my mother was off and running again.

Chapter Eighteen

And that was how Julian Emerson bumped St. Bart out of first place in the Mother Race. He clinched it by taking the coffee cups and service to the kitchen and suggesting that mother and I relax and visit while he washed up.

Even I appreciated that.

When Julian came back, we chatted a bit more. Finally I asked about Bruno's little delivery.

"I put it in your room, Dietlinde," my mother said. "It looks pretty big. Probably heavy. Maybe you should ask Mr. Emerson to help you with it."

My mother was sending me to my room—with a *man*? Well, with a vampire, but my mother thought he was a man. According to my mother, men only had one thing on their minds. From my experience, vampires did too, but that wasn't the point. The point was...oh. I remembered my mother saying a man wouldn't stay with the cow if she didn't give him milk.

I didn't tell her the cow had already been milked. And that the man probably wouldn't stay with her anyway.

But Julian seemed to want to stay with me at least for now, so I led him to the small room upstairs that was my childhood sanctuary. I found the bazooka almost immediately and headed back.

I stopped when I realized Julian wasn't behind me. Returning to the doorway, I saw him, face thoughtful, wandering around the room. Touching things, looking at them, sniffing at a few. He considered my Neon Genesis Evangelion poster and my TMNT action figures. My first Fender propped up in the corner, and my dartboard Justin Timberlake. He stopped the longest in front of my bookcase, sitting on his haunches to read the titles on the lowest shelf. Every once in a while he'd smile, like he'd caught the name of an old friend.

Then Julian saw my special oil on the top. He rose, picked up the slender bottle. Turning, he looked at me for the first time since we'd entered the room. "What's this?"

My cheeks heated. "Isn't it obvious?"

Julian pumped a little bit into his hand, tested the consistency. Thick, but not too thick. He brought it under his nose, took a small sniff. "Mmm. Nice. What's it for?"

My blush deepened. While I lived at home it was only for masturbation. But seeing Julian rub it, smell it...I swallowed hard. "It's for fapping."

Julian blinked. His eyes tracked in that way I was coming to know; searching for a translation.

Suddenly his eyebrows winged high. His eyes met mine. "*Fap*. The sound of intercourse on Internet porn sites."

"Um, yeah. Or in manga."

"Japanese comics?" His eyes tracked again. "Of course. *Baka*. Japanese for stupid. Could it be so simple? What about pwn?" I opened my mouth to reply when he said, "Internet, no...cultural reference...yes, it's computer gaming, isn't it? Pwn translates to *own*. To own or rule!"

And then, like Helen Keller breaking the sign language barrier, unlocking the door to understanding with the key word *water*, Julian got it.

"Fapping." He advanced on me, backing me into a wall. Abruptly, he thrust the hand with the oil down my pants. His fingers slid slickly over my pubes, began caressing back and forth. "I've been buckets of stupid, haven't I?"

"Well...not exactly." My hips rocked against his oiled hand. "What do you mean?"

His mouth hovered over mine. "Shizzle, Nixie. I've been a faphead." He kissed me, lips feather-light. "Feening over not understanding you. You must have thought my brain was rolled, as *baka* as I've been." His tongue flicked delicately over my lips. All the while his hand kept pumping, fingers caressing.

"Uh...not totally. *Baka*, that is." I was trembling, my body starting to perspire. "You're not Betamax about this hXc stuff.

You're wicked on that."

"Betamax." Julian kissed down my cheek, nipped my neck. I could feel his breath heat my skin. "Betamax cassette tapes? Ah. Old, obsolete. And hXc...hardcore?" He nudged aside my hoodie, wet the tee over my breast with his tongue. "Well, I can't help thinking hXc with you, Nixie. You're hawt." He clamped onto my breast and began to suckle. "Leet."

"Julian." I was starting to pant. "We're in my *parents'* house."

"So?" He pushed me harder into the wall, letting me know how really hawt he found me.

"So my door doesn't have a lock." The pressure was delicious. I arched against the wall.

"So?" I heard his zipper go. He removed his hand from my pants, but only to use both to push them down to my knees. Taking my bared hips in his hands, he raised me against the wall. While I was still trying to figure out how we were going to do this with my legs clamped together by my pants, he sliced his erection between my thighs and into my pussy.

With anyone else, that would have gotten them about one inch inside. With Julian's prodigious length, he stuffed me full. "Oh," I gasped, the heat searing me. "Wouldn't this be easier if you turned me around?"

"I want to kiss you as you come." He lowered his head.

His kiss was no longer delicate or light. His mouth opened on mine, his tongue driving, stabbing, dominating. His hips thrust in time to his tongue, hard and sure. Between his hands, hips, and my jeans, I found myself pinned securely against the wall. I could only hang in his grip and enjoy.

My fingers tangled in his hair. I gasped his name, and he growled mine. His deep, rumbling purr started, and I swear it vibrated clear through my chest and into the wall. And all throughout he thrust, thrust, thrust.

"Julian. Bite me." I offered my neck. "I'm so close...bite me."

"I can't." It seemed like he was speaking through an ocean of pain. "I would take too much. I want—oh, how I want. But your blood pressure's too low." His words were lisped around his immense canines, as long as I'd ever seen.

"Bite me." I yanked his head into to my neck. Felt his

175

breath steam my throat. "Bite me!"

"Nixie, no—"

"Bite me now!" I arched back hard, thrusting my throat into the pearl of his fangs. My blood rushed to meet them, kissing them with fluid red lust. I moaned and shuddered on the brink of a huge orgasm.

Julian *roared*. His mouth opened like a snake unhinging. He skewered my throat in a bite so powerful my eyes flew open and my entire body unfurled hard against the wall.

Forget bombs bursting in air. Forget lightning sizzling through the sky. Forget geysers of water and steam blasting out of the earth. This was so beyond.

I climaxed like a bullet train. Like a subway rocketing through deep, dark tunnels. Like running face first into a cliff at ninety miles an hour. The power of it was so far beyond anything I'd ever experienced, it destroyed me. Tore me in half, ripped out my heart, and smashed me back together.

And as Julian gushed and gushed into me, I realized with awful clarity that I would never be whole again.

Then I passed out.

♫ ♫ ♫

I woke facing a bright yellow wall decorated with cheerful rainbows and flowers. The *scrape-scrape* of a clock sounded from somewhere. At first I thought I was in a hospital, but I lay in a recliner, not a bed. And the woman who bustled in wasn't a nurse. "Feeling better, girl?" My friend Twyla Tafel's cocoa brown eyes watched me with concern.

"Twyla? The mayor said you were going to your sister's. What are you doing here?" I tried to sit up but felt weak as a puppy. Twyla put a hand to my shoulder, held me down with astonishing ease. I closed my eyes. "And where, BTW, is here?"

"Blood Center. I was on my way to my sister's when I got the call. Came right over."

The reason I was at the Blood Center was obvious, once I saw the needle in my arm. "What call?"

"Mr. Hottie Attorney. Said to come over right away, so I hustled my bootie right along."

"Julian? Where is he?" I looked around. The rainbows and flowers were actually only along one wall. The other three were concrete, two lined with refrigeration units.

"He took off. Something about a fight. So it's *Julian* now? Not Mr. Pricey Prude? Not the Lewtz at Law?"

Julian was anything but prudish, at least in the important things. And I'd found out he wasn't getting any of the money we raised. But I didn't know how much Twyla knew, so I only said, "Did he say what kind of fight? Or where?"

"No. Only that I was to keep you from following. He was quite insistent. Kinda scary about it." Twyla shivered. "That boy's got sharp teeth."

I tried sitting up again. This time I didn't feel so weak. "But Julian may be in trouble. I have to go. Where's my bazooka?"

"Your *what*?" Twyla's fine brows knit together. "Since when do you have a bazooka?"

"Uh, long story. Have you seen it?"

"No," Twyla said at the same time I saw it behind her. She glanced back. "And even if I had, sexy and straight took the ammo."

"Shizzle. Twyla, could you do me a favor? Could you call Bruno Braun, and—"

"No. No way, José. *Nein, nicht*, not, *nyet*, never, uh-uh." Twyla put up a long-nailed hand, today enameled in stop-sign red. "I know what you're thinking. And ain't no way. Leet lawman would have my ass on a platter if I let you one step out of this building, much less following him to that fight."

I sighed. "Fine. Can I at least make a phone call?" Digging in the pocket of my pants, I pulled out my cell phone.

"I guess. Lawboy went all testosterone protective over you leaving, not you calling."

That was Julian. "Yeah. He thinks I'm a kid." I hit Elena's speed dial.

"No way, girl. I saw him look at you. No way that man thinks you're a child."

Thinking about Julian looking at me, I got hot. "Then why won't he let me help him fight?"

"Oh, I don't know. Maybe because he's got fifteen inches and a hundred fifty pounds on you?" Twyla rolled her eyes. I rolled mine back.

My call to Elena went over into voicemail. Which meant she was probably at the fight too. With Bo no doubt. "At least tell me where Julian is. I know that you know. You know everything. I promise not to leave." In a low voice I added, "Before I'm ready."

"I heard that," Twyla said. "So, yes, I know, and no, I'm not telling."

"Come on, Twyla. Julian might need help."

"I'll be the one needing major help if he finds out I told."

"C'mon, Twyla. You owe me." When she tried to look innocent I hit her with, "I know you're the one who set the mayor on me, you haas."

She had the grace to blush.

"I vowed revenge, but if you tell me where Julian is, I'll consider us even. But if you don't—"

"All right, all right! It might be okay if you guess."

"I can live with that." Where would Julian, Bo, and Elena be? Well, where would a vampire fight be? The last one had been outside of the Roller-Blayd factory. My thoughts were accompanied by the *scrape-scrape* of the clock. I pointed at the bag of blood draining into me. "How long until this is done?" I frowned. "And why am I not at the hospital?"

Twyla crossed her arms and leaned against a rainbow. "Well, smarty, why do you think you're not at the hospital?"

"I guess because it was too far away from my parents'. And...because the Blood Center is closer to the fight!" *Scrape-scrape* went the clock.

"Now your wetware's working."

"So how long until I'm done?" I looked around for the clock. It occurred to me that clocks went *tick-tick*, not *scrape-scrape*.

"Another fifteen minutes. You didn't need a full unit. But your Julian wanted you to rest after."

"Like that'll happen." *Scrape-scrape.* "Do you hear that?" Such an odd-sounding clock. Especially when there was *no clock in the room at all.* "What *is* that?"

"What?" Twyla cocked her head. There was only silence.

Then—*scrape-scrape.* "That," I said.

Twyla frowned. "Sounds like mice."

"Like mice digging," I agreed.

"Huh. I'll have to call pest control when I get back."

"Except—" I strained my ears. "Don't mice go *scritch-scritch* instead of *scrape-scrape*?"

"Maybe they're using tiny shovels," Twyla said.

"Ri-ight." I wondered how many vampires Julian and company were fighting this time. Wondered if I'd get there in time. Wondered, if I did get there in time, whether bazookas were point-and-click. Bruno hadn't left any instructions. And Julian had taken the ammunition. Hopefully Elena's ammo would fit. "Are you going to pull this thing out of me when the time comes, or is there a nurse around?"

Twyla pushed off the wall to come sit in the chair next to my recliner. "I am. Don't worry, Lawboy showed me how. He's the one who fixed you up, you know. I was pretty impressed, how efficient he was."

"Yeah, well, I guess it's a hobby of his."

"Medicine?"

"No, blood." I looked around. Boxes sat on pallets. Refrigerators hummed. It looked more like a warehouse than a hospital. "Do they usually do transfusions at the Blood Center?"

"I don't know. They must, though, right? I mean, they have the equipment." Twyla indicated bag and pump. "That looks like the last of it." She unhooked me.

But when I tried to get up, she *sat* on me. "Let me go!" Only it came out more like *mumph miggle mumph.*

"Nuh-uh. Hunkalicious would take a bite out of me if you followed him." Twyla sounded wary. If only she knew how incredibly orgasmic Julian's bite was, she'd be spritzing herself with barbeque sauce.

"Not...going to follow...him," I gasped.

"Promise?"

"Yes," I said with the last of my oxygen. She got off. I sucked in a bushel of air.

I had told her the truth. I wasn't going to *follow* Julian.

I knew where he was. So I was going to go straight to him.

Chapter Nineteen

But when I got to the corner of Fifth and Grant, there was no crowd of ravening freaks. No bodies flopping heartless to the ground. No heads rejoining in a creepy-weird dance of rebirth.

Instead, a suspicious orange glow came from the east. I trotted toward it. As I got closer, I could see the orange halo was shot through with plumes of black smoke.

Shouldering my bazooka, I ran. It felt like miles. But only half a block further on I got a clear view. I screeched to a halt.

Kalten's Roller Skating Rink was nothing but a big camp fire.

If there'd been a fight, it was long over. Stunned, I stumbled closer, wondering where Julian and Elena were. Wondering if they were okay. Wondering where the hell I'd stage my bands now. As I stood mired in my stupidity, flames began licking the building's windows.

"Nixie! Don't go any closer." A hand clasped my shoulder, long-fingered and pale. "It's dangerous."

I turned. Behind me was Bart Bleistift. His nice boyish face was concerned. And strangely, a little wary.

"Bart? What are you doing here?" The wary expression, coupled with the time of night, made me suspicious. Butler had said Bart wasn't a vampire, but who else would be out so late?

I mentally smacked myself. Did I think everyone in the world was a closet bloodsucker? I was getting way too vamparanoid.

"I was walking home," Bart said. "Working late."

See? I told myself. Totally non-weird explanation. "Big case?"

"Some meetings that took all afternoon. Then I had to finish up a few things." Bart smiled his nice boyish smile, and I felt better.

He threaded his arm through mine. "So, how about I walk you home?" He gave me a saucy wink.

The wink implied I'd get laid. If Bart had asked me last night, I'd have shouted yippy. Since then I'd had deal-breaker sex with Julian. I knew until that memory faded, no one else could compare.

Of course, the memory of sex with Julian might *never* fade, but I didn't want to consider that.

"Some other time." I slipped loose and started toward the fire. Bo and Elena might have been fighting here. Julian might have been fighting here. I wanted to make sure they were not lying helpless nearby.

"Nixie, wait." Bart grabbed my arm, swung me around like a yo-yo. "You do *not* want to get any closer." He glanced toward Kalten's, then back at me. His stare was hard, like blue marbles. "You shouldn't even be *here*!"

The music in his voice was wrong. The emphasis should have been on "be", as in "You shouldn't even *be* here." But it wasn't, meaning... "What's wrong with *here*?"

It was hard to tell in the red glow, but I think he flushed. "Alone, I mean. At night. And, um, near a fire." He kept hold of my arm.

"Bart, I'll be fine. I just want to make sure no one needs help." I tried to tug away but he was strong.

"The cops'll handle it, Nixie. Look, I'm going your direction. Let me walk you home." Bart started dragging me northeast, toward my parents.

"I don't live that way!" Exasperated, I tried one more time to pull away. Bart wouldn't let go. So I gave him a twist and a hard yank.

"Hey!" He rubbed his wrist. "You didn't have to do that."

"Then let go, next time I ask." I started toward the fire, felt Bart reach for me again.

So I drew the bazooka. It wasn't loaded, but even an empty bazooka pointed at your chest makes you stop and think.

"What the hell?" St. Bart said.

"Leave me alone." I spoke each word clearly. "Do not touch me again."

"Okay, okay." Bart raised both hands, backed off. "Just don't say I didn't warn you."

"Warn me about—?"

An explosion rocked the street. I spun. Flames belched from every orifice of the Kalten, window and door. Glass burst onto the street. I put up one arm to shield my face. Heat roared around me.

I whirled back. "How the hell did you know that was going to—"

But Bart was gone.

♫ ♫ ♫

"So when did you find out about Bo? When he bit you on your wedding night?"

Elena and I were eating breakfast at the Caffeine Café. It was Tuesday morning, and she'd just gotten off shift. I played with my scone, chocolate chip this time (warmed with butter). I was too unsettled to eat. The incident with Bart was still on my mind. But this breakfast was about finally getting the 411 on vampires. And about a very huge apology from my best friend because she had lied to me and made me feel like an idiot.

Had I known what the future held, I would have at least tried to choke something down.

"I knew sooner than that." Elena smiled slightly. "I suspected long before, but didn't want to believe it."

"Come on. You must have known something was up when Bo's love-nips turned into real bites." Elena's smile widened and her eyes sparkled naughtily. Oops. Apparently Julian wasn't the only maestro at fangilingus. "Er, I meant neck. Neck bites."

"Of course you did. Look, if it's any consolation, I was as much in the dark as you in the beginning."

"Consolation? Hardly. *Your* best friend wasn't in on the secret."

"My sister was."

"You deliberately misled me! After that first attack on Julian and me, you said I was imagining the blood. Imagining things. Like I was Bruno, or something."

"Actually, I said 'I'm *not* saying you're imagining things.'"

"Whatever. I felt like an ID-ten-T."

"You're not an idiot. Eat your scone. You'll feel better."

I used my fork, but only to torture the damned scone. "I'm not joking, Elena. This time, the truth. All of it."

"Fine." She held up both hands in surrender, which looked a little funny with a forkful of muffin still held in one. "What do you want to know?"

Everything about Julian. Starting with his age. Could he really have done Renaissance dances when they were hip tunes? "How old is Julian?"

"I'm not sure. But Bo just turned a thousand a few months ago." She said it offhand, like she was just telling me the time.

"A thousand?" I sputtered. "Like a millennium?"

"Give or take a few years. I get the impression calendars have changed a bit since he was first born."

"Sweet chocolate Venus, Elena. A thousand years. Have you any idea how long that really is?"

She shrugged. "Your Julian might be even older."

My cheeks heated. "He's not *my* Julian." I smashed scone in my agitation. And then it hit me. "No wonder he's so good."

"He's good, is he?" Elena raised one eyebrow.

The heat in my cheeks became Bunsen burners. My scone became crumbs. "Moving right along. How did Bo become a vam—"

Elena mashed a finger into my lips. "We don't use the v-word, even here."

"Sorry. Bad case of the stupids." I tried to come up with a code word, mauling what remained of my scone as I thought. "So how did Bo...get his extralong dentures?"

Elena rolled her eyes. Apparently she didn't think much of my secret word. And I'd gone to such trouble, too. "You mean his *ang-fays*?"

"Like that's any better. Look, not just Bo, but how does anybody turn? I always thought it was getting bit that did it. But with as often as Julian bites...um, yeah." I broke off because Elena was grinning madly again. "Anyway, if it was all about the bite, I'd be sporting size extra-long pearlies by now.

Julian said only dead people turn."

"Julian's right. So's folklore, as far as it goes." Elena forked up muffin. "You have to be bitten, and you have to die. But that's not a guarantee you'll turn."

"It isn't? Is there some sort of blood exchange ritual thingy?"

Elena's pale cheeks colored. "Not exactly. I mean, an ampire-vay's blood works as well as a bite. As long as it gets into the human's bloodstream. The human doesn't actually drink it."

"Don't you mean uman-hay?"

"Ha-ha."

"But I still don't get it. How *exactly* does a human turn fangy?"

"You mean the mechanism behind it?" Elena's color returned to normal. "We don't know, exactly. We know certain steps that have to take place. We know a human has to be exposed to v-blood or a v-bite. We know the human has to die. We know three days later, the human wakes up, new and improved and bloodthirsty. Other than that, we're pretty much in the dark."

"But if vamp—I mean fangy guys have been around for thousands of years, *someone* must have figured out how they get that way."

"You'd think, but no." Elena popped a bite of muffin, washed it down with her mocha latte. "We don't even know what makes them different from humans."

"*What*? Isn't that pretty obvious? Pointy teeth, great reflexes, really bad sunrash?"

"I mean physically. At the cellular level."

"Cellular. Like phones?"

"Ho, ho. Like DNA. V-guys don't have doctors, don't need 'em. But there are a few. And the mystery is—V-DNA is entirely human."

"That's impossible!" DNA was a building plan, like blueprints for a house. Only instead of building a house, DNA built a body. Mouse plans built mice, camel plans built camels. Chicken plans were without lips. Human plans built *humans*. And if there was one thing Julian was not, it was merely human.

"Well, subject tissue under the microscope has holes. But no one is sure what that means."

"Not even the wise and mighty 'Ancient One'?"

To my surprise Elena put a hand over mine. Looked me straight in the eye. "Nixie. I know you're confused. It's natural. And I know you're feeling crabby about it. But you don't want to mess around with the Ancient One. You just don't."

Elena Strongwell, supercop. Warning me about a mysterious vampire like he was some daggy ruler of Oz. "Thanks. Everything's so clear now."

She sighed, removed her hand and sat back. "Look, three things to remember. First, most dead people stay dead. Second, for those who do turn, it's bite, die, three days, done. Third, *most dead people stay dead.*"

"I would guess the staying-dead part is kinda important." I pushed my much-abused scone away.

Elena's face turned pensive. "Bo and I have discussed it a lot. About making me like him. I'm going to age, and he's not. No problem now, but forty years down the road...well. He refuses to try. Not until we have better odds for me actually turning."

Wow. And I always thought marriage meant happily-ever-after. Guess there were still problems to overcome. And from Elena's frownie-face, that one hadn't been overcome. The frown, and the fact that she was stabbing her muffin like public enemy number one. Time to get her mind off it. "So what happened to Bo? How'd he do option two?"

Elena stopped her muffin-mangling to smile briefly at me. She knew why I'd changed the subject. "Bo was killed in a Viking raid."

"A real Viking. Somehow that doesn't surprise me." I drank coffee. "I always thought he'd look good in a bearskin with an axe over his shoulder."

"Yeah." Elena shivered. A bedroom shiver. Like maybe the image of a hot Viking warrior in nothing but a bearskin and sweat was more than a fantasy for her.

"TMI!" I plunked my mug down. Coffee sloshed onto the table. "I don't want to know. So Bo got it in a raid, and then what? 'Thor' bit him?"

"Thorvald? No, he's younger than Bo by several centuries."

I'd meant the Norse god-guy, but apparently Elena wasn't into sarcasm this early in the morning. "Fine. *Someone* bit him. And then three days later Bo woke up, saw his shadow, and we had six more weeks of winter?" I waited for a reaction.

"I know you're being sarcastic, Nixie. I'm just ignoring you."

Friends are so annoying. "Love you too. Bo?"

"He doesn't remember. But there were some v-rogues following the Viking raiders. The V-raiders feasted on the spoils, and the v-rogues feasted on the spoiling, if you know what I mean."

Ew. My turn to ignore her. "So a rogue drank Bo's blood, and by the luck of the dice, he turned."

"It might have been several rogues. You have a better chance of turning if there's more than one. Or if the one is very old. That's why I think Bo should at least take the chance of turning me...old topic. Never mind."

"And Julian? Do you know what happened with him?"

"I think it had something to do with Druids and ritual skull-bashing."

"Oh goodie." There was a hot bedroom discussion in the making. *Not.*

"So are we good, now? I'm sorry I lied to you about the blood. But you can see why. The world isn't ready for the reality of—" She did a quick scan of the room. Whispered, "Vampires."

"Especially not the Meiers Corners corner of it. Yeah, we're good." I dug into the remains of my scone, finally calm enough to eat.

That's when I got the first of the Munster calls.

♫ ♫ ♫

Thursday at what should have been supper time, my cell phone tweedled the theme from *The Munsters*. That meant someone from the Meiers Corners's Common Council. *Now* what's wrong? I wondered, swinging the phone open. It was the day before the festival opened. I was at home, staring at empty cupboards.

The elderly voice on the other end of the phone was

panicked. "The refrigeration went out at the Deli Delight, Nixie! Half the cheese balls melted and I don't know what to do!"

"Cheese balls don't melt, Brunhilde," I said, opening another cupboard. Also empty. Except for the cricket chirping.

"These cheese balls did. They were running grease all over the place! It was like someone took a flame thrower to them." She paused. "I think we're going to have to cancel the tasting. There's no way we can get more balls by tomorrow. Especially with the tasting opening so early. Why did it have to be three thirty? Couldn't you have picked four?"

"I didn't pick the time, the mayor did. And we're not going to cancel."

"We can still run the cheese contest," Granny Butt said.

"It won't have the same draw. Call Lew Kaufman." Mr. Chee$eball $alesman. "He can pull some strings." I hung up and took out my frustration by kicking all the empty cupboards closed. Even the ones over my head. Then I stomped into my bedroom to take a nap.

I flopped down on my bed. My stomach growled at me and my head ached. I rolled over to go to sleep. My mind refused to shut down. Tuesday. It had started Tuesday.

Tuesday morning, after breakfast with Elena, the first of *The Munster* calls came. Kurt Weiss, practically yipping with panic. "The truck with our shipment...all over the road...like vultures on a dachshund carcass..."

"Slow down, Kurt. Is it the corn 'n weenie roast?"

"The hot dogs. Sideswiped by a Winnebago camper!"

I swore. "No weenies, no roast." I rubbed my forehead. "Okay, look. Raid every grocery store within fifty miles. Buy all the weenies you can."

"Oh...great great great! You have insurance money!"

"Um. No. Not quite yet." Fuck. So I had to give Kurt the money I'd saved on bands to buy wieners.

Out of the blue, Julian called. Obviously in a hurry, he told me he'd be unavailable for a while. With a "sorry" that sounded anything but, he hung up before I could even ask what he meant by "a while".

On the heels of that disappointment, the mayor's sister, advisor for the Wauwatosa Applied Math Organization, showed up. At *my* townhouse. That was the first I knew that the mayor expected me to find a place for the WAMO kids to stay. After making a few hurried phone calls and getting nowhere, I ran up the white flag with my mother. Mom knows everyone in Meiers Corners, and what's more important, she's owed favors by the entire city. Even Bo Strongwell owes Mom. She found a place for all twenty little geeks to stay, and made me promise to come to dinner for a month in return.

I really hate owing my mother.

I needed groceries, but between one thing and another, the shopping didn't get done Tuesday. Wednesday morning I got up an hour early and skipped breakfast just to get a grocery guerrilla-hit in. Not that I had any breakfast in the house anyway.

The instant I arrived in the parking lot of Der Lebensmittelgeschaft (you got it, The Grocery Store in German), I was intercepted by Donner and Blitz. They were so drunk I could barely understand them. I had to drag them to the Caffeine Café and pour a gallon of coffee into them to even make out a word. And by the time I finished paying for their coffee, I had no money left for food.

Finally I deciphered the story. When Donner and Blitz pulled the tent for the beer tasting out of storage, it was half-eaten by moths. Going with them to City Hall, they showed me the huge holes in the seemingly indestructible canvas.

The unnaturally large holes.

All right, maybe I was vamparanoid. But those holes looked too big to be caused by moths. Unless, of course, the moths sported inch-long fangs.

I spent the whole morning chasing down a replacement tent. Without cash or a credit card, no one would sell me one, much less rent one, even used. I finally called Bruno. "Please, Bear! It's only for three days."

"Well, I'd like to, Nixie. You being a friend and all. But without credit—"

"I'll pay you out of the profits for the festival."

"I only have the one tent big enough to run the store out of. If something, you know. Happens."

That's how Bruno thinks. Everything's in terms of the Apocalypse. "We're just borrowing it."

"Yeah. But if something happens...unless you have insurance?"

Not that again. "I'll...I'll have to get back to you, Bear," I said as I whacked my head against the wall.

Noon was already a two-hour memory by this time. I ran to the kitchen. Flung open cabinets and refrigerator. The only thing I had in the house was a box of mac and cheese. Literally. No milk, no butter.

I found out you can actually make mac and cheese with only hot water.

Stomach partially satisfied, I set off for the grocery store. Only to take a *Munster* call from Buddy. A month ago he had ordered five hundred packs of cards for the Sheepshead Tournament, but they never arrived. When he called the company he'd ordered from, they said they'd have to trace it. It took them two weeks to get back to him. Monday they told him the shipment had been lost.

Not one to idly bemoan fate, Buddy started hitting the local department stores. The first store was out of cards. Coincidentally, so was the second. Not so coincidentally, so was the third. And the fourth.

It took me the rest of Wednesday into early this morning to solve that one. After calling practically every store in northern Illinois, I finally thought of the little geeks I'd traded my soul to my mother for. Geeks were gamers, right? Well, maybe not all of them, but luckily, these geeks were. They called their parents back in Wauwatosa and I had nearly two hundred packs promised by tomorrow morning.

So Tuesday and Wednesday I had a total of ten hours sleep and a box of mac and cheese to eat.

And after that first phone call, I didn't hear from Julian once.

Today was Thursday. My stomach growled. I had a headache. Things were getting screwed up left and right. I'd used up my emergency money. I had no food for dinner. I didn't have a place for the bands to play. I didn't have a tent for the beer tasting.

And I hadn't had sex for over forty-eight hours and my pussy was screaming at me.

What else could go wrong?

Chapter Twenty

At that point I did what any sane woman would. I got up and went to the kitchen, to get something to eat.

Like I'd gotten to the store in the last ten minutes. Still, I checked one more time. One cabinet contained a half-eaten package of cellophane noodles. Another revealed a soda cracker and a spider web. A third had an open bag of cherry licorice sticks so dry you could dig to China with them. In the fridge was a moldy can of spaghetti and an apple that looked like a shrunken head. My stomach growled again.

Damn. Everything was going wrong with the festival, I didn't have a place for the bands, and I had no food. *And no sex.* I flopped down on a kitchen chair and fought the impulse to cry.

My phone played "Hey Jude". "Yeah," I snapped.

"Hey, Nixie. It's Durango. Listen, I have some bad news."

Just what I needed. More bad news. Please turn off my lights and leave quietly.

"I can't make the gig tomorrow night."

"What?!" Guns and Polkas is a five piece band. Lob, Rob, Cob, me, and Durango. We need every one of those five pieces. We'd sound like a kindergarten band without any one. Not having a lead guitar would sound like...like rap! "You can't back out. We're the headliners!"

"Nixie, I'm really sorry. But they got a kidney for my Dad. I have to be at the hospital."

I rubbed my aching head. "Yeah, okay. I guess you have to do that."

"You can get a sub. Otto—"

"Played everything like a Viennese waltz last time."

"Well, what about Stung? Or Goober?"

"Stung's girlfriend broke his fingers. And Goober plays the Alpine Retreat Friday nights."

"Oh, yeah. I forgot about Goober. Why did Stung's girl break his fingers?"

"She found them in another girl's thong."

"Well, I'm sure you'll think of something, Nixie."

"Yeah, something," I whined, or rather groused, and hung up. *What else could go wrong?* Why, oh why did I Have To Think That?

It wasn't fair. Why were so many things going wrong in the first place? Why the hell did everyone expect *me* to solve all the problems? And what Evil Fairy of Responsibility did I piss off that *I* had to run this feckstravaganza?

Summerfest. Miller pavilion.

Dietlinde, I am so proud of you.

Well. There it was, of course. My mother was proud of me. And the gig of a lifetime.

As if those weren't answer enough, who else was there? Dirkenstein? Who else knew entertainment like I did?

There was no one else. Because *no one else* knew about the vampire threat.

I was the only one who knew how truly disastrous not raising enough money would be. Well, Bo and his watch group knew, but I guessed they had their hands full with gangy Lestats.

No, I was it. It was time to Grow Up.

It was time to buy insurance. Which meant taking the clerical job.

I phoned CIC Mutual and accepted the job. I hung up, too dead inside even to cry. As of Monday, my life was over.

I sat down at my kitchen table and contemplated the long, bleak life ahead of me. No more Guns and Polkas. A year off would kill the band. Which meant no more music at all. I used to think if I was lucky, I wouldn't make it to thirty. Now even twenty-six seemed too old.

"Is this a bad time?" a cultured baritone came from right behind me.

I jumped. "Don't sneak up on me like that!" I twisted, beheld Julian in all his male, suity glory. Two days and I felt and probably looked like a herd of cows had run me over—cows with diarrhea. *He* looked like Chippendale Business Edition. "How did you get in, anyway?"

"You shouldn't leave your key under the doormat."

"Well, now that you're here, *go away.*" I sat down again, contemplated salt and water soup for dinner.

"Ah. I did come at a bad time."

"Really? Define *bad.* Skeletal-bloodsuckers-attacking bad? Fire-burning-down-my-best-friend's-apartment bad? Everything-in-the-festival-going-wrong bad?" My stomach growled.

"I think it's worse than that. I think you're hungry."

"Congratulations, you have eardrums. Now leave me alone."

"I don't think so." Julian put a hand under my elbow and lifted. "You're awfully crabby."

Without meaning to, I stood. "I am not crabby!" I yanked my elbow out of his grasp. I would have sat again in defiance but Julian gently took me by the shoulders and turned me to face him.

"Nixie, darling. You're being a crabass. Let me take you to supper."

"I am not a crabass!" I tried to shake loose. "And I'm not hungry." My stomach promptly spoiled everything by growling again.

"Of course you aren't." Julian drew me gently from the kitchen. "So you wouldn't like a big, greasy burger." He lifted my coat from the back of the couch where I'd tossed it. "Or a thick, cold milkshake. Hold out your arms." He dressed me like I was a little girl. For some reason, I stood for it. "Or a malted. Extra-thick. *Chocolate.*"

"Chocolate?" I asked in spite of myself.

"Mmm. And sizzling hot fries."

I resented that I was hungry. I resented Julian knowing I was hungry. I *really* resented Julian being so calm and reasonable after two days of *no sex* while I was a basket case. Unless he had gotten some in the meantime.

Fuck. I was surprised how much that hurt.

I had my pride. "You think you can ignore me for *two whole days* and then make everything all better with some *food*?"

"I can try." Julian opened the door.

"Two *days*, Emerson! Forty-eight hours! You're going to have to try a whole lot harder—" My eyes lit on a vehicle parked at the curb. I felt them widen as big as a football field. "What's that?"

"It's a motorcycle."

"That's not a mere *motorcycle*. That's a *Harley*." I floated toward it.

"Well, yes. A Cross Bones." Julian followed.

"A Dark Custom." I ran a hand down its sleek side. A Harley-Davidson Dark Custom. Built from blood, sweat, and chrome. And sporting a nonstandard sidekick two-up seat. I was in love.

"I hope you don't mind. It took a while to drive from Boston."

"Is this why you were gone?"

"I had to take care of a few business things. But it's why I went in person. To buy the Harley. I thought you might like it." He added softly, "I promise I'll drive better than your sister's boyfriend."

Several emotions hit me at that. Warmth, that stodgy old Julian brought a motorcycle—for me. Loss, my sister's death on a similar vehicle. Security, Julian's gentle promise that I wouldn't end up the same.

And was Julian *my* boyfriend? That just made me hot. "Are you sure you're really Julian Emerson? Mr. Staid N. Sober? Leader of the boy band 'N Control?"

"I've recently had something of an epiphany."

"Epifan-huh?"

"The time at your parents' home. The oil?"

"Oh." I remembered the fapping oil, the Helen Keller moment, and the anything-but-staid sex that followed.

"You do have to wear this." Julian handed me a helmet as he fastened his own.

Whew. For a moment there, the theme from *Invasion of the Body Snatchers* was running through my brain (the 1956 version, not the 70s remake).

"Hold on," Julian said, mounting. As soon as my hands wrapped around his lean waist, he kicked off from the curb and we were racing down the streets of Meiers Corners. I peeked around him. The wind was on my face and I could feel the freedom beneath our feet. It was better than flying.

All too soon we stopped. But when I saw where, I jumped off. "Der BurgerHimmel." I sighed. Home of the Buttery Burger with Angel-soft Bun, the Mount Ararat 'o Onions (golden and crispy), and real live *custard* malts. I checked my emergency stash of cash. Five bucks. I dashed inside and ordered the most artery-clogging combo I could find for five bucks. And when Julian took out his wallet and paid, I gleefully added the Hog Heaven Sundae for dessert (five scoops of delicious creamy custard topped with hot fudge, raspberry syrup, chocolate sauce, crushed pecans, marshmallow cream, and five—count 'em, five—maraschino cherries).

Stuffed full, I sat back, and felt a contented smile drift onto my face. Life, I realized, did not look that bad. There were problems, true. The festival had hiccups, I still didn't have a place for the bands to play, I had no lead guitar for my own group, Monday I would start a Real Job, and Julian would leave soon.

But my stomach was full. I had managed to stave off the worst of the festival disasters. I still had twenty-four hours to find a guitarist and a venue for the bands. I only had to pull oars for a year.

And Julian was here now.

I felt massive body heat, Julian sliding onto the bench next to me. I opened my eyes, smiled warmly at him. "Want to take a ride back to my place?"

His eyes turned that peculiar shade of violet that I was coming to associate with sex. "I'd love to," he growled. Oh, boy. Growly-guy, my fave. Maybe he had two days of horny stored up, too.

Of course, my cell phone chose that moment to *Munster*.

I snapped it open. "What!"

"Nixie, this is Josiah Moss." Another alderman backup. Aw, hell. He said, "I may have found a place for the bands to play."

I was speechless for a second. "But that's *good* news."

"Not exactly. See, it's the old Roller-Blayd factory. The place is big enough, and better yet, mostly empty. But there's no heat. And no sound system. And, um, no chairs."

"It's better than nothing. Reserve it, and I'll see what I can do about the other things."

"Can do."

"Problems?" Julian asked, rubbing my shoulder with one strong-fingered hand.

"Yeah." I told him about needing a place for the bands, and how Moss had found something but there were problems. It felt good talking about it. And somehow, I got talking about all my other problems. I wound up with, "The worst is Durango canceling. I don't know where we'll find a lead guitar on such short notice."

Julian hadn't said anything but a few "uh-huhs" while I was spewing. But as I slowed down, he said, "Well, let's look at the easier things first. The mortuary has chairs, don't they?"

"I hadn't thought of that."

"Call Moss back and see if he'll deliver them. And rental companies have large-sized space heaters. Unless the place is an abandoned oil refinery, that would probably do the trick for heat."

"It's an abandoned skate factory. Should be safe enough." I was impressed. Julian was not only smart, but a problem-solver. I could definitely fall in love. I might even be able to overlook the three-piece suits. Especially with the added Harley incentive. "And the sound system?"

"Know of any place that sells equipment? Maybe they'd loan some to you in return for advertisement."

"I wanted to rent stuff from Woofers 'R Us. Their equipment is perfect. Better than perfect. Real high-end."

"It was too expensive even to rent?"

I blew a frustrated breath. "Yeah. After the fucking insurance. Do you have any idea how much the insurance for this shindig is costing?" My life. But that was another story. One I wasn't admitting to anyone.

Julian eyed me closely. "Well...several local businesses owe Bo one way or another. I bet he could get them to loan you the equipment. Then it'll be covered by their own insurance."

I blinked. "I hadn't thought of that." I wondered if that

would reduce my forty thousand soul-weight. "That'd be fantastic." Two problems solved. I began to relax.

"As far as the lead guitar goes, what about me?"

I was still thinking about the sound equipment. If Bo could talk to Woofers 'R Us, then...I gaped at Julian. "You? As *lead*? But...but you don't play guitar."

"The viola da gamba happens to be tuned the same. A step off, but I don't have perfect pitch. It'll be fine."

"Fine? Last I looked, gambas weren't electric."

"But they're tuned alike, which means I can probably pick up electric guitar pretty quickly."

"Julian, we don't play sixteenth century bransles! We play polkas—"

"Which are nineteenth century. I can manage. And besides, what choice do you have?"

When he put it that way, it seemed like none. Still... "We won't have time to rehearse."

He shrugged. "I was pretty good at improv back in the fifteen hundreds. I've heard it's like riding a bicycle. You never forget."

"Ha-ha. Improv *then* was nothing like now—wait. You aren't kidding, are you?" Had Julian Emerson really done improv on his viola da gamba in the sixteenth century? In the courts of Henry VIII and... "You! *You* were the relation who served Elizabeth I!"

He bent his head in a graceful acknowledgment. "And James I. Not Charles I, though. I had emigrated by 1625."

Shit. Had the man...vampire standing before me actually met kings and queens of England? It seemed impossible, outrageous. "Didn't they know? Didn't any of these paragons glom on to the fact that you're a *vampire*?"

"Shh," he said gently. "Not so loud. Not everyone in Meiers Corners know we exist."

"Could have fooled me."

"And no, they didn't. We pass easily as humans, and we're very careful not to be discovered. We're powerful, but we're still vulnerable, after all. A few million of us in no way balance billions of human beings."

"Mm...million?" I stuttered.

"More or less." Julian shrugged. "Though all but a few thousand are fledglings."

"Fledglings," I echoed, still trying to come to grips with *millions* of vampires.

"Twenty years dead or less. There was a large upswing in the population with the advent of autoimmune diseases. Possibly there's a correlation. But that's not the point."

"No. The point is you're still a secret society."

Julian kissed me gently. "No. The point is I can help you. If you'll let me."

I stared into his eyes. I saw from their deep, intense blue that he meant more than just helping with the band, or even just with the festival.

But how much more? And how much would it hurt when he stopped helping? When he left?

I already knew I'd never forget Julian Emerson. He was smart, handsome, and a problem-solver. He was generous and thoughtful. He was an amazing lay.

He had blown the competition, not only in the Mother Hunt but in the Orgasm Grand Prix, out of the water.

He had written on my heart with indelible marker.

Oh, no. So not going there. Even lusting after Suitguy was simple and unthreatening compared to falling in love. If I were in love...not just freewheeling sex, but hearts and rings and *commitment*—who was I then? Not sassy, independent Nixie.

And worse, if I fell in love with Julian Emerson—moldy old vampire and stodgy attorney—who was I becoming? Bright, exciting Nixie would be lost, drowned in a tide of forever and family. No longer Nixie the Pixie but Dietlinde the Drab.

Names have power. My mother called me Dietlinde because she was trying to force me into the conservative, responsible mold. Dietlinde Schmeling was bad enough. But I wouldn't recognize Dietlinde Emerson...shizzle. Where did that come from?

Julian, with that almost supernatural perceptiveness said, "It might be *you* who changes me."

"Oh, now that's just too scary. How did you know what I was thinking?"

"The degree of panic on your face. The frown lines between

your brows." Julian smoothed my forehead with a warm thumb. "You fear nothing and no one. Except losing your freedom."

"My mother calls it restraint. *Caution.*"

"She just wants you safe," he said gently.

"Yeah, well, why is safe so boring?" I crumpled my greasy papers and got up. "I almost envy my sister, dying on a motorcycle. At least she got to live before she died."

"You're living." Julian rose behind me. "You get paid for doing what you love. You have your own apartment and car."

"I don't earn much," I said, devil's advocate. "I have to visit my parents three or four times a week or I'd starve." I got to his motorcycle, touched the chrome wistfully. "And if I'm so free, why does it seem I never get five miles beyond Meiers Corners? I had more freedom as a kid. At least then we took field trips to Chicago."

"You could get out more." Julian handed me my helmet. "You could visit me in Boston."

The helmet nearly dropped from my hands. The truth hit me so hard I felt like screaming. There, in a nutshell, was what Nixie the Pixie would become, tethered to aristocrat Julian Emerson.

Nothing but a joke.

I pictured me in Boston, city of Ivy League schools and conservative blue-bloods. Like Meiers Corners but older and actually stodgier.

With the added incentive of being way too classy for a punk like me.

In Meiers Corners I was an anomaly. Funny, but kind of sexy, too.

But in Boston, Julian's old-money friends would make me look like new garbage. They'd all laugh at me.

I was exciting to Julian here because I was different. A vacation fuck. But if I showed up there, I'd be just one of a long line of women vying for his attention, and not in pole position, either.

Sure, Julian might ask me to visit. But once I got there...once he saw me amid his sophisticated friends and his gorgeous and elegant women—

He'd reject me.

And what was worse was that I would *care*. His rejection would break my heart...fuck. "No! No way I'm setting foot in the Home of the fucking Hoags!"

Julian blinked at me. "I thought you wanted adventure..."

"Ooh, adventure galore with Snobby, Priggish and Prude. As invigorating as swimming in concrete. Be still my frantic, girlish heart."

"I thought you might like it." If I didn't know better I'd have thought he sounded slightly hurt. "But you don't have to come if you don't want to."

As I thought! A charity invitation, extended out of pity. "You're so kind," I sneered. "How thoughtful, to invite me and then yank it away! I'd rather get run over by a truck!"

"No need to get sarcastic," Julian said, vowels flattening. "You complained about not getting out enough."

"Complained?! I *never* complain. Are you trying to pick a fight?"

"Me...? What is wrong with you? A trip to Boston—"

"Is my idea of a personal hell!"

"Stop interrupting," Julian snapped, temper obviously starting to fray. "If you would just listen—"

"And anyway, it's your fault, Mr. Head-fapping Hoag. You asked."

"I didn't ask. I simply said...oh, what does it matter what I said. I just thought you might like to visit Boston. With me. Maybe meet—"

His condescending, superior gorgeous *friends,* I mentally finished. "Julian Emerson, you can just take your snobby bitch crew and...and poke them up your prostrate, you...you ignoranus!"

Julian's eyes narrowed dangerously. "Please do not interrupt." His words were clipped. He crossed his arms over his broad chest. "And calling names won't help. It makes you sound like a child."

"I am not a child!" I could have screamed. Instead of meeting my anger, Julian was getting all superior, looking down his nose at me. His condescension made my blood boil. Here I was, losing it, and *he* only got more reserved. It pissed me off even more. "You always treat me like a fucking child!"

"Enough. We'll continue this discussion at your place." His tone had gone ice-cold. His eyes were glacial. He straddled the Harley and put his helmet on. Nodded stiffly at the seat behind him. "Where we can indulge in temper tantrums in private."

We, meaning *me*. This was what I hated most about fucking stifling Puritans, whether they be German mothers or frigid Boston attorneys. They made me look like a stupid, overreacting bitch. My anger turned lava-hot. "Fuck you, Lawboy. I'll walk." I tossed him the helmet.

Julian caught it one-handed, grabbed me with the other and flung me onto the motorcycle. "You are not walking *anywhere* alone at night." Jaw rigid, he stuffed the helmet onto my head.

"You're not my keeper, Emerson!" I tried to yank the helmet off but somehow he'd already fastened the chinstrap.

"You know what you need, little girl? A good spanking. Sit *down*."

"Don't you dare!" I gasped. "I'm not a little…!"

"Then prove it. Sit. Still." Julian slewed me a red violet look, and kicked into gear.

Chapter Twenty-one

I yelled at him the entire ride home. Half of what I said was carried away by the wind. But he got the gist. I know that because the instant we reached my townhouse Julian hauled me off the motorcycle and kissed me, just to shut me up.

There was something about sex when you were in the middle of an argument. Something *wicked.* Gloves were off. You were mad at the other person, madder at yourself—and you didn't care who got hurt.

So I bit Julian's lip, hard enough to draw blood. Surprised, he loosened his grip. I used the opportunity to grab him by his tie and drag him through my door. There, I pushed him onto the floor. Buttons popping, I ripped away his shirt and tie. He was wearing an undershirt, but I tore it out of his pants and shoved it past his armpits. With my crotch on his rapidly heaving belly, I leaned down and bit his nipple.

Julian's eyes went blood-red. He arched under me. I palmed his pecs, those huge sleek mounds of muscle. I licked my way across the valley, bit the other nipple. He snarled, reached under my coat and ripped my shirt in two. Half-sitting, he tore bra, shirt, and coat over my head, baring me to the waist. Immediately he latched onto one breast and suckled, hard. I would be sore later but right now it felt like fire from heaven.

His sit-up made his belly a hard, rippling washboard. I was in Japanese schoolgirl mode, knee socks and a pleated skirt and nothing else, not even a thong. My damp crotch scrubbed over his washboard, and my clit swelled in instant response.

Julian grabbed my breasts with both hands, fondling me like a rag doll. He left one hand pumping and tangled the other in my hair. Holding my head trapped, he took my mouth with his.

This was no gentle kiss. Julian's mouth dominated, demanded. I was just as forceful, tongue plunging into him like a pile driver. We kissed like two wrestlers vying for mastery, driving to conquer. He flipped me onto my back, ripped my skirt from my hips, and returned to kissing me, his body crushing mine to the floor. Pushing hard I rolled us over, broke off the kiss. Throwing my leg over his torso, I faced his feet and tore off his pants. His erection snapped up, into my face. It wept his arousal, visibly pulsed with it.

Well, I had to, didn't I?

Without turning back, I rammed my head down on Julian's stiff cock. My lips tightened around the shaft. My throat opened, sliding his head past rippling cartilage.

Julian roared. His fingers bit into my buttocks, convulsed as he flooded my throat with hot cum. I half-swallowed several times, working him mercilessly. He roared through all of it, an almost endless rush of climax.

I started to get off. But as my mouth opened, Julian's fully erect cock hit me in the face again. I stopped, mouth agape.

Julian, taking advantage of my momentary shock, shoved me back onto the floor. He rolled his hips over my face, thrusting his cock ruthlessly down my throat again. His strong hands gripped my thighs and spread my legs wide. Plunging between, he ravaged me with his hot, steamy mouth.

I went dizzy with arousal. His cock drove repeatedly down my throat. His tongue stabbed into my slit, while his mouth sucked me wetly. His fangs, full-length, pressed hard and sleek against my labia, which felt very slick and swollen by now. I writhed, but his hands held me down firmly for his plundering.

My ears were ringing. My eyes were tightly shut, my chest heaving. My belly felt hot and distended. My body arched helplessly into Julian's muscular strength. In the fight for domination, I was about to lose. I held back as long as I could, making him work for it, making him use every century of his experience.

And then I could hold out no more. Waves of contraction and release hit me, hot as sin. Powerful as the surf. Terrible as love.

I experienced a little moment of blankness. Switched off, just for a second. No sound, no sight, no sensation. A warm, soft cocoon enveloped me, completely outside of time and space.

Reality snapped back. I heard my heart thudding. Felt Julian's heart pound against my belly. Warm, wet fluid slid down my cheek, and I realized he had lost it, too. I opened my eyes. His legs were spread on either side of my head. His butt was in front of my face. Julian, I thought dazedly, had an absolutely gorgeous ass. I worked to lift one hand, found it incredibly heavy. Finally I managed to skim a finger over taut muscle.

"Again?" a dark voice murmured against the inside of my knee. Even cooling from climax, his breath instantly heated my skin.

"Eventually." I nudged him half-heartedly. The floor was hard and cold on my back, but my front was deliciously warm.

He sighed, rolled off me with a grace and surprising technique that brought me up with him, cradled in his arms. "Bedroom?" he suggested. His eyes were already warming to violet.

"Weren't we arguing?"

"Let's skip to the part where we make up."

"I think we already did." I smiled and raised myself in his arms just enough to suckle his earlobe.

♫ ♫ ♫

Toward dawn, just after Julian left, a man broke into my bedroom.

The guy must have been waiting for it. Before Julian's side of the bed even cooled, mist swirled through the wall. Dark mist, curling out like clouds of smoke. The mist floated in, snapped into a man.

A red-eyed, skeletal man. A man with very long, very sharp fangs.

"If you're looking for Julian," I said, more boldly than I felt, "he just left. You can probably catch him if you scoot now."

"It is not Emerson I seek." The man's voice was hollow and lisping, like a fifties radio with too much treble. "It is *you* I seek,

Dietlinde Schmeling." On the *you* he pointed one long, pointy finger at me.

One *claw*.

From the voice I knew that this was the infamous Lord Ruthven. For one second I was scared. Then I remembered Julian saying Ruthven was a bit melodramatic. Over the top. Like a musician's makeup. The voice, the claw, was all part of the Ruthven act.

Besides, Ruthass used my daggy name, *again*. That was like a red flag to a bull. "Me? What do you want me for, Deep Throat?"

His eyes narrowed and went ruby-red. "I am Lord Ruthven. Fear me, Dietlinde Schmeling. Fear me, and flee. Flee from the city, lest I destroy you."

"Uh-huh. Well, I would, Ruthie, but I've got this festival thing to run. Maybe you've heard of it? The crunk-fest to raise enough kiss-ass-cash for Chicago's leet?"

The creep frowned, ever so slightly. Apparently being second in command of a gang didn't make him fluent in street language. "Do not fool with me, Dietlinde Schmeling."

The last refuge of the incompetent. If you don't get it, make threats. "Not fooling with you, Ruthie. Just explaining why I can't flee in terror. At least, not today. Talk to me again on Monday." And, heart thudding just a little, I turned my back on him and pretended to go to sleep.

He roared. "You will not ignore me, Dietlinde Schmeling!" Claws raked my shoulder, tearing away the covers. "You will fear the name of Lord Ruthven!"

I sat up abruptly. "Trim the nails, Ruthven!" Huffing, I checked out my shoulder. Four thin red lines marked my skin, one oozing a little. "Oh, great. I just got some new blood, and now you've let it out." I gave him a raised eyebrow. "Julian will not be happy about this."

Beast Boy smiled, not nice. "Emerson will do nothing, not after I finish with him."

"Don't you threaten Julian, you creep!" I lost it. Jumping out of bed, my hands went for his throat. I forgot I was naked.

Ruthven's eyes widened, and changed to a simmering blood-red. "Very nice."

I stopped in my tracks. "Hands off." I yanked my robe off the footboard of my bed. "Because if you touch me, Julian will be pissed. And so will I." I threw the robe on and tied it tight.

"It matters not. I will get my way in the end. I always do." Ruthven stalked closer. "The only question is, will you do as I say? Or will you *die*?"

"Threats," I sneered.

"Promises. You will fear me, Dietlinde Schmeling. For I am Ruler of the Night. I am *Undead*." He stretched menacing claws toward me.

"Ruler of the Night, huh? Now, that's a problem." Jumping back, I evaded his grasp. Smiling sweetly, I continued edging back.

"It is not a problem. It is *power*." Ruth-vain stalked after me.

"You might want to reconsider that." Without warning I snapped open my drapes. Dawn flooded the room.

Ruthven choked on a scream. His eyes squeezed shut and he took two stumbling steps back. His arm raised in front of his face, as if he was blocking a blow. Little wisps of smoke rose from his skin. "This isn't over, Dietlinde Schmeling!" Turning, he fled from the room.

"Yeah, yeah," I taunted, a little cocky. Vampires weren't so almighty infallible. And this Lord Ruthie guy wasn't such hot stuff.

I admit it. I was pleased with myself. After all, my showing this time was much better than the last. I didn't always need hulking great Julian Emerson to save me. Smug, I pulled out my cell phone to call him and give him the 411. And maybe to gloat a little.

The line didn't even have a chance to ring before Julian answered. "Nixie?" His voice was a little hoarse, but I'd made him yell a couple times last night. Kinda loud. "Is something wrong?"

So I boasted about what had just happened. Julian listened without interrupting, which I wasn't expecting. But his reaction at the end more than made up for it. "What the hell did you think you were doing? Ruthven is no fledgling, to be taunted without fear of repercussion!" He added, almost muttering to himself, "Why did it have to be Ruthven? Of all of them, why him?"

"Don't be so upset, Julian. You're the one who said he's more bark than bite."

"I beg your pardon?"

He was so language-challenged. It was kinda cute, actually. "A real drama-llama. You know. Melodramatic."

I heard some Boston-accented sputtering. Finally Julian said, "Melodramatic doesn't mean Ruthven's not dangerous!"

"But I beat him. Last I saw he was running for the hills."

"Ruthven was running for *shade*. Which means he'll be somewhere close!" Julian added several words, vehement enough to be cussing, but no words I'd ever heard. Weirdly, they sounded a little like Latin.

"Julian...what do you mean by 'close'?" The hair on my neck stood up, thinking of that creepy vampire somewhere...close.

"He's probably in your basement. But that's not important now."

"Excuse me?! I think a vampire in the basement might be very important!"

"No. Happens all the time. The problem is that this time it's Ruthven, and he's been challenged by a pint-sized chew toy! Damn. I can't get there. Butler's out with the limo."

"Wait, wait...this happens *all* the time? There are vampires in the basement and nobody knows!?" I couldn't help it, my voice went high and squeaky. It is a measure of how much the idea of vampires in the basement freaked me out that I completely ignored the chew-toy comment.

"Well, where do you expect them to be if they're in a human's house when dawn comes? Fuck. Ruthven's *there* and I'm stuck on the other side of town!"

"Stop, stop! What do you mean, inside a human's house? You mean humans invite vampires into their homes?"

"That's just an old wives' tale, Nixie. Vampires can break into homes as easily as humans. Easier."

"Burglars, right? You mean vampires steal money? And...small electronics and stuff?"

"Some of that, yes. But mostly they steal blood."

"Blood!"

"Of course. Surely you're not that naive? Not all vampires live in civilized households. But this is all utterly and idiotically beside the point. How fast can you get to the Strongwells?"

With vampires-in-the-basement motivation? "I'm there already."

"You'd better be," Julian said, and hung up.

Chapter Twenty-two

In the end, I couldn't leave without Oscar.

I rationalized it, telling myself I'd need my instruments for tonight's gig. In reality, the thought of my baby, alone in the house with a crazy vampire, scared me shitless. Besides, Ruthven was playing Toastie-Os the last I saw him. He'd have to hang out in the basement a while to heal, right? Maybe an hour or two?

I had forgotten it took Julian less than three minutes to recover.

It was more like five minutes before I was ready to go. Finally, Oscar in one hand, clarinet over my shoulder, I ran through the living room to the front door.

A black cloud rose in front of me. I screeched to a stop.

The mist resolved to Ruthven, fire-free this time. "You aren't going anywhere, blood-bitch."

"That's what you think!" I swung Oscar's case hard. I was scared, I was desperate, and I was willing to bet all my chips that one hundred seventy pounds of vampire couldn't withstand a full-bodied smack from a Strat case.

Lord Ruthie decided he didn't want to play Las Vegas odds. Fast—almost too fast to see—he moved behind me. Grabbed me by the neck. I turtled. Snatched at his fingers to peel them from my throat. Jerked my hands back in shock. My fingers felt like I'd shoved them down the garbage disposal.

His were crowned by inch-long claws. My blood dripped over them.

I nearly went all trembly-shocky again. Nearly did the great digestion ejection. After all, I was still pretty new to this whole vampires-are-real thing.

Then Lord Ruthass said, "You are now mine, Dietlinde Schmeling. You will become my helpless blood slave. You will do as I say. Everything I say. I look forward to your submission."

"You *what*?"

My whole life people have been trying to make me conform. *Do this, Dietlinde. Do that. Why can't you be more like that nice Anna Versnobt?* Sometimes the whole of Meiers Corners seemed bent on jamming my round peg in their square hole.

I tried to fit in, for my parents. Failed often and miserably, but at least I tried. I tried for my friends. I even tried, sometimes, for Vice Principal Schleck.

But for Ruthven? Who'd this jerk think he was?

My stomach settled, my mind cleared. All I had to do was get out the door. I was small and human, slow compared to a superhuman.

But I wasn't helpless.

Ruthven stood directly behind me. With the difference in our heights, I was in effect under him, like a set of Russian stack-dolls. Without warning I launched myself upwards.

I caught Ruthven good, the top of my skull crashing into his jaw. Even with his supernatural reflexes, he couldn't avoid getting a nasty crack. Oh, sure, it hurt me, too. Stars of pain exploded in my head. But Ruthven got the worse end of the deal. Skull trumps jaw, every time. Even vampire-hard jaw.

The surprise blow gave me only a few seconds. But with my training, that was long enough. I back-kicked Ruthven in the stomach. Feeling his gut implode and hearing a satisfying wet retch, I yanked up Oscar and tore out the door.

Julian was pacing the foyer of Bo's apartment building when I got there. The door was propped open despite the chill of the day—and despite the bright sunshine. Little wisps of smoke came off Julian's face and hands. I thought it was vampire reaction to the light, but he might have been just that pissed.

He saw me and was instantly there, sweeping me off my feet into a great hug. Little flames began to dance on his skin. He ignored them. "What the fuck took you so long?"

"I ran into a 'spot of trouble'." I was grinning like an idiot.

"Let's get you inside before I have to find those asbestos gloves."

"You're enjoying this!" He held me at arm's length and gaped at me. His eyes were red, his face plated as if he was fighting. At the same time his skin was flaming and he was gasping, as if it was hard for him to breathe.

"I'm not enjoying it." I pulled him toward the door. "It's just nice to know you can lose your cool once in a while." Especially when I actually was keeping mine.

"I lose my cool, as you put it, far too often around you." We dragged each other into the foyer. I dumped my instruments while Julian doubled over, panting.

Elena came running into the foyer. "Nixie! Are you all right?"

"Dine and fandy. Everything set for tonight? Beauty pageant and all?"

"How can you worry about the festival? I heard that awful Ruthven attacked you!"

"The festival is my anti-Ruthass spray. How else am I going to make sure Ruthie never shows up again? This town ain't big enough for the both of us." All right, maybe some of the cheerfulness was dumped adrenalin and delayed reaction. But it felt so damned good to be safe. So good to be with my friends and loved ones.

I meant Oscar. Loved ones, as in Oscar. And...my clarinet.

"Elena," Bo's voice came from the kitchen. "Where's Julian? I just got a call—" He emerged from the kitchen and saw us all in the foyer. "What's going on?"

So I had to explain it again, including the part where Ruthven came on to me a second time, which Julian hadn't heard. When I finished, he grabbed me. "Damn it, Nixie. Until this thing is over, I'm not letting you out of my sight!"

That abruptly sobered me. "This thing" would be over Sunday night. And with it, *my* thing, with Julian. He would leave, fly back to Boston, I would never see Not-So-Stodgy Suitguy again.

"That's one of the reasons I came up," Bo said. "I just took a call from the Watch. The Lestats are planning to disrupt the fundraiser tonight."

Elena said, "Why am I not surprised?"

"The Watch?" I asked. "Your neighborhood watch?"

Elena put a hand on my arm. "Nixie...I'm sorry, but I fibbed about that, too. The Watch is a network of vampires who protect humans. They're sometimes called Lords of the Night. They have eyes and ears everywhere. Bo's one of them. So's Julian."

While I tried to absorb this, I heard Julian speaking to Bo. "We'll have to put guards at every function."

"Yes, of course," Bo said. "I'll contact all my people immediately."

"Do you have enough?" Julian asked.

"Wait." I frowned at Julian. "Guards? What do you mean, guards?"

It was Bo who replied. "One of us will have to be at every event. I'm already on the beauty pageant. Thorvald can guard the families at the church."

"One of—*us*?" I was shocked. "You mean vampires? You're placing *vampires* at the festival?"

Julian said, "Don't worry, Nixie. No one will know. We'll pass as humans."

Bo said, "As would the Lestats, until it was too late."

"It's the only way to identify the gang," Elena reassured me. "Vampires can recognize other vampires even when humans can't. I guess it's a smell thing. So we'll have Thor at the church, and who else?"

Bo was ticking up fingers. "Steve can enter the Sheepshead Tournament at Nieman's."

"That still leaves the beer tent, the VIP reception, and the Pie Delight," Julian said. "And the bands."

"Wait." I was struggling to keep up. "*Steve*? As in Elena's brother-in-law? I don't mean to be insensitive but...isn't he dead?" I'd attended the funeral last year.

"Living-impaired," Elena said. "The Sheepshead Tournament is perfect for him. He plays a mean leaster."

"But...Steve's a vampire? I thought he died during a mugger's attack."

"He and Gretchen were attacked, but by vampires. Bo got there in time to rescue Gretchen. They killed Steve."

My head was spinning. "But...he's not dead? He's a

vampire now? How long have you known? Does *everyone* know but me?"

Elena put a comforting hand on my shoulder. "Remember, I didn't know until a few months ago. And no one outside of Bo's household has a clue."

"I can't believe you didn't tell me that Steve's still alive!" I thought our talk at the Caffeine Café had bared everything, or at least most everything. It had hardly scratched the surface. I saw why people go zip plus four, if coworkers were half as aggro as *friends*. "I'm gonna grill you like a Polish sausage after this festival is over. Fine. If no one knows Steve is semi-alive, how can he show up at the tournament? Won't people talk?"

"Nah. Remember, Steve had a closed coffin. We'll say he wasn't really dead. That when he revived, he'd lost his memory and wandered off. He only recovered his memory recently."

"Stark will back us up," Bo said. "He'll say he found Steve's coffin empty, but was too embarrassed to say anything, and simply closed the casket."

I put a hand over my eyes but it didn't stop the kaleidoscope in my brain. "Stark...you mean Solomon Stark, of Stark and Moss Funeral Homes? Why would he do that?"

"He's one of us. Hey." Bo ticked up another finger. "That's who can take the VIP opening."

My jaw hit the floor so hard it bounced and I bit my tongue. "Wait, wait! Steve and Stark are both vampires? Is *all* of Meiers Corners vampy?"

Elena laughed. "No, of course not. Only Steve and Thor in Bo's household, and Stark. And the occasional rogue passing through. Oh, and Drusilla."

"Yeah, Dru." Bo ticked up a fourth finger. "She can take the beer tent."

That cut through the merry-go-round in my head. "No," I said. "No way. Good idea—having guests for Thanksgiving. Bad idea—having Tom Turkey as a guest for Thanksgiving. Good idea—putting a vampire guard at the beer tent with a bunch of drunks. Bad idea—putting Double-D Drusilla in with a bunch of drunks."

"I see your point," Bo said. Elena slapped his arm. Bo gave her a quick kiss. "All right, Dru can do the cake contest. We'll have to bring people in to police the beer tent and bands. And to watch over the pedestrians."

"Not people," I said to no one in particular. "Vampires."

"I'll call down to Iowa," Julian said. "The Ancient One should be able to loan us a few trained helpers."

Bo shook his head. "That's the other thing I came up for. He's already sending us half a dozen. They'll arrive at sunset. That's the other piece of news.

"There's going to be a hit on the Blood Center this weekend."

♫ ♫ ♫

"This is suicide," I said, watching Julian. "That's a high-tech piece of equipment. Much more powerful than you're used to. You'll never learn to use it in time."

"Don't worry so much," he replied. "It's no more complicated than Elena's SMAW. It'll just take some adjustment."

"It's not a damned bicycle, Emerson. And you hold it this way!"

I grabbed the borrowed Gibson (a Les Paul Classic) from between his folded legs and thrust it at his chest. "Sideways! Not up and down. Oh, it's hopeless."

"I was just recalling the finger positions." Julian put the guitar back between his legs like some punk cello, and touched his fingertips to the wire strings. "There's more tension in the strings than I remember."

"You don't do finger *positions*. You do chords." I twisted his hand on the fingerboard, bent his second and third fingers down. "That's E minor." It was the easiest chord I could think of.

"I know that, Nixie. I played gamba, remember? Tuned a step lower, but the fingerings are the same."

"Oh, don't get so superior on me! That's like saying you can drive a car because in the eighteen hundreds you knew how to saddle a horse!"

"It's not that different—"

"It is too!" I paced the small bedroom where we were

213

practicing. "We are so screwed."

"Have you ever saddled a horse?"

"No, but—"

"Then don't jump to conclusions." Still with the guitar between his knees, Julian strummed a quick Em-G-D-Bm progression.

"Fine. So you know some basics. But as lead guitar you can't just do chords. You have to do riffs and melody and—"

"No problem. I also played a bit of psaltery." Julian laid the guitar across his lap and plucked "Greensleeves"—melody and harmony and a rather impressive interlude.

"Okay, maybe it's not hopeless," I said, wavering. "Do you know anything post-Renaissance?"

"A little." He turned the guitar flat to his abdomen and picked in quick sequence a Bach theme, a Mozart motif, a Tchaikovsky melody, and something that sounded remarkably like Stravinsky's *Firebird*. My jaw dropped. In thirty seconds he'd done a four-century hit parade, then to now.

"Showoff. Okay, you're good. But can you hardcore?"

He pointed to the CD player. "You were going to play me an example."

Guns and Polkas had made a couple CDs by now. I started with the one where Durango had been drunk.

"Seems a little sloppy." Julian frowned as he fingered along with the recording.

"Uh, yeah." Julian had a good ear, too, if he could tell that. "Let me play you another." I put on the CD where Durango had actually practiced. Julian's fingers flew over the fingerboard, not making a sound, but it looked like he knew what he was doing.

After the track ended, Julian nodded. "I've got it. Play the next one."

"Don't you want to hear it again? Or try it with the amp...?"

"It's two o'clock, Nixie. I have a half-hour's worth of music to learn and we still have to build me a costume. That's not including the time you'll need to get ready. And both of us have to make sure our people are in place at the festival venues."

"Uh, yeah." No rehearsal, and a single run-through of the tunes. I could only hope Julian Emerson was half as good as he thought he was.

As he fingered along, Julian said casually, "So are you going to tell me?"

"Tell you what?"

"Why you've been so irritable?"

"I'm not irritable." I might have snapped it.

"No, of course not. Or even a little blue." Julian fingered a complicated set of chords that had taken Durango two months to learn.

He was so dangerously perceptive. Even when I wasn't thinking about my life ending Monday, he got it. He saw it. I crossed my arms over my chest, an ineffective shield for my far-too-visible emotions. "I'm *not* irritable. Or sad. Just...harassed. Because of the festival."

"It was worse when I came back from Boston."

"Yeah, well, you try going two whole days without sex. See how irritable you get."

"I did. And I was. But not like you." He flew a solo across the fretboard.

"The festival—"

"—isn't the reason. Or not the main reason. I know you by now, Nixie." He stopped playing and hit me with his most penetrating stare. "What's wrong, sweetheart? Maybe I can help."

Fuck. I caved. "It's...the insurance. I need it, because of the Lestats. But the only way to pay for it was to...I have to...Julian, I'm selling myself!"

Years of Vice Principal Schleck hadn't done it. Seeing blood hadn't done it. Hordes of revenant monsters hadn't even done it. But this did.

I threw myself into Julian's arms and started bawling.

He patted my back and made soothing noises. The Les Paul lay between us, strings cutting into my breasts. I didn't care. The pain seemed right, somehow. Clean.

As I wound down, Julian offered me a box of tissues. I pulled one and sopped tears. "It's just that...I'll be like everyone else now. Nine-to-five Jane Doe."

"A martyr to pantyhose and heels." Julian smiled and wiped under my nose.

"And I'm not even doing it so I can buy a new guitar or

something cool. I'm doing it because of the festival. Because I'm *responsible*. Following the Rules. Damn it, Julian. I'm becoming my mother!"

"Nixie. What would happen if I played viola da gamba with Guns and Polkas instead of this guitar?"

It took me a second to switch topics. "Julian, you can't! It would sound...weird. Like music frosted with Muzak."

"And if I played guitar, but tuned a quarter tone sharp?"

"*What*? What kind of musician are you? Do you scrape your nails down a chalkboard and call it music?"

"So are you saying that in music, you follow the rules?"

My lips kept flapping but no sound came out. I think because my face had hit the floor. "Well...I guess I do." Me. Free Nixie. I followed rules. "But not always!" I grabbed onto the thought like a lifesaver. "I also improvise."

"You improvise solos." Julian started fingering along with the CD again. "But if everyone improvised at the same time, what would happen?"

"It would be disaster..." I frowned. "That wasn't a change of topics, was it."

"No." Julian smiled. "Freedom in music is all about knowing *when* to be free. Follow the rules when playing together, and improvise the solos. Life can be the same way."

"It can?"

"Do you remember me telling you I had an epiphany at your parents' home?"

"Yeah. I looked it up on dictionary.com. Epiphany. Means a flash of insight."

"Well, my flash of insight had to do with the time I fell in with William the Bloody and his out-of-control crowd. When I burned down a building in the name of artistic *freedom*."

"Sure. Guilt made you the tight-assed guy you are today." I dropped a look at his ass, grade super-tight, and licked my chops.

Julian grinned, then sobered. "I thought *freedom* was the problem. But I was wrong. The problem was being creative at the wrong time."

I started to get it. "Like driving on the freeway. It'd be hell if everyone decided for themselves which way to go."

"Exactly. As long as I'm careful and controlled in public, what's to stop me from being a little creative in private?"

Thinking of just how creative Julian got in private, I shivered. "So how does this all apply to me?"

"One thought springs to mind."

I tried to see what he meant. Failed utterly. "Um...make that thought pole-vault?"

He laughed. "The same thing applies to you, but in reverse. You need coverage for liability and damages. That's following the rules. But how you get the coverage can be creative."

I sucked in a breath as it clicked. "Like having Woofers 'R Us insure their own equipment?"

"Yes. And Nieman's Bar has insurance. Probably all the commercial venues do."

"And the city will cover things that happen on the street and sidewalk. But...what about the beer tent?"

"Are the exhibitors paying an entrance fee?"

"Yes, but I can't ask for more at this late date."

"No, but the spaces they rent can be considered their storefront. And thereby under *their* insurance."

"And the general area?"

"Buy an umbrella liability policy. At one-tenth the space that's only $2,000."

"Two thousand through CIC Mutual. It's even less if I go with one of the other companies. CIC was fifty percent off because of the employee discount—what?"

Julian's eyes had flashed instantly to red and his strumming had changed to picking. Claw picking. "CIC? You were going to work for CIC?"

"Well, only because of the employee deal. Why?"

"CIC Mutual. One of the Coterie Insurance Companies."

"Fuck."

"I agree."

I pulled out my cell phone. And before I even canceled the insurance policy, I called CIC to quit.

Chapter Twenty-three

I felt a hundred pounds lighter. In fact I was floating on air when we left the practice room to find Julian a costume.

We decided with the crunch factor to check Julian's clothes for something suitable. As we headed for the basement steps, Elena stopped me and gave me a flashlight.

I looked at her strangely. "Didn't you pay your electric bill either?"

"Not exactly." She opened the door to the basement, and I traipsed down, Julian following.

At the bottom of the stairs I stopped. Looked around, bewildered. It was a basement, okay fine. But it was an *unfinished* basement. Laundry machines, some clothesline, and a few storage shelves. No bedrooms. Not even a spare cot. Nothing beyond the washers, dryers, boxes, and shelves.

Until Julian opened a door at the far side of the basement wall. Flicked on a light switch.

I joined him. "Whoa. Where'd that come from?" A hallway stretched beyond.

Beautiful hardwood floor. Long, plush runner, looked Oriental. Eight carved wood doors, four on each side. Oil paintings hung between the doors, not your starving-artist kind. Old-fashioned crystal wall sconces gave the hall an eighteenth-century glow. "Last door on the right." Julian held out his hand, indicating I should go first.

I slid into the corridor. A smell tickled my memory, like fresh rain. It gave way to lemon polish and scented candle wax as I moved toward the far end.

Opening the last door on the right, I felt around for a light switch. Nothing. "Where's the light?"

Julian took my flashlight and flicked it on. "As I said, a little dark." Handing the flashlight back, he made his way into the room. I followed more cautiously. As soon as I let go of the door, it slammed shut behind me.

I jumped. "*This* is where you're staying?" Just a little spooked, I shined the light into Julian's face. His eyes glowed red like an animal's at night. It was not reassuring.

He pulled me into his arms, gave me a quick hug. Fears receded. "Bachelor's quarters. Bo and Elena have lights. The bathroom is over there, if you need it." He nudged the flashlight until it shone on a doorway to my left.

"You don't need light to see?" Even cats needed some light.

"No. We think our eyes generate their own light. Or maybe it's some kind of heat vision."

"You mean you don't *know*?"

"We heal too fast to need doctors. And we stay clear of human medics. Our physiology isn't exactly normal."

"I guess not, with your mouth leading to your blood system and all."

"But we're here for a costume." Julian left me and I heard the sound of drawers being pulled, punctuated by muttering. "I wasn't expecting this kind of performance."

Slowly turning in place, I shined the flashlight over the room. Good-sized. He was right about that. The floor had thick carpeting over what felt like a plenum. More art hung on the walls...was that a Goya? Bookshelves were stocked full. An armoire and two chests of drawers for clothes.

And a huge four-poster bed. Ooh. That had possibilities.

"What about this?"

I twitched the flashlight from the bed to Julian holding a black V-neck sweater to his chest. "Cashmere?"

"Yes."

"Uh, no." I pointed the flashlight at the bed again. Four black walnut spires. Lapping the shore of the bedrails was the Pacific Ocean of mattresses, a mile wide and two miles thick. Looked really soft.

And really bouncy. Ideas flew through my brain involving me, Julian, and that trampoline of a bed.

"This?"

I flashed back and nearly choked when I saw what he held. "Three-piece suits for rock and roll went out in the fifties."

He gave a disgusted snort. "You look, then."

Curious as to what a bloodsucking supernatural vampire might wear, I did.

Turned out supernatural bloodsuckers wore pretty much what regular bloodsuckers did. Suits, ties, shirts. Italian shoes.

Then, in the bottom drawer, I came across leathers. "Biker leathers?"

"I bought them with the bike."

"Sweet." I pulled out the buttery-soft black pants, considered them. They were big in my hands, but they'd be tight on Julian. "You have boots to go with these?"

"Of course."

I dug until I found a wide, studded belt. "And a jacket?"

"Yes, but...oh, I see where you're going. But I don't have any pop music tees. The closest I have are white undershirts."

I smiled, pulled loose his old school tie. "Oh, I think you have something perfect for popular music." I removed his shirt and slipped my hands under his tee. "Your naked chest will be very popular." I pulled off the undershirt, and rubbed my palms over his silky-smooth skin.

"Nixie. We don't have a lot of time." He grimaced. "And the bed's been made..."

"We have three minutes." I pressed a kiss to his lovely abs. "And let me show you what I can do standing up."

♫ ♫ ♫

We left well before sunset to check out the venues. I wanted to make double-sure everything was set for the festival opening at four thirty. We took the limo. Before I got in I whispered a slight change in route to Daniel Butler.

As we rolled away from the curb I checked Julian's costume. He looked every bit as yummy in his tight leather pants as I thought he would. And his muscular torso was as gorgeous as a da Vinci oil in the sleek frame of his open leather jacket. I adjusted the jacket collar, couldn't resist touching the smooth, round pectoral beneath...encountered something long and hard.

Pulling the jacket open I stared at a handle sticking out of an inner pocket. "What's this?"

"My weapon." Julian pulled out a rod about a foot long and a couple inches around. He touched somewhere on the rod. A long blade snicked out, so fast it was only a silver blur. "It's a swing-guard stiletto."

"A stiletto, huh?" I ran a finger along the handle. It was covered in black leather lacing, with a brown Celtic-looking knot woven in. It looked like the hilt of a sword. In fact, the size of the thing made me think less "knife" and more "sword". "Do you all carry these?"

"At times. Depending on where we are and what we're doing. This is my patrol blade. I have a smaller one for general public wear and a larger one for ceremonial purposes."

I traced my finger onto the metal. A groove down the blade made it look more like a sword, too. Oddly enough, a bead of silver-colored metal ran just behind the edge. And there was a strange little etching near the hilt. "What's this?" I pointed at the etching.

"The symbol of my allegiance. A sickle-sword."

"Vampires have countries?"

Julian smiled. "No. We have factions, though. There's been infighting since the beginning. So we have alliances. And at certain points in our lives we go through changes. It helps to have an older vampire guide us through them."

"So you have allegiances. Huh. And the line of stuff that looks like silver?"

"Is silver. It helps make vampire flesh more vulnerable to the blade."

"Wow. Then the whole silver allergy thing is real?"

That made Julian laugh. "Not as you're thinking. Pure silver burns a little. Like a cut stings from alcohol." He flicked the blade closed.

The limo slowed. Julian sat forward as he stowed his weapon. Frowned as we pulled up in front of Dolly Barton's Curl Up and Dye. "What are we doing here?"

"Just a last-minute addition to your costume." I jumped out and ran to the door, held it open. Smiled encouragement.

Shaking his head, Julian jumped out after me. He didn't flow, because there were a dozen people staring at him from the shop windows. But he ran fast.

I worried he'd be smoking by the time he made it inside, but it wasn't noon, and he only looked unusually flushed. Hot. But that was okay, because with his leather pants tight over his taut ass and the leather jacket framing his bare muscular chest, he *looked* hot.

In fact, half the women were panting. The other half were drooling. And I won't say what the men were doing because there were only two, and one was Doyle "Doily" Hartung, the only openly gay man in Meiers Corners. The other was Bruno. Though Bruno cross-dresses, he's not gay. But I got a fleeting impression that for Julian, he'd reconsider.

"Hey, sugar!" A small, buxom blonde swept over, scissors in hand and an intent look in her eye. Dolly Barton is the world's leading gossip. She knows everything that goes on in Meiers Corners, sometimes before it happens. Even God gets his gossip from Dolly. "Is this that hunk of yours I keep hearing about?" She eyed Julian like a tall T-bone steak. "Mmm-mmm."

"Uh, yeah." Not *my* hunk, but still. Mine for tonight. "Julian is playing with the band. He needs a bit of jewelry to complete his costume."

"Jewelry?" Julian gave me a sharp look.

"Jewelry." Dolly considered him with hand on chin and nodded. "An earring, of course."

"Of course," I echoed.

"An earring?!" Julian looked at me like I'd gone mad. He motioned me to him and bent. "What are you thinking?" he hissed in my ear. "My skin heals too fast to poke a hole for an earring!"

"Does your DVD flash twelve?" I asked in wonder. How did this antique male ever function in the Quark Age? "They use a gun, now. *Kerchunk*, in." I made a shooting motion.

Julian frowned, but when Dolly brought over a selection of starter studs, he let me pick out a very hawt one-carat diamond.

Then I saw the price tag. "Um...can I pay for it in

installments? Maybe, uh, ten bucks a month?" For the next twenty years.

"I'll pay." Sighing, Julian whipped out his credit card.

I craned my neck to see what an über-successful attorney used for plastic these days. He tossed it to Dolly too fast for me to see clearly, but it might have been platinum—or maybe white gold, studded with pearls and emeralds and featuring a very nice five-carat radiant-cut diamond. Okay, I was exaggerating with the diamond.

Julian wasn't very happy, but he would try it. For me. He was trying it, for my sake. Because I wanted it. I felt...I don't really know what I felt, but it was warm, and a little fuzzy, and a lot tingly.

Dolly ran the card, whistled. "A quarter million limit?"

"Dolly!" I said. "How did you find that out?"

Dolly shrugged. "I have the extended credit service. Here's your card, Mr. Emerson. Have a seat."

Almost gingerly, Julian sat. When Dolly approached him with the gun, he winced. His eyes found mine and he glared. As if saying, "If this goes wrong, it's on your head." Dolly put the gun to his ear, moved it up and a bit forward. Then—*kerchunk*! It was done. Julian didn't even flinch.

"Do you like it?" Dolly held up a mirror for Julian to see. Now all the women were both panting and drooling. Doily Hartung adjusted his pants, and Bruno started looking at the remaining studs like maybe he'd get one too.

But Julian ignored the mirror and looked straight at me. "Do *you* like it?"

Did I like it? Ab-so-fucking-lutely. It looked just like I knew it would. I couldn't wait to taste his earlobe with that sparkly nonpareil in it. "Oh, yeah," I breathed. "It looks utterly hawt."

Julian nodded and stood. "Thank you, Ms. Barton." It looked like he was going to stride straight out, but at the last moment he turned and faced the drooling women. "I hope you all will patronize the festival tonight." He stood extremely straight, his chest jutting out, and I think one nipple winked.

"Oh, we *will*!" the women cooed, practically in unison. When Julian turned and we left, one actually fainted. I heard the thud even though I didn't see it.

Or maybe that was Doily Hartung.

Our first stop was the Roller-Blayd factory, where the bands were playing. We had to drop off our instruments before checking the other venues. Wouldn't do to meet any fangy-gangy guys with our hands full.

Since Julian would already be onsite, performing with Guns and Polkas, he was going to be the band guard. While he wouldn't quite blend, he wouldn't stick out in a fangy sort of way, either.

I almost didn't recognized the factory without boards. The inside was still the same, though—concrete slab floor, metal walls, and air. And *live*. Sound bouncing everywhere, booming and echoing like a cathedral, or like putting your head in a tin can. Hopefully it would be different with a crowd. Otherwise there would be a lot more people with handicapped parking stickers and I'd be buying stock in hearing aids.

As we walked in, activity churned around us. The high school football team, hired by Josiah Moss, were setting up chairs and stages. Guys from Woofers 'R Us were installing four six-foot-tall speakers. Lob was there to test all the equipment. The bands would sound good tonight.

Toward the back someone had cleared off a couple wooden pallets for stacking instrument cases and coats. Boxes of old roller blades and the rest of the pallets were pushed into the unlit area behind the stages. Julian and I headed back.

"Mr. Emerson. Mr. Emerson, wait up!" a voice like a cheap trumpet brayed. With a burgeoning sense of dread, Julian and I stopped.

Up swept a cheesy bow tie. Yellow and red tonight, but the ripsaw grin was the same. Lew Kaufman, $uper$alesman. "How ya doin', Mr. Emerson? And Nixie Emerson! Glad to see you, glad to see you!"

I stopped at the name. Names have power, and I waited for the kick in the gut from this one. Nixie Suit. Nixie One-Step-To-Death. Nixie...Emerson.

No kick came. It sounded, well, kind of nice.

Lew stuck out his hand for a shake. Julian, who was brave in the face of ravening vampires and earstud guns, turned and would have run if I hadn't put hands to his chest. His hard, muscular chest, yum. But now wasn't the time.

I grabbed Lew's mitt, put it in Julian's. Lew pumped his, then mine. "Glad to see especially you, Nixie, 'cause I have some news."

"News?"

"Yeah, I got on the horn to my suppliers. But, well, this is kind of embarrassing."

I wondered what he was talking about. Then I remembered siccing Brunhilde Butt on him when someone had torched the cheese balls. At the time I stamped it "problem solved" and hadn't given it another thought.

"I tried, Nixie. But I couldn't get enough."

"Enough what?" I really didn't know. Lew could sell Buddhism to the Pope. It really hadn't occurred to me that he meant what he did.

"It would have been fine if the ones with the nuts had melted. My suppliers had plenty of those. But the plain cheese balls...well, they won't have any in until tomorrow."

"What?!" Like the Royal Canadian Mounties, it was unheard-of for Lew not to get his man...er, balls...er, well.

"So I did what I had to do, Nixie. It's not like most people will notice."

"Most people won't notice what?" I got a cold, foreboding feeling. "What have you done, Lew?"

"I, um, called your mother."

"My mother!" I already owed her for the little math geeks. And now I owed her for cheese b—oh, no. Please, no. Not even Ruthven was as deadly as the peril facing me now. "Couldn't you have tried your backups? Why did you ask *my mother*?"

"I had to, Nixie," Lew said, almost pleading. "It was the only way I could supply for tonight. I tried my alternate vendors. I even tried my alternate-alternate vendors. Nobody had any balls, except with nuts. Which we already have."

Or a nut with balls, I thought, giving Lew the evil eye. Unfortunately he did not burst into flames and melt too.

"Tomorrow we'll have plenty, of all kinds. I've got a rush shipment coming from Munroe. But tonight...well, it had to be the Lutheran Ladies Auxiliary Mothers Association."

"But Lew! The LLAMA ladies make the worst cheese balls in

the state! The world!"

"They're not that bad," he said, but his wince told another story.

"They *are* that bad, and you know it! Who the hell else makes cheese balls out of head cheese and blood sausage?"

Head "cheese", for the blissfully unaware, was not cheese at all. It was boiled-down head of baby cow. Barfarific. You could also make head cheese out of pig head. But that wasn't really any better.

And blood sausage? Yep. Boiled-down blood. Yum-yum. You were never supposed to watch the making of sausage or politics, but it weren't nuthin' on the Lutheran Ladies Auxiliary cheese balls.

"I really don't think anyone will notice, Nixie," Lew repeated, giving me a pat. "Well, I only needed to tell you the sad news. Got to run. Nice seeing you, Mr. Emerson. Knock 'em dead." He stopped, gave Julian a frown. "Is that a new shirt?"

Julian shrugged, pulled me with him toward the far end of the warehouse. Lew let us escape, but it didn't matter. I felt like falling to my knees and whacking my head on the concrete. "We're ruined, I tell you. Ruined!"

"Because of cheese balls?" Julian dropped off his Les Paul. He pulled Oscar from me and set him down next to the Gibson's case. Oscar sort of leaned into the Gibson, like he was snuggling up. It would have been cute if I hadn't been Doomed.

"*Cheese* balls. Hah. Like they're made out of cheese. That's as optimistic as school lunch mock-chicken legs." I shook my head. "I watched my mother's church group make cheese balls one time. They use pus and mayonnaise, Julian. And that's just the base. Then they mix in the most disgusting things they can find—goat entrails and bull semen and heaven knows what else. Meiers Corners regulars avoid the LLAMA's cheese balls— even when they're drunk! Oh, those poor unsuspecting tourists!" Remembering the schedule, I slapped my forehead. "And the cheese ball tasting is already open. I have to do something!" I ran back toward the entrance, intent on getting to the Deli Delight before too much damage had been done.

Only to snap back as Julian caught my arm and tugged. "We can't worry about that now, Nixie." He nodded toward the door.

Five huge guys had just entered, wearing ripped jeans and sporting enough jewelry to count as the national treasury of a small South American country. They were carrying instrument cases.

"They're a band." Although I didn't recall which one.

Julian's nostrils flared. "They're vampires."

"OMG." The last band at auditions, when I was so desperate to get laid I would have signed up the Martian Kazoo Band. "How come you couldn't tell Monday?"

"They were downwind. And my senses were concentrated on a—different smell." Julian's growl had gone to his chest, like some feral cold.

"Shit. Are they Lestats?"

"Maybe. I know all of Nosferatu's lieutenants, and those aren't his. They might be Ruthven's specials."

"I thought Nosferatu and Ruthven were part of the same hinky group of suits. The Dove-ery."

"The Coterie, and they are. But that doesn't mean they work together. Damn it, Ruthven himself was bad enough. We don't need his lieutenants on top of it."

I was still trying to work it out. "So Nosy sends his gang to rough us up. But Ruthie sends a separate gang—why?"

Julian shrugged, but his stance was all aggression, and his eyes never left the five vampires. "Ruthven thinks Nosferatu is too soft on humans. Ruthven hasn't actually challenged Nosferatu for leadership, but it's just a matter of time. Oh, why the hell Ruthven, and why now?"

Ruthie was a vampire. Ruthie wanted to run the Coterie. The Coterie wanted Meiers Corners's blood. I stared at Julian while the pieces fell into place in my mind.

I turned the completed puzzle over in my head. It explained why Ruthven was here. It explained why his goons were here. It explained why now. It also predicted exactly when the attack on the Blood Center would be. But could it really be so simple? "You couldn't have told me this any earlier? Like, in time to stop thousands of tourists from coming tonight?"

"Even Ruthven's not insane enough to give us away to a large group of humans. The tourists are safe." Julian watched the approaching vampires with the attention of a hunting tiger.

The five vampires, trooping menacingly toward the humans setting up the stage, caught sight of Julian and stopped. Dropping their cases (the cracks as the instruments hit concrete made me wince) they huddled to confer.

"That big one next to the guy with the mullet is Billy the Kid," Julian said. "Definitely Ruthven's."

I felt my eyes widen. "*The* Billy the Kid?"

"His father. Although he doesn't acknowledge it." Julian's jaw clenched. "Damn. I wish I knew why Ruthven was taking such a personal interest in this."

"*The* Billy the Kid's *father*?"

"He's one of Ruthven's best. Why is he here? Hell, why is Ruthven here?"

"You mean...you really don't know?" That surprised me enough to forget the Billster. Usually Julian was as quick, or quicker, than me. "Julian, think. There's only one answer."

His head swiveled instantly toward me. "There is?" I had his full attention, and even though it wasn't *that kind* of attention, it made me shiver and lick my lips.

Down, girl. I had some exposition to do. "Sure. Why is the Coterie trying to take over Meiers Corners?"

"Because of the Blood Center."

"And Ruthven wants to take over the Coterie."

"Yes, but—oh. Damn. Damn, damn, damn." Julian went on to swear in another six languages. I was impressed.

Ruthie's interest made sense if you knew Meiers Corners had a blood distribution center. It made even more sense when you factored in the big shipment of blood going out tomorrow.

Because that meant hundreds of gallons were sitting there *tonight*. "Wouldn't Ruthass be in a better position to challenge Nosferatu if he controlled three thousand pints of blood?"

Julian's answer was to swear even more. Which, I guess, was answer enough.

While he was reciting the Oxford Dictionary of Cuss, I phoned Elena. She put me on speaker phone and I relayed my theory to her and Bo. For a moment I heard stereo swearing, Julian in one ear and Bo in the other. Only Bo's swearing sounded more like *føkka bjeller drittsekk*.

"I'm sure you're right," Elena said to me. "It all adds up."

"Except one thing. With the Blood Center locked up tight, how does Ruthven expect to get in?"

"He can mist in," came the stereo growls.

"Yeah, but the place is crawling with tourists. Not to mention the rent-a-fangs we'll have after sunset. How's he going to get the blood out?" There was a stunned silence on both ends.

That's when Ruthven's gang broke huddle.

Chapter Twenty-four

Ruthie's pseudo-musicians rumbled down on us like the Bears. A dozen fullbacks couldn't have been scarier.

Julian stood next to me, jaw working as if his fangs were barely in check. But nothing showed. There were still a dozen humans around, after all.

The Ruthven gang was fully armored and clawed, but their backs were to the warehouse. The only one to see them was me.

And, I realized after a squeak and a thud, Lob.

I'd have to worry about that later. The lead vampire, Billy the Kid, *the* Billy's dad if Julian was to be believed, was a rough-looking male. He was only a couple inches shy of Julian's skyscraper height, and a whole hell of a lot bulkier. The Kid flowed in until he was almost nose-to-nose with Julian.

Julian didn't back off a millimeter. In fact, he pumped up and leaned forward a bit. "What do you want, *yearling*?"

The vampire's eyes fired red. "I'm almos' two hunnerd," Billy TK hissed.

Hunnerd meaning hundred, I translated. Two hundred years old was decent, but only Queen Victoria instead of Queen Elizabeth I.

"Yearling," Julian said clearly. "Look me up when you're a thousand."

Oh goody. My belt is longer than yours. Boys.

But the Kid's red eyes faded, as did some of the armor. "We want somethin'." He glanced back at his gang, the wall of muscled plate behind him. That seemed to pump back some of his courage. "Not from you, oh semi-Ancient One," he sneered. "From her." He thrust a gnarled thumb-claw in my direction.

Julian jumped in front of me and pumped even bigger, his back radiating his fury. "You'll have to go through me."

"This ain't your business, Emerson," I heard the Kid say beyond Julian's bulk.

"The hell it isn't! You've got exactly five seconds to get the fuck out of here—"

"We got a contract!" There was a crinkly sound, the Kid thrusting paper into Julian's face. "You can't threaten us, Emerson, and you can't send us nowhere!"

"What...do...you...want?" Julian growled, so low and dangerous even I felt it.

"We want to be first," the Kid said. "To play. We want to open."

I jackknifed around Julian at that. "No. No way. You guys are awful. You'll freak out half the audience. And the other half will hurl beer at you."

Julian hissed, shoved me back behind him, and glared—at me. "What?" I said, frowning. "Beer would short out the equipment. We don't have insurance." Woofers 'R Us did, but BTK didn't need to know that.

"You'd better let us play first, blood-bitch. Because if we don't play, we chomp."

Julian slid one hand slowly into his jacket. Anybody who'd ever seen a gangster movie would have recognized that threatening gesture. "Not on my watch, Billy."

The Kid had the audacity to laugh. "How you going to stop us, Emerson? You don't want to frighten the *humans* so you can't fang up...*ack.*"

The *ack* was because Julian did his faster-than-sound thing, the one he did the first night I met him. The whistling flash of silver that sliced, diced, julienned, and spurted blood like a squirt gun. I peeped around his back.

The Kid's throat was sliced open. His head lolled awkwardly on his shoulder, held on by a few gristly bits. Blood spurted haphazardly over his tee, spattered the floor.

With trembling hands, the Kid picked up his head and plopped it back onto his neck. He shoved a little, like he was popping a doll head on. The muscle and skin reattached. With a crick of his neck, the Kid was as good as new.

He sneered at Julian. "Nice trick. But I'll be prepared for it next time. You won't...*ack.*"

Julian, without even moving very much, had done it again.

"Nice," the Kid said when he'd reattached again. "But you can't...*ack.*"

"Okay," said the Kid when he'd pulled himself together a third time. "Maybe you can. But you can't do it all...*ack.*"

This was followed by a blur and four more *acks*. When I blinked, the blur was gone and Julian was standing right where he had started.

And all the vampire guys were picking up their heads.

The guys assembling chairs and speakers stopped and stared. I peeked around Julian and smiled. "Magic act, folks. For closing night. The red stuff's Kool-Aid." I nudged Julian with my elbow. "Psst. Do your Obi-Wan thing again."

"My what?"

"I am so taking you to see *Star Wars*. Do the mind control thing."

"It's called suggestion," he muttered, but dutifully called out, "You only saw a magic act." His voice was that weird hollowness that got inside your head and rang. Even I almost started believing it was all hocus-pocus.

By this time the vampires had gotten their heads back on. Julian faced them, discreetly tapping wicked, six-inch curved talons against his chest. Wow. What Dolly wouldn't give to have *his* nail technician. "Gentlemen," he said in a cold, contained voice. "Please do not make me go through this all night. Because the next time, your heads may get lost before they can be reattached."

The Kid's eyebrows tightened in a frown. "What do you mean, get lost?"

"You don't want to know."

Which might have been scary and might not. So I suggested, "We could take them to the bowling alley. They'd be a little scuffed up after a few frames, but..."

"Thank you, Nixie." Julian clapped his hand over my mouth. "But I'm sure Billy here can imagine for himself what I might do."

"Just trying to help," I mumbled into his palm.

"We'll go," the Kid said. "But we'll be back."

"Thanks for the warning, Terminator." My clever remark was lost in Julian's hand.

When Julian finally released me, the gang was stalking out the door. He stared after them, his mind obviously working hard. "Why the hell did they want to play first?"

"To drive away the customers. Which is better than killing them." I grabbed his hand and yanked him toward the door. "Which is what the Ladies Auxiliary's cheese balls will do unless we can get there fast!"

Julian didn't move. "But how does it fit with Ruthven and the Blood Center—"

"Come *on*, Julian! Save the world now. Brood later."

He didn't like it, but he came.

When we got there, it was worse than I could have even imagined.

Three people were in charge of every event—a chair, a council producer, and a vampire protector. The chair for the cheese ball tasting was Twyla Tafel, conveniently out of town helping her sister with the new baby. Brunhilde Butt was the council member, but she was also doing the opening reception and couldn't be in two places at once, no matter how fast she shimmied. The vampire guard was one of the rent-a-fangs, who wouldn't arrive until dark.

Not a single in-charge person was there.

Zillions of LLAMAs were, however—including Mrs. Ruffles, Dirk the Duck's mom (picture a girl duck with big high heels, pearls, and an overbite). Lutheran Ladies were everywhere, feverishly laying out large, smelly balls. I couldn't call them cheese balls, not with what the Ladies did to them. Macbeth's witches couldn't have come up with nastier stuff.

Fortunately no tourists were there yet. I still might beat off disaster.

"Fire!" I yelled.

Mrs. Blau turned immediately. "Why, hello, Nixie. What a lovely party." Mrs. Braun, Mrs. Gruen, and Ms. Gelb added their smiling concurrence.

Mrs. Ruffles waved. Friendly, except she had a cheese ball

in her hand. The ball catapulted like a major-league pitch. I ducked just in time to avoid pus-ball face. The ball hit the door with a splat, sliding slowly down like snot. There's an image you don't want of something that's supposed to be food.

"Tornado!" I shouted. "Evacuate!"

"Yes, dear," Mrs. Blau said. "Could you get a few more napkins?"

They were ignoring me. Could things get worse?

Sure. While I was trying to think of something else to yell, a bus from the retirement community pulled up. Thirty or forty little old ladies and a dozen little old men shuffled off, headed straight toward us.

I swore, but only in my head. There were church ladies here, after all.

Just before the door opened to the tourists, I saw the snot-ball lying on the floor. With a swift kick, I sent it under a table. But some stuck to my shoe. Eww. I shook my leg frantically. Slime-ball sprayed all over the floor. Shit. The tourists would think someone had barfed. Oh well. At least things couldn't get worse.

Then I saw my mother swooping down on Julian and me.

Apparently things could *always* get worse.

"Mr. Emerson! Julian! It's so wonderful to see you again! *Such* a delight!" It was all Julian this and Julian that. Mom was so effusive I thought Julian might go into a diabetic coma. If vampires went into those sorts of things.

"Good evening, Mrs. Schmeling," Julian replied, kissing both her cheeks. Whoa. I guess two could play at the gigasugar thing. Or maybe his Old World courtesy ramped up when greeting his future mother-in-law...oh, I did *not* just think that.

My mother got a load of what Julian was wearing and jerked visibly. I palmed my aching forehead, knowing what she was seeing. Black leather jacket, naked chest, black leather pants, naked chest, black leather boots...and of course, naked chest.

But all she said was, "What a nice earring, Julian. Is that new?"

Ye gods. I was doomed.

Sure, not a word about the naked chest, so I should have

relaxed, right? But my mother was cagey. Like "have you stopped beating your wife", her question posed all kinds of danger.

Because what could Julian say that would not get us both burned at the maternal stake?

He could say, "Yes, Nixie bought the earring for me." Then my mother would think, ahah! A diamond, so an *engagement* present. And if not an engagement diamond, what the hell was I doing spending that kind of money on a man? Moreover, what crime had I committed to get that kind of money?

Julian could say, "No, the earring's not new," but then my mother would think he was a closet punk. Since in my mother's mind punks committed all sorts of atrocities, maybe Julian had been—gasp—lying about other things. Like being a lawyer. Strangely, I thought the small omitted fact of his being a vampire wouldn't bother her half as much as finding out he'd lied about being a lawyer. There's a reason Gainfully Employed is number one on the Mother Test.

Julian could also answer, "Yes, I bought the earring for myself." That was just admitting he was a girly-man. Because what other kind of guy buys jewelry for himself, especially a one-carat diamond earring? Yes, I know that's *baka*, but that's how my mother thinks.

I signaled frantically, doing the round Obi-Wan gesture. When Julian ignored that, I began to flail in my best *Team America* manner. Still nothing. The man was a total pop culture moron.

I had forgotten that Julian, while he hadn't seen any movies in this century, had quite a lot of experience with human nature. He smiled blindingly, said, "Why, thank you, Mrs. Schmeling. I'm glad you like it," and left it at that.

Hit with Julian's best twenty-four carat smile, my mother blinked several times. "Oh, yes. Nice weather we're having." She seemed to have forgotten that she ever asked a question. It probably didn't hurt that his nipples winked at her.

Imminent disaster averted, I took the opportunity to scope out the cheese ball damage.

The Ladies were working clockwise from the door, putting out atomic bombs...er, cheese balls. They looked like lopsided toy basketballs—the cheese balls, that is, not the Ladies. As they put out their ticking bombs, they pushed the gourmet (i.e. edible) balls back out of reach.

Dirk's mom was working twice as fast as everyone else. So I started with her. "Mrs. Ruffles?"

"Hello, Dietlinde, how are you? I heard you are running the festival. Do you like that? Who is that lovely young man you're with? Does he play music? My Dirk plays music, you know. He plays a big brass flute. Do you still play the black flute?" She was laying out balls as fast as she was talking.

With all the LLAMAs watching, I couldn't simply make the bad balls disappear. I could only do like Sleeping Beauty's third good fairy godmother and cast a mitigating spell. As quietly as possible, I pulled the good, tasty, *normal* cheese balls back in front. "I'm fine," I said, answering the only question I remembered.

"That's good," Mrs. Ruffles said. "Oh, hello."

The last wasn't to me. I looked up to see two rich-looking old ladies approaching. As they came they dipped into aged cheddar and wine with almonds, brie with chives and cashews, and Wensleydale with walnuts. They also dropped twenties in the donation buckets like monsoon season.

Yay! Donors. And generous donors. We might win against Ruth-ass-ven yet.

Mrs. Ruffles chose that moment to set a pusball down right in front of them.

I stared for a moment in stunned horror. At best, the little old moneybags would nibble a bit of pus and run out screaming, plucking up their twenties on the way.

At worst, they would keel over dead from instant food poisoning.

I didn't have time to think. I simply acted. I snatched up a good cheese ball and threw it, aiming between the old ladies and death.

My aim wasn't so good. The ball smacked Mrs. Ruffles in the back of the head. She lost her balance, went flailing. She tried to catch herself on the table, put her hand *splat* into her cheese ball.

Okay, not what I intended. But it worked. Got rid of the pusball *and* took Mrs. Ruffles out of the balling race. And I'd only lost one good ball.

Before I could congratulate myself too much, Mrs. Ruffles tried to get rid of the glop—by shaking her hand like a wet dog. Gobs of pusball went everywhere, over walls, over the tables, over me. Pusball spatter hit the little old ladies in the face like bugs on a windshield.

The two little old moneybags stood frozen like corpses in rigor. Cheese pus slithered down their cheeks and jowls, dripped off them onto the floor. One took off her glasses and, without seeming to notice what she was doing, polished them on a pus-covered sleeve.

Mrs. Ruffles held her hands to her mouth to stifle a gasp. "I'm so sorry! I'll get you cleaned up in a jiffy!"

"No!" I cried. Ruffles genes and LLAMA pusballs—duck.

Mrs. Ruffles swept up the first clean cloth she saw to wipe pus spit off the old ladies.

It happened to be the tablecloth. Cheese balls went flying. Good *and* bad. Plop, plop, plop went cheddar and Wensleydale. *Splooshhh* went pus. The brie stuck to the ceiling.

Shit. Maybe I could rescue the good cheese. Five-second rule, right? Just scoop up the slightly flattened gourmet balls and put them back on the table. We'd call them baroque cheese balls. Baroque, get it? Like "broke", only baroque also means squashed pearl and these balls certainly qualified...okay, not funny. But I was under pressure.

Anyway, like a birthday wish spoken out loud, the five-second rule doesn't apply in public. With witnesses watching, I couldn't pick up the good cheese balls. We were now out three more gourmet cheese balls (with nuts) and only one more pusball. The odds were getting worse.

Mrs. Ruffles panicked, running around like Daisy Chicken with her head cut off. Her foot hit the ball of pus and she went skidding. *Slam!* she went, into another table, sending more cheese balls flying.

Then *I* panicked, because most of these were the good balls. Without those cheese balls, we were *ruined.* I flung myself onto the ground. Maybe if they landed on me at least it wouldn't be the floor. Does the five second rule apply to skin?

I had forgotten Julian's supernatural reflexes. Even before I landed I felt a breeze, heard tiny sonic booms. Maybe not real sonic booms, but when I got to my elbows and opened my eyes, there sat the cheese balls on the last standing table, nice as you please.

There was a collective silence as we took in the damage. Mrs. Ruffles and I were on the floor, both of us ass-deep in pus and mayonnaise. Two tables were overturned. The floor was littered with bits of cheese, pus, and nuts. Little bits of pusball clung to one old lady. The other one had died and was now a ghost. No, that was only the tablecloth covering her.

Julian reached up and snagged the brie off the ceiling. My mother went for the overturned money buckets. Mrs. Ruffles tried to get up to help her. I tackled Ruffles harder than a Cowboy fullback. I'd found out things *could* get worse. If I let Mrs. Ruffles up, who knew what more damage she could do? Like mother, like son. Except, thinking of my mother, what did that make me?

It wasn't worth worrying over. Anyway, I had my hands full, holding Mrs. Ruffles down until Julian and my mom came. As my mother led Mrs. Ruffles out, I rose with a sigh of relief.

Until I remembered the rich old pus-covered ladies.

"Well," said one ex-donor. I cringed.

"Well," said the other, kind of muffled.

The first one drew the tablecloth off her. Her hat was skewed and her brillo hair stuck up in clumps. She said, "That was...interesting."

The first one slowly smiled. "That was the most fun I've had in years!"

The second one clapped her hands. "Me, too. It makes me feel so alive!"

"Let's go get drunk at the beer tent," suggested the first, tossing a handful of twenties on the table.

"Wonderful idea," said the second, tossing on another. "Maybe we can meet some handsome men and get laid."

I gaped at them as they left. "She didn't say that. Please tell me that little old lady didn't say what I thought she did."

Julian came up behind me and rubbed my shoulder. "Isn't it nice to know life doesn't stop at fifty?"

"Eighty, and I didn't think *life* stopped. Just...ew."

"I'm over a thousand," he said, starting to purr just a little.

"Don't get creepy, Emerson." We needed to get rid of the

pusballs, without the Ladies Aux noticing. An idea struck me. "Hey, Julian. You can move faster than the speed of sound. Can you move faster than the speed of light? Or at least the speed of sight?"

Chapter Twenty-five

Before leaving the Deli Delight, I phoned Elena to ask about the Blood Center. I breathed a sigh of relief when she told me Bo had sent Stark there. Stark could keep an eye on things until either the Ancient One's ringers came to relieve him or we figured out how Ruthie thought he was getting the blood out. Then, because none of us could guess why the Ruthiettes wanted to be opening band, Julian and I decided we might as well finish our rounds. Five of Ruthven's lieutenants were accounted for. But that left a whole lot of Nosferatu's hench mutants to cause trouble.

We got to the beer tent, where we met yet another disaster.

People were weaving around the tent, glasses, bottles, and cans in hand. Already drinking. I gaped in horror. "The festival's not open until four thirty!"

"Apparently they don't know that," Julian said.

"We've got to stop them!"

A tourist, carrying a tray laden with two pitchers of beer and six glasses, passed. Julian tried to pluck the tray from him. Despite Julian's lightning-fast vampire reflexes, the tourist was faster, jerking away and running. He growled as he escaped, a hunter protecting his kill.

Julian shook his head. "I don't think we're going to be able to stop them by ourselves. We'll need help. Who's the protector assigned to the beer tent?"

"One of the fill-in fangs." Like the cheese tasting, this was one of the events guarded by a ringer. Sent by the "Ancient One", whoever that was. Someone in Iowa, which left out George Carlin. Yes, I knew he was dead. That was the whole point to being a vampire, right?

"They won't be here until sunset. Four thirty, at the earliest. Who's the chairperson?"

"Daisy Mae Sattel. But this isn't her work." My mouth set in a grim line, and I put hands on hips. Knuckles smacked skin; I was wearing superlow skinny jeans with spike heels and spangled sports bra.

"No?"

"No. Donner and Blitz, Meiers Corners's town crunks, have been at it again."

"I don't believe I've had the pleasure," Julian said. Not "I've never met them" or "whozat". Which just shows you can sleep with a man/vampire for literally days and still be surprised by him. Who said a marriage has to be boring?

No, no, *no*. I did *not* just think that.

"Nixie? Why are you hitting yourself on the head?"

"Uh, no reason. Look, we've got to find them. Can you do your supernatural senses thing? Sniff them out?"

"I'm not sure locating those two would be the best solution, if crunk means sloppy drunk. Far from being helpful, wouldn't they cause more trouble?"

"Oh, no. If ever there were such a thing as gentlemen drunks, Donner and Blitz are it. They're *responsible* drunks." At Julian's frankly skeptical stare, I added, "No, really. I can prove it. The bartender at Nieman's didn't want to serve me beer with the rest of the Common Council after meetings. But they talked him into it."

"How old were you?"

"Well...fifteen. But I suffered through those meetings, same as the grownups. It was only fair."

"You don't know everything at fifteen." Julian shook his head, obviously not agreeing with me that this nominated Donner and Blitz for responsibility. "What do they look like?"

"Like a perfectly matched carriage set. Donner's the horse and Blitz is the carriage. As polite as eighteenth century vicars—and a touch more mellow."

"Well, I don't see—Nixie, look out!"

I hit defensive stance, expecting fangs and claws. I also expected Julian getting all pushing-me-behind-him overprotective. But to my surprise he just stood there. That stunned me so much that I didn't see the kid until he bear-hugged me, picking me up and twirling me until I almost puked.

I looked down. Holding me was a skinny, pimply teenager. He gave me a big sloppy kiss. "You're cute!" he burbled, grinning like a maniac. "Are you a freshman?"

I gaped. Who was this little creep? "Put me down!"

He hugged me and continued to bubble. "I'm in high school too. I like your curly yellow hair. It looks like a doll's."

"I am not a doll! And I'm not in high school! And *put me down!*"

He *giggled*. "What's your name? I bet you're Barbie. My name's Bill. Like Bill Gates, the Alpha and Omega of computers. Did you know that's why you click on 'Start' to shut down?"

"Your name will be Dead if you don't put me down!"

That apparently did it. He finally set me down. I took a deep breath, winding up for a good lecture. Just as I opened my mouth he planted another big sloppy on me. I stood there, completely speechless. Julian was also apparently dumbfounded.

The kid's power of speech was unfortunately fine. "Are you in middle school then? I'm a junior in high school. You're cute," he repeated happily. "Do you know why computers get Halloween and Christmas confused?"

"Now listen here—"

"Because October thirty-first equals December twenty-fifth!" The kid guffawed like a maniac, actually slapping his leg. "Get it? Thirty-one in base ten is the same as twenty-five in base twelve!" As the kid's chortles disintegrated into hiccups, I rolled my eyes at Julian, who returned my look with sympathy.

"You're *drunk*! How old are you? Where are your parents?" I demanded, for once almost sympathizing with my mother. "Do they know what you're doing?"

"Ms. Meier knows," the kid said with a hiccup. "She's our advisor."

I slapped my skull. The mayor's sister, advisor to the twenty little geeks I'd foisted off on my mom. Only the geeks weren't so little—and at least one was definitely drunk.

"I don't believe you. I can't believe a respectable matron would introduce you to alcohol!"

"She didn't," the kid said, hiccups increasing. "Mr. Donner did."

Didn't that just figure.

"Ms. Meier only bought the second pitcher."

"What!?"

"Well, gotta go. We're going to see the bands later. You're cute!" The kid ran off, weaving a little.

"I'm doomed."

"It's all right." Julian pulled me tight, caressed my hair.

"No, it isn't! Do you have any idea how much the insurance deductible is for this gig if we have to make a claim? What kind of crappy parents do these little hoodlums have? Can't they control their own kids?" My mouth dropped open in horror. "I cannot believe I just said that." I stared at Julian. "Did you change me?"

He shrugged, making his pecs jump nicely. "If I did, it was Newtonian."

"Newton...oh. The apple-dropping guy."

"Newton didn't drop the apple."

"Yeah, I know. The tree did."

"Actually, I did. To get back at him for the time he dumped a bucket of ice water on my head."

"I do not want to hear this. Leave dead dry guys alone. The idea of Sir Isaac playing tricks is just wrong." I narrowed my eyes. "I thought you said you emigrated by 1625."

"I went back for a little visit in the 1680s."

"*Sure* you did. I suppose you helped Newton develop calculus, too."

"Of course not." Julian looked a little offended. "That was twenty years earlier."

I shook my head. "No. This is wrong on so many levels."

"All I'm trying to say is that if I had an effect on you, you had an equal and opposite effect on me." Julian pointed to the earring.

As yummy as a chocolate chip in a cookie. And even more distracting. I smacked my lips.

Julian smiled. "Come on. Let's check out the rest of the venues. Maybe it'll give us a clue as to why Billy the Kid's band wants to go first." He took my elbow and started to lead me out.

"But the drunk little geeks—"

"Will be fine. Ms. Meier and Donner and Blitz are with them."

"Oh, good. That's so reassuring. Dante and Randal, minding the store."

Julian cocked a questioning eyebrow at me. "Was that a pop culture reference? Some sort of television show?"

I let him guide me. I was starting to like the feel of his square, competent fingers on my arm. "Movie. Say, want to play Scene It? I'd whomp you."

Chapter Twenty-six

On the way to the next venue, we argued about what Ruthven might be up to, but got nowhere. At the Fudgy Delight another disaster met us.

Actually, Bo and Elena met us. But they were so worked up I knew something had gone disastrously wrong.

"It's horrible." Elena's eyes were wide and her face as pale as I'd ever seen it.

Bo collapsed in one of the chairs and buried his face in his hands. "It's...I can't believe...oh, the humanity!"

"What?" I cast frantically around for Ruthven, or the Lestats, or at least one of the drunk teenage geeks trying to get into the beauty contestants' dressing room.

Julian snarled, all vampire-fighting systems engaged. "What's the problem?"

"It's the pageant." Elena choked, and sank into a chair next to Bo. She shook her head, as if whatever it was, was so horrible, the words refused to come.

"What about the pageant?" I was beginning to panic. "Did Headless Horseman Cutter bite all the contestants? Did Ruthven scare off the judges? *What?*"

Elena was still speechless, so Bo answered. "Worse." He took a deep breath. "The contestants have been rehearsing all week. Talent skits, walking down the aisle, answering questions. That sort of thing."

I sat down next to Elena and shook my head in confusion. "But—that's good, right? Practice makes perfect?"

Elena found her voice. "We were happy about it. They were taking it seriously."

"We thought it would make for a more polished pageant," Bo said.

"We were *happy* about it," Elena wailed.

I was bewildered. "So what's the disaster?"

"They were practicing all week!" Elena jumped up from her chair. "*Here!*"

"Here?" I looked around at the old wooden floorboards, the thick wood tables. The raised stage with its uneven stairs. "Is this building dangerous, somehow?" A thought struck me. "Did someone fall on the stairs? Are we going to have a liability claim?"

"It's worse," Bo said.

"No. What could possibly be worse than an insurance claim?"

Elena took me by the shoulders. "Nixie...they got into the fudge!"

"So they ate a little fudge," I said, relieved. "We'll take it out of petty cash."

"It's not the money! It's—"

Just then the contestants sashayed onto the stage for a final dress rehearsal. They wore polka-dot purple/red, polka-dot eye-splitting green/orange, and other polka-dotted hues not found anywhere in nature. I thought maybe someone should have tried to color coordinate them, or at least introduce them to stripes.

I watched the ladies slink down the runway. "I didn't know we added a muumuu contest. Or is this a politically correct version of the bikini contest?"

"They *are* in bikinis!"

I stared harder. The women were indeed wearing tiny swimsuits—in solid colors. The garish polka dots weren't on the cloth. They were on the contestants' skin.

"What...what happened?" I could barely speak around the sudden tracheotomy someone had done on my throat.

"I told you," Elena wailed. "They got into the fudge!"

"No." I clapped hands to head. "This is a disaster!"

They looked like Binky the Clown with the measles. Or the plague. Or like they were painted by a really bad Warhol imitator with a tie-dye fixation.

Sauntering down the runway, those women looked like deadly disease on the hoof. And they looked horribly contagious.

"What will we *do*?" Normally Elena is a kick-ass detective, but this really seemed to throw her.

Then I found out why.

"Bond girl," Bo said distinctly.

"No!" She whirled on him. "I am not taking off all my clothes—"

"You have before," he said reasonably.

"Not on purpose!"

"You'd be wearing more this time," her husband said hopefully. "A bra. And a gun belt."

"You didn't want me to do this when Dirk suggested it!"

"That was Dirk. This is different. *This* is an emergency."

I chimed in. "It may be the only thing that will distract the audience from...that." I waved a hand at the spotty brigade.

"No. No way." Elena crossed her arms, glared at us all.

Julian put up his hands and said mildly, "Hey, don't look at me. I didn't say anything."

"You were thinking it!"

The first of the audience entered, took one look at the apparent smallpox epidemic, turned and left.

I joined in. "Elena, please."

Elena: "Not in a million years."

Me: "We could ask someone to do it with you. For moral support."

Elena: "Like?"

Helpful fucking husband: "Drusilla?"

Elena: "Not in *two* million years."

"We can ask other people," I said, trying to smooth things over. "The Widow Schrimpf. Hey—how about Rocky Hrbek?"

Elena blinked at me like I had gone completely nuts. "Rocky? That chunky girl you went to high school with? Bad hair and glasses?"

"She wears glasses because she thinks her eyes are too big. And you haven't seen her lately. Tell you what. I'll phone Rocky and Josephine. Bo, why don't you call Dru?" Catching the snarling badger look on Elena's face, I amended, "No, wait, Julian can do it."

Bo beckoned to Kurt Weiss, the pageant's aldermanic coordinator. "Even Elena, Dru, Rocky, and Josephine might not be enough to stave off this disaster." He spoke to Kurt. "Quick. I have an errand for you. Our very lives may depend on it!"

"Yes, sir, Mr. Strongwell!" Kurt, the nervous wiener dog, nearly saluted in his eagerness, turned, and took off. He was out the door in seconds. Julian and I exchanged a look. Kurt sheepishly stuck his head back in. "Er, what is the errand?"

Elena jumped in. "We need you to go shopping, Kurt. Two dozen one-piece maillots, pronto."

"Yes ma'am." Kurt saluted, raced briskly off. We waited patiently. Two seconds later, Kurt slunk back. "Uh, what's a maillot, ma'am?"

"A one-piece swimsuit. Get the kind with high back and front."

"And maybe those little skirts," Bo said.

"Yes, sir!" Kurt raced off again.

"And Kurt..." Bo didn't even raise his voice but Kurt screeched to a halt.

"Yes, sir?"

"Better pick up some opaque tights."

"Yes, sir."

Next Julian and I checked out the church. With all the disasters, I was expecting a flood at the very least. But when we got there, all the kiddie games were set up. The wall at the entrance had been decorated, some sort of cartoon sponge painting. Gretchen, Elena's sister and the Common Council member helping out, was sitting calmly at the door, knitting.

Standing over her was six-foot plus of very menacing, long-haired Viking male.

"Hey, Gretch," I said. "Have any trouble yet?"

Her needles clicked rapidly. "Thorvald and I had just a bit. A couple large men tried to get in."

Julian hissed. I asked, tentatively, "Were they...you knows?"

Gretch nodded. "They had slight overbites, if that's what

you mean."

I looked around. No creepy gang guys now. "What happened?"

"I explained there were children's games here, and that they had to leave."

"And they just walked away?"

"Sure." She dimpled up at me. "After Thor showed them how to play some of the games."

"Really? Which games?" Did vampires even play games?

"Skee ball. Did you know if you throw the ball hard enough at someone's chest, it makes a hole you can see clear through?" She smiled up beatifically at us, needles still clacking.

The sponge painting, red, took on new meaning.

"Okay," I said to Julian. "I think this one's good."

Approaching the Pie Delight next, Julian's nostrils flared. "Vampire."

"Shit. How many this time?"

"Two, maybe three."

A loud shriek came from the direction of the store. We ran, only to stop outside, dumbfounded.

Two large men lay comatose on the stoop of the Pie Delight. As Julian and I stared, the door opened and another gave a dazed sigh before tumbling down the stairs to the pavement.

I looked up. In the doorway lounged Drusilla, the most sensuous woman since Mata Hari—or Jessica Alba, if you were young enough to use the word "sweet" instead of "neat-o".

Dru smiled down at us. Julian glanced at the fallen vampires, raised an eyebrow at her.

In answer, Dru licked one finger and touched it to her butt—*tsah.*

In case I haven't mentioned it, Drusilla of the natural DDs is Meiers Corners's top prostitute—but she could have cleaned up in any market, including Chicago, Paris, or even New York.

Today she had apparently cleaned up right here. And taken out the trash to boot.

"Well," I said. "I guess things are under control here, too."

Dru simply turned and sashayed back inside.

If I thought things were looking up, I should have remembered two non-disasters in a row was an omen like two sunny days in Chicago was a spring. Didn't mean jack shit, brother. Lake Michigan way, April showers brought May snowstorms. I'd'a had a better chance to win the Powerball.

But hope sprang eternal. Our next stop was City Hall. Actually, our last stop was City Hall. The whole shindig was starting there at four p.m. with a speech by the mayor. Since Stark had shifted to guard the Blood Center, we needed to stay for the opening ceremony.

In the limo on the way, Julian and I had a pretty good discussion about how Ruthven planned to get the blood out of the Blood Center. Julian argued for the possibility of transporting blood through a hose running out a window. I argued for a blow job. I won. Mmm.

A huge line of people snaked outside City Hall. Since only VIPs were invited, a couple guards worked the door (turning people away with a free beer token. The mayor's no dummy). As we negotiated our way to the front, I asked Julian, "Do you think those toothy guys at the Pie Delight and the church were Ruthie's or Nosy's?"

"Only the band at the Roller-Blayd factory was Ruthven's. All the others were Nosferatu's."

"I wonder what that means. Ruthie's gang is trying to horn in on the bands, and Nosy's is disrupting the rest of the festival events. But neither of them are attacking the Blood Center directly."

"That we know of."

"Bo would have heard from Stark and called us. Oh, look. We're finally at the front of the line."

Just as we were about to get in, Murphy's déjà vu struck. A puckered powder blue suit whisked in front of me.

It was Vice Principal Schleck.

Apparently he didn't recognize Julian in his punk attire. "Excuse me, sir." Julian tapped gently on the vice-principal's shoulder. "I believe you have, er, taxed our place."

I nearly snorted to hear the phrase in Julian's highly cultured tones. Like carving lewd statues out of crystal. It was just weird.

"Not now, punk." The veep threw Julian a sharp frown.

"Dirty punk."

The door in front of us opened. Schleck moved.

Julian's jaw worked like his fangs were jumping to get out and play. And his eyes fired up, more red than violet.

I was going to enjoy this.

Vampire-fast, Julian grabbed seersucker coat. "I believe you're out of line, sir."

Schleck scrabbled like a bicyclist in neutral. "Let me go, shit-for-brains!" The veep got exactly nowhere.

Julian lifted the veep off the ground, twisted his coat until Schleck swung gently face to face. "Actually, you were never in line in the first place."

Slowly, Julian grinned. Schleck was treated to the sight of two very long, very pointy teeth. Julian clicked his teeth together in a couple deliberate chomps.

Schleck screamed. The powder blue turned indigo across the front of Schleck's pants. His legs started pistoning well before Julian set him down. When his tread hit pavement, he shot off like Meatloaf's Bat Out of Hell.

"Bullies." I shook my head. "Always the first to pee and run." Julian held out his hand, and we entered City Hall.

The opening speech was going to be delivered in the council chambers, where I'd held band auditions. All the tables and chairs had been cleared from the room. The raised dais at the far end had a podium, but no mic. Apparently the mayor had joined the zeros and would use a wireless.

The first person I saw inside was Bart Bleistift, and he was not happy. His boyish face was dark with anger, his generous mouth tight. I thought maybe Mom had told him he had lost pole position in the Mother Race. That idea was reinforced when I saw him staring at Julian like he tasted month-old turkey loaf with mayo. Working himself up to confront us, I guessed— confirmed a moment later when he motored in our direction.

Bart grabbed Julian by the sleeve, walked him two paces forward. "What the hell are you doing here, *old fuck*?"

Hearing that, seeing them side by side, I reevaluated my two contenders in the Nixie Race. Bart admittedly had solid shoulders, but Julian's were broad and muscular. Bart's butt was trim, but Julian had a really tight ass. Bart ignored what he didn't understand, but Julian had learned my language for me. I wondered what I'd *ever* seen in the good Saint. Maybe my mother's approval, but even that had veered in Julian's favor.

His voice icy with disdain, Julian answered, "I might ask you the same thing, *child.*"

Men. More "my rocket's bigger than yours".

Bart clenched his teeth. "Negotiations are over, Boston legal. Why don't you pack up and go home and lie in your grave like a good little bloodsucking lawyer?"

"The battle's over, but the war is far from won." And, to my utter shock, Julian flashed Bart a lavish length of fang.

"Julian!" I slapped a cautionary hand on his wrist.

Julian's unblinking violet eyes did not waver an inch from Bart. "Bleistift knows all about us, Nixie. He's Nosferatu's human minion."

"Nosferatu's *what?*"

Staring right back at Julian, Bart hissed, "I told you not to get mixed up in this, Nixie."

"You didn't tell me anything of the sort! You told me I shouldn't be at the Kalten's Roller Rink, remember? Just before it...before it...oh my lord. Just before it exploded. You knew!"

Revelation on top of revelation. Good thing I was quick on my feet. First, Bart was a vampire's human minion. I didn't know everything that meant, but I knew it wasn't good.

And second, the explosion at Kalten's. I already suspected the Lestat gang was involved somehow. But apparently Nosferatu had ordered the destruction. And Saint Farty Booger was in it up to his trim pimply ass.

"I told you to stay out of it!" Bart snapped, spinning on me. He didn't have fangs but his anger was scary enough.

And I had thought he was *nice*. "How can you be working for Nosferatu? Don't you know what he's trying to do to people here? What about Denny Crane?"

"Denny Crane?" Julian asked, distracting me.

"Bart's boss," I snapped. "Not the *Boston Legal* character."

"Boston Legal character?"

I sighed and turned to Julian. "You know. Played by William Shatner?"

"*Star Trek*'s William Shatner?"

I was surprised. "Shatner was in a TV show before *Boston Legal*?"

"For shit's sake!" Bart sneered, snagging my attention back. "Stick to the point."

Oh, yeah. My rant. "What about Denny Crane? What about Meiers Corners?" I glared at Bart. "What about *my mother!*" What about me, I wanted to add, but didn't. I had some pride.

Bart stared at me, his upper lip curled in disdain. "I don't know what I ever saw in you."

Any residual sympathy or affection died. "I was just thinking the same thing," I muttered. Louder, I asked, "Did you do it, Bart? Did you blow up the Rink?"

He snorted. "You really think I'm going to tell you?"

I did. With him doing "my fang's longer than your fang" with Julian, I thought he'd boast to high heaven if he'd been playing with explosives.

But he wasn't boasting. Either he had amazing self-restraint, or he hadn't done it. I knew which I favored. "Nosy doesn't let you play with matches, hmm?"

Bart flushed. "I was the one who told them about your using Kalten's. I planned it."

"But you didn't *do* it. I guess it was too important for a human minion," I taunted. "Some fangy guy did it, then. Cutter?"

Bart's red face told me I'd hit it. "Yeah, well, as a disruption it was second rate." He speared me with a nasty look. "*You* screwing up the negotiations by screwing Emerson far surpassed *my* feeble attempts."

Now it was my turn to flush. "How can you side with Nosy? Don't you know what he wants?"

"Nosferatu wants blood. No different from any of the suckers. No different from *him*." He sniffed at Julian. "Or will you try to tell me beastie-boy here hasn't sucked your blood?" He made "suck" sound like a dirty word.

"He has, yes. But that's different."

"Because he's too pretty to be a monster? Because he *asked*?" Bart scoffed. "Oh, please, purty please, Miss Nixie. Let me sippy your sweet neck. Sure, that makes it all okay."

I was starting to get angry. Didn't Saint Barty get it? Could he possibly be that dense, or was he willfully ignorant? "It's *okay* because it's not Blood Center blood. Not the blood slotted to *save human lives.* Julian is protecting that. Which is more than I can say for you, human." With my own sneer I added, "Between you and Julian, I know which is the monster."

Bart, whose job was arguing, was speechless.

Julian poked Bart in the chest. "Which returns me to my first question. What *exactly* are you doing here, Blei?"

Julian, I realized, was right to worry. If Bart was on the Nosferatu team, he wasn't here to cheer the mayor on.

Bart was here to throw a monkey wrench into the works.

I grabbed Bart by the wrist, yanked him close. "What are you going to do? Tell me!"

Blei-shit had the balls to laugh. "Oh, look at me, I'm the evil villain, gloating over the hero and spilling my guts."

"At least you know which character you are." I released him with a small shove. "Julian...can you see or smell any fangy monsters here?"

"Any *other* fangy monsters, you mean," Bart corrected.

St. Bart was starting to get on my nerves. Starting? Make that three repeats and into the coda. "Julian?"

"No." Julian's eyes were narrowed. "But you don't have to worry, Nixie. Nosferatu won't stoop to frightening tourists."

"Not with supernatural weirdness, no. But if Team Nosy means to disrupt the opening ceremonies, they could use *gangland* weirdness." I scanned the crowd. "But if no fangy-gangy guys are around, then what?"

"Blei's here to do something," Julian said. "Obviously."

Yeah, obvious. But what? Bomb, or something Mr. Pencil-pusher had up his sleeve?

"Goot EFFNINK, mine goot LADIES"—a high squeal—"entlemen." Mayor Meier stood behind the podium, fiddling with his lapel. Wireless mic, yes. But that still didn't mean he'd joined the Higgs Boson age.

As he fiddled, Heidi marched onto the dais. Heidi was Twyla Tafel's cohort in the mayor's office. She looked like the title character from the book *Heidi*, all blonde braids and airhead blue eyes. Except she tended toward leather, spike-heeled hip boots, and lots of studs. She was almost as sharp as Twyla, and a hell of a lot more tyrannical. Even I was a little scared of Heidi.

Heidi slapped Mayor Meier's hands away from the mic. It sounded like the crack of a whip. "Stop fussing, Mayor!" we heard at eight hundred decibels. He stopped. Finally she got it fixed.

The mayor cleared his throat. "Welcome, welcome everyone to the First Annual Meiers Corners International Fun Fair, Sheepshead Tournament, and Polka Festival!" He smiled, all jolly Wiener schnitzel. The crowd on the floor quieted instantly, and several people started smiling in response. Mayor Meier was really good at this, I thought. If anyone could get a bunch of tourists happy-happy enough to spend several hundred thousand dollars, he could.

I was distracted only for an instant. In that instant, Bart vanished.

So did Julian. He snapped, "Stay here," so it wasn't like he dipped out without a word. But he puffed into smoke so fast I couldn't say boo, much less follow.

But did Julian *really* think I'd stay put?

Chapter Twenty-seven

I had two guesses where Bart might have gone. If a bomb was set to go off, St. Barty had run away. Out of the room, out of the building, out of the city if I was lucky.

But I had begun to suspect there was no bomb. Sure, Nosy's Lestat gang had exploded Kalten's Roller Rink. But there weren't any people involved in that. I didn't think he would blow up an occupied building.

Not that I thought Nosy was weighed down by scruples. No. I bet Nosferatu would dynamite a room full of self-warming blood like I could throw away a package of cookies.

Not going to happen.

So how was St. Barty going to frighten off our happy, money-spending tourists? Only one way I could think of. There was no gang inside, ergo the gang had yet to get in.

Bo had said older vampires could mist into buildings, those a century or more dead, like Nosferatu. If Cutter and his gang were less than that, someone would have to open a door.

Bart hadn't run out. He had run to let the Lestats in.

But where?

City Hall had four outside doors. The main entrance was too exposed. The one Julian and I had used this evening was guarded.

That left the door I'd exited by the night I met Julian, and a corresponding door on the other side of the building. I thought Julian would cover the one he knew about, so I ran for the other.

Which really didn't make sense, when you think about it. Assuming Julian was following Bart, it didn't matter whether he knew about the second door or not.

Except Bart Bleistift, Nosferatu's human minion, knew vampires. Somehow he lost Julian. Somehow he got to the door Julian *didn't* know about, alone.

I ran up, breathless, just as Cutter floated in.

"Quick." Bart gestured frantically. "Emerson's onto us. I just barely evaded him."

"Yeah?" Cutter said. "Then what's *she* doing here?"

Oops. Busted.

Bart's shocked face would have been funny, except three more toughs in leather swirled in around him. I guess even Opie looked wicked in a dark forest.

So there we were. On one side of the hall was the Nosy Gang: Cutter, he of blond body-building physique; three big, tough vampires in long leather coats; and nice-guy Bart, who at the moment looked anything but nice. Four strong vampires and a strong human man.

All against a pint-sized punk with great makeup.

Time for Attitude. "She," I said, popping out some gum and swaggering into their midst, "is sick of being priggy old Emerson's chew toy. *She* is here to play. Right Barty?" I winked at Bart. Not to try to get him to cooperate. I saw *Dracula*. Human minions were fly-eating insane. The best I could hope was to confuse him.

"Uh...yeah," Bart said weakly. Confused.

Well, nail the *B* in BINGO.

It gave me time to think up a cunning plan. A plan so cunning you could slap a wig on it and call it my mother.

All I had to do was delay the bad guys until the mayor finished. When the speech was done, the people would leave for the other delights of the festival. The Lestats could terrorize an empty room all they wanted—as far as I knew, floorboards didn't scare easily.

If I could delay them until the VIP tourists dispersed, Nosy's Gang was screwed.

I took a quick look at the clock hanging on the wall behind Cutter. Four-oh-eight. The festival started at four thirty. Whooboy. I had my work cut out for me.

"So. You boys here to brawl?" I cocked a hip, checked out

my nails, and slewed a catty glance at the lead leathercoat.

Mr. Lead Leather wore his hair spiked and his leather studded. Yum—if I hadn't already developed a taste for Julienned vampires. At my come-hither smile Lead Leather gave a start of surprise, then smiled back—with a hint of fang. Not as long or sleek as Julian's. I wondered if size of fang and size of *thang* were related. Probably. If so, I had gotten extremely lucky in the fang lottery.

I nearly slapped myself. Julian, I reminded myself, was going home as soon as this was over. It wouldn't matter how long his fangs were. They wouldn't reach from Boston.

Mr. Lead Leather's smile faltered. Oops. Too much thinking, not enough seducing. I deliberately tipped my head back, just enough to expose some throat, and winked. Well, I figured if a flash of panty can do it for a regular guy, a flash of jugular must be a vampire voyeur's dream.

Leathercoat's fangs grew and his eyes turned red. Nail me an *I*. He took one step forward before Cutter held up an arm. "Bludgeon! Hold up."

Cutter? Bludgeon? Could they get any daggier?

Cutter turned to me. "How do we know you're telling the truth?"

"Don't you guys have a truth ray, or something?" I widened my eyes in waves, like I was some sort of Rasputin. "Laser vision?"

Cutter's gaze went ruby hard, and not the kind of red that Bludgeon-Leathercoat had. Angry red, not lusty red. "If you're not Emerson's minion, prove it."

Okay, now I was out of my depth. How did you prove you were *not* a vampire's human minion? "Glad to, Ichabod. If you'll just tell me what the difference is between minion and sex slave." At five simultaneous gasps and four sets of suddenly stiff—er, fangs—I added, "Hey, he's an old guy, but he is pretty well-endowed. A girl would be *baka* not to indulge. And being a sex slave's kind of fun." I hooked my thumbs through the belt loops of my superlow skinny jeans and did a grind, ending in a bump of my nearly naked hips.

Nostrils flared at that. Bludgeon Leathercoat's eyes got even redder. Like I was super-delectable now. Apparently having an old guy in the vampire world was a good thing.

Give me a *B*, give me an *I*, give me an *N*!

Cutter was the first to get his er, fangs under control. "What has bakery got to do with this?"

"*Baka*," said Bludgeon Leathercoat under his breath. "Means stupid, stupid." He winked at me, a sign we were on the same wavelength. I gave him a conspiratorial smile and blew him a kiss. He knew what *baka* meant! Either he kept up with his slang, or he'd died quite recently. Which meant he wasn't that powerful.

So it was one pint-sized punk against three vampires, a human, and a fledgling.

Not much better odds, but hey. I'd taken on Ruthass and won. How hard could it be?

I studied my naked hips. "You wouldn't think such a fusty old lawyer dude would be any good," I said thoughtfully. "But apparently they teach more than legal briefs at the old Paper Chase. They must teach bikini briefs." I released my belt loops and slowly unbuttoned the top button of my jeans. "Boy-cut briefs. French-cut briefs." I pulled out my waistband and took a look in. Gave my panting audience a naughty smile. "*No* briefs."

If vampire eyes were stove burners, those boys would have been set on Inferno. Even Bart looked like he was smoking a little out the ears. *B-I-N-G.*

"And Emerson certainly knows how to handle all those briefs. Especially the no-briefs. Mmm. What he can do with a fang"—I touched one finger to my neck—"a finger"—I flicked my butt—"and a cock." I made a riding gesture with *two* fingers. "Well. He's a real *stallion.*"

The vampires were actually drooling blood out the corners of their mouths.

And the big hand of the clock behind Cutter was on the three.

I polished more fingernails. "So you boys were here to disrupt the mayor's speech?"

Cutter sucked his tongue back into his mouth. With a vestige of bluster he said, "We're here to scare your rich donors, donor. Ha-ha."

"Good idea." I polished the other hand. "Too bad you're too late."

Cutter flashed a look at his Rolex. "What are you talking about? It's only quarter after four. Fifteen minutes yet."

"Right. Sure. Good timing." I paused, looked him straight in the eye. "If Meiers Corners were on Standard Time."

He laughed. "I adjusted for that, blood-bitch. Daylight savings, central time-zone. It's four fifteen."

"Uh-huh. But that's not what I meant."

"Wha...?"

"Meiers Corners time, Nimrod. Everything's twenty minutes early. The mayor's speech ended five minutes ago."

Cutter looked shocked. Bart swore. All four vampires plus semi-human ran from the hall toward the council room. Going to check it out, but I knew it'd be empty.

"BINGO!" I crowed after them.

"Very nice," a deep, cultured voice said from behind me. "You know they'll just go on to the next venue."

"And we'll deal with it," I said without turning. "But at least the VIPs aren't RIPs. Speaking of Meiers Corners time, aren't you a little late, Emerson?"

"You didn't seem to need the cavalry." He came up behind me and slid his arms around me. "And I so enjoyed hearing about my exploits. Am I really a stallion?"

"Don't let it go to your head." I rubbed back against his leather-clad hips. "If I thought you were really hot, I'd have compared you to a Maserati or Quattroporte."

He leaned down, flicked his tongue across my earlobe. "I'll just have to try harder, won't I."

Whoo-boy. Rev my engine up. "Yeah," I breathed. "After."

"After what?"

"After we check out the sheepshead tourney."

His tongue took an interesting detour. "That doesn't start until four thirty. It's only four-seventeen."

"Weren't you listening, Emerson? Meiers Corners time!" I turned in his arms and tapped his nose.

Julian released me with a sigh. "Since when are you the responsible one?"

"Alien body snatchers!"

We emerged from City Hall into wisps of smoke. The tail

end of a limo streaked down Main. Apparently the Nosy Gang hadn't used umbrellas to get to their ride.

Daniel Butler opened the back door of our limo. "Sir? Miss?"

As we ran for cover, I asked Julian, "How come they're all smoking and you're Ice Cube?"

"An advantage of age." He smiled, revealing gorgeous long and sleeks. Much better than Bludgeon-Leathercoat's. Coolness was not the only advantage of age, I thought. As Butler shut the door, I said, "We have about three minutes."

Julian's smile widened. "What I have in mind takes only two."

He underestimated. When Butler popped open the limo door exactly two minutes, twenty seconds later, I was still pulling up my pants. But in his defense, Julian had gotten rather creative.

Just outside Nieman's door a very red-looking Steve Johnson blocked Cutter and his trio backup. They'd apparently lost St. Barty along the way.

Steve, who'd died a year ago, was...has been...had been Gretchen O'Rourke Johnson's husband. Damn, this living-dead thing was hard to conjugate. Was Julian *was*, or was he *had been*?

Anyway, it became evident to me that Julian was right—age did make a difference. Cutter looked normal but the leathercoats were starting to smolder. And looking closer, Steve's red face might have been because he was about to burst into flames. "Better get those canvas gloves," I murmured to Butler.

Before Towering Inferno III could happen, Julian took over. "Inside," he said, muscling all five vampires into the bar.

"What?" Steve exclaimed. "Letting in this gang of hoodlums is suicide!"

"A scene involving spontaneous combustion is worse." Julian pushed them all the way through the bar into the back room. More of an expanded hallway, really, but tables had been set up for the tournament here as well as in the bar area. Some were already occupied.

Julian glared at the half-dozen players, eyes flashing violet. "*Scram.*"

They took one look at him and ran.

"Scram?" I echoed. "Scram? How trite is that? Why not—'Begone!'? Or 'Off with you!'?"

"Nixie," Julian said warningly.

"Or even, 'Out of my way, peasant!' Really, Julian, what's happened to you?" I cocked my head at him. "Where's the 'I believe you're out of line, sir' Julian I fell in love with?"

He stared at me, his eyes suddenly bright blue. "Why, Nixie. I didn't know you cared."

I could have cut my lips off. "Yeah. Well." ATTITUDE deflated to attitude, which slunk away, whimpering.

"Aw, isn't that cute," Cutter sneered. "Little chew toy's in lo-ove."

I swatted Cutter's mohair-clad arm. "Fuck you, fang-boy."

"Ooh. Witty."

"That's enough." Julian's low growl was annoyed enough to make even me shut up. "You are here to disrupt the Sheepshead Tournament, correct?"

"Yeah," Cutter said, sounding kind of sulky. "And don't think you can stop us by yakking. *This* event goes all night."

"I wouldn't dream of it." Julian crossed his leather-clad arms over his magnificent naked chest. His earring winked in the half-light coming in low through the smoked-glass window. The guy looked good enough to eat. And we'd just done that in the limo ride over. Whoo boy. Julian continued coolly, "But you should know the Ancient One has sent us six of his best. They're due to arrive shortly. Including—Logan."

"Logan?" Cutter went suddenly pale. "Logan...Steel?" he repeated, as if numb.

"Who's Logan?" I mouthed to Julian.

Julian just gave me a quick "no" with his eyes. He'd tell me later, I guessed. He'd better.

"Not *Logan*," Cutter said. "Aw, shit." He started pacing the confined area. Stopped. Demanded, "When will they be here?"

Julian shrugged. "Around sunset. Which is just about...now."

"Fuck!" Cutter whirled. "We've gotta go!"

"But boss," the lead leathercoat said. Bludgeon, I remembered. "Nosferatu said to disrupt the festival. He's not going to like it if we don't even try!"

Cutter stopped hard. He stood there, quivering, as if caught between a rock and a wrecking ball. "Shit. Oh, shit."

Suddenly he lifted his head and his nostrils flared. "Fuck. He's here. I'm doomed." He went from quivering to full tremble, his eyes riveted on the doorway.

A man sauntered in. Tall, movie-star gorgeous, the man had gold-flecked hazel eyes and a mane of bright blond hair that shimmered down his back like a river of sunshine.

With a nod for Julian, the blond glided up to Cutter and patted his cheek. Cutter took it, simply standing there, shaking like a leaf. "Hello, Cutter," the man said. "How nice to see you." His voice was deep, and lazy. "How very nice. Because I seem to recall you owe me money."

"Ye...yes, sir. Yes, Mr. Logan, sir. I just don't have...much with me. That's it, I don't carry cash..."

"That's all right, Cutter." The blond man smiled gently. "I'll let you have another chance." He extended a strong hand toward the other room. "Sheepshead? Double or nothing?"

Cutter groaned. Like a man walking the green mile, he trudged through the doorway.

"Nicely done, Logan," Julian said, holding out his hand.

The blond man shook it, grinned. "Can't stay long, Emerson. Got a fish to fillet." He nodded in the direction of Cutter.

"Of course. Just wondering if you brought anybody with you who could take care of three yearlings." Julian flicked his eyes toward the three coats, who had begun shivering.

Logan's smile broadened. "Oh, I don't think anyone else will be necessary." He crooked a single finger at the three coats. "Come with me, little minnows. Let me teach you a man's game."

Steve made a choked sound. "Five-handed sheepshead with four players against you? Begging your pardon, lord Logan, but are you insane?"

"Why don't you come and see?" Logan's eyes glittered rose-gold, and just the tips of his fangs showed as he spoke. When Steve hesitated, he said, "C'mon, it'll be fun. I'll buy the first round of drinks. How about a Red Special?"

"Well..."

Bludgeon, the one who seemed to like me, who knew what *baka* meant, clapped his hands. "All right! Red Specials are the best! Let's go!"

Everyone stared at him for a moment, including Logan and Julian. Bludgeon shrugged. "He knows how to play sheepshead and he's buying a round of Specials. He can't be all bad."

Logan laughed. Clapped Bludgeon on the back. "How right you are, fledgling. Come along now. Let me show you how to win on three jacks and an ace—without a partner."

"All right!" Bludgeon said again as they disappeared into the bar.

Chapter Twenty-eight

"And no one's tried to get in?" Julian paced the back of the Fudgy Delight, speaking low on his cell phone. "All right. It'll be some time tonight. Call me the instant you hear or smell anything."

"Nothing?" I asked as he flipped his clamshell shut.

"Not even a mist."

"Maybe I'm wrong." I watched the audience fill up. It was seven thirty-five, past time for the beauty pageant to start—and really late according to MC standards. But Kurt had just dashed in with the maillots. It would take at least ten more minutes for the contestants to squeeze into costume.

"You're not wrong." Julian slipped the phone inside his jacket. "The blood is there now. It ships out tomorrow morning. Ruthven has to steal it sometime tonight."

"Which could be a minute from now or ten hours from now."

"Don't worry. The Ancient trains his lieutenants very thoroughly. If anyone can protect the Blood Center, they can." He continued pacing, belying his own words.

"We could go there ourselves," I said. "The band doesn't play until nine. You wouldn't worry as much if you were there, onsite."

"No." Julian stopped pacing, turned his slightly violet eyes toward Bo. "Then I'd worry about him."

Elena's husband was near the stage, pacing even more frantically than Julian. His eyes were shading toward red, and his jaw worked continually, like he was fighting to repress his fangs and not succeeding very well.

"What's he so amped about?"

"Amped...oh, worked up." Julian breathed deep, nostrils distending. "We—my kind—we're rather possessive of our mates."

"But he's the one who suggested Elena do this!"

"To serve a bigger purpose." Julian shrugged, a jerk of one shoulder. "Doesn't mean he likes it."

"So you're staying here to make sure he doesn't go all red-eyed fangy?"

"Something like that." He tensed. "Here they come."

I scanned the stage. "I don't see anyone."

"I smell them. Come on, let's go prop up the Viking."

That must have been one hell of a sniffer, because a full minute passed before the first of the contestants came onstage. Anna Versnobt, who had no doubt insisted on going first. I'd gone to school with her, and she delighted in making my life hell. Picked on my size, my weight, and my way of talking. She looked sicker than all the rest combined. Of course, I could hope she simply hadn't aged well.

Before half the audience could leave, I signaled to the first of my ringers. Drusilla glided into view. She wore a bikini that was more painted-on than worn. From the audience, I could practically hear the drool hitting the floor, men and women both.

Another spotty, fudged-out contestant came on behind her. Still stunned from Dru, the audience didn't even notice.

I watched very carefully. Each ringer had to offset at least three contagious-looking contestants. I'd led with Dru, my heavy hitter. Heavy hitter, ha-ha. Watching her DD's bounce, I realized how apropos that was, if not entirely tasteful.

But as the second fudgy followed the first, the audience started coming out of their stupor. Anxiety attacked me with a stick. Two contestants. Only two, and Dru was the most distractingly gorgeous of the ringers. I signaled frantically.

Josephine Schrimpf sauntered out. Jaws hit the floor.

The Widow Schrimpf wore nothing but hair. She was utterly, totally naked. Like Lady Godiva without the horse. Elena told me later Josephine had a peach-colored bikini, but from here, I couldn't see it. And fortunately, neither could the audience.

That was good for another two. But no more. As the second polka-dotted lady came downstage, a couple people even got up to leave. Desperately, I signaled.

Elena herself came out. She had gone with Dirk's suggestion, her gun belt strapped low over her hips. Normally Dirkenstein's suggestions are like gonorrhea—recurring, and to be avoided. But in this case...wow. The people leaving fell back into their seats. Even I stared at Elena's tight, muscular body, limned by steel and an air of violence.

That was good for another three.

But there were still four contestants left. Four, and only Rocky to distract the audience. Rocky Hrbek, who in high school was overweight and acne-prone. Who dressed in muumuus because they were comfortable. Whose body-image was even more fucked up than most of us double-Xers.

The curtain parted. A gold tube slid out from between. Rocky followed, gliding onstage like a nymph. She put flute to lip, started playing.

Besides auditions, I'd heard Rocky play before, in orchestra. Blending with three so-so violins, a flat tuba, and a punk rock clarinet, she was pretty good.

Playing solo in a bikini, she was breath-taking.

She was playing something exotic, her body swaying to the beat of the music. And what a body! Even Dru stopped for a look, and I caught a glimpse of fang. Fang, dripping with drool.

Totally unselfconscious, Rocky played. She was one with her music. The flute was a living extension of her, as only the best musicians can make it. The sound, blended with her very soul, spread out in waves over the audience. Captivating them. Capturing their attention, their imaginations—their hearts.

The final four contestants, looking like refugees from an isolation ward, slunk out without even a whimper from the audience. We were all far too enthralled by Rocky and her music.

When Rocky finished playing she folded in on herself, all the poise of a scared bunny. But it didn't matter. The magic had wrapped up the entire room.

The pageant was going to be fine.

Julian and I stayed the whole hour. Rocky won. Even with the Widow Schrimpf, Elena, and Drusilla to choose from, the judges picked Rocky. For her beauty, for her talent, but also for her innocence, that sense that she truly had no idea how beautiful and talented she was. That sweet naivety just enhanced her appeal. The emcee took the sparkling crystal crown and set it on Rocky's chestnut head.

And you know what she did?

She took the crown off. Walked over to Elena. Said, "There must be some mistake. This is obviously yours." Reached up and put the crown on Elena's corkscrew curls.

But that was Rocky for you. And I couldn't complain. She had saved the pageant.

The festival was in full swing, going fine. A competent fangy guy guarded each event, and though I kept checking my voicemail, not one problem was called in. I was actually starting to relax.

I should learn not to do that.

Because when we got to the Roller-Blayd factory, the Ruthiettes were setting up. On the *main* stage.

Where *we* were supposed to open.

Lob ran from Billy the Kid to each of his posse, yelling. BTK et al ignored him, plugging in equipment and generally taking over the stage.

I waved impatiently to Lob. Thanks to a suggestion from Julian, Lob was fully recovered from his brush with fangy weirdness. He saw me, came over. "You've got to do something," he yelled. "Moss and I both tried, but...these guys are a disaster!"

"Set Guns and Polkas up on the second stage," I told him.

"What good will it do?" Lob asked, pulling on his already-spiky hair. "The speakers are wired to the main stage. Nobody will hear us."

"The speakers are wired to both stages." That was Woofers 'R Us's idea, but I thought it was pretty froody.

The sound equipment was set up so either stage could use it. While one band was playing, another could be setting up on the other stage. When the second band was ready, the system would switch to the new band. Slick.

Lob made a face. "Yeah, but the equipment is preset. It switches every half-hour—and it starts on the main stage!"

"Great. Simply lucking fovely." I cast an eye over BTK and the Ruthiettes. The guy with the mullet had grabbed an electric bass. He hung it upside down from the strap around his neck. He tried to plug into his preamp by sticking one of the tuning machines in the socket. When the tuner didn't even come close to fitting, the dweeb decided to be clever. He used his mighty vampire strength to strip off the knob. Too bad his brain power hadn't increased with his muscle power. When he stuck the denuded pin into the amp, a zap of current lit him up brighter than a light bulb. His eyes turned red and his mullet stood out like the bill of a baseball cap. He jittered around the stage for a bit, until the guitar came unplugged. Then he just stood there, the occasional zap quaking his body, bits of smoke rising from his nostrils and ears.

BTK was smarter, but not by much. He plugged in his guitar okay, but the volume knob was dialed all the way down. He hit the strings and nothing happened. He fiddled with all the keys on the guitar including the tremolo bar—in fact, everything *but* the volume control. Still nothing. That pissed him off so much he broke the guitar over mullet guy's head. I winced but the growing audience applauded.

Josiah Moss, the alderperson for the bands, jumped on the stage where Julian and I stood. "We've got to do something," he said. "I don't know who these guys are, but they don't listen worth shit. And they're stronger than hell." He rubbed his arm, where I saw four distinct finger-shaped bruises.

Julian started purposefully forward. "I'll take care of it."

I put a hand on his arm. "There's already too many people here. Somebody will see."

"I'll be discreet." The tips of Julian's fangs were just poking out his lips.

"There are five of them, Julian. One of you."

"I've done five against one before." His chest muscles, just visible between the edges of his jacket, were pumped up like boulders. "I can handle them."

"I'm sure. But five bodies...twelve pints each? That's a huge mess, Julian. I'll be a good little wifey, but I ain't cleaning up all that."

His fangs disappeared like slingshots. "Wifey?"

Oops. Talk about Freudian slips. Julian would run like the wind.

So I was utterly shocked when he pulled me tight and kissed me like he'd like to crawl down my throat. "Yes," he said.

"Yes?" I echoed faintly, not even knowing what the question was.

At that moment the Ruthiettes struck their first chord.

We both flinched. It was so bad it hurt. They had figured out how to plug into the sound system but they still didn't know how to make music. Bass, lead, rhythm, and keyboard all joined in a cacophony of tsunami proportions.

They clashed like they'd thrown their instruments in a blender, along with a sixties Volkswagon bus. And the bus sounded best.

All around us people were staring at the band on the main stage. Not upset or unfriendly, exactly, but confused. Apparently they thought this was simply a new style of garbage rock. One or two tried to dance to the beat, but as the Ruthiette drummer entered the fray, it became obvious the beat was the musical equivalent of thrown paint.

"We've got to do something!" Lob and Josiah wailed at the same time.

"If not my solution," Julian said, "what, then?"

"Can we cut their power?" I asked Lob.

"I tried. There's a backup supply on each stage. It'll die, but not before we do."

"Where's the backup?"

Lob pointed at a dark gray box nestled between Billy the Kid's feet.

Shizzle. As friendly as BTK was with that backup power supply, even Julian couldn't get to it.

Julian pointed to the crowd. "You'd better come up with something soon. We don't have much time."

People were milling restlessly, some starting toward the door. We were counting on a full night of bands to keep the people—and money—hopping. The Ruthiettes could shut us down before we even started.

Suddenly Julian snapped his fingers. "*Star Trek.*" He motioned Josiah Moss over.

"What?"

"*Wrath of Khan.* They may be stronger, but music is *our* world."

I was surprised that Julian knew any pop culture but wisely kept my mouth shut.

"We'll take advantage of their ignorance." Julian shouted instructions in Moss's ear. Then he pushed him toward the door. "Hurry!"

As Moss ran out, Julian clamped hands to ears. Apparently his vampy hearing was even more sensitive than mine.

"What did you tell him?" I asked.

He told me.

"Shit. You're kidding, right?" Our fate rested in the hands of the most frightfully unreliable people in the world—teenagers. And worse. Drunk teenagers.

"Can you think of anything else?" Julian winced at a particularly loud Gm7 with added 13, 19 and yowling cat.

Josiah Moss returned in short order. Twenty drunken teen math geeks reeled in behind him. But not *just* math geeks, *applied* math geeks. That was what Julian was counting on now.

The lead geek was Bill Like Bill Gates. The one who'd kept smooshing me with kisses. "He likes you best," Julian said to me. "You'd better explain."

I glared at him, and I think my eyes turned red. I know I was snarling. But I did it. This responsibility thing was no fun, but it did get easier. "How much do you know about acoustics?" I shouted in Bill's ear.

"Enough to know when waves are seriously clashing." Bill closed one eye like he was getting a hangover. "Why?"

Twenty, drunk, *uninsured* teenagers. Maybe this wasn't the only solution. Maybe—

As I hesitated, three people near the door left. Another two started after them.

I took a deep breath. "We need some help."

"You need help from us?" Both of Bill's eyes snapped opened and swung to me. "Do I get a kiss?"

"No," I said. Julian *growled.*

My voice was lost in the overwhelming ruckus, but the growl cut through.

"Okay," the kid said, eyes switching to Julian. "No kiss." A beat. "Nice earring. Engagement present?"

Julian opened his mouth to answer. Since I did not want to hear what he would say, I yelled, "So do you? Do you guys know anything about acoustics?"

"Sure," the kid said.

"Great. Here's what we have in mind."

Chapter Twenty-nine

Billy the Kid and the Ruthiettes had control of the main amp and speakers until nine thirty. Lob had set up our equipment on the second stage.

Normally our speakers wouldn't make a dent in the hell-sound that the BTK posse was spitting out. Even our five-foot Big Daddy was seriously underpowered compared to the six-footers.

But I had a secret weapon. Twenty little technogeeks. They combined and boosted our small amps and speakers. Serious boosting. As the final fillip, Bill-not-Gates whipped out a black Sharpee and drew an extra click on the volume knob.

He'd ramped us up to eleven.

At least half a dozen people had already left. The rest of the crowd was heading toward the door. I gave the nod to our singer and frontman Cob, and held my breath.

"Are you ready to rock, Meiers Corners!" Cob boomed.

People stopped in their tracks. Turned hopefully.

Guns and Polkas started our signature tune, fast and furious, at about five thousand decibels. It was so loud it had to be good.

The crowd started wandering back. I crowed with triumph. Of course, with our style of music my crow sounded like a duet with Cob.

We ripped out that tune like we were *American Idol* megastars. Manic energy poured from us; we were light-years better than our very best. We were tighter than tight, louder than loud, driving music out like a speeding semi.

And Julian was *amazing*. It was as if he'd played punk all

his life, complete with muscular riffs and rippling abs. The audience was blown away.

The intent however was to blow away BTK and the Ruthiettes. We were counting on vampire hearing being more sensitive. I was hoping we were so loud the bad-guy vamps would stop playing and run away.

Half the plan worked. They stopped playing.

They didn't run away.

When Billy the Kid saw the audience returning, he smashed another guitar over mullet-boy's head. I guess he was pissed. So I gave him a friendly, one-fingered salute.

BTK, sprouting fangs, came straight at me.

I wasn't worried. The ramped-up speakers were pointed strategically toward the vampire band. When Billy TK leaped onto the edge of our stage, it put him right in front of our Big Daddy.

I slipped behind the head-high speaker. Nodded to Julian, who squished in a set of earplugs.

Then I hit Billy and his homies with a seriously ramped-up power chord.

Set to eleven, the amp smashed that chord through the air like a hammer. Waves of sound pumped out so big and hard even I could feel them. They would pound a vampire's brain to mush.

The vampires screamed. Jumped off the main stage like deserting rats. They headed straight for the backstage area, darker and cooler than the rest of the warehouse. They didn't bother to take their instruments.

But even though his head should have been hollowed out by my power chord, Billy the Kid came straight for me.

I saw it with the clarity of a nightmare. BTK mere feet away, fangs extended and dripping saliva. Cob, nearest me, had just seen the fangs and was paralyzed, shock clear on his face. The rest of the band hadn't even seen the danger.

Except for Julian. Out of the corner of my eye I saw Julian leap toward me.

But he was on the other side of the stage. Billy the Kid was within spitting distance. I knew there was only one male who could protect me now.

Oscar.

Heart breaking, I slammed Oscar into the stage. Oscar broke, his rosewood fingerboard separating from his body. As BTK ran toward me, I swung Oscar's neck up to my shoulder like a bazooka.

We were invisible to the audience, behind the Big Daddy speaker. Good thing, because the Kid had dropped any semblance of humanity. His face was plated, his fangs and claws were flared. He absolutely dripped rage as he lunged for me.

I stood stiff, Oscar's headstock braced against my shoulder.

Billy the Kid impaled himself twelve inches deep. His eyes widened. He took one gaspy breath. His claws closed and opened spasmodically, then disappeared. He didn't vanish in a poof of dust, but no more breaths followed. His eyes rolled back into his head. Slowly he collapsed.

I stood there, heart pounding. Bo would be proud. I had done it. I had staked a vampire, the old-fashioned way. Without a bazooka.

The Kid fell off the back of the stage with my improvised stake still embedded in his chest. Oscar's neck slid from my grasp. Hell. I wish it had been a bazooka. A tear ran down my cheek.

A hand gripped my shoulder. I jumped, only to freeze when Julian's warm voice sounded in my ear. "Ruthven's gang is escaping!"

I shot a look toward the door, but the Ruthiettes weren't there. Then I remembered they had run toward the back of the warehouse. Toward the dim, dark corner where our coats and cases were. "What do you mean? There's no escape that way. No doors, and the windows are a story up. Unless they can fly?"

"Not old enough. But if there's no escape, why did they run that way?"

"I don't know." And I didn't care. Oscar lay broken at my feet. Behind me, Lob and Rob had finally figured out something was going on. Well, with half the band not playing, they were bound to sooner or later. Cob was still paralyzed.

"We've got to follow them," Julian said urgently.

"We can't." Oscar was gone. And while I could play on a borrowed guitar for the rest of the set, the guitar wouldn't play itself. Take away rhythm, take away lead..."Guns and Polkas sounds like a kindergarten band without guitars!"

Raising both eyebrows, Julian said, "Is the band's sound more important than catching *vampires*?" He ran an exasperated hand through his hair. "Sorry, I'm being buckets of stupid. Of course it is."

A muddy rasp turned both our heads. "Am I late, Nixie?" Dirk Ruffles, his sax hanging from his neck, climbed onto the back of the stage. He gave BTK a glance as he passed. "That's a funny place to take a nap."

"Dirk!" Here was an opportunity marked quack. "Do you remember 'Take Five'?"

"Of course," he said. "Why?"

"Lob! Grab the keyboard off the main stage. Hook it in and use the auto-chords. You want E-flat minor/B-flat minor." I turned to Dirk. "Okay, wing it until I get back."

"You got it, Nixie!"

Julian and I rushed after the vampires. Back of the warehouse, no way out. It should have been like a box canyon. We should have confronted four mean and fangies.

But when we got to the unlit corner, all the Ruthiettes had disappeared.

I stared, disbelieving. It was like a locked room mystery. Three walls, a ceiling, and a floor covered with wooden pallets piled with instrument cases. No doors, no windows, nowhere to go. Yet four big vampires were gone.

"Did they mist?" I asked, remembering Ruthven, and Julian's easy-off clothes.

"Billy was the only one old enough." He cast around him, nostrils flared. "They're not far." His eyes were so red they almost glowed.

Red glow. Like an *exit* sign.

And I thought, what if?

There's an old story about PT Barnum. He put together a museum of exhibits and live acts—Tom Thumb, the Feejee Mermaid, various stuffed animals, and the like. People came to see them, but were so enthralled they didn't leave. And even in the dark ages, you hadda have throughput to make money. So PT posted signs saying, "This way to the Egress". People thought "egress" was another exhibit. Maybe some kind of bird. But it's not—it's an exit. In PT's case, an exit with no way back in. And people would exit, whether they intended to or not. Instant throughput.

PT Barnum's egress was an exit that didn't look like an exit. What if there was an egress here? Not a door, or window, or something we'd normally think of as an exit. But something else? I dove to my knees in front of the mountain of cases, and pulled them aside to bare the wooden pallet underneath.

"What...?" Julian crouched down beside me. His eyes widened. Something was under the pallet.

Or rather, *nothing* was under the pallet. I had revealed a big hole in the concrete floor. "WTF...a tunnel! This must lead to the Blood Center. *This* is how they planned to get the blood out."

Julian nodded grimly. "Call Elena. I'll contact Bo, have him send us Logan and the rest."

The calls took less than thirty seconds. After we passed the information on, Julian dropped into the hole. "Jump, Nixie." His voice sounded echoey, like he was far away.

I squeaked. "Don't you want to wait for Elena and Bo?"

"No time." Julian's voice floated up from the pitch black. "Ruthven's lieutenants will know we're not far behind. With the element of surprise gone, they may decide to break the blood out another way. They may even destroy it, if they can't have it."

"But they won't know we've found their tunnel." It was so *dark* down there. And...deep-sounding.

"They'll figure it out. Come on, Nixie. Jump. I'll catch you."

I couldn't see a thing. I didn't know how deep the tunnel was. From the far-off sound of Julian's voice, I was afraid it wasn't just a few feet.

I would need to trust him to catch me.

Did I trust him that much? Did I trust a man I'd met less than two weeks ago to keep me from jumping to my death, or at least a couple broken bones?

Fuck. Yes. Yes, I did. I jumped.

The fall was longer than I expected. My stomach flew to the roof of my mouth. Nothing, nothing...suddenly Julian's warm arms caught me.

Then, to my utter shock, we dropped more. But slower, gentler. We floated like a feather to a stop. "Can *you* fly?" I gasped.

"Not exactly," Julian murmured, setting me down. "It's a form of shape-shifting."

The blackness engulfed me. I grabbed for him, caught his jacket in my fist. Gently, Julian disengaged me, murmuring soothing nonsense. I seized his hand instead.

He curled his fingers protectively around mine. Led me forward, slowly. I started relaxing. It was so much like the night at the *Kosmopolitisch* I nearly laughed out loud. But there were four big vampires somewhere in the darkness. I didn't want them hearing me.

Or maybe, I thought with a pang of panic, more than four. After all, some of Ruthven's gang would have to be inside. Inside, passing blood down from the Blood Center. Carting the blood back this way, to pass it up into the Roller-Blayd factory. But only after the tourists had been scared away. I choked back my laugh.

The tunnel went on for what seemed like miles. Any second I expected to run into Ruthiettes. I couldn't hear anything above my own pounding heart, so I strained my eyes, hoping for some light. I thought a couple times I could see...something. But no. Nothing except my own eagerness and fear playing tricks on my brain.

So it was a complete surprise when a small golden glow appeared, and didn't disappear when I blinked. "Julian. Is that light?"

"Shh. It's the Blood Center. Nixie—we don't know what we'll find. I don't suppose I could convince you to wait here?"

"NFW." *No fucking way.*

"All right. Be careful, please. Remember that though they're young, these males are vampires. Their reflexes are still much faster than yours."

"I staked one." I was hit by a momentary twang of mourning for Oscar.

"No stakes here," he said reasonably. There was a momentary silence. The sort of pause that said Julian was working to choose his words.

"What," I said. Julian the Vampire always knew what to do.

Julian the Lawyer always knew what to say. For him to have to think about it meant I would not like it.

We were about to do battle and we might not win. Hell, we might not even both survive. Maybe Julian was about to say something we'd both regret later. Maybe he was about to go all emo with the *L* word.

"Julian," I started.

"I need you to do something for me, Nixie."

Oh. Not the *L* word. I was not disappointed. Really. "What?"

"I don't like it. I'd rather you stay back or stay with me. But..."

"Just spit it out, Julian. What do you need me to do?"

He sighed. "I could normally handle four of Ruthven's lieutenants by myself. But with the blood at stake...and in case there are more of them...well, it would be better if I had help. I don't know how long it will take Bo and Logan to get here. So while I engage the vampires...I need you to open the Blood Center front door."

"To let in the Ancient One's ringers?" It sounded like Julian was just manufacturing an excuse to get me out of the way. "Can't they mist in?"

"No. Only Logan and the one at the beer tent are old enough to mist. The three guarding the Blood Center entrance are well-trained, but they can't get in. Unless you let them in."

"Okay. No problem."

"One problem. You'll be on your own. If I screw up, if I let one vampire through and he catches you—" Julian's arms came around me, hauled me to him. He planted a quick, hard kiss on my mouth. "I'd kill myself. I don't know how it happened, but you've come to mean the world to me." He kissed me again, then released me as suddenly as he'd embraced me.

"Well," I stuttered, embarrassed. "You mean...a lot...to me, too."

"Good. I hope that means you'll be careful."

The light winked four or five times as we got closer, as if bodies were passing in front of it. Maybe bad vamp reinforcements. Aw, hell. "Julian—I do lov—"

The first of Ruthven's vampires attacked.

We were in a small cave, or actually a wider area of the

tunnel. All-terrain carts waited to transport blood. Along with rogues to push them.

Julian shoved me toward the wall. The sound of growling came from behind me. Whistling slashes, and the sound of blood hitting dirt. I sure as hell hoped it wasn't Julian's.

A shadow passed in front of the doorway. Paused. I couldn't see a face, but the shape and eerie way of flowing looked like Ruthven.

The shadow turned toward Julian and stiffened. It waved someone forward. Pointed at Julian.

Ruthven. It had to be. Ruthie had seen Julian. I ran toward the doorway.

The shadow silently disappeared.

Ruthie had seen Julian, and now the scaredy-rat was fleeing. Damn it!

I sprinted after the mega-slime. I didn't know what I thought I'd do if I caught him, but him bending over and pointy spikes loomed large in my imagination.

Dirt gave way to concrete. The light improved dramatically. I saw a ladder, scrabbled up it. I recognized the Blood Center storage/donation room—just as a hand grabbed my neck.

"Well, well. Emerson's little chew toy." The hulk hauling me up was bigger than Ruthie but not as big as Julian. His hair was long and gnarled. His breath smelled of stale blood.

I didn't recognize him, although he obviously knew me. His fingers pricked my neck, like his claws were out. His mouth was open, his fangs dripping with menace.

Time for Attitude. "Nice fangs, but a little small, if you know what I mean." I gave the hulk a once-over with my baby-blues. "I've met all of Billy the Kid's band, and you ain't one. How many of you Ruthiettes are there, anyway?"

I was gratified to see his fangs recede, his snarl turn to confusion. "Ruthi-whats?"

"Ruthiettes. You know. Ruthven's boy band. His posse."

The hulk drew himself straight, his chin flying up. "We are Lord Ruthven's *lieutenants*."

"Oh, *lieutenants*. Like the Army." I cracked imaginary gum. "Only without the training and the discipline."

"We have discipline." The vampire crossed his arms and

tapped his foot to let me know how offended he was...incidentally letting me go.

I shrugged. "Sure. Never meant to imply otherwise. I'm sure even the Ancient One's homies don't get *your* level of training."

"Well..."

"I'm sure you're *more* than capable of beating Julian Emerson, who's just through that door." I jerked my head toward the hole in the wall.

"Well..." The vampire's eyes tracked nervously toward the hole.

"And I know you've seen right through my ploy to keep out of that front office. You know I've been trying to delay you until Julian can rescue me. And to *keep me out of that front office.*"

"Well...yes. Of course I have!"

"Oh darn. I was hoping you wouldn't figure it out. Maybe if I ask nicely? Please, may I wait here?" I clasped my hands in an attitude of supplication. "Just don't throw me into that front office, Mr. Lieutenant. Please-oh-please. Anywhere but the front office."

I thought for a second maybe I'd laid it on too thick. If he'd ever seen a Bugs Bunny cartoon or read Brer Rabbit...

"No!" The hulk's fangs sprung out. "No mercy! You're not keeping me here, blood-bitch. I'm taking you into that front office no matter how hard you plead!"

The front office, with the front door. How lovely.

Then he hesitated. "Unless you plead really, really hard. I might be merciful."

Shit. A vampire with a conscience. I pretended to ignore him. "You won't take me willingly!" I said as I rammed a spear hand into his gut.

He sucked in a breath and doubled over. Got him right in the solar plexus, paralyzed his diaphragm. For a moment I considered running, but I might only run into another vamp— who might be smarter. So I waited patiently for this one to restart his diaphragm.

Eventually he did. Gasping, he grabbed me. "That's it, blood-bitch! No mercy. You're going to the office!"

Heh-heh.

He hustled me into the front office. Once there it was easy.

"No, please, no!" I cried in a fairly good imitation of a girly-girl, making sure I was pulling and tugging toward the storeroom for all I was worth. Even with supernatural strength he had to put his weight behind it to move me.

So all I had to do was stop resisting him.

He tumbled ass over tea kettle into the office. Released, I feinted toward the back. When he grabbed for me I reversed and headed straight for the front door. The office was all of three steps deep and I made it before the hulk even got to his hands and knees. I caught the knob, flipped the lock, and flung open the door.

Three good-guy vampires flowed in, eyes red, fangs and knives out, loaded for bear. "Back room!" I shouted, pointing. They disappeared faster than a chocolate bunny on Easter.

As I punched in the alarm shut-off code, a low growl came from behind the desk. Oh, oops. Forgot about the hulk.

He rose from the desk like Godzilla—angry, pumped, and just a little green around the gills. Blood ran from a gash in his forehead. Apparently he'd hit his head when I'd pulled my little maneuver. "You're toast now, blood-bitch!"

"Yep. Scared." I worked frantically on options. I rejected half a dozen, including just screaming like a girl. While I had no doubt Julian would fly to my rescue (maybe even literally) I didn't think I could live with myself if I did that.

But what could I do? I had no bazookas and no stakes. I had an office with a filing cabinet, a desk, and a cup full of...pencils.

"Ah-ha!" I snatched up a number 2. "You'll only wish you were dead after five minutes with me and this pencil!"

The hulk paled. Went almost sheet white. Well, yay! Maybe Bo was wrong. Maybe it didn't have to be forearm thick. Maybe it was the wood that did it.

From behind me, an insouciant voice said, "Hello, Blaxx. Long time no see. Do you have that thousand you owe me?"

If anything, the hulk went paler. "Lord Logan! What a surprise. Um, I'm a little short of cash at the mo'." The apparently named Blaxx patted down his coat.

Behind me the gorgeous blond vampire Logan stepped with lazy grace through the door. "Oh, that's all right. I'll just take my payment in blood."

One second Logan was in the doorway, the next he towered over the hulk. A gleaming white, sharp smile made his face look slightly feral. "You don't mind, do you?"

"Uh...*gack*," the hulk said as Logan open his throat with two flicks of what looked like a rapier. Fountains of blood spurted from the severed neck, splashing desk, wall, and pencil cup. Logan followed up with a dagger, digging out the heart with a round slash that he made look impossibly elegant.

"Hmm. That'll leave a stain." Sheathing the dagger, Logan picked up the cup, plucked out the pencils. Overturned the cup. A stream of red liquid poured onto the desk. Dropping the heart calmly into the cup, he arched a blond brow at me. "Where's the party?"

"Back there," I said, feeling a little sick. I was a kick-ass black belt, but I didn't seem to have all the necessary prerequisites to be a vampire slayer. Oh, well. In each generation, there was only one anyway.

"Good," Logan drawled. "I was getting bored."

"What happened to the Sheepshead Tournament?" I asked before I could help myself. It was supposed to go on all night.

He arched the other brow. "I won, of course. Coming?"

"Uh, yeah." Covering my nose and dodging the desk, I followed Logan's broad back into the storage room.

Chapter Thirty

In the storage room the fight was going hot and heavy. Three ringers and Julian were pitted against a dozen vampires. Though Julian was holding his own, the ringers looked a little the worse for wear. "Well," said Logan, gold-flecked eyes bright on the ruckus. "This ought to be entertaining."

"A little less talking," Julian bellowed as he swiped his foot-long blade through a vampire's neck, "and a little more helping, if you please."

"If you're sure," Logan said. "I would hate to spoil your fun."

"Don't hesitate on my account, Steel." Julian caught the falling body, dug out the heart with a quick efficiency that looked more like he was pitting a cherry. Dropping the body, he lobbed the heart into the wall. "There's more than enough to go around." The heart went *splat*. I felt sick again.

"You're doing quite nicely without me, though," Logan said. "I don't want to interfere if—hey!"

Enough was enough. I pushed him. "Get the fuck in there and fight."

To my surprise, Logan laughed. "Oh, you'll have your hands full with this one, Emerson." He caught the neck of a passing vampire, spun the vamp to face him.

The vampire's eyes opened wide. "Steel? Oh, shit no, not Steel!"

"Hello. And good-bye!" Faster than I could follow, Logan's arm moved. More blood, ick. And when the body fell, there was an alarming hole in its chest.

"Nice work," Julian said.

"Well, ya gotta have heart." Logan tossed something red and muscley in the air like a ball and grinned.

I groaned.

"Huh. No sense of humor," Logan said to Julian with a toss of his blond head at me. "Now why am I not surprised?"

One of the ringers passed by, retreating from two of Ruthven's gang. "Hey," Logan called. "No fair herding. This is Illinois, not Wisconsin or Texas. You can't steer around here. Leather you want to or not." He tapped one of the gang on the shoulder. The vampire whirled, eyes red, fangs extended. "You don't cow me." Logan's dagger flashed out and bit deep into the rogue's neck.

I stood in the doorway and covered my eyes. I wasn't sure if I was more appalled at the destruction or the puns.

With both Julian and Logan fighting, the tide turned. Soon there were only two of Ruthven's vampires left standing. Both were from the Billy the Kid band, the keyboard player and the mullet.

Two Ruthiettes, and five of our guys. Julian, Logan, and the three ringers stalked slowly forward.

The keyboard player took one look and quit fighting, his hands held high in the air. "I give! Please don't slice off my head."

But Mullet guy, standing near the blood refrigeration units shouted "Coward!"

And pulled out a big red button.

Uh-oh. I had seen enough movies to know a Big Red Button was never a good thing.

"One step closer and the blood's had it!" Mullet guy squealed.

Logan stowed rapier and dagger and leaned lazily against one wall. "Can you be any more trite?"

"The threat is real," Julian cautioned.

"Yeah, but could Razor be any cornier? 'One step closer and the blood's had it.' What kind of self-respecting villain uses such hackneyed dialog?"

Razor? What was it with these guys? Stupid-Name-of-the-Month Club?

Julian shook his head. "Whatever he says, Logan, we can't

take chances."

"Listen to Emerson." Razor backed toward the office doorway. "After all, he's the smart one."

"I think I've just been insulted." Logan clapped both hands to his heart.

Ignoring him, Julian said to mullet guy, "I'm smart enough to know that button has only a limited range. How far do you think you'll get, Razor?"

In a flash, Razor reached out. Grabbed *me*. Winched me in, held me tight against his body. "Far enough."

I huffed a disgusted breath. "I can't believe I fell for that."

"Nixie!" Julian's nostrils flared and his eyes were instantly red. "If you hurt her, Razor, I will tear you in pieces."

"I won't hurt her—if she behaves." Razor continued backing toward the doorway, forcing me with him. "This time. But you won't always be here, Emerson." He cackled. "Or you, Steel. Or your precious Ancient One or any of his oh-so-wonderful lieutenants."

"Bo will be here." Julian was obviously holding himself in check only with the greatest difficulty. "And his lieutenants are every bit as well-trained."

I wondered about that. Bo had Steve and Thorvald. There was also Stark of Stark and Moss Funeral Home, but he kept pretty much to himself. Dru, too, but as far as I knew, that was the entire permanent vampire population of Meiers Corners.

While Razor and the rest of Ruthven's shorties lived less than an hour away in Chicago.

Well. Looked like I was going to have to learn to save myself.

I still had the pencil. While it probably wouldn't do much good as a stake, it was quite pointy. Driven through a body part, it would still hurt like hell.

The particular body part I had in mind was Razor's Big-Red-Button hand. I'd learned enough to know I couldn't go for it directly. In a straight speed and reflex contest, a vampire would win, every time.

But I'd learned from fighting Mr. Miyagi in my black belt classes that old age and treachery win against youth and agility. So, mix those up, sort of, and you get human treachery winning against vampire agility. I hoped.

I feinted, twisting in Razor's grip like I was going to pull away. In reality I was getting my pencil hand free. When he followed and tightened his arm around me like a vise, I let him. I'd gotten what I wanted.

A free stab.

The sharp pencil went satisfyingly deep. I felt a gasp. Razor emitted such a high-pitched squeal I thought he'd shape-shifted into a pig.

Julian peeled Razor off me in an instant, while Logan caught the button that fell from his injured hand.

"She...she *stabbed* me!" Razor gasped in disbelief.

"So she did." Wrapping me in his arms, Julian's tone was a mixture of relief and pride. "My Nixie can take care of herself, and you'd better not forget it."

My Nixie? Face sheltered in Julian's yummy abs, I wondered when I had become *his* Nixie. I also wondered at the burst of pleasure I felt hearing that. Hadn't I already established I was only his Nixie as long as he was in Meiers Corners? Once he went back to Boston, he would become his tight-ass lawyerly Emerson again.

And I would go back to being my own punk and lonely Nixie.

The pain of that made me suddenly want to do something, anything, to make him stay. To be *my* Julian. To be *his* Nixie, maybe forever.

Oh, fuck. I *was* in love with the jerk.

"Nixie?" Elena's voice, from the front door. "Are you all right?"

"Fine," I told her wearily, turning away from the beguiling, silky warmth of Julian's skin. "As is the Blood Center."

Hitching her SMAW on her shoulder, Elena came through the door. Behind her hovered her husband Bo, fanged and ready. "What's going on?" he asked. "I only got part of the story."

Julian released me. "Ruthven's lieutenants were going to highjack the shipment of blood through a tunnel. They must have been here for some time, digging from the Roller-Blayd warehouse into the Blood Center."

I said, "But the festival put a crimp in their plans. Especially having all those people listening to bands in the Roller-Blayd factory."

"That's why they wanted to play first," Julian said. "To drive everyone from the warehouse."

"So no one would see them bringing up the blood," Elena said.

"Exactly. When we foiled that, they tried to blow up the evidence. Nixie saved the day."

"Nixie?" Elena looked startled.

"My Nixie." Julian pulled me tight.

"*Your* Nixie?"

"His Nixie," Logan said helpfully.

"Well," said Bo to no one in particular. "That explains the state of the limo."

I blushed. "Okay, okay!" I pulled away from Julian's possessive arms. "But we've got a festival to protect, people! Let's get organized. Ruthie's minions are taken care of, but they're not the only Lestats in Meiers Corners! And Ruthie's not the only member of the Coterie interested in us. Because while we've been dealing with the Ruthiettes—"

Behind me, Julian sucked in his breath. I have to say, the boy was quick on the uptake. "Nosferatu."

"Exactly. So let's get going, guys and gals. Logan—you keep the ringers here to guard the blood. Elena, Bo, Julian...let's hope it's not as bad as I think it'll be."

While we were dealing with the Ruthiettes, Nosy's Lestats had free run. I bolted out of the Blood Center, afraid of the havoc they might already have wreaked.

"Oh, shit, there's a couple vampires." Bo pointed to the Deli Delight. "Four more." In front of the Fudgy Delight.

We ran down Fifth. "Three over there." Julian indicated Nieman's Bar. "And I smell at least half a dozen in the beer tent."

Nosy's lieutenants were everywhere. Like cockroaches. Spread out all over the four blocks of the festival.

How would we stop them? Especially, how could we stop them without scaring away the tourists?

Rounding a corner, we saw Cutter and his three

leathercoats—headed directly for us.

Well. Stop these four, first. Worry about scaring tourists later.

Bo and Julian tensed, eyes going fighting violet. Elena unhooked her SMAW. She looked discreetly around her, realized she couldn't blow up Lestats without torching a couple handfuls of tourists. Put the SMAW back with a grimace.

Cutter and his gang were fangy and snarling. Red-eyed and clawed.

But people passed them fearlessly. Some of the tourists even waved and called out good-natured ribald comments. Huh. Maybe they thought fangs and claws were festival costumes.

As the Lestats got closer, though, I realized something odd.

That wasn't snarling.

They were *singing*. Poorly and off-key, but singing nonetheless. They sounded amazingly like the drunken teenage geeks.

And as the Nosy Quartet reeled up, a smell of beer and brats washed over me. "Hello, pretty lady," Cutter called to me. "Hello, pretty lady with the bazooka," he said to Elena, a goofy smile on his face. He actually sloshed over to Julian and tried to embrace him. "Julian! My very good bestest friend in the world!"

"You're smashed," Julian said, holding Cutter firmly away.

Cutter's eyes widened. "I am?"

"He can't be," another Lestat said. He was young and fresh-faced, sort of like I thought Bart was before I found out Bart was a puke. "He didn't have any beer. Or liquor or Red Specials or antying...anthying...*any*thing."

"What have you all been doing?" Elena asked suspiciously.

"I don't remember." Cutter blinked. The other Lestats echoed him.

"Do you remember anything?" Bo asked the fresh-faced Lestat.

"Nothing much," the vampire said. "We were supposed to cause trouble. So we bit a few people." When Bo growled, the young vampire added, "Not much! Not to hurt them or anything. Just to scare them a little."

"Oh, no," I said, a giggle bubbling up.

"This is hardly a laughing matter, Nixie," Bo said.

"No, of course it isn't." I was trying to control myself and failing utterly. "So you bit a few people?" I asked the Lestat.

"Just a little," he admitted, eying Bo warily.

"Which people?"

"Well..." He waved his hand vaguely around him. "People. Tourists," he added, as if he'd just thought of the word and was proud of himself.

"Tourists. On the streets?"

All four vampires nodded.

I pursed my lips. "Hmm. Tourists...at the festival events?" They nodded harder. "At Nieman's bar?" They nodded like spring-loaded goony birds. "In the beer tent?" They nodded so hard Bludgeon threw up.

Both Elena and Julian were laughing by this time. Even Bo was starting to smile a little. "Tourists with a blood alcohol level well into intoxication," I said. "Do you suppose a vampire could get crunk on alcohol-laced blood?"

Julian and Elena were laughing too hard to answer. Bo said, "We learn something new every day. In fact—"

He was interrupted by a loud bray. "Mr. and Mrs. Strongwell! Mr. and Mrs. Emerson! Nixie, nice to see you and your little hubby!"

Julian took one look at Lew Kaufman, bearing down on us, and turned heel to run. He was stopped by Bo's and Elena's wide-open mouths. "Mr. and Mrs. *Emerson*?" Bo gasped, starting to laugh. "Oh, now that is rich."

I blushed. Elena clapped an arm around my shoulders. "Congratulations, Nixie! You got yourself a keeper." At that I flushed hot. I couldn't look at Julian.

"Mr. Kaufman!" one of the Lestats called, distracting me from my embarrassment. "Mr. Kaufman, remember us?"

"'Course I do, m'boy!" Lew said. "I always remember a customer!"

"Customer?" I echoed, more to turn the subject from me and my little "hubby" than anything.

"I was at the Deli Delight and couldn't believe it," Lew said. "Someone packed all those perfectly good cheese balls away in back!"

"Cheese balls?" I asked faintly. "Which cheese balls?"

"The LLA's, of course! Well, we couldn't have that, could we?"

"We couldn't...? Oh no. Lew, what did you do?"

"I sold them!" Lew chortled gleefully.

"Sold...them?" I asked in horror.

"Sure. Well, the head cheese and blood sausage ones." He shook hands with all four Lestats. Gestured toward the other vampires reeling around. "My new best cheese ball customers."

I looked around me with fresh eyes. Sure enough, several people were bent over like they were sick. Only now I knew they weren't people.

They were vamps with tummy aches.

"Here's the money, Nixie." He handed me an envelope. "Well, got to run. Got to make sure the regular cheese ball shipment is good for tomorrow."

♫ ♫ ♫

Monday morning we sat in Bo's kitchen, Elena and me, Julian and Bo. Counting money. "Four hundred ninety thousand, four hundred ninety-one thousand."

"Here's another three thousand," Elena said, pushing a stack of money over.

"And the bank just called. We got a thousand in change."

"Four hundred ninety-five thousand." Bo stared at the money. "That's not enough."

"Damn." I'd failed. Tears gathered in my eyes. I had worked so hard. But I had failed.

"It's okay, Nixie." Julian put an arm around me.

"No it's not!" I wiped my eyes. "Fuck. I didn't want to run this. Why did the mayor put me in charge? I know about organizing, not fundraising and shit. Did he *want* us to bomb?"

"We're not beaten yet." Elena squeezed my hand. "We'll get the other five thousand somehow."

"How?" I said bitterly. "Raise taxes? Ask for a donation from Chicago? Put on a relief telethon for Needy Attorneys?"

"Nixie." Julian rubbed gently between my shoulder blades. "We'll figure out something." The soothing hand moved down.

Rubbed my spine, the small of my back. Tickled my hair further down. Slid into my low-cut jeans...stopped suddenly.

"What's this?" Julian pulled out an envelope, held it in front of my face.

I took it from his fingers. "Oh, just the money from Lew. For selling those god-awful cheese balls." I tossed it onto the pile, unopened.

"But how much is it?" Elena asked.

"Come on, Elena. We're talking LLAMA pusballs. We'll be lucky if it's not a class-action lawsuit."

"You should at least open it," Julian said.

"Forget it. You open it. I'm done with this being-responsible shit."

"Pouting doesn't become you, little girl," Julian said softly.

"Who cares?" I groused back.

"Aren't you even curious?" Bo asked. "I know I am."

"Then you open it."

"I think I will." Extending claws, Bo slit the envelope. Pulled out a sheaf of bills.

Two Ben Franklins were on the outside. I snorted. "A Kansas City bankroll." Lew was a salesman to the end.

Bo fanned it open. "No. Looks like turtles all the way down."

"What?" Sure enough, even from across the table I could see every bill in the pack was a Franklin. "Fuck. How many?" My heart beat faster.

"Well, let's see, shall we? One hundred." Bo laid down a bill. "Two." Another. He made ever so sure the edges of the two bills were square.

"Stop that." Elena smacked her husband in the shoulder. "Just count the damn things."

Bo looked across at Julian. "No sense of drama."

"It's the shorter life span. Always in a hurry."

"Ah."

"I'll give you drama," Elena said, eyes narrowing.

"How's that?" Bo peeled off another $100, set it carefully on top of the other two.

"No sex," Elena said distinctly.

"Well, that's different, isn't it?" Bo began to count quickly.

Fifty Franklins later, I was ready to kiss Lew Kaufman. "We did it," I said, hardly believing it. "We made five hundred thousand dollars!"

"Ironic, isn't it?" Bo slipped the stack of hundreds back into their envelope. "That the funds that put us over the top were contributed by Nosferatu's own gang?"

"I'd say justice," Julian said.

And so Meiers Corners had a happy ending.

But not me. I tried to be grateful. Truly I did. Meiers Corners was safe from the bad guys. The public had won. And Guns and Polkas would get their shot at stardom.

But at an astronomical personal cost. My baby was gone.

Oscar had died nobly, saving my life. But I was a little lost without him. It felt like part of myself was missing. I'd bought Oscar with the first money I ever earned. He was with me most of my life. I loved him more than many people.

I missed Oscar, terribly.

I had a feeling I'd miss my snarky lawboy more.

Chapter Thirty-one

I hoofed out from Bo and Elena's alone. No need for Julian to chaperone me. Vampy guys were all dug into snug graves nursing their hangovers. Or wherever v-guys slept when out of town. Was there a vampire motel chain? The Vampada Inn? The No-Tell Motel? Swan-necked Sylvia's Bed-and-Breakfast?

Even without the threat of gang guys, Bo pressed me to use the limo. I nearly took him up on it, thinking I'd get farewell sex.

But Julian said he had to pack.

I hung around a bit before going. I thought maybe Julian would try to get me to visit Boston again. Even invite me to leave with him tonight. But Julian had phone calls to make.

And he had to pack.

So I left Julian to his packing. I wondered if he would even come say goodbye after sunset. Or if he was eager to just get the hell out of Dodge.

Maybe I should suck it up and visit him on my own. He'd asked once, after all. Visit him in his blue-blood, country-club Boston environs, where I'd see the Stuffius Lawyeranous in its natural habitat. Where both of us would see how painfully I did not fit in. I could go home and we could both move on.

I wiped my strangely wet cheeks. Hell. Maybe I could go to Boston but just hide out in Julian's bedroom. After all, we fit there well enough. And on the sidewalk. And in limousines...double hell. How would I get along without him? And why hadn't he at least tried one more time to get me to come?

As I passed each of the festival's venues the sense of loss

deepened. There was Nieman's Bar, where Logan Steel had tromped everyone at sheepshead. Good Shepherd Church, where Thor and Gretchen "just said no" to a couple vampires and made it stick. The Fudgy Delight where Rocky Hrbek won the beauty contest and Elena got the crown. The Roller-Blayd factory where the music—

Where the music was still going.

I couldn't quite hear details. Curious, I tried the door.

A saxophone was playing "Take Five".

"Dirk?" I ran in. "Dirk, it's Nixie! Oh, Dirk! You can stop now."

On stage, Dirk Ruffles took his sax from a mouth so swollen it looked like a collagen implant gone wrong. He was wringing wet, sweat and spit both. He tottered to the edge of the stage where he didn't so much sit as collapse.

"Dirk! The festival's been over for hours. The bands were done days ago! Why were you still playing?"

"'Ooo 'old 'ee 'oo 'ay," he said in a voice thick from disuse. His swollen lips made the consonants into mush.

"What?"

"'oo," he said, pointing at me. "'old," making a talking motion with one hand. "'ee," pointing at himself. Then he just pointed at the sax, lying on the stage.

"Me?" I said, getting it. "I told you to?"

When he nodded tiredly, I thought back. I'd asked him to cover for me, sure. But what exactly had I said that Dirk would still be playing days later...shit.

Wing it until I get back.

I had never come back.

Julian and I had been so busy chasing Lestats, protecting the blood, and protecting the festival that I had never come back.

And Dirk went on winging it.

"Oh, Dirk, honey!" I sat next to him on the stage, put an arm around him. "You must be exhausted."

He nodded mournfully.

"I know just what'll take care of that." I dragged him to his feet. "Let's go put something cool on those lips."

"'ere?"

"Nieman's Bar." When he perked up, I knew I had a winner. And hell, I could use the amnesia.

♫ ♫ ♫

I was pleasantly wasted by sunset. When Granny Butt came to dance I barely even noticed. I did swivel slightly on my stool, to watch the door. Sun was down, now. Any moment. Any moment *he* would come to say goodbye. Maybe he would even come in the limo. We could do a lot of goodbying on the way to O'Hare.

Two hours later I was totally crunk. Julian had not come.

"I don't care," I repeated to whoever would listen. "He's just a stupid shrink-wrapped shark. A vacation fuck. I don't care he didn't say goodbye. And I especially don't care I didn't get goodbye sex. Buddy, gimme a refill."

"That's your fourth pitcher, Nixie." Buddy was sweeping up after Granny's latest promenade knocked all the peanuts to the floor.

"So? I'mn-not goin' anywhere. Gimme a refill."

"Why don't you get a little fresh air first?" Buddy gave me a sympathetic look.

Sympathy, because a snarky lawyer stood me up. Skewer me and call me shish kabob, why don't you? "I wanna refill!"

Buddy's answer was to quietly take my glass and pitcher and put it in the washer.

"Fine. No tip." I slapped a few yuppie food stamps on the bar, to cover both me and Dirk, who was still anesthetizing. I swung off my barstool and stomped away.

Only to find out I didn't have my hoodie and jacket. Nothing spoils a dramatic exit like not exiting. When I finally found them ten minutes later (groping blindly like a Ph.D. in stupid), I left quietly.

It was dark out but no one cared. No one was going to sneak up on me and inform me in that highly aggrieved tone that I should not be out alone at night. I blinked rapidly. I was glad! I was glad oppressive Daddy was gone. I was...fuck.

I fell back against the brick of Nieman's. My breath huffed

out. I was not glad. I missed him. Only a few hours, and I missed Julian Emerson so much it was like a knife in my chest.

"There you are."

The voice was female. I peered into the wet mists. Wiped my eyes with an angry swipe. Elena strode up to me.

"What are you doing here?" She took a sniff. "Have you been drinking?"

"I *was* drinking. Buddy cut me off."

"Just in time. How are you going to enjoy the party if you're drunk?"

"Party? What party...the mayor?" It occurred to me the mayor must have put together a shindig for the people who worked the festival. Strange that it was on a Monday night. But maybe that's the only time he could get caterers to come. "No thanks. I don't wanna drink bad wine and eat pusballs." I stumbled toward home. My empty home, with no vampires in the basement...or in my bed.

Elena hooked my elbow. We spun like a mini merry-go-round, with me as the tiny pony. "Whoa!" She caught me by the shoulders. "You're drunk already, aren't you? Why?"

"Why?" I practically bleated it. "I'll tell you why. And it has nothing to do with that hoagy lame-ass lawyer you brought in who turned out to be neither hoagy nor lame-ass."

Elena marched me across the street. "You mean Julian?"

"It has nothing to do with him! Just because not-hoagy not-lame-ass dipped out without even a poke at goodbye sex—"

"Julian hasn't gone anywhere."

"But...but..." Finally I managed, "He was packing."

"Well of course," Elena said. "That's what you do when you move."

"He's moving?" I blinked, my brain apparently still on daylight saving time. "Emerson's moving?"

"I thought you knew."

"You mean...he's moving in with you and Bo?" Was it possible that Julian was staying in Meiers Corners?

But before I could even get a single hope up, Elena said, "Let me explain something." She dragged me into a nearby doorway (it was the local comic book shop, closed for the night) and propped me up against the door. Casting a glance around her and apparently seeing no one, she said, "You need to house at least six human donors for each vampire. Our household is full. So Julian's starting his own."

"Joy and rapture." Julian was starting a "household" in Boston. A household with sexy Julian and his human minions. Bye, Nixie. Hello, minions. Minions...and sex slaves too, no doubt. "How kewl. Another nest of vampires."

"Nest of...certainly not!" Elena looked almost insulted. "A household is more like a co-op."

"A co-op, uh-huh."

Elena knew sarcasm when she heard it. "No, really. Good-guy vamps protect humans from rogues. In exchange, humans give the vampires the blood they need."

"Sure. And sex has nothing to do with it." I pictured Julian surrounded by his new "donors". Six lovelies, his mouth at their throbbing arteries...oh, sure sex had nothing to do with it.

"It's not about sex, Nixie! Good grief, what has Julian been telling you?"

"Come on. Why would anyone want to get bled, if not for the sex?"

Elena's eyes widened in shock, then narrowed dangerously. "I'll tell you why. *Fear.*" She ticked up her index finger, directly in my face. "My sister Gretchen was attacked by a vampires. They *killed* her husband. She feels safer at Bo's."

"Oh. That makes some sense. But—"

"*Security.*" Elena raised her voice and ticked up a second finger. I had to turn my face not to get my nose roto-rooted. "Rogues often raid funeral homes for blood. Josiah Moss has to live with Stark just to stay in business."

"But—"

"*Tradition.*" Another finger and a very dirty look. "Daniel Butler grew up in a vampire household. It's his way of life."

I couldn't let that one pass. "Puh-leeze! Butler 'donates' blood because his father did? How medieval is that?"

"Householding's been going on since Victorian times. Earlier. Think castles and manor houses. Hasn't changed much since then."

Huh. Daniel Butler really was a butler.

"There weren't very many households, up until recently.

But lately, the number of rogues has skyrocketed."

"Because...?"

"No one knows, though we have some theories." Elena shrugged and stepped back, finally out of my face. "But, bottom line, it means we need more protection. So Julian's starting a new household."

"In Boston." I said it out loud this time, surprised by how much it hurt. The beer had pretty much numbed everything else. Why not my *baka* heart, too?

"No, in Meiers Corners." Elena looked surprised. "On the southwest side of town. I thought you knew."

"But..." I should have had a joygasm. Instead I felt awful. Julian was staying. He was staying and *he hadn't told me*.

"The housewarming party's tonight at eight." Elena tugged on my arm. "C'mon. We need to put a move on or we'll be late."

"No!" I jerked away. "Not going nowhere." Why wouldn't Julian tell me he was staying, unless *he didn't want me anymore*? I was no longer numb, just heavy. My legs, my heart...my head felt like a sixty-seven Chevy. I let it hang. "I don't think I'm invited."

"Of course you're invited." Elena tugged harder. "Now let's get going before all the good party eats are gone."

"The party," said a cultured baritone, "was *supposed* to be a surprise."

Julian! My head rose like a dying plant given a deluge of water. Or maybe my head was just attached to my heart. "What the hell, Law Boy? Where do you get off packing like you're leaving and not saying goodbye and then not even leaving—" Anger burned off the last of the alcohol.

He grabbed me and kissed me. "I love you too."

Damn. My lips flapped but nobody was home.

"It was supposed to be a surprise," Julian repeated, his eyes intent on mine. "A *good* surprise."

"I thought you were gone." Forever, my heart added.

"I apologize. No, I'm sorry. I thought you knew I couldn't leave without"—and here he rubbed his delectable hips against me in a blatantly sexy motion—"at least one more time."

"Well, what do I know? Maybe I wasn't that special."

"*Not that special?*" Julian put me at arm's length, a

flabbergasted expression on his face. "I can't even begin to explain how much you mean to me." He shot a look at Elena. "At least not here." He raised one eyebrow suggestively. Like he would do some explaining later...lots of hot, wet explaining. "Anyway, I have a present for you."

I perked up immediately. "Present?"

"At home."

"Okay." I set off toward Elena's.

"*Our* home."

My stomach dropped. "Um...*we* have a home? As in, you and me?"

"Yes."

"As in, four walls and a roof and a yard for the dog to play?"

"Yes."

"As in, mortgage and responsibility?"

"It's paid for," Julian said. "And it's more of a multi-family dwelling."

"Oh, goody. All of the responsibilities and none of the conveniences." Flippantly, I added, "How can we have sex in the backyard with the neighbors looking?"

"Privacy hedge." The tips of his fangs peeked out. Ooh.

Elena crossed her arms and tapped her foot. "Are we going or not? I want to see what you've done with the place. And I especially want to see Nixie's present. Is it sparkly and ring-like?"

"No."

"Oh. Well, then I at least want to see what you've done with the place."

The "house" turned out to be two side-by-side townhouses, four units each. A driveway separated them, leading back to a parking lot with garages. The buildings were two-storied, only the second story looked more like a roof. Shingles came all the way down the wall, and only a few small windows clued that it wasn't actually an attic. Fortunately, picture windows on the first floor made the rest look open and inviting.

Elena eyed the setup critically. "Enough room for at least fourteen donors. That's good. But if you're in one building how will you protect the people in the other?"

"The buildings are connected at the basement level. There are a couple more apartments down there."

"Oh! You're taking on two lieutenants?"

"Since I'll be out most nights, yes."

"You'll be out?" I thought he'd bought the place, decided to stay here, because he wanted to stay with me. Where was he going?

Julian smiled at me like he knew what I was thinking. "Guns and Polkas' lead groupie."

That made my panties twinkle. "Or Guns and Polkas' lead viola da gamba."

"Only if you add sixteenth-century bransles to your repertoire."

"Sure, if you wear your twenty-first century leathers."

Julian laughed out loud at that, surprising me. "Deal."

A door banged open. Bo leaned out, a bottle of beer in one hand. "Hey you guys! Your party's already started. Get in here!"

"Parties wait for no man." I offered my elbow to Julian.

"Or vampire." He took it and escorted me in.

The front room was crowded with bodies. It looked like Bo and Elena's entire apartment building had shown up, along with half of Nieman's. Julian introduced me to a few new people. An older couple with teenage sons named Mr. and Mrs. Hinz. Two young men, Richard and Andrew, who held each other and giggled.

"My donors," Julian explained.

"Wow." I yoinked a brew from a washtub of ice. "The mind boggles."

"That I have donors?"

"That Doily Hartung isn't the only gay in Meiers Corners. So are they donors out of fear, security, or tradition?"

"I beg your pardon?"

"Elena gave me Donors 101. She said people don't donate blood to you guys just for the sex." Stashing the beer in a pocket I grabbed him by the ears and brought his head in close. "You *don't*, right?" My eyes weren't lasers, but I did try to bore through his head.

He blinked. "The Hinz family was attacked by rogues in

Chicago. One of the Watch saved them. The Hinzes moved here because they'd heard about Bo. They were devastated that he didn't have room for them and their kids. Practically mowed me down when they heard I was starting up a household."

"And the other two? Richard and Andrew?" Rich and Andy were young and handsome. And they probably thought Julian was as delicious as I did.

"Similar to the Hinzes. Rich and Andy had a run-in with some rogues in San Francisco. Sweetheart, my ears."

I let go. "And your household in Boston? Won't your donors there miss you?" I tried to keep the pathetic jealousy out of my tone, but wasn't entirely successful.

"I don't have donors in Boston, Nixie. Or a household. I've been a troubleshooter for the Ancient One for the last fifty years. Running all over the country. I'm not home long enough to be master of a household." Rubbing his ears, Julian frowned at me. "Why all the questions? What is going on in that sweet, curly-haired head of yours?"

"No donors? You don't get regular sex...I mean blood?" I blushed, having Janet Jacksoned exactly what was going on in my *baka* head.

Julian looked as shocked as Elena had. "Donation *isn't* about sex, Nixie. And even if it was, *I'm* not. For your information, I drink mostly bagged blood. Sometimes the households I visit will offer their donors. But it's a courtesy. And I would *never* take advantage of it by making sexual advances."

"But lore says vampires are like sex parties waiting to happen. Carnal-vals." I had firsthand experience of that. "V-guys and gals can have sex with anyone. And make it orgasmic. So why wouldn't they?"

"You mean why wouldn't *I*." Julian reached out to brush my hair tenderly from my forehead. "Yes, vampire senses are much keener than humans. Our skin feels pleasure on a level you can't even imagine. We're like walking erogenous zones."

"Sounds painful."

Julian threw back his head and laughed. He wore an open-necked polo shirt, and the sight of his strong bronzed throat nearly made me want to turn vampy, just so I could bite it. Not about sex, hah.

"Vampires can have sex with anyone. And many frequently do. But because of our heightened senses, some people are much more appealing than others. Scent, sound, feel. Taste." He took me in his arms, bent to kiss my nose. A soft purr started.

"So I'm...appealing? Like a juicy burger?"

"You're beyond appealing. You're perfect to me." Julian's lips touched my cheek, temple, ear. His tongue swept lightly over the small hairs on the lobe, making me vibrate with anticipation. "You're a delight to my senses, all of them. You're sweet, tasty, and supple, and a balm to my soul. With just a bit of tart personality for tang. And there's more."

"Wait—there's more," I echoed, eyes closing. "If you order now, you get Hemoglobin Flavored Intimacy Gel with Tartar Control...for that special fangy guy in your life."

He chuckled, kind of weird frosted with purr. "Nixie, have you ever wondered why, in all the times I did my 'Obi-Wan' as you call it, you were never affected?"

"Huh?"

"You were present at least twice when I used suggestion to alter people's perceptions."

"You mean your mystic mind-control thing?"

"That's my artless Nixie."

"Have I been insulted?"

Julian laughed again. He seemed to be doing that a lot, tonight. Like he was...happy or something. "I can't manipulate you, Nixie. I'm old enough to compel most people and many vampires. Of course, I can't manipulate myself. And I can't manipulate *you*."

"Is that important?"

"It is if we want to share the rest of our lives."

My heart started to pound double-time. Fear? Or excitement? "Well. I guess. So, um...so you aren't in it for the sex."

"You're the only one I have sex with, Nixie. And now that I've found you, you're the only one I want to have sex with. Because it's more than sex. It's a *joining*. We're two halves of the same whole, you and I."

Thinking of how snugly his Tab A fit in my Slot B, I

shuddered in agreement.

"Now let me show you around." Julian took my hand and walked me through his...*our* new home. The townhouses had been modified extensively, with connecting hallways and several common areas. There were still separate entrances and the illusion of separate units, but he showed me the entire place without going outside once.

The most interesting thing was the bedrooms. Though there were windows galore in the other rooms, none of the bedrooms had windows. And the bedroom doors were reinforced so heavily they looked like entrances to a bank vault.

I ran my hand over one of the doors, feeling cool steel under my fingers. "What's with the bedrooms? They're like bomb shelters."

"For protection. The vampire population is increasing rapidly. We don't get a lot of rogues here, but it's only a matter of time."

"So when the bloodthirsty hordes attack, humans will have a safe place to sleep? I thought older vamps could mist in."

"That's why the walls are reinforced with metal. And electrified." Julian drew me into a bedroom and closed the door. He shot a deadbolt with a quick twist. To my surprise, a green light flicked on, and the room seemed to hum. "Logan Steel discovered vampires can't get through electrified walls. Not even as mist."

"The bedroom walls are live?"

"Only when the locks are engaged." Julian unbolted and opened the door.

"Oh." I followed him out into the hallway. "How many people will base here?"

"We could fit as many as fifty donors, but that wouldn't leave room for children and old ones."

"Excuse me. Did you say 'old ones'?"

"Children and the elderly can't donate. Not safely." Julian shrugged. "Have to think of things like that."

"Responsibility." I shook my head. "So how many people do we have to think of things like that for?"

"Couple dozen, more or less. It won't be so bad. I'll hire a housekeeper and cook."

"Live-in?" I asked, brightening.

Julian only smiled. "We'll have plenty of people to share the burden of responsibility. A couple dozen adults. Two other vampires."

"Vampires in the basement," I said, remembering Ruthven.

"Not just vampires," Julian replied, tracing a finger up my neck. "You and I will sleep in the basement."

"Together? I don't suppose you'd like to show me?"

"I thought you'd never ask." He took my hand and led me down.

The double basement was divided into two sides. On one side were washers and driers, workbench and pool table. On the other side was a hallway.

"Over here." He opened a door and flipped on a light. "I thought this could be our room."

The room revealed was bright and airy. I poked my head in, saw a door off the side, open to what looked like Mediterranean tile. Another seemed to lead to a walk-in closet.

Like Julian's bedroom at Bo's, this room had soft, luxurious carpet. I stepped in, felt my feet sink in bliss.

After indulging a few moments, I opened my eyes and looked around. Not only the carpet was the same. I recognized that ocean-sized bed, two-foot thick mattress looking soft as cotton candy. "Is that from Bo's?"

"Well...yes. You seemed to like it."

"Oh, yeah. I had some ideas to try out. You did this for me?"

Julian shrugged, looking a little embarrassed. "I didn't know if you'd want to move in with me. I wanted to offer you some enticement."

"Julian, this is the best present I could have asked for."

"It's not your present."

"It isn't? But—"

"Your present's upstairs."

"No. My present is right here. Or at least it will be." And I pulled his yummy face down to mine and kissed him.

Chapter Thirty-two

We had all the time in the world, now. A lifetime. I didn't tongue-dive immediately or push my hand into his pants. Instead I rubbed my lips slowly against his, just enjoying the touch of skin on skin. The warmth of his breath. The sound of his light purr. I licked his lower lip and got high on the taste of him, male and tangy and all Julian.

He folded me in his arms and caressed me with his lips. He backed me toward the bed, kissing me all the while. When my hips hit comforter, he lifted me in his arms, never breaking mouth contact. He laid me reverently on the bed. Eased himself on top of me, letting just enough of his weight fall on me to be arousing. I pushed up with my hips, my pubic bone meeting an already-heavy arousal. *Oh yeah.*

Julian broke the kiss. Before I could moan a "no", he began to scatter little butterfly busses over my face, over cheeks and eyelids and jaw. His square, competent hands came up to cup my face while he kissed my mouth again, deeper this time, but no less sweetly. All the while his hard and sleek erection throbbed against me.

He left my mouth to kiss down my neck. Gently, lightly. Heating me with tiny tastes rather than branding lust.

His mouth skimmed over the sunny side of my breasts. The nipples poked their heads up in curiosity. He breathed on one and I swear she began purring too. I kissed the top of his black head. His hair smelled like fresh rain, felt like silk.

Julian slid his hand under my cami top, pushing it off my breast. I caught a glimpse of my nipple, pink and alert, before he lowered his head and suckled gently. Little points of pleasure lit up all over me. Everything was so light and silky that when he scraped his teeth ever-so-slightly against my nipple I nearly shot off the bed.

Shifting down my body, Julian licked the shade side of my breasts. His hands skimmed down my ribs, onto my hips. He lifted himself just enough to unsnap and unzip, and to peel back my denim. His mouth followed his hands, burning a light trail down my belly to my thong-covered mound.

Julian kissed and tongued me through the silk until it was damp and clingy. I arched, following the waves of need rolling through my body. Anchoring his lips in the cloth over my pussy, he opened his mouth and breathed. Heat spread over me. I felt slick moisture dew the thong.

His nostrils flared. He smiled up at me from between my legs. His fangs were long and graceful. Bending his head he slipped one under the thong. Levered the thong up and out. Replaced it with his tongue.

Hot passion licked my lips, slicked my slit. I jerked against his mouth, unseating him. The thong snapped back into place. Julian let loose a frustrated oath.

He slapped an arm over my hips, a band of steel holding me fast. I wiggled a little, found myself trapped good. Ooh. No more Mr. Nice Vampire.

"Now. Let's try this again." Julian slid his square, competent fingers into my thong. Pulled it slowly aside.

He gazed at my pussy, a look of awe on his beautiful face. His nostrils flared and his eyes closed, black lashes long and thick against his sharp cheekbones. He took two deep breaths, pulling in the last one like a man preparing for a deep sea dive.

And then he went down on me.

He licked me, kissed me, tongued me, suckled me. When I thought I couldn't stand any more he latched onto my clit and sucked it like a cherry. Erotic hunger sang through me. It was so sweet it almost hurt. When he finally let up, it was only to raise his fangs over my mound.

He bit me and all hell broke loose.

The elegant teeth sank into my mound like tasers, zapping me with a thousand volts. My clit screamed and popped up. He lapped its little red head like a paddleball. My vagina began spasming, hard waves working me until my head spun. The orgasm turned me practically inside-out.

Julian phased out his clothes and climbed over me. "You rev all my senses, Nixie," he said, his voice roughened by his purr. "Scent, sight...but especially *touch*." He mounted me in one hard thrust.

As his enormous cock drove home it took my slickened lips with it, rolling them over. Not so much tugging at my clit as yanking it halfway inside. I gasped, half-sat. He pulled out. Rammed home. Pulled out. Drove in. Each thrust rolled my swollen clit like a marble between fingers. I felt myself ready to come again, an orgasm so deep it began in my throat.

Which is where Julian bit me.

His fangs sank into my neck, igniting the climax like a bomb. Fizzing down the trail until—*boom*! My insides exploded, starting at my vulva and rushing back up through my body, a *foosh* of flame to my head. It burned my brains out.

I lay in a daze. Julian collapsed on top of me, the duet of thudding hearts gradually slowing. "Uh," he grunted eloquently.

"Uh," I agreed. I would be living here, with Julian. I could get this any time. I could get this kind of sex *every day*.

My head burned out again.

Eventually he rolled off me. Lying on his side, he smiled down at me and stroked the damp hair from my forehead. "I do love you, you know."

I looked down at myself. My nipples were soft and happy, my belly well-kissed. My pussy was happy-looking too, in an exhausted, drippy kind of way. "I kinda got the picture. Great present, by the way."

"That too." He kissed me. "But your real present is upstairs. We should get dressed and go get it."

"Do we have to?" I closed my eyes. Did it get any better? Soft comforter under me, silky-skinned male next to me, warm love inside me. Not just the physical kind, but I didn't say that out loud. "It's a lot of work to put on clothes."

He rolled my thong and jeans up. "Mmm. But think of the fun of taking them off again." Growly-guy, my fave. "Okay." I yawned. "Let's go."

We spent a little extra time dressing each other. Belts and shirts take a bit longer when you're doing them backwards—especially when you add lips and tongue.

As we humped stairs, I said, "How long have you known you're staying in Meiers Corners?"

"I only decided two days ago, although I think I knew the first instant I saw you. Why?"

"How did you get the remodeling here pushed through so fast?"

"The buildings were actually remodeled months ago. We knew from the Coterie's rumblings and increase in rogues that we'd need more vampires protecting Meiers Corners. I just added a few finishing touches."

Like the bed. Yum.

Upstairs, the party was even more crowded. All my friends and neighbors were there. Elena and Bo. Dolly Barton and lawyer Denny Crane. Rocky Hrbek and Drusilla. Chief Dirkson and his nephew Dirk Ruffles, lips still puffy but face not so haggard. Bruno Braun was even here, discussing security with Logan Steel.

Play by the rules when playing together. With family and friends. Improvise the solos.

"Ladies and gentlemen," Julian called out. "If I could have your attention?"

His voice was mildly hollow, with just a touch of what I was coming to recognize as vampire compulsion. Conversation dropped off. "Your attention, please. I have an announcement to make. As you know, I have decided to take up practice here in Meiers Corners."

Cheering greeted that, along with some good-natured ribbing of Denny Crane.

Julian cleared his throat. "But while I have made many new friends in Meiers Corners, living here would be very lonely without company. Without someone special to share my life." He signaled, and Bo brought him a package.

"Nixie?" Julian held the package out to me.

It was beautifully wrapped, gold paper with a huge satin ribbon. And the weirdest shape since the breaking of the continents. Not a box, or a tube. Not even a garment bag. No, this package looked more like a—guitar.

I took it like a zombie. How could Julian think...so soon...I couldn't replace Oscar. That would be like getting a new puppy the day a beloved dog died.

I peeled back the paper with brittle fingers. Julian meant well, I told myself. He meant to make me happy. He didn't mean to break my crayons.

A new guitar. With Oscar barely cold. My heart was shredding.

I looked up. Julian smiled brightly at me. *He didn't get it.* I wanted to rail and scream. I had hoped...had dared to believe...but Suitguy didn't understand me after all.

The paper stuck. I gritted my teeth, pulled it away. Saw the neck. Oh, fuck. He had gone to a lot of trouble to copy my defunct Strat. The Schaller machine heads were exactly the same. So was the rosewood fingerboard, even including the custom black opal inlays.

How could he? How could the Boston wonder hoag be such an ignoramus? With everything we'd been through...he didn't get it!

I'd think of Oscar every time I looked at the guitar. It was exactly the same—C-shape maple neck with satin polyurethane finish, twenty-two medium jumbo frets, and the bent tuning machine on the E string.

And the bent tuning machine on the E string. Where my sister had stepped on it.

It wasn't exactly like Oscar—it *was* Oscar. Reborn.

Julian went down on one knee. "Nixie Schmeling. I love you. I want to live with you, forever. Will you marry me?"

His face was even with my neck. Cupping his cheeks, I tilted his head to stare straight into his gorgeous blue eyes. "Julian! You do get it! This is better than a ring. Yes," I said, laying a big smoochy one on his lips. "Yes, yes, yes!"

My friends shouted and toasted us with beer. And new Oscar—and my heart—riffed right along.

About the Author

Mary Hughes is a computer consultant, professional musician, and writer. At various points in her life she has taught Taekwondo, worked in the insurance industry, and studied religion. She is intensely interested in the origins of the universe. She has a wonderful husband (though happily-ever-after takes a lot of hard work) and two great kids. But she thinks that with all the advances in modern medicine, childbirth should be a lot less messy.

To learn more about Mary Hughes, please visit www.maryhughesbooks.com.

GREAT
cheap
fun

Discover eBooks!

LaVergne, TN USA
10 November 2009
163620LV00011B/4/P